Hurray for Me

HURRAY
FOR ME

A NOVEL BY **S. J. WILSON**

CROWN PUBLISHERS, INC. NEW YORK

Second Printing (before publication), January, 1964

© 1964 by S. J. Wilson
Library of Congress Catalog Card Number: 63-21122
Printed in the United States of America

To honor my mother,
For the memory of my father.

For groups, as well as for individuals, life itself means to separate and to be reunited, to change form and condition, to die and to be reborn. It is to act and to cease, to wait and rest, and then to begin acting again, but in a different way. And there are always new thresholds to cross: the thresholds of summer and winter, of a season or a year, of a month or a night; the thresholds of birth, adolescence, maturity, and old age; the threshold of death and that of the afterlife — for those who believe in it.

— Arnold van Gennep: *The Rites of Passage*

Hurray for Me

chapter 1

What a discovery! What a find! Two new, empty cans, one right next to the other in the gutter. Luck was in love with me. I swooped down, scooped them up and holding them above my head—some soupy remains dripping on my sweater sleeve—ran back, calling, "Look what I found! Hey, Libby, look what I found!"

Libby sat on the steps of our apartment building, busily setting an imaginary table on the top step and ladling food from a pot-covered stove visible only to her, and didn't so much as lift her eyes.

"Look!" I held out my treasures triumphantly. "They're brand-new!"

Libby slowly set what appeared to be a heavy plate on the step, then, placing hands on her hips, turned and scolded, "Why are you so late getting home from work? I had dinner ready an hour ago. Now everything's cold like molasses. I ought to give you a piece of my mind. I work and clean and wash and iron and sew and bake and cook and everything all day from morning to night to make your dinner—"

"No, Libby. Look. You know what these are? They're silver skates. And they're all mine. And I don't have to go halfies with nobody in the whole world."

I put one can on the ground, squashed it to fit under the sole and around the sides of my shoes.

"I'm going to skate," I announced.

"No you're not!" Libby grabbed the back of my sweater. "You're going to play house with me. I got the dinner all ready. Besides, you promised."

"Leggo," I cried, "you're tearing my sweater, you Fifi la-la Libby, you. And I didn't promise."

"Yes you did. You promised if I told you what I know about my brother, you would play house with me. You did! You did! A hundred times you did!"

"I didn't promise," I insisted. "You asked me, would I promise to play with you if you told me what your brother had under his belly button. And I asked you, what? And you said he had hair growing. So I didn't promise nothing and I'm going to skate."

"No you're not! You promised to play house with me. And if you break your promise you're going to turn black and die in twenty-four hours."

I pulled my sweater free. "That's crazy. Even if I did promise, I wouldn't turn black and die. I asked my mother and she told me, so you're crazy, Libby, 'cause you think crazy things. Fifi la-la Libby Jackson is crazy like a daisy," I yelled to all the listening world.

"I am not," cried Libby as she lunged, grabbed the other can. "You got a head full of cockamamies," she shouted, and darted across the street. "I got your other skate," she taunted, holding up the can.

I started after her. The can fixed to my shoe scraped the pavement.

Libby hooted as she ran. Realizing that my "skate" was slowing me down, and that if I didn't catch her by the time she reached the corner she might, to get even, throw the can into the sewer, I shouted, "If you don't give me back my skate, I'll tell everybody and my brother what you told me about your brother."

She stopped, and threw the can at me. "Here's your rotten old skate. It's only a can and not a real skate, anyway . . .'cause you're not old enough to have real skates. And I'll never tell you anything secret again long as I live. I swear it and hope to die."

I picked up the can, squashed its middle, fixed it to my other shoe. Then, tramping loudly, I marched back across the street singing, "Fifi la-la Libby has googly, googly eyes and a feather in her hat and calls it macaroni."

The time had come to show the skates to my mother.

I hobbled up the granite steps into the hall, up the marble stairs until I reached the door of our apartment.

I pounded on it. No answer.

I pounded again until I heard my mother say, "I will not open the door until you knock on it the way you're supposed to."

I scratched the door with the edge of my fingernail.

"I didn't say 'scratch,' I said 'knock,' " came her voice.

I kicked the door with the heel of my shoe.

"You'll stay out there until gingersnaps grow on blueberry bushes."

I made kissing noises into the crack of the door.

"You can wear your lips out, but that door isn't opened until I hear a knock."

I knocked very lightly.

I knocked slightly louder.

Just as I was ready to pound on the door again, it was opened.

"Come in, light of my life," my mother said softly. And as she turned and started for the kitchen, she added, "Close the door as if it were your best friend."

I began to follow, and she said, this time louder, "Take those cans off, you'll scratch the linoleum."

"I just found them. I just put them on," I complained.

"Then just take them off."

"I'll walk light," I offered.

"You'll walk right out of here if they're not off before I can say, Solomon Grundy."

"I can't get them off. They're on too tight."

"Off they come, or out you go. Take your choice."

"But they're not cans, they're silver skates," I protested.

"I predict," her voice was ominous, "that it won't be very long before it will be very hard to tell the difference between a certain Robert Benjamin Hirshman's eyes and open faucets."

I mediated by slipping out of my shoes. Going into the living room, I threw myself on the couch, picked up one of my father's magazines, and although the words were mostly sticks chasing each other across the page, I read slowly and loudly:

"Once upon a time there was not such a good mother. She wasn't a real bad mother but she wasn't a honest-to-good mother. And she had a wonderful son. He was the light of her life. He was a prince, too. And she found him in front of her door where his real mother left him by mistake 'cause she went to buy him a pair of silver skates. But he knew his real mother's name—"

"What was it?" my mother asked.

"It was . . . it was . . . it's a secret."

"If I ever find out, I'll ship you to her, express collect."

"Wait till I finish," I shouted.

"I beg your pardon, your highness."

"The prince had a good fairy whose name was Nelly Belly Foo," I went on, and then called, "Did you hear that name?"

"When did she change it? It used to be Tinkerbell."

"Tinkerbell, stinkerbell," I muttered, and continued, "So Nelly Belly Foo told him how he should get rid of his not-so-good mother and find his real one with the silver skates. So she gave him a harti-choke. And he cooked it for a year and a day, and gave his fake mother the hartichoke and she ate it. And she choked and choked.

14

But she choked so hard that he felt sorry for her because she wasn't very bad, she was just not so good. So he quick gave her his best cough medicine and a mustard plaster and a half a aspirin and a hot-water bag under her feet and made her all better."

"Thank you for saving my life," my mother said. "Now do me another big favor and turn off the radio."

"I don't want to."

"Why?"

"Because I didn't turn it on."

"Turn it off anyway."

"Who turned it on?"

"It doesn't make any difference who turned it on. I'm asking you to turn it off."

"It's not fair."

"We'll take it up with the Society for the Prevention of Cruelty to Children next week. Meanwhile, turn it off."

"Why do I have to do everything around here?"

"Because you're the only one smart enough."

"You're just saying that because you want me to turn it off."

"I wonder if a certain someone is going to come around in a little while asking for a nickel so he can buy a jelly apple?"

I flipped the switch. "All right, I turned it off. Now will you do something for me?"

"I'm doing something for you right now."

"What?"

"I'm making an upside-down cake."

"That's for everybody, not only for me."

"Believe me, it's exclusively for you. You're the only upside-down one in the entire family."

"That's because you don't like me and you never did."

"It doesn't pay to argue with the truth."

"Sing like a bird, please," I asked, knowing that if she were really annoyed or angry with me, she would not sing and would reply instead with "The bird has flown the coop," or "The bird's on strike for better pay." But a soft, velvety trill came. It seemed to start from a great distance, grew nearer, fuller, rose, fluttered and then, falling, faded to a shimmering quiver.

"What kind of a bird was that?" I asked.

"A nightingale."

"I never heard of such a bird."

"It keeps late hours."

The doorbell rang. From its complaining impatience I knew at once who it was. "If that's Fifi la-la Libby, I'm not here."

"Come in, Libby," I heard my mother say.

"I just climbed up the beanstalk," I called.

"Don't come back without the hen that lays the golden eggs," my mother said.

"I wouldn't come to see you even if you were old and sick and had a big bile on your head," said Libby. "I came to see your mother, anyway."

"She's not the real one."

"But my punishments are," my mother retorted.

Libby spoke in her very polite voice: "My mother asks if when you're taking Bobby to register for school tomorrow, you'll take me too."

"I won't go if she goes," I threatened.

"Tell your mother I'll be glad to take you. And also tell her we have to be there by seven-thirty, so you be ready and dressed by seven-fifteen."

"I'm going to wear all my new clothes. And my mother said that I'll look prettier 'n a doll. And she's going to make me special curls. And I'm going to wear my new Mary Janes that have two straps instead of one. And—"

My mother interrupted her with, "I know, dear, you'll light up the sky, but don't forget to tell your mother about having you ready by seven-fifteen."

"I won't," said Libby. I heard her open the door. But before closing it, she called, "And I hope you fall down the beanstalk and all
the king's horses and all the king's men couldn't put you together
again."

As soon as the door sounded shut, I ran into the kitchen, climbed
a chair and sat on the table.

"Bobby, we eat at that table."

"My pants are clean."

"Robert!"

"All right." I slipped onto a chair. "But why can't her mother take
her to school? I don't want to go with her. Everybody's maybe going
to think she's my sister."

"She's your best friend."

"Not any more. We're mad on each other. For a long time, too."

"At least as long as last time."

"And she didn't say why her mother can't take her."

"Her mother doesn't feel well."

"What's wrong with her?"

"Never mind."

"What's wrong with her?"

"She has diabetes."

"What's diet beetles?"

Rolling her eyes upward as if in prayer, she said, "God in heaven,
what have I done to deserve this?"

"I don't think she has diet beetles. I think she doesn't want anybody to know she's Fifi la-la's mother. Maybe if she took the other
way and didn't go past Mr. Goodman's candy store, then no one
would see them and they wouldn't point and say, 'Look at that Fifi la-
la Libby and her poor mother who has to live in the same house with
her.' And her mother wouldn't have to feel sorry and cry."

"Your words are like birds," my mother said.

"Why?"

"Do you understand what a bird means when it says, 'peep-peep'?"

"No."

"Neither do I." She went to the drawer in which she kept her change purse. "Here's a nickel. Go buy a jelly apple and please take two days to eat it."

I pocketed the nickel. "It's not fair," I said, and squeezing my feet into my shoes, I hobbled out singing, "An apple on a stick will make you sick. An apple with cheese will make you sneeze . . ."

My skates struck sparks from the pavement as I ran.

I passed my friends, Davie, Henny, Moey, Tony, Clara, Tilly, Milly and Danny, Eric, Ray and Tommy McCarthy, who, though he was six years old, had been circumcised that summer with permission of his Church and had been the closest thing to a national hero our street had known. I shouted to them. They shouted back. My skates pounded and clanked.

"Bobby, stop that noise," Mrs. Greneker complained as I passed.

"Mrs. Greneker, I can't stop. These are The Red Shoes. I got to keep going. I love you Mrs. Greneker, but I can't stop because it's The Red Shoes."

Mrs. Greneker, who was childless, thanked God that she had never had one like me, hoisted her bundles higher against her bosom and walked on.

I pushed open the door to Mr. Goodman's candy store and made out the white-fringed top of his head as he knelt behind the penny candy case.

Irwin and Melvin Baker, the twins, couldn't agree on what to buy for the penny they shared. "Make up your minds, already," Mr. Goodman complained. "For a penny you'll be here all day. Which is it, the chocolate babies or the chicken corn?"

"Chocolate babies," said Irwin.

"Chicken corn," said Melvin.

"I know what I want, right away, Mr. Goodman," I called, holding the nickel above my head.

"You wait till it's your next," said Mr. Goodman.

"Yeah," said Irwin.

"Yeah," said Melvin.

"I'll go 'round the corner to Mrs. Spector and you won't make any money today," I threatened.

"It won't be different from any other day, so go where you like," Mr. Goodman replied.

I went up to the case and examined its contents on the chance it would speed up their decision if I made some suggestions.

There were penny pies in pink, green and yellow, two-for-a-penny marshmallow twists, licorice whips, chocolate licorice, sour balls, gumdrops, light fudge, dark fudge, silver-wrapped kisses, non-pareils, caramels, cornsticks, chicken corn, Italian dreams, jelly beans, lemon, orange and lime slices, paper ribbons with candy buttons pasted on them, pumpkin seeds, polly seeds, red pistachio nuts, salty white pistachio nuts, sesame-honey bars, Indian nuts, bubble gum, coconut marshmallow puffs, chocolate babies, cinnamon hearts, peppermint leaves, pretzel sticks, lollipops, snowballs and butterscotch squares.

I was about to recommend that the twins buy two-for-a-penny marshmallow twists to get the most for their money, when Irwin asked if they could have a half-penny each of chocolate babies and chicken corn.

"Why not?" replied Mr. Goodman, and he slowly counted out four chocolate babies and six chicken corn and put them in a small brown-paper bag.

"You'll grow up to be another King Solomon," he said as he gave Irwin the bag and collected the penny from Melvin. "And now let's hear from the big butter-and-egg man. What do you want, Bobby?"

"I want the biggest, fattest jelly apple in the world."

"This one?" asked Mr. Goodman, pointing at the napkin-lined tray on which sat a dozen or more glistening pot-bellied apples with sticks in their heads.

"No," I said automatically, "the very big one."

"This one maybe?" asked Mr. Goodman, knowing that there had to be at least three choices.

"I think it's right behind that one."

"Oh, I see," said Mr. Goodman. "This one here." And he daintily picked up an apple and set it in a paper napkin. "Here, take it in two hands and be careful don't drop it."

"How can I give you the nickel if I have to hold it in two hands?"

"I'll come and get it. Just don't drop the apple." He came from behind the counter and took the nickel from between my fingers.

"I'm gonna have this one for two days," I boasted.

"You're lucky if it lasts two minutes," Mr. Goodman said, and opened the door for me. "Good-bye and good luck."

With jelly apple in hand and cans on my shoes, I paraded out into my world—a world that consisted of one street, bounded on the east by Dawson Avenue, on the west by Prospect Avenue—yet as limitless as the universe to me in my five-year-old imagination.

It was called Union Street. It had little houses and tall apartment buildings, two trees, four manholes, four street lamps, and it tilted slightly to the west, which made it right for roller-skating and pitching marbles. It had two groceries, one candy store (the competition was around the corner), a barbershop and a tailorshop which combined a laundry as well. And it had a lot, a private heaven that stretched half the length of the next block; there must have been buildings there at one time but now only two signs remained, one that read "M. Ruffino & Son Monumental Granite Works," and the other "P. Lascari, Ice, Coal & Wood." One end of the lot, the end that faced our street, was enclosed by billboards and thus was favored for important prizefights, secret club meetings, treasure hunts, roasting marshmallows and potatoes, playing king-of-the-hill and, more importantly, for hunting lions in Africa, digging holes to China and adventures that could use the assistance of a few clumps of grass, ailanthus trees and make-believe.

The street had its noises. The early-morning sparrow peepings would be drummed out by the garbage trucks and the milkman's bottle-clanking. A cat would sing. A dog would complain. A janitor's wife would scat them with her broom, yelling something in Polish as she did; then the drumfire of roller skates and homemade scooters. A girl bouncing her ball would twing-twang:

> "One-two-three a-lairy
> I spy sister Sairy
> Sitting on a bumble-airy
> One-two-three a-lairy."

And eventually, as the morning unfolded, the sounds would collide with one another into a thunderous concert of noise.

But the street also had the sound of my mother's voice, which, when she sang, flooded it like soft sunlight. Whenever he heard my mother sing, Steve Calabrese, the barber, would always come to the door of his shop, wipe the ashes of his gnarled cigar from his jacket and making a circle of his thumb and forefinger, would say, "Like wine." Mr. Fisher, the tailor, would lean across his sewing machine, adjust his pince-nez and contradict his next-door neighbor, "Like honey."

And it had its smells. Smells of cheese, bread, garlic, poppy, caraway, cinnamon and dill pickles; smells of lilac hair lotion, glycerine and rose water and Mavis talcum powder; smells of urine, perspiration, cigars and garbage. It had clean Monday smells and rich, mysterious Friday dinner smells. It had the kerosene smell of Sunday's funny papers. It had the milky smells of mothers, the pipe smells of fathers, the buttery smells of sisters and the fierce body smells of older brothers.

The street was like an immense basin gathering everything that fell into it, from horse dung to rainbows reflected in its oil slicks. It was redecorated daily with squares for the potsy players, circles for the immy players, triangles for the stickball players. It was chalked with threats, promises, rumors, romantic announcements and magic symbols.

21

An aphrodisiacal cloud must have hung over the street. It was always filled with children. Some were in carriages or strollers, some were just starting to toddle, some walked, ran, jumped, and flew like winds upstairs, downstairs, across the street, around the corners, appearing first in a window, then in a doorway, then waving wildly from the roof. Everywhere I turned I had friends, or ex-friends or half-friends or quarter-friends. I had poor friends, rich friends and in-between friends.

The street was all life, and gave itself up to its children. Their voices woke it. Their games and laughter, frights and tears, kept it in an upsurge of constant wildness. It seemingly defied change and time, each generation taking over where the preceding one left off. And if names, rhymes, catcalls and markings were different, the spirit and the fiery youth of it remained the same. Thus, when loss, sadness or bereavement came, the street and its children gave it one tremulous look and turned their backs until all signs of grief were gone.

chapter 2

My mother woke me next morning by kissing my eyes and saying, "Wake up, Mr. Schmeckel-Peckel."

"What kind of a name is that?"

"It's a love name."

"Well, don't tell it to that Fifi la-la Libby, or she'll call me it all the time."

"All right."

"Promise?"

"I promise, but now get up and go brush your teeth and wash your hands and face. And let me know when you're ready for me to come and comb your hair, Mr. Schmeckel-Peckel."

My brother Peter, supposedly asleep in the next bed, began to giggle. "That's just the name for you, Mr. Schmeckel-Peckel," he jeered.

"You shut up," I shouted, "or I'll get a big pin and stick it in your—"

"Sh-sh," my mother admonished. "A brother is a friend given by God."

"Why don't you tell him that?" I complained. "He's older than me."

"He heard," my mother said flatly, and left the room.

During breakfast, while I wondered if the satisfaction I'd get from spitting an orange pit down my sister's back would be worth her retaliation, the doorbell rang. My brother opened it only after he was convinced nobody else would.

It was Libby Jackson as I had never seen her before, as I never dreamed she could be. A great red bow like a glistening butterfly sat on top of her head. Her curls hung in fat, shining spirals. She wore a dark blue pleated skirt, a middy of the same color; its wide collar, edged with three white stripes, hung outside her blue, white-buttoned coat. A huge red kerchief softly folded in a half-knot was draped around her neck. In her hand she held a small, imitation-leather schoolbag. And her face shone like Sunday morning in the park.

I spit the orange pit into my plate and said, "Libby, you look like a blueberry shortcake with strawberry ice cream."

"Oh, don't bother me," she said shyly, and turned her back.

My mother went to her, turned her around and knelt before her. "Libby, my love, you may be happier than you are at this moment, but you will never be more beautiful." She kissed her cheek. Libby returned the kiss.

"Gee," Martha said, "she looks a little like Mary Pickford. Of course, she has black hair."

"Black hair is very nice," I said.

"All the big movie stars have blonde hair," said Martha authoritatively. At that point in her life—she was twelve—my sister lived on, in and for movies.

"Mother has black hair," I said.

"Mothers don't count," said Martha. We knew what she meant, but it had come out all wrong.

My mother turned toward Martha, who was busy straining milk through her teeth, and placed her hands gently on her head. "Martha, my child, I have but one prayer for you. And that is that you grow up to be a great actress; that you marry a millionaire; and that you have a daughter just like mine."

Martha looked up at her uncomprehendingly.

"We're going to be late." Libby swung her schoolbag impatiently.

"All right," said my mother, slapping her hands together, "let's have some action. On the double, make like a bubble." She pointed to me, "Go get your jacket."

I ran into my bedroom, snatched the jacket off the back of a chair, dodged a shoe my brother threw at me, whipped into my parents' bedroom and waved good-bye to my father, who said, "Remember Bobby, keep your eyes and ears open and your mouth shut."

"Shut like a letter box," I promised, and ran out to find my mother putting on a hat.

"Why do you have to wear a hat?"

"Because whenever you go to a place you respect, you should wear a hat."

"So why don't I wear one?"

"Because your father isn't on talking terms with the Secretary of the Treasury."

The year was nineteen hundred and thirty—a stock market crash had shaken the world awake to the meaning of money; and those of us whose families were not yet affected by the Depression, whose fathers, like mine—he was a head librarian—continued to work, were apprehensive. So ingenious substitutions were made and it was the vogue for boys to wear beanies cut of men's worn-out felt hats, the brims fashioned into a circle of points, and rounds and squares punched out of the crowns. My head, however, was still too small to wear one.

A minute later Libby and I were running down the steps, tailed by my mother's voice warning us not to fall and to be careful.

The street was alive with the exaggerated noises of excited children and proud mothers. There were questions: "How old is she?" And answers: "She's small for her age, she's really five and a half." Libby and I wound our way between islands of people, Libby complaining that she shouldn't run because her curls might fall out, while I thought how funny it would be to find one of her curls lying on the sidewalk.

Mr. Goodman was standing in front of his store and called to us as we passed. "Here," he said, giving us each a chocolate kiss. "Do you know why I give you this free with no charge?"

We shook our heads.

"Because I want you to remember that learning should always be sweet for you."

We popped the kisses into our mouths and ran toward the school.

My mother caught up with us, ushered us into line. Looking around, I realized for the first time how much taller and straighter my mother stood than the others. I compared her with the woman directly ahead of us whose face, tired and dark, had the look of bitterness which I thought could come only from tasting laundry soap. I studied the boy whose hand she held. He had large brown eyes that darted from side to side, his lips tightly pressed; I imagined that if they parted, they would release a frightened cry.

"You know," my mother said, surverying the huge indoor playground, "thirty years ago I stood in line like this with my mother, and the only change I can see is that the place is thirty years dirtier than it was then."

The woman in front of us turned and examined my mother carefully, squinting, furrowing her forehead as if she had difficulty seeing. My mother smiled at her.

"I beg your pardon," the woman said, "but could you be Frances Kirchner?"

"I used to be," my mother replied, "but fortunately I traded Kirchner in for a married name, Hirshman."

"What's your name?" I asked the boy. He turned his head away.

His mother's eyes widened. "I was Jeanette Frank," she said.

"Jeanette Frank?" My mother's voice could not conceal her surprise. She took the woman's arms and held her at a distance, examining her from head to foot. "Jeanette Frank." She repeated the name as if she didn't quite believe it could belong to this woman. And then changing her tone, she quickly added, "The most beautiful girl in the school. . . What am I saying? The most beautiful girl in the world!"

"Not any more," the woman protested.

"Oh please," my mother said, and hugged the woman to her. "Am I glad to see you, Jeanette! What a wonderful, wonderful surprise! How long have you been in the neighborhood?"

"Only about a month."

"And who is this?" my mother asked, releasing the woman and kneeling beside the boy.

"This is Johnny, he's my oldest." The woman patted the boy's head.

"Hello, Johnny," my mother said softly.

The boy turned to his mother and buried his head in her coat.

My mother looked up and asked the woman what her married name was. "Schafer."

"All right," my mother said, turning to the boy. "Johnny Schafer, I want you to meet Bobby Hirshman and Libby Jackson."

We exchanged feeble hellos. Anyone introduced by a parent was hard-set to prove his eligibility for friendship.

"How old are you?" I asked.

He mumbled. His mother prodded him gently and he finally said, "Five years." Having spoken, he felt it his privilege to ask my age.

"Five going on six," I replied.

"You are not," Libby contradicted. "You're only five and I'm five and a half and I'm going on six faster than you."

This began an argument, and Johnny joined my side when Libby announced that her mother told her that girls get older faster than boys.

"Fight it out among yourselves," my mother said, and stood up to

27

talk to her friend.

"How many more do you have?" she asked.

"Just one, Arthur is three. And you?"

"I have three altogether. The oldest is fourteen and he's in high school. Martha is twelve and she's in junior high, and Bobby here. So tell me, how long have you been Jeanette Schafer?"

"Seven years, last December. Who did you marry, Frances?"

"Jack Hirshman. You should remember him, Jeanette, he went to the same high school."

The woman shook her head.

"Of course you must. He was head of the debating team and the Arista, and he was voted most likely to succeed—he was valedictorian at our graduation."

"Oh. . .oh. . .now I think I do remember. Tall, slender, with brown hair. . ."

"He's still tall and slim but the brown hair disappeared gradually down the bathroom sink."

"What does he do?" the woman asked.

"He's a librarian."

"That's nice. That's very nice."

"Of course, we can't as yet afford a yacht."

"Didn't you do anything about your singing?" the woman asked.

My mother was about to reply when suddenly we heard a thunderous voice demand, "QUIET!"

"I'll tell you about it later," my mother whispered, and herded Libby and me back into line.

"All children whose last names begin with the letters A to M," the voice boomed, "please form a line on the right. And the others please form a line on the left."

Everyone began to shuffle. People collided, children refused to leave their friends. My mother waved to the woman and to Johnny, who were now in the other line.

"Who is she?" I asked my mother.

"She was my friend, a long time ago." My mother's voice was distant, abstracted.

"Like Martha and Henrietta?" I mentioned my sister's best friend to determine how close my mother and this woman had been.

"Yes. . .no. . .well, I suppose so." Her voice was still distant. Her face chased a memory.

"You suppose what?" I asked. I had to know what she was thinking.

"What?" she asked.

"You haven't been listening to me."

"I can assure you," she said, patting my head, "my ears are glued to your lips."

Before I could inflate the argument, I heard Libby say, loudly and angrily, "Keep your cockamamie feet off my brand-new Mary Janes." This was directed at the girl in front of her.

"What happened?" my mother asked.

"She stepped on my shoes and scratched them all up," Libby complained.

"I'm sure it was an accident, dear," my mother said. Taking a handkerchief out of her purse, she wet an edge of it on her tongue and started to clean the shoe. But before she could, a woman asked, "Are you this child's mother?"

"No, but I'm responsible for her," my mother replied.

"Well, someone should be responsible for her language." The woman shook her shoulders indignantly.

"What did she say?" my mother asked.

"It sounded like a very dirty word to me."

"What word was that?"

"I have no intention of repeating it," the woman said.

"Then you've got no case in my court."

"All right, you asked for it. Exactly what does 'cockamamie' sound like to you?"

"To me it sounds like a five-year-old trying to say decalcomania, those pictures they buy in the candy store and transfer to paper. But to you it sounded like a dirty word. I'll tell you what. . .I'll be responsible for this child's language, if you'll tell me who's going to be responsible for your dirty mind."

The voice issuing instructions brought the argument to an end, but I felt my mother had won.

Our registrations completed, Libby and I ran ahead in an attempt to beat all the others out of the building. We found ourselves caught up in a tide of people inching their way out of the only door that had been opened.

"I hate school," Libby announced. She then listed the ingredients of her discontent. They included the girl stepping on her Mary Janes; the teacher forcing her to lift her dress to show her vaccination mark; the uselessness of having taken her schoolbag—she had thought school would begin that day—and finally that she was put into the same kindergarten class as I was; she felt that being older and being a girl, she should have been assigned to some "higher" kindergarten.

I found some sense in all but the last of her complaints. Although several months younger than Libby, I had learned how to read the alphabet and to write—somewhere in the three-letter-words area. I felt, therefore, that if anybody deserved going to some "higher" kindergarten, assuming there was such a thing, it should have been I. But I could not use this as an argument, for my mother once heard me boast to a friend that I could read and write while he couldn't, and threatened to punish me if I ever did it again.

(I never knew why she didn't take pride in what I thought of as my talents, except that perhaps she may have felt they were more the results of circumstance than precocity. Since my brother was nine and my sister seven when I was born, my first awareness of them was connected with their doing homework—the only periods when they were home for any length of time. Searching in their books, scratching on pads, became an absolute necessity if I were to catch up with them.

Reading and writing became such urgent ambitions, my mother said, that at the age of three I could not get my fill of being read to, and at four I would spend hours copying the alphabet that was printed on the wooden frame of the blackboard. These, in addition to my habit of creating my own versions of the fairy stories read to me so that they worked out to my advantage, may have explained my facility with language. But whatever the reasons, the results were never commented upon as being unusual.)

Libby and I found Johnny and his mother waiting at the foot of the school steps.

"Where's your mother, Bobby?" she asked.

I turned to look, suddenly aware that I had, for the moment, lost her in the crowd. She was at the top of the steps; she waved at me. But I had to be sure that it was at me; I stood on tiptoes, stretched up my hand as high as I could and called, "Here I am! Here!"

When she joined us, Johnny's mother asked if she had a few minutes, and as they slowly walked they talked in low voices, earnestly. My mother's face became attentive and the lines between her eyebrows contracted. I tried to listen, but she pushed me ahead, saying, "Go play with Libby and Johnny."

I did so reluctantly. Libby had been busy collecting vital statistics from Johnny: that he lived on our street in a building diagonally opposite from ours; that he was assigned to the same kindergarten class; that he didn't believe she was a princess; and that he didn't think he wanted to marry her. As she ran up the steps into our building, she turned, stuck her tongue out at him and shouted, "I wouldn't marry you if you lived to be a hundred!"

Since Johnny's mother and mine were still engrossed in conversation, I sat on the step and pulled Johnny down next to me.

"Let's talk secrets," I whispered.

"What kind?"

"The kind that you don't tell no one."

"What kind is that?"

"Well. . ." I searched for a starting point, "who don't you like best?"

His eyes widened. "I don't know," he said. Furrows formed above the bridge of his nose.

"Think hard like a squirrel with a nut and he don't know where to hide it," I suggested.

The furrows grew deeper. "I'm thinking hard like a rock in school," he said. His face shadowed.

I sensed the game of secrets would soon come to an end if I didn't rescue it. "All right, now you're supposed to ask me the same thing."

His eyes cleared as he asked the question.

"First," I announced, "I don't like Fifi la-la Libby best because she's got skinny teeth and fat cockamamies in her bloo-boos."

"Where's her bloo-boos?"

"Her bloomers. Then I don't like Grub-Tub Linderman because, you know why?"

"Say why."

"Because he's so fat that if you put a pin in him, he'd bust like a bomb and everybody'd die from off'n gas poisoning." I thought. "No, I take it all back, I don't like Tub third best. Second best I don't like the Baker twins because I can't tell which is Irwin and which is Melvin except when it's cold and Melvin has a runny nose. Then I can tell which is which because Melvin wipes his nose on his sleeve. But the real reason I don't like them is because if one of them pushes you, you don't know which one it is so you can't push back. . . . What does your father do? Do you have any brothers or sisters?"

"I have a little brother."

"How little?"

"Three years little."

"That's little like a baby. I got a big old sister and a bigger very old brother. My brother's so old that you know what?"

"What?"

"He had a Bar Mitzvah 'cause he was promoted from Hebrew

school when he was thirteen. And everybody gave him lots of presents. He lost lots of them already. And he got a real, live watch. But he broke it, my father said, before it could even tell him the time. And biggest of all, he got a key to our house. What does your father do?"

He sucked his underlip; again his face grayed. I thought it was going to be more difficult to continue the game than it was worth, when he blurted, "He sells."

"What?"

"Things for ladies."

"What things for ladies?"

"I don't know," he said, looking across the street and as if through the building and beyond to a place I couldn't see.

I knew I had lost him. He had gone into his private world, where I could not follow. There was only one way I could bring him back: by making lots of noise that didn't say anything. I knew, because I too had such a world, and it always worked with me.

"Maybe he sells, smells, yells, tells, bells?" I cried.

"No," Johnny said, clasping his hands and pushing them into his stomach, "he sells, pells, dells, shells, hells!" and sewed up his lips. "Ooh, what I said."

"What?"

He looked to make sure no one else was listening, and putting his lips to my ear, breathed, "Hells."

"Is that bad?"

He nodded emphatically.

"I say it all the time," I boasted.

He twisted his mouth to one side in disbelief.

"You wanna see?"

"Yes, yes, yes," he said gleefully.

"Hail, hail the gang's all here," I sang out. "What the *hell* do we care? What the *hell*—"

"Bobby!" my mother's voice shot and silenced mine.

"I'm just singing."

"Not by popular demand," she said. "Keep your voice down."

I turned away and bellied out my tongue. "She doesn't like anything I do, never. She'll feel sorry."

"Why?" Johnny asked.

"I'll tell my father on her." The idea had the thrill of impossibility.

"What'll he do?"

"Maybe he won't give her an allowance."

"What's that?"

"That's something they take away from my brother and sister when they're bad and they can't buy anything or go to the movies for a long time. You know what my father does?"

"Say what."

"He's a liberrian."

"What's that?"

I knew that it had something to do with books, but it did not seem splendid enough. "Do you know what a strawberry is?" I asked.

He nodded.

"And a huckleberry?"

He nodded again.

"Well, my father works in a liberry."

"Does your father play with you a lot?"

I considered the question for a moment. "About ten per cent, but he reads a lot. He reads and reads until sometimes he reads everything off the page and there are no words left. How much per cent does your father play with you?"

He leaned forward, rested his elbows on his knees and dropped his chin into the cup of his hand. "He goes away lots of time 'cause he sells far away. And sometimes he comes home but it's dark and I don't see him."

"So why don't you put the light on?"

" 'Cause I'm sleeping."

"Does your mother play with you?"

"She plays more with Artie, like, 'This little piggie went to market.' But then she has bellyaches and she has to lay in bed on her belly, and then I say, 'Pain, pain go away come again some rainy day,' until maybe it goes away. But it comes back all the time."

"Why doesn't she eat Ex-Lax?"

"She eats big white pills."

"So who do you play with?"

"With my brother, but most I close my eyes and think."

"What do you think?"

He glanced at me, then staring directly ahead, said, "I think like I had a big bag full of a hundred thousand hundred jelly beans; and I stuck my head out of the window and I threw a jelly bean to everybody in the whole world and even to the birds and all the stars; and everybody yelled, hurray for me forever."

"That's no game," I said.

"Yes it is," he replied mildly, as if he knew it beyond argument.

"No," I insisted. "A game is when someone has to win."

"I win the game because everybody says, hurray for me."

It was strange and intriguing. Why did everybody have to say, hurray for him? I didn't care if nobody said it to me, except my mother—and she said it in hundreds of different ways, but not in those words. I wondered if his mother said it to him. I was sure she did; all mothers did. But if she did, why did he need everybody? I could see that there was something different and odd about him; that he didn't belong to the street, but to that other world of his into which he had once more drifted and from which I felt it vital to rescue him. I was about to do that and also to prove that he could win games without giving away jelly beans when a slight cough caught our attention.

We turned to see Libby coming down the steps slowly and solemnly. She carried a slotted spoon, held it majestically before her. Around her shoulders she wore a wide pleated collar, a remnant of one of her mother's blouses. And to a bobby pin in her hair she had attached a streamer of toilet paper, which flowed down her back to the ground and behind her into the hallway.

"What's the game?" I asked.

"It's no game," she said imperially.

I peered past her to see how far the paper extended. From where I sat I couldn't see the end. "Did you take the whole roll of toilet paper?"

"It's not toilet paper. It's my velvet train." She walked past us, gently tugging the paper after her.

"What kind of a queen are you?" Johnny asked tentatively.

She looked pleased at the question. "I'm not a queen. I'm a princess. And I'm going to the Chester Avenue five-and-ten to buy some jewels."

"What's the spoon for?" I asked.

"It's my wand, can't you see, you booby-head?"

"Let me and Johnny carry your train?"

"No."

"Why not?"

"Because you both have to bow in front of me three times."

After seeing me place my hand across my stomach and bow three times, Johnny did the same. Libby touched our heads with her spoon, and we ran back to the hallway to find the end of the paper.

We discovered it halfway up the steps to the second floor, and in a moment were back in the street waving it triumphantly.

"Let's play another kind of game," I shouted.

"No!" Libby shook her head and spoon emphatically.

"You gotta! You stand still and we'll bandage you up."

We ran in a huge circle to the other side of the street, past Libby and across the street again.

"I don't want to be bandaged up," Libby shouted. "I want to play princess."

Ignoring her, we continued to run faster and in narrowing circles hoping to swathe her completely with toilet paper.

Convinced that we were not going to obey her, Libby began to chase us, calling, "Drop my train—drop my velvet train!"

We were around the corner when she caught up to us. Grabbing Johnny, she tried to tear the paper out of his hands. When he resisted, she pushed her fist into his stomach.

"My belly!" Johnny gasped. He folded his arms in front of him and bent over them.

I fell on Libby and ripping paper away from her, yelled, "Look, Johnny, I'm gonna make a dead popsickle out of her!"

Libby defended herself and we pummeled each other madly as shreds of paper floated over the street.

"You got herrings in your nose," I shouted at her. "And you got pins and needles in your behind," she shrieked, trying to get at my hair. "You're a big, fat spittoon!" "You're a dirty potty!" she retorted. I tried to kick her and at the same time elude the clutch of her hands; I yelled, "You're crazy you, Fifi la-la Libby, and your mother has diet beetles—"

Libby's flying arms froze. Her face crumpled into a blubber.

"I'm gonna tell my mother what you said," she wailed, and disappeared around the corner before I could apologize.

I knew the moment I uttered those last two words that I had done something unforgivable. There was an unwritten but inexorable law that allowed us to call each other names of all kinds without risking punishment. We could say disparaging things about brothers, sisters and sometimes fathers, but even to suggest there was the slightest thing wrong with someone's mother was forbidden. I knew I would hear about it from my mother before the day was over.

"Look what you do!"

I turned. There was Mr. Calabrese, the barber, staring angrily at me. "Look what you do!" He waved his twisted di Nobili cigar first in my face and then in Johnny's. "You make duh whole street dirty with toilet paper. What d'ya think, it's Fourth of July? You should-a be ashamed. Who's-a gonna clean it all up? You gonna do it?"

Johnny made a gesture at stooping to gather a few remaining bits of paper, but I stopped him and moving back beyond the range of Mr.

Calabrese's admonishing cigar, said, "It's Libby Jackson's toilet paper. Let her clean it up."

"You not going to clean it up?" Mr. Calabrese asked with amazement. "All-a right," he declared as he started for the corner. "I'm-a gonna go in-a my store and call up the street cleaner for you, and he's-a gonna come and put you in duh garbage jail. . .the two of you!"

"And I'm not gonna come to your store for no more haircuts, never again. You betcha!" And to further demonstrate my bravery to Johnny, when Mr. Calabrese had disappeared into his store, I yelled, "Shave and a haircut, shampoo. Go to bed and scratch your head, don't tell me what to do." Then, putting my arm across his shoulders, I said, "Let's go and hide someplace so they can't find us."

"Is he going to call the garbage jail?" Johnny asked, his eyes widening, his lip beginning to tremble.

"Sure," I said, "but we'll hide in my cellar and even if they look for a hundred hours they won't find us."

But he suddenly broke away and turned the corner, crying, "Mommy. . .Mommy!" and ran to where our mothers stood.

I knew the barber had not been serious—at one time or another he had threatened every child in the neighborhood with this same punishment—and that I had allowed Johnny to believe otherwise only to inflate my importance. I was sorry. I was very sorry, but it was too late. Both Libby and Johnny had gone off in tears. I decided to go into hiding at once, and ran down the metal steps of the janitor's entrance, through the back yards and around to the cellar of our apartment building. Crouching just below the top step, I could see Johnny, his face buried in his mother's coat, crying and blubbering about the barber and the garbage jail.

She patted his head to calm him, but without success. Then she lightly touched my mother's arm in farewell and led him home. I saw my mother look up and down the street; she called me twice before entering the building, but only casually as if all she wanted was for me to come change my clothes.

Once certain she had gone, I ran across the street to Johnny's building, where I found the Baker twins on the steps playing "match" with baseball cards.

"What floor does Johnny live?" I asked.

"I don't know," said Irwin without lifting his eyes.

"We don't like him," Melvin volunteered, and blottered a drop at the end of his nose with his sleeve.

"Why not?"

" 'Cause he ain't friends. He don't play with us, and he won't let us come in his house and show us his toys. And that's why we don't let him come in ours," Irwin explained.

"And," Melvin continued, "my mother says that his mother is stuck up like flypaper and she don't talk to nobody even when my mother once said hello to her in the hall. . ."

"And," Irwin went on, "nobody sees his father, my mother told my aunt, and she don't like the looks of it, 'cause who pays the rent?"

I was about to argue that his mother was wrong and to tell what I knew about Johnny's father, but keenly aware that I had already broken the mother "law," I kept silent. Instead I made my way down the steps, involved in these new and tantalizing questions: Why didn't Johnny play with anybody? Why didn't he let the twins into his apartment? Why didn't his mother talk to theirs? They were beautiful problems . . . with endless possibilities for asking questions and for guessing.

I decided I would take the matter up with my mother, and automatically looked up at the window of her bedroom, the only room in our apartment that faced the street. Then I remembered that it was about the time for me to get my nickel, but if Libby had already told on me, my mother wouldn't let me have one. Rather than run the risk of doing without what I thought was an important essential of my day, I went at once to Mr. Goodman's store.

"What do you want, Bobby," Mr. Goodman asked suspiciously after I had very carefully closed the door.

"Can I please have some water, Mr. Goodman?"

"Why don't you go home and get water?" Mr. Goodman returned to his newspaper.

"There's no one home," I lied.

"Where's your mother, if there's no one home?" he asked indifferently.

"She's helping Mrs. Jackson to kill her diet beetles."

"So why don't you go to Mrs. Jackson for some water?"

"Libby is telling my mother something bad about me right now."

Mr. Goodman groaned, folded his paper and finally stood up.

"A person wants to live, but they don't let him," he said to a box of chocolate marshmallow twists. Taking a glass from the metal tray behind the counter, he filled it to its halfway mark. Less than half-full would have meant that he was really annoyed at having been disturbed.

I finished the water, brought the glass to Mr. Goodman's table and set it down in front of him. He didn't look up. I decided it would appear too abrupt and pre-planned to come right out and ask him to let me have a jelly apple on credit, so I took the more lengthy approach.

"Mr. Goodman," I announced, "I have a new friend and his name is Johnny, and he lives in the same house with Melvin and Irwin. And they told me just now that once when their mother said hello to his mother in the hall, she didn't answer. Why?"

He looked at me doubtfully. "If I tell you why, you promise to go away and leave me in peace?"

I agreed.

"Because maybe when their mother said hello, it sounded to his mother like good-bye."

"That's no answer," I objected.

"Sorry." He shrugged his shoulders. "If I can think of a better one I'll send you a special delivery—meanwhile, good-bye and tell them I sent you."

"From now on I'm going to Mrs. Spector for water."

"That will be the blackest day of my life. Good-bye and give my best regards to the President when you see him and tell him I wish on him what he wished on me." Mr. Goodman drew the paper across his face.

I was farther from the subject of a jelly apple than ever. There was no longer any alternative but to attack directly.

"Mr. Goodman," I asked hesitantly.

He didn't reply.

I tried again, inserting a tear in my voice. The paper closed slowly.

"I will tell you something very confidential, Bobbeleh," he said. "You can make miracles."

"I can?"

"Absolutely. It used to be, a man had to live for ten years to become ten years older, but now with you and your questions, he can get ten years older in ten minutes, maybe less."

"I didn't ask for anything, yet."

"So I've got something else to look forward to?"

"Can you please trust me a jelly apple?"

"Do you see that sign?" he asked, pointing to a printed card tacked to the wall.

"Yes."

"Can you read it?"

"No."

"I knew it was thrown-out money when I bought that sign," he said, but to himself. "Half the people can't read it and the rest make believe it's not there." Then, directing his voice at me, "It's printed on there, 'In God we trust. Everyone else pays cash.' "

"Does that mean, if my mother asked you to trust her a jelly apple, you wouldn't?"

"What's all of a sudden with the mother?" he asked. "Did you hear from my mouth one word about a mother? You didn't give me so much as a chance to say, yes, no or efsher I'll trust you a jelly apple, but quick you throw up the mother to me. You think, maybe, you'll throw a scare into me? Why in the first place didn't you ask your mother for a nickel, you shouldn't have to come to an old man who doesn't know where his next piece of bread is coming from—a choleryah should take the whole Republican Party—to trust you?"

"But—"

"Don't be such a Mr. Buttinsky. Since when do you say 'but' to an older person? Make no mistakes, mister. I love your mother like she was my own daughter, maybe even better. I knew her even before I let my wife talk me into going into business for myself. Some business. On J. P. Morgan should be wished such a business. He'd be on Easy Street in no time, with a broom and a shovel.

"So let's get down to cases. I'm going to make an exception this one time. It's what they call in business, good will. Today I'm trusting you a jelly apple, but if it should ever happen again that you ask me to trust you and all of a sudden you give me a song and dance with the mother, then I'll ask you to do me a favor and go with good health to buy by Mrs. Spector. See how far you'll get with her. Mrs. Spector is also a mother, and mothers don't have to trust each other. Understand?"

I didn't, but nodded.

"And another thing," he said as he walked behind the counter, "when you trust a jelly apple, it's not like paying cash on the line. You don't get no picking, no choosing. You take the one I give you the first time. Here," he said. "Hold it with both hands."

"I will, thank you Mr. Goodman." I took the apple. "I have no hand to open the door."

"Just a minute," he said, coming around the counter. He opened the door, but before letting me out said, "Just in case you should take it in your head to talk to anybody about our private transaction, you can tell your mother that I would trust her with my last penny. Understand?"

"I'll tell her, I promise. And I'll pay you right away, tomorrow."

I worked away at the apple and had finished it by the time I was halfway up the street, when I saw my sister, Martha, walking rapidly toward me shaking a "where-have-you-been-finger" at me.

"Do you know what time it is?" she asked.

"It's time for you to leave me alone."

"For my part," she said, "I could leave you alone for the rest of my life, but your mother wants you."

"I'll tell her what you said."

"What did I say?"

"You said that she was my mother, like she wasn't your mother too."

"Stop talking bushwa." She took my hand and quickly dropped it. "What have you been playing with? Your hands are like glue."

I put what I thought was a mystery look in my eyes and said, "The janitor in Melvin and Irwin's building keeps frogs and we went down there to see them. I picked up a frog and it peed in my hand. Their pee-pee is like glue. And you're going to get lots of big warts 'cause you touched my hand."

She pushed me toward the house. The moment we were inside the apartment I realized that her friend Henrietta was there; I could smell her toilet water. And also that my mother was angry with me; she didn't say a word.

I walked into the kitchen and found her at the sink, peeling tomatoes. "I'm here," I announced.

This usually brought some retort such as, "We'll have the flags flying in a second," or "Now my joy is complete." Now she merely said, "Change your clothes, wash your hands and come eat."

"He's filthy," Martha reported to my mother. "He's been playing with frogs."

"I was not," I objected as I pulled the sweater over my head and went to wash.

My mother had placed a dish of lettuce, tomatoes, onion rings and sliced hard-boiled eggs with mayonnaise dressing on the kitchen table when I returned.

"I don't want the onions, they make me cry," I said.

"You'll cry anyway before we're through."

"Why?"

"Eat first, you'll find out later."

"Then I won't eat."

"You'll just make it harder for yourself. You'd better eat."

I could tell she was not going to change her mind. I finished the salad, but when it came to the lamb chops I could feel the tears collecting, ready to spill out at her first word. I pushed the dish away. "No more," I said.

"Why?"

"Because you hate me so much you don't even want to talk to me." The tears ran down the sides of my nose.

"Why do you do things that make me punish you? Wherever do you get such fantastic ideas? Whatever made you say that Libby's mother was full of dried beets? Where do you hear such things?"

"I didn't say that," I sobbed. "That Fifi la-la Libby lied."

"What did you say?" Her voice softened slightly.

"I said that her mother had diet beetles. And that's what you told me."

A smile appeared and faded on her face. "It isn't what you said to Libby, it's just that you know you shouldn't say anything against anyone's mother. How would you like it if Libby, or any of your friends, said something against your mother?"

"I'd stick them with a pin." The sobs had lessened.

Martha came into the kitchen, her face alive with a question, when she noticed my tears. "What's he crying about?" she asked.

"He did something wrong today," my mother said.

"For my money, he should be crying all day, every day, because he's always doing something wrong."

"Since you have no money, we'll discount that last statement."

44

"Of course, nothing I say is ever right." My sister shrugged her shoulders up to her ears.

"Your batting average is pretty low."

"Why do you talk that silly baseball talk?"

"Because I'm trying to drive something home to you, but it seems I keep on striking out. Now, what did you want to ask?"

"Can I wear your crystal beads?"

"Where are you going that you need my crystal beads?"

"Nowhere. After dinner Henrietta and I are going over to her house and we thought we'd dress up for a change."

"Who's going to be there?" my mother asked in all seriousness. "Richard Barthelmess or Ronald Colman, or both?"

I laughed.

"Why do you always make fun of me . . . especially in front of him?" Whenever my sister became indignant, her voice rose to a squeak.

"Martha's got a mouse in her mouth," I shouted gleefully.

My sister started for me but my mother quickly slipped between us. "All right," she said, "you can wear the beads, but not until after dinner. Now go back to Henrietta, you shouldn't leave a guest alone for so long. As for you," she turned to me, "finish your meal."

When I learned that my mother was not going to allow me to have any of the cake she had made that day, I objected with: "But I cried already."

"So you don't have to cry again. You are not getting any dessert because of what you did today. Just be content with the thought that if you behave, you'll have some tomorrow."

"It'll be old and stale by tomorrow."

"You'll be older tomorrow but will you be stale?" I shook my head reluctantly. "Well, neither will the cake. Here, have some milk."

"You're going to be sorry not giving me some cake."

"I'm not going to be sorry, I'm sorry right now. After all, I made the cake for you. Now I'm going to have to wait a whole day to find out if you like it. Finish your milk."

"If I told you something Mr. Goodman said could I have some cake?"

"Bribery may get you something but it won't be cake."

"Don't you want to know?"

"Not if I have to pay so much as a crumb for it."

"He said he would trust you with his last penny."

"That's very nice of him. Meanwhile, what did he trust you?"

"How do you know!"

"I have eyes in my pocketbook. What did he trust you?"

"A jelly apple."

"Did you tell him that I said you could have it?"

"No."

"Then it can be fixed up with no damages. The nickel you get tomorrow will pay for today's jelly apple."

"Then will I get two nickels tomorrow?"

"Only one. You weren't supposed to have a jelly apple today, so today's will have to take the place of tomorrow's as part of your punishment."

"But you already punished me with no cake."

"That was only one part of it. The idea was that you would have nothing sweet today at all. Get it?"

"Yes, but I don't like it."

"That's all right as long as you still like me."

This was beyond argument. I left the kitchen, went into my room and crept under the bed. It was my own shelter, and in the half-light I pondered the imponderables.

My world was the dot under a question mark. Things did not merely happen in this world, there had to be a reason for their happening. And there was, I was certain, an answer to every question, with a question to follow every answer. The most important question at the moment was this new boy, Johnny. I had met him only that morning yet felt as though I had known him a long time, longer even than

Libby. He was different from me and my other friends. I could sense that he lived much more in his private world than we did; that he had lots of dark places inside him where he hid his secrets and the things that frightened him instead of telling them to people.

I knew that I would not be able to talk and play with him as I did with my other friends; I would have to be careful not to touch the sore spots. For instance, I had to be sure never to ask him to let me come to his house, or ask him any more questions about his father.

I had trouble understanding my feelings about Johnny. They were yes and no. Yes, I wanted him to like me, especially because I was sure he didn't have any friends and liked only his mother and maybe his brother. No, I didn't like the way his eyes looked. They were afraid and dark most of the time. And it made me feel strange that he never smiled but only burst into sudden laughter that would vanish as quickly as it had come.

It wasn't easy to think out and it was further complicated by the way I felt about his mother. I could have bet that he had learned not to smile from her. She wasn't like my mother, or even any of the other mothers. I remembered how excited my mother had been to meet her, but she held back, like someone afraid to run or skip or jump because something might fall out of her pocket.

These were hard questions, but that's the way the questions were. The brighter butterfly ones, though more insistent, lived only briefly. The darker crawling ones, such as the crash, the Depression, selling apples, the shame of home relief, the disgrace of being dispossessed, were more difficult to ask about and were, it seemed, continually underfoot. But whether my questions were soaring or earthbound, I was certain there was one person who knew all the answers.

I remember once coming to her with the problem of Mr. Fisher, the tailor, and his nephew. Mr. Fisher swore that his nephew was a famous Hollywood actor, but he would never reveal his name. Every now and then, he would wave an envelope in front of me and say, "See! Here is a letter from him. Now will you believe?"

47

"From who?" I would ask even though I knew whom he meant.

"From my nephew, the actor, the rich one. He's not fancy-shmancy like the others. He writes his uncle."

Practically nobody I knew believed that Mr. Fisher's nephew was a famous actor. And then what could be more impossible to believe than the existence of a famous actor without a name?

But my mother replied, "If Mr. Fisher doesn't have such a nephew, he certainly should have one. And if someone thinks he should have something so badly, he usually gets it. So I am sure Mr. Fisher's nephew is a big deal in Hollywood."

I believed.

On the other hand there were things I saw with my own eyes, yet she taught me to doubt them—such as Carmella and her bruises. Mr. Calabrese, the barber, had an only child, a fifteen-year-old daughter named Carmella, who was fleshy, round and wide. Everything about her was wide. Her hair, like wires straightened with stove black, stood away from her head. Her cheeks plumped out like enormous polished olives. Her breasts, which seemed incapable of confinement, pointed away from each other. And her hips were like great goose-down pillows tucked under her skirt.

But wider than any physical part of her was her expansive nature. She loved everyone, especially children. If she could, she would have engulfed every child on Union Street. She fondled them, babied them, kissed them, watched them hour after hour while sitting outside her father's shop on one of his dainty brass-backed, brass-legged chairs, which she completely obscured. Without the restraints imposed on her by her mother and her Church, Carmella would have happily given birth to an army. At the sight of a handsome man or older boy, her nostrils would dilate, would quiver with the intensity of her passion as her eyes followed him down the street. Time and again she would say to my mother, "Mrs. Hirshman, I love your son, Peter. I'm going to eat him up alive one of these days." To which my mother would reply, "If you can digest him, you're welcome." And pointing to me,

"And you can have this one for dessert."

Carmella was plagued by ghosts, ghosts that pinched her at night. They were not, according to her, ordinary pinching ghosts but rather ghosts of the saints whose pictures hung on the walls of her apartment. "I can tell when they're going to pinch me," Carmella would say. "At night, when I pray to them before I go to sleep, I can see their eyes moving around. They go around and around in circles. And then when I fall asleep, they come down from the pictures and they pinch me here and here." Carmella would lift her skirt and proudly exhibit deep, plum-colored bruises on her thighs. "There are more in other places," she would add, "but I can't show them to you until you grow up."

For all their vivid reality, for all Carmella's proofs that the effects were not achieved through the use of indelible pencil—she once stole a cake of soap from her father's shop and performed a washing demonstration on the street—I found her pinching ghosts difficult to accept.

Then one day when Martha was describing a particularly large bruise on Carmella's upper arm supposedly inflicted by a ghostly saint, my mother established the official attitude by saying, "You can bet your bottom dollar it was a ghost by the name of Dominic Fastafazoola, who lives a few blocks from here."

From that moment Carmella could turn as purple as her bruises with rage, I would not believe.

chapter 3

My father's voice was gentle, his face rough even when freshly shaved. If I was still awake when he returned from work, after he kissed my mother and Martha, he would kneel and press my face against his. I cannot remember his ever having lifted or kissed me.

On the evening of my first regular day at school he was home early. Peter had come up the stairs with him and they were still in the hall. "Can I, Dad?" I heard my brother ask him. "Can I?" "We'll talk about it inside," my father said in his talcum-powder voice, which meant the answer was, practically, no. "Gosh, Dad, I got to know right away!" But my father was immune to such pressures and entered the apartment without answering.

I asked my brother where his books were. "Geez!" he shouted, turned and flew out the door. Peter was the fastest runner, skater, bicycle rider and swimmer in the neighborhood, which prompted my father to remark that he was greased lightning, except for his brains.

My mother came from the kitchen and kissed my father on his lips. This never failed to embarrass him, but if he objected—as he sometimes did with, "Fran, not in front of the. . ."—she would silence him with, "When I don't kiss you hello like that, then you've got trouble, Mr. Hirshman."

"Well, how good was Bobby-boy today?" He knelt, patted my face.

"Ninety per cent," I replied.

"Not even fifty," came my mother's voice from the kitchen.

"More than fifty," I whispered.

"What did you do?" he whispered in return.

"I lost my new ball so I can't get one for three days. And also I put chewing gum in Leatrice Aronowitz's hair by mistake."

"Then it must have been about seventy per cent." He rose and went to wash.

My brother returned, threw his books on the couch.

"What do you want from Daddy that he's not going to give you?" I asked.

"What *don't* you want from me that I *am* going to give you," he replied, and broad-jumped into the kitchen.

"What?" I called, knowing that he expected it.

"A boot in the poot," he said.

"Your hands, Peter." This, from my mother.

He broad-jumped out of the kitchen into the foyer and collided with my father coming out of the bathroom.

"Do you think the day will ever come," my father asked, "when you'll develop into something higher than a kangaroo?"

Peter didn't reply.

Martha, actress-walking, crossed the living room, stopped suddenly and turned to me. "Who do I look like?"

I examined her carefully. "Like nobody's sister."

"Oh, you idiot! You're supposed to say, Vilma Banky." Then, walking into the kitchen, she asked, "Mother, don't I look like Vilma

Banky?"

"Around the mouth," my mother said, and told her to wash her hands.

Invariably at this point in the evening, just before the rest of the family were ready to have their dinner—I had already had mine and was not allowed to "bother" them—the dumbwaiter bell would ring. My mother would habitually protest at the timing, saying it was as if the janitor somehow knew they were just sitting down to eat and did it on purpose. Nevertheless she had the pail and paper bags under the dumbwaiter door in readiness.

From the complete silence in the kitchen, I knew that they were also waiting for the sound of the buzzer.

"He's late," my mother said. Then, after a few moments, "He must be at the bottom of the bottle again."

More silence, followed by my mother's "I feel just like a trained animal. I just can't go ahead and serve dinner until I hear that bell."

All the while they ate, I heard a faint but prolonged humming of bells, which could only mean that tenants were ringing to get the janitor's attention. Then a voice called, "Hey, Sobieski, put the bottle down and bring the dumbwaiter up." This was followed by more voices and finally Sobieski's guttural, "Shod hop! The goddamned lousy dumbwaiter is broken. No garbage today!"

"Again?" my mother asked. "One of these days it will die altogether, like in The Poorhouse."

There was something disturbing in what she said, but I was diverted by the Niagara of voices in the dumbwaiter shaft, and above them all, rising full and clear, was Mrs. Greneker's, "If you don't collect today, you won't collect on Christmas."

"How duh hell can I collect, if duh sonofabitch lousy rotten t'ing is broke. Tell the landlord to go fix it. I'm a super, not a dumbwaiter fixer!"

"Why don't *you* tell him to fix it?" I called to my mother.

"If you don't do the things I ask," she replied, "what makes you

53

think Mr. Sobieski would?"

"Because he likes you."

"Don't you?"

I went at once to see what sort of look she would give me. But attention was now on Peter, who had asked, "So can I, Dad?"

"Can he what?" my mother interjected.

"I got a chance to join the football scrub team but I gotta have your permission."

My father slowly folded his napkin. He placed it on the table and pushed his chair back slightly. "Tell me if I'm right—you are on the swimming team, the relay team, the lacrosse team and the basketball team. Anything else?"

"High jump," Peter replied, "but it's not really a team. You do it by yourself."

"Which reminds me," my mother interrupted, "there's something else I'd like you to do by yourself."

"What's that?" Peter asked suspiciously.

"Take the garbage down when you go."

"Whaaaaat?" Peter's voice rose from indignation to outrage. Martha, who had been examining her baked apple with disdain, began to eat it. "Since when am I the janitor in this family?"

"Since I gave up the job," my mother said.

"Well, I don't wanna!"

"Why not?" my father asked.

" 'Cause I just don't wanna go down into that stinking cellar. The floors are all mud and there's all kind of dirt hanging from the ceiling. And besides, that Polack's always after me. Why can't Martha go?"

Martha, her mouth filled with apple and protests, began to choke.

"All right, Camille," my mother said, slapping her back, "you can stop, *you* don't have to go."

"Well, that settles it," my father said, "the scrub team is out."

Peter let out a long, anguished, "Why?"

"Because anyone who is so afraid at the thought of getting a little dirty would be a washout at football. Besides, how about taking a couple of minutes a day to huddle over your schoolbooks?"

"Aw, gee," my brother complained. "You never let me do what I want to. I never have any fun."

"Neither do I," said my mother. "The Republican Party has a monopoly on all the fun. Maybe we'll have some after the next election."

My brother pushed himself from the table and muttering, left for the living room, where, from the sounds, I guessed he had thrown himself on the rug.

"Ready to hear from the next county," my mother announced.

I walked to the middle of the kitchen and stood at attention.

"Can't you wait until I finish eating?" Martha complained.

"If we wait for you to finish we'll be hearing about his first day in college," my mother said. "Come Bobby, tell us about school." Martha left, holding the dessert plate.

"After all the mothers went home," I began, "we marched into a room that had colored paper pasted on the windows and little, little seats like everybody had a dolly ass."

"Stop trying to be cute," my father said.

"Behind?"

"All right, go ahead."

"The teacher said that her name was Miss Diamond and that we should say hello to her. So all of us said, 'Hello, Miss Diamond,' then we sat down. Libby was on this side, Johnny on that side, and I was in the middle.

"Then the teacher said that we should stand up one by one and say our name and say who we like very much. And when Libby stood up, she said that her name was Libby Jackson and that she liked Mrs. Hirshman because Mrs. Hirshman took her to school last time to register when her mother was sick and had to stay in bed. So I didn't know what to say because I was going to say that I like my mother best and Libby said it before me. So I stood up and I said that my name was Robert Hirshman, and that I liked Libby Jackson. Then the teacher asked me why I liked her. So I thought very hard and said, 'I like Libby Jackson because she has lullaby eyes. . .' "

"What kind of eyes?" my father asked.

"Lullaby eyes."

"What kind of eyes are lullaby eyes?" he asked.

"I don't know. Everybody laughed. I laughed too."

"I think lullaby eyes are very nice," my mother said, and turned to my father. "If he can think up something like lullaby eyes now, just imagine him when he's grown up. I can hear the cherries popping all over the neighborhood."

"Fran, watch what you're saying," my father admonished.

"What kind of cherries?" I asked.

"The kind they put on top of banana splits," my mother said, and laughed.

"Anyway, then the teacher said for Johnny to stand up and he wouldn't. I told him in his ear to stand up but he wouldn't. He just sat there like a duncebell. So the teacher asked him his name and he wouldn't answer. He wouldn't say nothing."

"Anything," my father corrected.

"Anything. And then the teacher started to walk over to him and I was sure she was going to give him a good hard smack, so I stood up and said that I knew his name was Johnny Schafer. And do you know what the teacher did?"

"No, what?" my mother asked.

"She told me to sit down right away and not to meddle, that Johnny knew his name and was just a little bit bashful because it was his first day of school. And she told me never to answer when she was speaking to somebody else in the class. That's what she said."

"She's right," my father said. "You have to learn how to mind your own business and to speak only when your teacher speaks to you. Didn't I tell you to keep your eyes and ears open and your mouth shut?"

I nodded.

"Then what happened?" my mother asked.

"I don't want to tell any more."

"Just because your teacher was right is no reason to sulk." My mother stroked my head. "Believe me, Robert Hirshman of the sensitive Hirshmans, this will not be the last time that you and your teachers won't see eye to eye. School is like business, the customer is never right."

"Well," I went on, "she came over to Johnny and asked him to stand up. But he wouldn't. So Marcia Weissbaum turned around and said that he was being naughty and he should be put in the corner with a dunce cap on his head. Then Johnny began to cry hard. So Libby stood up and said that Marcia Weissbaum should put her head in the toilet and pull the chain three times. Miss Diamond got very mad and she clapped her hands and told everybody to keep quiet or she would take steps. What does 'take steps' mean?"

"Steps are the things you take when you don't expect to get anywhere," my mother said.

"It means punishment," my father asserted, giving my mother a thin look.

"So then she went in between the chairs and she took Johnny's hand and took him out of the room. And you know what Libby did when the teacher left the room?"

"You're not tattling on Libby now, are you?" my mother asked.

"No. The whole class saw it. I swear."

"You don't have to swear. We take your word for it," my father said.

"All right, what did she do?"

"As soon as the teacher left, she turned around and took her schoolbag and hit Leatrice Aronowitz, who is Marcia Weissbaum's best friend, over the head. But the teacher came back right away so Leatrice Aronowitz couldn't hit back. And Johnny didn't come back."

"Not at all?" My mother looked puzzled.

"No, not even when they gave us milk and a box of animal crackers, he didn't come back."

"Why didn't you tell me about this when I called for you this afternoon?"

"I started to," I protested, "but you told me to save it for later when Daddy came home."

"Yes, I did. I remember," she admitted as she stood.

"Where are you going," I asked. "I'm not finished."

"Tell the rest to your father. I have to make a phone call." She left.

"I won't," I said angrily, and ran out of the room and threw myself down next to Peter.

"Let's run away," I whispered to him. I heard my mother jiggle the telephone receiver.

"Don't bother me." Peter pulled away.

"We can run away and sleep in the park."

"You know what I'm gonna do?" Peter asked, turning to me. "I'm gonna quit school and get a job."

"What kind?"

"I know a guy whose brother made as much as a buck and a half shining shoes, and all he had to do is buy the shoebox. They call it a permanent investment. And then on Sundays I can deliver the papers straight to people's doors. There's lots of money in that, too."

"But you can't quit school."

"Why not?"

"Because you'll become a bum in the gutter begging people to please give you a penny 'cause you're starving."

My mother passed us on the way back to the kitchen.

"They only say that to scare you. There's lots of famous people who quit high school. But not according to this family. You know what?" he asked, bracing himself on his elbow. "I don't think I really belong to this family."

"Yes you do and me too," I whispered into his ear. "Only Martha doesn't belong here. Her real name is Heartburn."

"I like you a lot, Bobby," my brother said reflectively, "but I think you get more loony every single day. By the time you get to be my age you'll be in a straightjacket, you know that? Where do you get such ideas that Martha's name is Heartburn. Martha hasn't even got a heart."

"Mother once called her Sarah Heartburn when she was making believe like an actress."

"Well, let me let you in on something, kiddo, your mother isn't so straight up here either," he said, pointing to his head.

"Maa-aa-aa," I yelled.

He clamped his hand over my mouth. "If you tell what I just said I'll never talk to you again."

I pulled away from him and ran into my mother's room. Opening the top drawer of the sewing machine cabinet, I took out a pin, rushed back and jabbed it into his behind.

Peter screamed, "You little bastard!"

I ran into the kitchen, threw myself into my mother's lap. Peter was right behind me, his face twisted with rage and indignation. "Do you know what he did?"

"What did he do?" asked my mother innocently. "You're still alive, aren't you?"

"He stuck me with a pin, right here." He pointed vaguely.

"Did you do that?" my father asked.

I nodded.

"Why?" asked my mother.

" 'Cause I promised you that if anybody said something against you, I would stick him with a pin. But I can't tell you what he said because he'll never talk to me again if I do."

"I'll do worse than that," Peter threatened, "I'll beat the feathers out of you when I get my hands on you."

"You'll do nothing of the kind," said my mother.

"But it hurts," said Peter, rubbing his behind.

"It will heal by the time you get married. And if it doesn't, your wife will kiss it and that will make it better."

Peter's face turned red and he flew out of the room and into our bedroom. Before slamming the door, he yelled, "How did I ever get into this crazy, crazy family?"

"Einstein has been working on that problem for some time," said my mother. "He should have the answer any day now."

"And as for you," my father turned to me, "defending your mother is all very fine, but you're not going to do it by making pincushions out of people. If you really wanted to punish Peter, you should have told us what he said. You can't now because you promised you wouldn't. But if you had, it would have made him feel worse than he does."

"All right, enough is enough," my mother said impatiently. And then, "They don't have a phone. I think I ought to go over and see if anything is wrong."

"Where?" my father asked.

"Over the hill to The Poorhouse," she replied, nodding her head toward the front of our building.

"Do you have to?" my father asked.

"No, but then I could sit here and feel like a fool wondering what happened." She went to the hall closet and slipped her coat off its hanger.

"I want to go with you," I said.

"You stay here and finish telling your father about your first day in school."

"No."

"What do you mean, no?"

"I don't want to tell him without you."

She looked at me for a moment, then said, "You know, you're too small to be my shadow and too old to be holding onto my apron, don't you think?"

I had no answer. I had nothing but the need to be with her, especially if she were going to Johnny's.

"Why don't you take him along?" my father asked.

"But I'll only be a minute."

"It may help the other one feel more at ease tomorrow," he said softly.

With a sigh of exasperation, she said, "All right, get your blue sweater, the heavy one."

I ran into my room, got the sweater from the lowest drawer in the bureau and struggled into it, at the same time telling my brother I was sorry I stuck him, and ran out while he hunted vainly for something to throw at me.

The street lamps were golden moons. A satisfied silence hung suspended as if the street had just finished a large meal and was sighing with well-fed contentment. Rose, white and yellow lights shone from the tenement windows, each curtained with its private mystery. From a distance, as if trying to pierce the insulation of silence, a woman called her child's name, and in her voice could be sensed: "Where are you? It's late. I'm worried. . ."

We crossed to the opposite sidewalk, and walked up the steps of the building. It was the oldest tenement in the neighborhood and was called "The Poorhouse" by those fortunate enough not to live in it. For though there was a strong sense of equality among the residents of the street, differences were measured mainly in terms of money.

The knowing eye picked up the significant details: the kind of fur on a woman's coat collar (the furriers' wives were experts at distinguishing kolinsky from a masquerading belly of fox); the pin in a man's tie (the jewelers wore invisible loupes in their eyes); a woman who shopped at the A & P was called an AP (Almost Penniless); she who bought Nova Scotia smoked salmon in place of lox had more than stuffing in her mattress; and she who opened her window and called sweetly and clearly to her son, "Samuel, darling, shall I wrap you up and throw you down an imported skinless and boneless sardine sandwich with sweet butter and crispy lettuce with a spritz lemon in a new-bought roll?" was lying in the teeth of adversity.

The laundry was another excellent clue. A clothesline hung with men's shirts and bedsheets meant the family was living from hand to mouth. If these same articles were sent out as wetwash and were then ironed at home, the family lived from day to day. But when they were sent out and returned ready for wear, that family had "the bundle."

The itinerant ear picked up additional statistics. The sound of a radio prevailed over the music of the Victrola; the scratching of a violin or a scale plodded on the piano indicated that there was money to be thrown out; an automobile for pleasure implied there was money to burn; but the family that was incessantly quarreling obviously didn't have a nickel to its name.

These and other considerations notwithstanding, the final and irrefutable method of estimating a family's means was by where it lived. For this purpose, the houses were named in order of precedence: The White House, The Mansionette, Double Dreckers (two families above, two below), The Pigwam, The Flop Garden, The Cave, Sonia's Hole, The Craphouse, The Coffin and, finally, The Poorhouse.

And as I climbed those steps, I recalled my mother's comparing our broken dumbwaiter to the one in The Poorhouse that hadn't been running for years. Inwardly I rebelled at the thought of living in a place like The Poorhouse, which was also called The Winter Palace because they rarely had heat. To me the building had all the connotations of hunger and poverty, such as Melvin and Irwin with their one penny to share for candy and their torn sweaters and cardboard linings in their shoes.

I didn't want our dumbwaiter to stop running. I didn't want to miss hearing its bell every time my mother was ready to serve dinner. It was all part of the order of my day and any change was a threat to happiness.

I was about to ask my mother whether the dumbwaiter really would be fixed by the next day, but we were already in the hallway, so thick with darkness that even by groping along its walls my mother couldn't find the bells and nameplates. She finally gave up and asked me to go to Mr. Goodman's for matches.

Mr. Goodman, as usual, was seated at the small table in the rear of his store, and when I asked for matches, he slowly lowered his paper to the table. "When you going to burn up City Hall?"

"It's for my mother, quick," I said, jumping from one foot to the other to convey the urgency.

Mr. Goodman drew out a long, "Oh." Then resettling his glasses on his face as if to draw me into sharper focus, he said, "If it's for your mother, tell her to get the matches from the same place she bought the cigarettes."

"My mother doesn't smoke," I said angrily.

Mr. Goodman waved a hand at me. "This you didn't have to tell me, you young robber, you. This I could have told you before you were born that your mother would never smoke. But now, gonif, you fell head-first into the trap."

"What trap?" I asked impatiently.

"If she doesn't smoke, what does she want matches for, eh? So, it's you who wants the matches, not your mother. And believe me, God Himself would have to come in here and ask me personally before I give you so much as one single, solitary match—He should forgive me for bringing Him into the conversation."

"But it's not for smoking. It's to find the bells in Johnny's house."

"By me the conversation is finished," Mr. Goodman announced, and had reopened his newspaper when there was a tinkle at the door. It was my mother.

"I should have known," she said, half-smiling and placing a hand on my shoulder, "that there would be a little argument about matches."

Mr. Goodman stood as soon as he saw her and walked toward us.

"Would you mind letting me have a book of matches? I'm trying to find a neighbor's bell and the hall is dark."

"For you, you don't even have to ask," and he thrust two matchbooks at her.

"One will be enough, thank you," she said. Then to me, "Take the matches, Bobby, and thank Mr. Goodman."

"Thank you," I said aloud, but to myself wondered at Mr. Goodman's saying that God Himself would have to personally ask him to give me the matches.

It took five matches before my mother could locate the bell. She pushed it; waited; pushed again.

"Push harder," I suggested.

"You don't fix broken bells by pushing on them," she replied. Then, lighting another match and peering closely at the nameplates, she said, "Anyway, they're on the top floor."

She opened the inner hall door. "Even if no one's home, the exercise will do us good."

The halls were dim, and a smell of wet decay hung suspended. "It makes you appreciate fresh air," my mother said as we started up.

The stairs whined and cracked beneath us. A rung of the banister squeaked at my touch. We finally reached the top floor, where four faceless, nameless doors stared at us.

Stopping only to take a deep breath, my mother walked lightly up to one of the doors, sniffed, walked softly away to the next, sniffed and moved to the third. Here she knocked.

"Who's there?" A woman's voice.

"It's me . . ."

"Who? Who?" The woman's voice was frightened.

"It's only me, Frances," my mother said but with the pacifying quality that was always present whenever she commiserated with me over a bruised elbow or knee.

The "Oh" reflected relief, and Johnny's mother opened the door. "If it's inconvenient—"

"Oh no, Frances, not at all. Please, please come in." With one hand she took my mother's arm, drew her into the apartment; the other tightly clasped a bulky sweater, which was now a time-grizzled green. The skirt of her stiff cotton dress hinted of what was once a print of pink roses. Her face was sallow defeat; only the eyes were determined with a searching ferocity.

The room was knife-clean. White-enamel walls harshly reflected the light of the single, hanging unshaded bulb; two dining-room chairs against the wall on either side of the one window, a bridge table surrounded by four metal folding chairs, were the only furniture.

"Where's Johnny?" I asked.

"He's in his bedroom with the baby," she replied, but made no move to get him.

"Is anything wrong?" my mother asked.

"Oh no . . . not at all," she pressed her assurance. The corners of her smile were stiff, unyielding. The thought of "something wrong," which I invariably associated with illness, made me aware of the piercing smell in the room, a smell that brought to mind Friday afternoons in our apartment when my mother would pour a brown bitter liquid into the pail to capture every last germ, she would explain, and "kill it flat on its back."

As my mother walked to one of the chairs, Johnny's mother quickly said, "We've ordered furniture, but it hasn't come yet."

"I don't stand on ceremony, or even sit on it," my mother said.

I asked, "Can't Johnny come out?"

"Of course, of course," she said as she went to a door on the right, opened it slowly and whispered, "Johnny? Johnny, come out."

He appeared wearing pajamas, his eyes bothered by the light, his face shining with an after-bath brightness.

"Look who's here," his mother coaxed.

He looked around vaguely.

"It's me,me,me,me,me," I shouted.

His eyes widened, and he laughed as he pointed a finger at me and imitating, bubbled, "You,you,you,you,you."

"Not so loud," his mother warned, "the baby's asleep."

"You too." My mother poked a finger between my shoulders.

Turning to Johnny's mother, she asked, "What happened in school today?"

She shrugged. "Who knows? He missed me. A regular mama's boy . . . couldn't bear being away from me . . . not for a minute."

I went up to Johnny. "Did you?"

"Did I what?"

"Did you miss your mother in school?"

He nodded shyly. Signaling him to follow, I walked to the farthest corner from where our mothers sat, and slid to the floor. Johnny sat beside me and I told him what had happened after he left, taking extra care to blow up everything to its fullest, yet remain believable.

"Do you know our dumbwaiter's broke?" I asked.

"What's that?"

I knew at once that I had made a mistake. It was like my boasting about my ability to read and write again. "Do you know what a dumbbell is?"

He nodded.

"A dumbwaiter's a dumbbell's father."

The mention of a father brought back that lost, distant look. I had only gotten in deeper. Somehow I had to assure him of my intentions to be his friend. "Do you know why my mother came here?"

"No," he replied.

"Maybe because they're friends like us. Are we friends?"

He thought. "I don't know," he said finally.

"I know."

"How can you tell?"

" 'Cause if I had something I'd go halfies with you."

"What have you got?"

"Nothing. Would you go halfies with me if you had something?"

"Maybe."

"Only maybe? Wouldn't you give me jelly beans like you said you would give everybody."

"It's gumdrops now."

"Then would you give me gumdrops?"

"Yes."

"How many?"

"Two or three."

"How many would you give Miss Diamond?"

"Nothing."

"How many would you give Libby?"

"One."

"But you'd give me two or three?"

"Yes."

"We're friends. I know."

"How do you know?"

" 'Cause you'd give me more than Libby and lots more than even Miss Diamond."

His face lit. "Sure!" he cried. "We're friends!"

His mother shushed him. "Tell me, Frances," she asked my mother, "didn't you ever do anything about your singing?"

"Frankly, Jeanette, I started to, but let me put it this way—"

"She can make like a night bird," I offered.

"Don't interrupt," my mother said, and went on, "I started singing lessons after I left high school, but they were terribly expensive. So I got a job selling at Zelda's Takes-the-Cake Bake Shop and studied at night. Jack Hirshman asked me to marry him, my singing coach said, 'No.' Then I got a job taking money at Schechter's Original Authentic Kosher Cuisine. Jack Hirshman asked me to marry him, my singing coach said, 'No.' Finally I got my great opportunity. I was offered five dollars to sing "O Promise Me" at Sylvia Krumholz's wedding. The bride's father told me I was another Rosa Ponselle and gave me an extra two dollars. That night I said, 'Yes,' to Jack Hirshman—'No,' to my singing coach—and I've been living happily ever after. What did you do when you left high school, Jeanette?"

"I took a course in a secretarial school . . ." She suddenly gasped, "Ai . . . ai . . ." then screamed; clasping her handkerchief to her mouth, she jabbed her fist into her stomach and rushed from the room.

"Jeanette?" my mother called, ran after her but stopped at the closed door. "Jeanette, what's wrong? Is there anything I can do? Jeanette? Jeanette!"

From inside there came the sound of strangled screams.

"What's the matter with your mother?" I asked.

"She gets that all the time," Johnny said without surprise.

"Jeanette!" my mother shouted. "What's wrong? You're frightening the daylights out of me. Jeanette! Jeanette!"

"What does she get all the time?" I asked.

"Jeanette!" I recognized that sound of determination in my mother's voice. "I'm coming in." She turned the knob and opened the door as she spoke.

I started to follow, but the door closed behind my mother as quickly and absolutely as NO!

"Why's your mother mad?" Johnny asked.

"She isn't mad."

"She sounded mad."

"That wasn't her mad sound, that was her worried sound."

"Why's she worried?"

"Something about your mother."

His eyes darkened. "What about my mother?"

" 'Cause she ran in there like something was hurting her."

"But I told you she gets that all the time."

"But you didn't tell me *what* she gets all the time."

"A bellyache."

"Must be an awful big bellyache," I said, going to the door.

"Sometimes they're big and sometimes they're little, but she goes in her bedroom and takes a pill. And you know what?"

"What?" I asked in a whisper, not wishing to reveal that I was eavesdropping.

"She swallows it without water."

This was not credible, but the time was not right for proving. I raised a finger to my lips and laid my ear against the door. The sounds were sharp, rustling, like the angry buzz-buzz of a large fly against a window screen, then a breath taken deeply and with difficulty, followed by a moan as cold and brittle as the cracking of a puddle's icy skin. Silence.

"What are they doing in there?" Johnny asked.

I made a show of ignorance with my hand and continued to listen, but outside of a few sibilant whips there was nothing. I tiptoed back to Johnny and lowered myself to the floor.

"What are they doing in there?" he asked again.

"How do I know?"

"Why don't you go in?"

"Why don't you?"

"I'm never supposed to go in there. It's her bedroom."

"Never?"

"Never."

"I can go in my mother's bedroom."

"All the time?"

I thought. "All the time."

"Then you can go in."

"It's too quiet."

"Would you go in if there was noise?"

"Sure."

"But if there's no noise maybe something happened to them?"

That probability capped the issue. I stood, went to the door and knocked. My mother opened it, face flushed, eyes small with the suspicion of tears. I tried to look around her, but she stepped forward and filled the doorway.

"What do you want?" Her voice had no room for anything but immediate business.

I had to answer in kind. "I want to go home."

"Who's stopping you? There's the door. Be careful going down the steps and crossing the street. Tell your father I'll be home in a little while."

I wasn't prepared for marching orders. "I want to go home with you."

"In that case you'll have to wait until I'm ready."

"When will that be?"

"Bobby, I have no time now for questions. Go play with Johnny."

"He has no games."

"Here," she said. Closing the door behind her, she went to the card table, picked up her purse, opened it with a quick twist and rummaged around inside until she found a small roll of string—the kind used to wrap the laundry, which she always carefully unknotted and scrupulously saved, as she did rubber bands, safety pins and buttons. "Play cat's cradle with Johnny," she said, pushing the string into my hand, and left the room.

I was considering the advisability of protest when Johnny asked, "What's cat's cradle?"

"Don't you know?"

He shook his head.

"You *don't* know cat's cradle? *Everybody* knows it."

"I don't."

"Are you *really* sure you don't?"

"Honest to God, I don't."

I slipped the knotted string over my hands and pulled it into the cat's cradle. "Here it is."

"It is?" He looked at it from all angles.

"Sure, can't you see it?"

"I didn't know cats slept in cradles."

Realizing I didn't know how to tell him the necessary moves to form the next shape, I said, "You know what kind of cat sleeps in such a cradle?"

"What?"

I recited:

"Who's that ringing at my doorbell?
A little pussy cat that isn't very well.
Rub its little nose with a little chicken fat,
That's the best cure for a little pussy cat."

"I know one," he said as he got up on his knees.

"Kitten, sittin' by the sea,
What do you see? What do you see?
I see a fish, a tasty dish
Swimmin' in the sea.

"Kitten, sittin' by the sea,
Put in a paw. Put in one more.
I'll step right in and catch his fin,
Swimmin' in the sea.

"Kitten, fallen in the sea,
What do you see? What do you see?
I seen no fish, no tasty dish
And say good-bye to me."

Before I could ask him where he had heard about that kitten, he
asked, "Do mothers die?"

The question was as startling as it was sudden. One minute we
were talking about kittens and the next about mothers dying. I didn't
know how he had gotten from one to the other, but I did know the
answer and also knew that it had to be delivered with absolute authority that left not the slightest chance for doubt.

"No!" I said, for if I was ever certain of anything it was that
mothers did not die, ever. It was not only a deepest conviction, I could
also prove it. Weren't both my grandfathers dead and both my grandmothers alive? Didn't every one of my friends, every single one of
them, have a mother? I didn't know all their fathers, but I knew every
one of their mothers. And wasn't it true that no one could ever say
anything bad about a mother, though the same did not apply to other

members of the family, even fathers? Then there was that mysterious private knowledge I had that mothers possessed a certain magic that other people didn't. For instance, didn't she know that when I was in the bathroom and the door was closed I was just running the water and not really washing my hands? Couldn't she see through the walls and say, "Why waste the water when you could be washing your hands at the same time?" Didn't she also know when she was in the kitchen that I was making faces in the mirror in her bedroom? Didn't she call out, "Just be careful we don't get a sudden cold snap—your face will freeze that way forever, and we'll have to pay someone to marry you." And how did she know, without having to look, that I was hiding under my bed, or in a closet, or under the table? Or how did she know that I had had a fight with someone in the street—I'd come in, no scratches, no torn clothing, no tears, and as soon as she saw me she would say, "Who won?" And when I came in after a battle with Libby that ended with our swearing never to speak to one another for life, wouldn't she, after a slight glance, ask, "Did she give back the engagement ring?"

I could prove it in a million ways, but up to now it never needed proving. I was as certain as sun, air, water and night that mothers could never die.

I was about to ask him why he asked the question, when the door opened. His mother came out first. Her face was yellow-green, the color of a smelly cheese that my father liked and which my mother kept in the icebox wrapped under several layers of wax paper. Her eyelashes were moist and tufted, outlining the redness of her eyes. My mother followed her, wearing what I called her "bad news" look. The corners of her mouth were drawn back, making a tight, sharp line of her lips. Her eyelids were lowered so that I couldn't see her eyes, but she had no way of hiding the shadowy bibs beneath.

Looking up, she said, "Don't tell me you've been here all this time with your sweater on?" Turning to Johnny's mother, she said, "You think they have all the brains in the world until they have to use them."

His mother nodded weakly.

"Why didn't you take *your* coat off?" I asked.

She looked down at her coat as if just realizing she had it on. "You want to know why?"

"Yes."

"Because you were in such a hurry to leave that I didn't want to waste time taking it off. And that will have to stand for an answer until I think of something better. Come on, the party's over. And your bathtub is so lonely for you I think I can hear it crying."

Still holding the string taut between my hands, I rose and started for the door.

"Aren't you going to say good-night?" my mother asked. I was sorry she had. I knew once I turned and looked at Johnny I would have to offer him the string. "Good-night," I said, and then slowly, "Do you want the cat's cradle?"

"Yes, yes, yes, yes," he shouted as he ran up to me and tore the string off my fingers.

My mother went to the door, nudged me out ahead of her and before closing it, turned back to Johnny's mother. "Listen, Jen, there's nothing to worry about. Believe me. I've known hundreds of such cases. And it's absolutely nothing. I'll get in touch with you-know-who first thing in the morning."

We arrived home, and my father lowered his paper as we came into the living room. "Is everything all right?"

Instead of answering at once, my mother pulled my sweater up over my head, held it there I thought a few moments too long, and then, slapping my behind, said, "Get into your bathrobe and slippers and come have your bath."

But just before going into my room, I turned and saw my father and mother exchange looks that signified there was much she had to tell him. . . .

The language of looks was developed to a fine art not only by my family, but by the entire neighborhood. People were more often than not characterized by their eyes. One had kind eyes, thieves' eyes, hawk's eyes, eagle's eyes. Wall-eyed and cross-eyed people were tolerated only out of the goodness of one's heart, and then while one's fingers were crossed. "If looks could kill," "She looked daggers at me," "She opened up a pair of eyes at me like I was dirt under her feet," "He looks at me like I owe him money," "She told me with her eyes," were but a few of the expressions in constant use. Not to understand the meaning of looks was to lose half the conversation. Certain jokes were told with sad looks. Someone's misfortunes were sometimes related with eyes laughing. When to start and to stop haggling over price was determined finally by looks. Kids ready to fight tried first to "look each other down." There were long looks, thin looks, loving looks, rotten looks, dirty looks, I-don't-give-a-damn looks, dead-and-buried looks, honey, sweetie, dearie looks, drop-dead looks, uptown looks, milk-and-honey as well as poor-as-paper looks, some that meant exactly the way they looked, others that signified the complete opposite. But they all spoke, reflecting the slightest shadings of difference, conveying thoughts over and beyond the power of words.

The look exchanged between my mother and father that night told me that what she had to tell him was not only long, but sad and difficult; that it was only the beginning of something that would take many tears before it would be over; that it would not be discussed in front of me under any circumstances—all of which meant that if I wanted to know what it was I would have to listen and watch more carefully than ever before, especially at night.

chapter 4

I awoke the next morning to hear my mother give the telephone operator a number and then say, "Hello, Dr. Reuben, this is Frances Hirshman. Everything's all right here, thanks, but I'm calling about a Jeanette Schafer who is coming to see you this morning. . . . Don't worry, she'll be there during visiting hours. You don't have to tell me. It's the eleventh commandment—don't visit your doctor except during visiting hours. Listen, do me a favor, don't ask her to pay. I'll take care of it. Do you understand? . . . No, just don't say anything. She won't think it's free and she won't go around telling the whole neighborhood about it. . . . Doctor, have you ever heard of *ts'dokeh?* Well, if someone wants to give, don't stand in the way. I won't tell anyone either, I promise. Thank you. Good-bye."

It was all very mysterious, intriguing, and a perfect seedbed for sprouting questions. As I lay there wondering how I might best use this information, I heard Martha call innocently but loudly, "Mother, someone didn't take something down he was supposed to, last night."

Peter bolted upright in bed.

"I not only saw," my mother called back, "I've already decided how much allowance it's going to cost him."

"That two-timing, double-crossing, snitching fink," Peter muttered angrily.

It was evident that something very serious was occupying my mother's mind: she had overlooked Peter's failure to do what she asked him last night, and that Martha was tattling this morning.

While she dressed me and all during breakfast I watched her carefully, but she said little, hardly looked at me, and moved about briskly. When we met Johnny and his mother in the street, my mother said hello to her, and then, "I called. It's all right," to which his mother said, "Thanks," and nothing else all the way to school.

Once in class, I was surprised to see that our chairs had been placed in a circle instead of rows as they had been the day before. Johnny and I ran to get adjoining seats. Libby tried to push between us.

Miss Diamond rapped the back of her desk with her ruler. "Were you or were you not told yesterday that you do not sit until we say good morning?" We were ordered to form a line near the door. "It is obvious to me," she said, "that we will have to appoint a class monitor. It is a very important job and I can give it only to the best-behaved person in the class."

Everyone stiffened. Gerard Shuminsky, who was tallest and heaviest, became wood.

"I am going to watch how each of you pays attention this morning," Miss Diamond went on, "and I will pick a monitor just after you have had your lunch. Now I want you all to go and stand in front of a chair—in an orderly fashion. Libby Jackson! I said in an orderly fashion . . ."

"I didn't do anything," Libby mumbled.

Holding hands and keeping very close, Johnny and I started toward the chairs. As soon as we found two together, Libby pounced in front of one. We moved in the circle until we discovered two others; once again Libby darted and claimed one. By this time there were none together, so Johnny and I had to drop hands and part.

"Good-morning," Miss Diamond said.

"Good-morning, Miss Diamond," we replied.

"You may all sit except for Libby Jackson, who will please step to the middle of the room."

As if she had been expecting it, Libby skipped gracefully to the center, took a little bow, and before Miss Diamond could speak, recited:

> "My name is Libby Jackson.
> I live on Union Street.
> My father's name is Irving.
> My mother's name is Gert.
> I have an older brother.
> And I'm a little flirt."

She curtsied and smiled.

"What is the meaning of that?" Miss Diamond asked.

"It's a poem my mother made up for me," said Libby proudly.

"Did your mother also encourage you to keep friends from sitting next to each other?"

"Huh?"

"You heard what I said."

"But the poem was special, by my mother."

"I understand that. Your mother writes very nice poems, but you're not a very nice girl."

"Yes I am."

"Not if you try to keep friends from sitting next to each other."

"I'm Bobby's friend before he is," she said, pointing to Johnny.

His hands flew to his mouth. He pinched his lips between his fingers.

"That's not the point," said Miss Diamond. "They were trying to find seats together."

"But I want to sit next to Bobby too, 'cause I even live in the same house and—"

"Libby, please hold your tongue."

"I wanna go home," Libby blubbered. "I hate kindergarten. I hate everybody."

Miss Diamond sighed deeply. "All right, Libby, stop crying." Then, separating two girls who had already begun stepping on each other's toes, she sat Libby, me and Johnny together in the circle. Still bawling, Libby fell weeping on my shoulder. I heard titters and snickers, and felt my face redden. I glanced and saw Johnny blushing and swore I would never talk to Libby again, ever.

Miss Diamond announced our first project. "I want you to think of something you'd like to collect during after-school hours. And after a few weeks you can bring in your collection for all of us to see, and the one who has the best collection will win a special prize."

Starting with Leatrice Aronowitz, she asked each of us what we would like to collect.

"False teeth," said Leatrice Aronowitz after studying the pleats of her skirt for a moment. Miss Diamond didn't think that was too practical and asked her to think of something else. After several tries, Leatrice Aronowitz settled for buttons.

When asked, Gerard Shuminsky, who was still wood, said he wanted to collect shoelaces.

"Why shoelaces?" Miss Diamond asked.

"I can get lots of them 'cause my father sells them."

Miss Diamond smiled gently. "You should choose something that's not so easy to get." So Gerard Shuminsky picked gum wrappers, which Miss Diamond thought a brilliant idea.

Libby insisted she wanted to collect jewels even after Miss Diamond said they were too expensive. Her reluctant second choice was cards, but when Miss Diamond learned she meant the cards her mother and father played with, she suggested that Libby make another selection.

She finally ended with stones.

"Not rocks, Libby, stones," Miss Diamond cautioned, and explained the difference.

I chose bottle tops, to which Miss Diamond simply said, "All right."

Johnny asked if he could pick bottle tops too. Miss Diamond said that he could, which made Libby furious.

"I wanna collect bottle tops too," she said.

"Libby," Miss Diamond said with a show of great patience, "you are not supposed to speak until I give you permission. You must raise your hand first."

Libby's hand flew up.

"No. I think two bottle-top collectors are enough. You'd better stick to stones."

Libby snorted her discontent. She made the same sounds later in the day when Miss Diamond announced that Gerard Shuminsky would be head monitor and Leatrice Aronowitz assistant monitor.

Solly Mink voiced the majority opinion when he muttered, "Shid!" for which he had to stand in the corner facing the wall.

I found my mother waiting for me at the usual place in the indoor schoolyard. But she wore her hat.

"Why do you have your hat?" I asked.

"Is that the latest way of saying hello?" She knelt, kissed me, brushed my hair with her hand. There was sadness in her touch.

"Why are you wearing your hat?"

"I have some important things to remember. My hat keeps them from slipping out of my mind." Then, standing, she asked where Johnny was.

"Why?"

"He's coming to our house today."

"Hurray!" I cried. This was a great event; Johnny's mother never allowed him to play in anyone else's home. Now I would have the chance to show him all my games, my books, places to hide—all the things I had told him about.

"I'll find him. I'll find him right away," I called, and ran off into the crowd. Inching and twisting my way through children and their parents, I bumped into Libby and her mother. "You know what?" I shouted. Libby clamped her hands over her ears. "I don't wanna hear." "Johnny's coming to my house!" I trumpeted. "He's coming to my house, now . . . right now!" "Who cares," Libby shot back.

I wormed and wriggled my way forward. A woman looked down at me and smiled. "For such a little boy, you're a big pusher." I heard Mrs. Jackson call, "Bobby, be careful," then shout angrily at the woman, "What do you mean, calling the child a pisher? What kind of talk is that to little children? And how do you expect anyone to move when you stand there like the Rock of Gibraltar?"

As always, I was secretly thrilled by Libby's mother's show of noise and anger. It sounded rough but I knew from Libby that in spite of all her threats she had to depend on her husband to carry them out.

I finally found a worried Johnny looking up and down the street. "Come!" I grabbed his hand, pulled him with me.

"I have to wait for my mother," he objected, and tried to hold back.

"No! No! You're coming to my house! My mother told me! She's in the schoolyard!"

Instead of the delight I expected, his face turned dark with fright. "It's all right. . . ." I assured him. "Come, fast!"

He ran, but at every third or fourth step looked back. My mother was not waiting at the door. She had wandered further into the empty schoolyard and I could see now that she was dressed entirely in black; in the silence, under the vaulting metal arches, she looked small and as if a great distance away.

"We're here," I shouted, mostly to dispel the stillness.

"Where's my mother?" Johnny asked as soon as we had reached her.

She knelt, opened her purse, removed her handkerchief and wiped a smudge from his face. "Do you know," she said offhandedly, "you were born in a hospital?"

He shook his head.

"Well, you were—"

"Me, too?" I asked.

"Yes, but let me talk to Johnny for a minute." Turning back to him, she said, "Your mother went to this special hospital when you were born. It's a very big place and it's filled with very smart doctors who can help people if they're not feeling well. So today your mother and I took a taxicab, a real taxicab, and we went for a little ride to this same hospital."

"Why?" he asked.

"Just so she could show me this important place where you were born. But when we got there and we saw all the wonderful things that were happening—people were coming in sick one minute and going out healthy the next—your mother decided she was tired of having those terrible bellyaches . . . you know they really hurt a lot, don't you?"

"Yes, but she had pills," he said.

"But don't you think it's better that she shouldn't have any bellyaches at all and not have to take those pills?"

He nodded.

"So, you know what she made up her mind to do right then and there?"

"What?"

"She decided she would take a little vacation and stay in the hospital and get rid of those bellyaches once and forever."

"For how long?"

"I'm sure the small bellyaches are gone already, but the big ones may take a little bit longer. A few days, not much more. And she'll be back before you can say Mr. and Mrs. Fineshmecker."

"Who are they?" I asked, but really thinking I had expected Johnny to come to my house for several hours, not a few days.

"The Gingerbread Boy's father and mother," she replied. "And"— she rose and took his hand, and after shifting her purse took mine and started toward the exit—"do you know what happened to your mother as soon as she stepped into her room?"

"What?" he asked.

"Somebody brought her a big beautiful bouquet of American Beauty roses. They smelled like honey cake with almonds and each one was the size of a beach ball. And she put them in water right away. Do you know why?"

"Why?"

"So she'll be able to bring one of them home to you and you'll be able to see that the most wonderful things in the world come from hospitals."

"What wonderful things from hospitals?" I asked.

"Well, Johnny's mother is going to come from the hospital, and what could be more wonderful than that?"

"I mean, for me," I said.

"Of course for you," she said. "Don't you think it's very wonderful that Johnny is going to stay at our house?"

"Yes," I replied, but with slight reluctance.

"Well, if his mother didn't go to the hospital he wouldn't be able to stay with you, and think of all the fun you would have missed."

"Do you hear that?" I asked Johnny. He tried to look pleased, nodded his head, but it wasn't enough so I began to shout at him that he was going to stay in my house with me.

My mother tugged me back to her side. "Let's wait until we're home before the noise factory gets going. And," she added, "to start the proceedings off on the right foot we'll get a couple of ice cream cones."

I dropped her hand and started for Mr. Goodman's.

"Not so fast," she said, catching my shoulder and pulling me back to her side. "Johnny is your guest. Do you know what that means?"

"He's getting an ice cream cone too, isn't he?"

"Yes, but more than that, you have to see he comes first."

"Why?"

"Because every guest is like George Washington. First in war, first in peace and first in the hearts of his countrymen, especially since his picture's on the dollar bill." Opening the door, she sent Johnny first, then me.

Children were jostling one another for positions in front of the penny candy case, but the moment Mr. Goodman caught sight of my mother he left the case and came up behind the soda fountain.

"In black," he asked her, "for a reason?"

She looked at her coat, thought for a moment, then smiled. "For the stock market." And then asked, "What's the latest?"

"Before the first of the year the Secretary from the Treasury got up from his gold throne and made a statement. What did he say? He said that he saw nothing in the present situation that warrants pessimism and that he has confidence that there will be a revival from activity in the spring; the country is going to make steady progress. And he was, for a change, right. It progressed from bad to extra-bad. By the spring there were four million unemployed and by now its almost seven million. And where it's going to end, nobody knows."

They both sighed.

"Well," he said finally, "what can I do for you?"

"The two gentlemen are going to have ice cream cones."

Leaning over the counter, he announced, "We have one hundred and twenty kinds flavors. What's your pick?"

"He's first," I said, pointing to Johnny.

"Why?" the old man said. "Because you didn't make up your mind yet?"

"What flavor would you like, Johnny?" my mother asked. He looked at her, his eyes wide with indecision.

"What kinds do you have?" I asked, thinking that making Mr. Goodman name the varieties would give Johnny time to decide.

"Vanilla, chocolate, strawberry," he recited.

"And what else?" I asked.

"From then on it depends what you like."

"Do you have pistachio?" I asked.

"Pistachio we have."

"Do you want pistachio?" I asked Johnny. He nodded. "He wants pistachio," I said to Mr. Goodman.

"And you?" Mr. Goodman asked.

"I want pistachio too."

Mr. Goodman piled two balls of vanilla ice cream on two cones, then took two red-coated pistachio nuts and placed one on top of each cone. "Goodman's homemade pistachio. Save the nut for last. And hold it with two hands."

My mother paid him. "Thank God they didn't ask for tutti-frutti."

"Why? By me tutti-frutti is strawberry with a cherry on top."

As we were about to leave I spied a bottle cap on the sawdust-covered floor and quickly pocketed it, hoping no one saw me. Outside, I explained the collecting assignment to my mother, but she seemed to ignore me until I reached into my pocket and offered the bottle cap to Johnny. She patted my head. "Getting may be pleasure, but giving is happiness . . . it says."

"Who says?" I asked.

"No one I know personally," she replied. I decided that having Johnny in my house was not going to be as much fun as I had first thought.

We finished our ice cream and my mother told us to go to the apartment while she did some shopping. I assumed that Martha or maybe even Peter was home, and went up and pounded on the door, expecting complaints. Instead, Mrs. Greneker opened it.

"What are you doing, collecting rent?" Folding her hands across her bosom, she asked, "Are you coming in or do you want to stay out and bang some more?"

I followed her in. "This is my friend, Johnny," I explained.

She didn't seem surprised, proceeding to unbutton first my coat and then his.

"So what did you learn today in school?" she asked.

I told her about the bottle caps.

"And what are you collecting?" she asked Johnny.

"Bottle caps," he replied shyly.

"Well, I always said there's no end of what you can learn from bottle caps. It's an education in itself."

"It is?" I asked, wondering at my wisdom in having chosen them.

"There's no question. How else would you know that on Thursdays Mrs. Greneker makes gedempfte fleisch that Mr. Greneker says is the most delicious in the whole world, but to digest he needs the help of Dr. Brown's Celery Tonic?"

Without warning, Johnny's face screwed up. "Where's my brother? Did my mother take him?" His eyes blinked in preparation for tears.

"Sh-sh!" Mrs. Greneker put her finger to her lips. "You want to see a surprise?"

"What kind of a surprise?" I asked.

"If I told you what kind of surprise, it wouldn't be a surprise anymore. Take a walk and you'll see for yourself."

Beckoning to us, she tiptoed across the living room. We followed closely behind. She opened the door to my bedroom. I peered in. Someone was in my bed.

"Who's in my bed?" I shouted.

"Shush!" Mrs. Greneker ordered, and quickly shut the door. It slammed on my finger.

I screamed.

"God forgive me, I didn't mean it," Mrs. Greneker gasped.

"You broke my finger!"

Johnny put his hands over his head, ran to the opposite corner of the living room and half-hid behind my father's chair.

"Who's in my bed?" I demanded between sobs. "My finger's dead!"

The front door opened. It was my mother.

"She broke my finger in two places," I cried. "Who's that in my bed? Get him out of my bed. My finger is going to fall off!"

"At least," my mother said, but quickly gave Mrs. Greneker her bundles and took my hand, which I held up as proof. "Let me see."

"No!" I screamed, pulling it away. "It's going to turn green and then I'll die."

Taking me by the arm, she led me, protesting bitterly, to the kitchen, where she rolled up my shirt sleeves and held the finger under the cold water.

"I want it to fall off," I insisted.

She wiped my eyes and nose with her handkerchief. "Don't worry, it will, but this way we can catch it in the sink and sew it back on again. You'll never know when you may need it."

"Who's in my bed?"

"You sound like Goldilocks and the three bears. ' "Who's been sleeping in my bed?" growled the papa bear.' "

"It's not Goldilocks, who is it?"

"Johnny's brother."

"Why?"

"For the same reason Johnny is here."

"I want to go to bed right now."

"Congratulations. That's the first time you ever said you wanted to go to bed. Most people wait until they're married before they ever say it. See how smart you are?"

She dried my hands, ran the hot water until it steamed, poured a teaspoon of epsom salts into a cup of water and plunged my finger into it. "Now if it falls off, it will fall in the cup."

Finger in cup and cup in hand, I marched angrily out of the kitchen.

Johnny sat stiffly on the couch as if in school. "Does it hurt?" he asked.

"It's going to fall off and it's all your brother's fault," I said, continuing to walk.

"Did you forgive Mrs. Greneker?" she asked, and when I refused to reply, she said philosophically, "So you won't invite me to your wedding. I'll save on the present I was going to give you."

Stopping in front of my room, I shouted at the closed door, "It's my room and my bed and somebody's in it and it's not me. That's what's the matter!" I marched into my parents' room, pushed open the sliding window screen, and with the help of a chair climbed out onto the fire escape.

I sat, my finger in the cup, sullen, hurt because things had not worked out as I first thought they would. Artie's presence changed everything. How, I wasn't as yet sure, but one thing was certain: He had already taken my bed. What next? All the bouncing plans I had for myself and Johnny were now deader than a punctured ball.

I sat, wretched like a King of the Mountain without a mountain. I looked down at my street, at friends who, now that I was miserable, were no longer friends. Some were playing Red Rover. Carmella in front of her father's barbershop, chewed—I could tell from the dainty way she held them—polly seeds and spat the hulls on the sidewalk. Libby bounced a ball and sang:

"My mother, your mother live across the way,
514 East Broadway.
Every night they have a fight,
And this is what they say:
Your old man is a dirty old man,
He washes his face with a frying pan.
He combs his hair with the leg of a chair.
Your old man is a dirty old man."

I began my revenge. I would get fake-sick and not go to school the next day. I would put a quarantine sign on Libby's door. I would rub soap on the edge of the apartment steps so that everyone would slip and break his neck. I would open the dumbwaiter door and shout, "Fire!"

None of the plans, however, included a way of getting rid of Artie. A thought came to mind: I would tell everyone in the neighborhood that Dr. Reuben treated Johnny's mother for nothing. But this thought, instead of leading to another, led to the question: What if it had happened to my mother instead of theirs? It was impossible. It couldn't happen. After all she was a *mother!*

Yet, a dark voice said, Johnny's mother was also a mother, and she had gone away. It made no difference where she had gone, or even that she would be back before he could say Mr. and Mrs. Fineshmecker, or with the biggest, most beautiful rose. The important thing was that she had gone without him—and his brother.

My mother wouldn't do that. She couldn't! What would happen to me if she did?

No! To prove to myself this couldn't happen I thought of mothers. I thought of Libby's mother and her cold compresses. I thought of Mrs. Weissbaum's backaches and of Marcia's telling me that her mother had to wear a cage under her dress; of Melvin and Irwin's mother, who coughed so she couldn't call them from the window but had to shake a bell to get them to come home; of Johnny's mother and her bellyaches. But my mother never had headaches or backaches or carried a handkerchief into which she coughed all the time, and she never had to take pills with or without water.

No one ever had to take me to school because my mother didn't feel well. No one ever had to shush me from making noise because my mother was sick. I remembered the last Fourth of July when some boys were throwing firecrackers in front of the Coffin house and a big girl came out to beg us to play elsewhere because her mother was very sick; she gave us money; she even gave me a penny although I didn't have so much as a wooden clapper noisemaker.

No, my mother wasn't like other mothers. She was different. She could never be sick. She would never go away. She would never leave me.

Dawns exploded. My mother was like God. She was!

As if in response to this revelation, my mother came to the window, sat, and leaned her elbows on the sill.

"Well, so how's the world's biggest herring salesman?"

I didn't understand. "What's a herring salesman?"

"Selfish, which is exactly what you were when you saw Artie in your bed."

"Is he still there?"

"Yes, you haven't got that much pull in heaven. And then you hurt Mrs. Greneker."

"Look what she did to me." I wiggled my finger.

"It was your fault. She wouldn't have shut the door if you hadn't screamed bloody murder. She was so upset she had to go home."

"Anybody else?"

"How about Johnny?"

"I didn't do nothing to him."

"You did more than enough by letting him know his brother wasn't welcome. "So, who's next on your list?"

"Nobody."

"Good. Now, tell me what's wrong with Artie being here?"

I had no way of putting it into words.

"Well?"

"I'm thinking."

"If you have to think about it, it means you're looking for an excuse that isn't there."

"It's there, but I don't know how to say it."

"You mean this apartment is not big enough for you and for Artie?"

"Yes."

"When are you leaving?"

"I'm not leaving."

"Neither is he. At least not until his mother comes home."

"Maybe he can go to his grandmother's house?"

"He can't, but I can take you to either one of your grandmothers in less than a jiffy. Which one do you want to stay with?"

"Can't he go and live with his aunt?"

"He doesn't have any."

"Not one?"

"Not a single, solitary one. But you're lucky, you've got a wide selection to choose from. You can visit your Aunt Shirley and play mahjong; or there's your Aunt Edith, who cooks everything with blackcrap molasses and drinks acidophilus milk like water; or maybe you'd like to live with your Aunt Bailke Shifre, known and loved the world over as Berenice Salome, the sweetheart of the Socialist Party. You could be of real help to her."

"I could?"

"Yes, you can keep her earrings from falling between the violin strings when she's playing with her quartet. Or—"

"I don't wanna go to them."

"Then we're back where we started. Artie can't go anywhere else and you don't want to. So it seems to me that unless you can think of another way out, you're going to stay here together."

"Couldn't he stay with Libby?" I suggested in final desperation.

"No! And listen to me, Robert Benjamin Hirshman, you keep this up and you'll get calluses on your heart."

"What's calluses?"

She held out her hand, palm up, and pointed to the puffs and ridges. "Just feel how hard they are," she said. "Calluses on hands are all right, they come from hard work. But when your heart gets calluses you end up by becoming one thing and one thing only."

"What's that?"

"A rent collector."

"That's bad?"

"The worst. How's the finger?"

I pulled it out of the cup. I was delighted. The bruise had a bloody red eye surrounded by brilliant mottles of purple and blue.

She wrapped it carefully first with gauze and then with tape. "Now, do you want me to kiss it and make it better, or would you like it to turn green and fall off?"

"Kiss it, please." She did. "Thank you."

"Now, I want you to do a favor for me. I can't leave Artie and

Johnny alone. I want you to find Martha and tell her I need her right away."

I hunched my shoulders. "Where?"

"Where else but Warner Brothers Studios, the one in Henrietta's bedroom."

"I thought they were mad."

"They're glad again. The show must go on." She took the cup and helped me inside.

"Can I ask you a question?"

"What is it?" she asked.

"Are you like other mothers?"

"No," she replied, "only I have you."

Flowers opened.

I found Johnny in the living room, looking as if he didn't know where he was and didn't want to be there.

"I have to go find Martha 'cause my mother needs her right away," I said. " 'Cause she can't leave you and Artie. And look at my finger. But when I come back, I'm going to show you some big games. And if you want, Artie can play, too. Wait till you see my sister. She makes like an actress but my brother says she hasn't got a heart. My finger's bouncing like it has a ball inside. Good-bye."

Once in the street, holding my finger like a decoration before me, I noticed that Red Rover had turned into a free-for-all. Libby was chasing Solly Mink, who had taken her ball, and just as I passed the barbershop, Mr. Calabrese came out and gave Carmella a resounding slap in the face for dirtying the sidewalk with polly-seed husks.

"Someday you'll hit me and knock my brains out."

"That'sa what I'm-a looking for," he roared, waving his cigar.

I held my finger up higher for Carmella to see.

"Shut up," she yelled at me, "my head hurts worst."

I crossed the street (Carmella shouted, "Look two ways, you dope.")

and my eye was caught by a large, shapeless clump on the sidewalk next to Henrietta's house. There were soft bundles of all sizes, some tied in frayed sheets, others in old coats held together with knotted sleeves. There were painted, peeling iron head and footboards; springs from whose metal network coils hung like frozen curls; thin mattresses twisted up like jellyrolls; a bureau painted chocolate understruck with patches where jags of missing veneer showed through; assorted grocery cartons overflowing with shoes, crockery, broken records; a pair of floor lamps with most of the bright glass jewels gone from the shades; a red plush mohair chair and couch, head- and hand-stained, their bottoms sagging, their seats as uneven as a broken pavement; three knurled brass candlesticks and a flared iridescent glass vase with paper and wax flowers stood tipsily on a warped vegetable bin whose open doors revealed a roll of toilet paper. And tied to an ironing board and a batch of curtain rods, a dirty gray, crazy-haired mop stood guard over all.

The owners either did not know that their possessions were on the street, or if they did, did not wish to acknowledge the fact, for no one was around. I didn't want to touch anything. I knew these were the ousted possessions of an evicted family, and could not understand why no one was there to protect them.

I walked quickly past, entered the hallway of Henrietta's house. But at the battery of doorbells I realized I did not know her last name. A little girl walked through the hall, and I asked if she knew where Henrietta lived. She put her finger in her mouth and walked away.

I went back outside to see if there was anybody around I could ask. Two boys had taken a grizzle-whiskered broom from the heap and were sawing off its head for stickball. I was sure they would be annoyed if I interrupted them, especially with a question about where a girl lived, so finally deciding there was only one sure way of finding Martha, I returned inside, went to the foot of the stairs and cupping my hands around my mouth, shouted, "Calling Martha Hirshman in Henrietta's apartment . . . calling Martha Hirshman in Henrietta's apartment . . ."

A door opened and an old woman, a white scarf around her head, poked her face out. "What are you doing here making all this noise? Go home where you belong, you crazy thing, you." She shook a twisted yellow finger at me.

"I've got to find my sister." I explained, and shouted again: "Calling Martha Hirshman in Henrietta's apartment."

"Stoppa dat goddamned noise down there," a voice came from above.

"You don't stop, I'll take a frying pan and hit you in your stinking head," the old woman warned.

"Just let me try once more," I begged her. "I got to find her because my mother's got to see her right away."

She looked at me suspiciously, and then said, "All right, one more time, and then I'll call the police on you."

Meanwhile angry voices continued to fall: "Who's calling who?" "Genug!" "Drop dead down there and go away!"

I cupped my mouth again and blasted, "CALLING MARTHA HIRSHMAN IN HENRIETTA'S APARTMENT!"

A shower of curses, threats and howls fell from above. "That's the last time," said the old woman. "One more, and I'll throw a sewing machine on your head."

Reluctantly, I had started to leave when I heard someone running down the steps, then Martha's furious voice: "I'll die . . . I'll kill him . . . I'll never be able to come in this house again."

"Is that your sister?" the old woman asked. I nodded. "Two crazies in one family. What a shame," she said, and shut the door.

"What do you want? Are you insane? What are you doing here?" Martha screamed at me.

I winced; I could feel her fingers digging into my shoulders in advance. "Mother needs you," I said quickly.

"You're lying." She raised her hand to slap.

"I'm not!" I insisted, getting ready to kick her the moment she touched me. "You better come home, because their mother went to the hospital . . ."

"What happened to mother?" Martha cried, and before I could explain she was out of the hall and in the street. I hurried after her.

She muttered, mumbled to herself as she ran, "Oh my God, if anything's happened I'll die. I'll fall right down and die . . ." Then stopping and giving me her look of deep suspicion, she threatened through clenched teeth, "If you lied to me, I'll cut your throat from limb to limb."

"But she told me to find you," I protested, trying to keep up.

"How could she tell you if she's in the hospital?"

"She isn't, their mother is."

"Oh, you don't know what you're talking about. You have less brains than . . . than . . ." and since we were passing the barbershop, she said, "than even Carmella."

"Is that so? Mother said today I'm so smart that I say things people don't say until they get married. And you're not even married yet."

We ran into the building and on the first landing met Mrs. Greneker, who said nothing to Martha but caught my arm. "Just a second, Mr. Pishponim," she said, "I have special news for you."

"What?" I was anxious to follow Martha into the apartment.

"Arrangements have just been made, they're going to hang Mrs. Greneker first thing tomorrow morning for hurting your finger."

"They don't have to," I assured her, "my mother kissed it and it's not going to turn green and fall off."

"So I'm forgiven?"

"Mrs. Greneker, I love you," I called back.

"I love you too," she said.

Even before my mother opened the door for me, I heard Martha asking, "Who are they? Who *are* they?" and my mother's reply, "President Hoover and Vice-President Curtis, in midget copies."

"What's going on here?" Martha's voice became edged with

hysteria. "Who are they?"

"All right . . . all right," my mother calmed her. "They're the Schafer children. Their mother's a very dear friend of mine. She had to go into the hospital and they have no other place to stay. It will only be for a few days. But I need your help Martha, so just do as I ask, please."

My mother went to the secretary, took an envelope out of the drawer and began writing. "Now look," she said, giving the envelope to Martha, "I want you to go over to the Schafer apartment—"

"I don't know where it is," Martha interrupted.

"I know," I said.

"Bobby will show you. Here's the key to the apartment—don't lose it, whatever you do." And she gave Martha careful instructions about where to find the children's clothing. "Once you've got everything and you've locked the door with the key," my mother went on, "wet the end of this envelope and paste it on the door. It's to tell anybody looking for the family that she's away for a few days and that the children are here. Do you understand?"

I already had the door open.

"Just a moment," my mother called me back into the living room. "If anyone asks you anything about the children and their mother, don't say a word. Give them a polite answer and walk away. That goes for you too, Martha, understand?"

On the way down, I asked Martha what kind of a polite answer she would give if someone asked her. She looked at me scornfully and said, "I would tell them, 'Iay egbay ouryay ardonpay utbay Iay ontday eakspay inglishay.' "

"What does that mean?"

"It's Pig Latin."

"So how can I say it if someone asks me?"

"Let me do the talking."

I wondered who Martha really was and why everyone made believe she was my sister.

Once in the apartment, the insistent smell of carbolic, the statue whiteness of the walls, the squeezed-out emptiness of the room, and the silence made sharper by Martha's rummaging gave me the feeling that nothing that had ever lived here, down to the tiniest germ, would come back again. It was as if someone had taken an enormous sponge, dipped it in disinfectant and cleaned the place of life, forever.

Then came the thought: What if their mother was never coming back? Johnny and his brother were going to live with us forever? Wasn't that the reason my mother had told Martha to take everything she could find? I ran into the bedroom, where Martha was busily stacking clothes on the swaybacked bed. "Don't take so much," I cried.

"Mother said to bring back whatever I find. And that's what I'm going to do, because if I don't I'll only have to come back here again."

She handed me a pile of clothing. My first impulse was to drop it and run—it was like bringing ammunition to the enemy. But I knew if I didn't, Martha would anyway.

We left the apartment, and Martha, clothing piled up to her chin, licked the gummed tip of the envelope and pasted it to the door after locking it.

"If I fall and break my neck," she said, "you know whose fault it'll be."

"Whose?"

"Your mother's. She sent me on this crazy errand."

"Me too."

"No, she didn't ask you to go, you volunteered."

The thought that I had only myself to blame made me miserable as rain on a picnic day. "Martha? Do you think their mother is coming back?"

"Of course she's coming back. What do you think we're running—a nursery?"

"How long does it take to have a bellyache fixed?"

"Bellyache, my eye."

"That's what Mother said she has."

"That's because she's so old-fashioned. If you ask me, she went to have a baby."

Dawns lit the horizon of my mind. I was astounded I had not made the association between the big-bellied women in the neighborhood and Johnny's mother's bellyaches, and astonished at Martha's wisdom. Could she possibly be my sister after all?

As we came down the stoop, I noticed several women bunched around Mrs. Greneker. They were staring and pointing at the clump of furniture and bundles near Henrietta's house. I heard their "tsks, tsks," as they sadly shook their heads and whispered to one another.

Martha held her head high as when she balanced books on it during her graceful-walking exercises, but I saw a possible chance of learning to whom the dispossessed articles belonged. I walked toward them.

"Hey, diavolo vecchio," Carmella Calabrese, standing on the fringe of the group, called to me. "Hey, fresca fritta baccala, what you carrying there?"

"You want to know?"

"Sure, tell me."

"It's a secret for someone."

"I won't tell anybody in the whole world, so help me God," she swore.

"All right," I said, "it's for President Hoover and . . ." Forgetting the other name my mother had told Martha, I blurted, "It's for President Hoover and the other midget."

Mrs. Greneker gave me a vanishing look.

"Bobby!" Martha shouted from across the street. I ran up to her. "I thought mother said you weren't supposed to talk to anyone?"

"She said we weren't to say anything about Johnny or his brother or his mother."

"Idiot!" she said.

I decided she wasn't my sister after all.

When we got upstairs, even the sight of Johnny drawing on *my* slate with *my* chalk and Artie crawling around in *my* bathrobe could not dampen my smiling knowledge of the baby.

Peter came home and was told there was no time for explanations.

My father arrived, and he and my mother had a long talk in their bedroom with the door closed.

Libby came to ask if she could play with me, to which my mother replied—before I could yell, "No!"—that we were fresh out of playing room. "But tell your mother to come over around seven-thirty tonight, dear—I'll tell her everything firsthand then." Libby left.

Martha called Henrietta, told her that she couldn't come to see her but couldn't tell her why. From the mingled expressions of anger and indifference on Martha's face I could tell that Henrietta had hung up on her.

"What with all the excitement, I never finished making dinner," said my mother in a tired voice.

"How about deli for a change," Peter suggested.

"For a change," she said. "He eats delicatessen for lunch five days a week, and now he wants it for a change."

"How do you know I eat deli every day?"

"Because I ate deli five times a week when I went to high school . . . and your father did, and so did everyone else. What else is there to eat when you go to school?" My mother started to chuck Peter's chin, but stopped and reminded him that she hadn't forgotten the garbage.

"I'm for deli, too," my father joined.

"And me," I added.

Martha was curiously silent. "It's not good for my figure," she said, running her hands down the flat sides of her body.

"I wouldn't let that bother me," my mother said. "I have it straight from her best friend that Jean Harlow lives on pastrami."

"All right," said Martha with a sigh of mock resignation. "But," she added quickly, "I'm not going for it."

"I'll go," I said.

"Peter and Martha will go together," my mother said firmly. "Get a quarter of a pound of each of corned beef, pastrami and tongue, a pound and a half of potato salad—"

"I'm too old to go shopping for deli," Peter objected.

My mother shook her head wearily, and my father said, "If you're too old to shop for it, you're too old to eat it."

"But why can't I go with them?" It seemed imperative that I belong to those who were going and not to those left behind. Also, it was the first time I could remember my mother's asking Peter and Martha to do anything together. I couldn't bear being excluded from the alliance, no matter how strange.

"I don't understand it," my mother said to my father. "All of a sudden there has to be an explanation for everything I do." Then, turning to us, "All right, here is the why and the wherefore. If Martha went alone, the deli owner would weigh everything with his fat finger on the scale; same holds if Peter went. But if Peter and Martha go, Martha can watch the scale and Peter can watch his hand." Beckoning me to come to her, she whispered, "The real reason you can't go is that you wouldn't want to leave Johnny here alone with his brother, would you?"

Shame and remorse and resentment played tag inside me. I left the kitchen as my mother continued: "A pound of deli rye; some pickles and sauerkraut, but not for the money. And tell him to give you enough mustard 'toots' for everybody."

Johnny was on the floor vainly trying to teach his brother to play cat's cradle. Artie wanted only to pull the string away. I sat down next to Johnny. "I'd play with you, but I got a broken finger."

"Does it hurt?" he asked. From the pinch in his voice I knew that tears, dammed up, were close to overflowing. I thought of the games we might play but they all seemed unimportant; to change his mind from crying, we would have to do something serious. "Would you like me to read you one of my books?" I asked.

"Yes," he said with little enthusiasm.

"Let's go to *our* room," I said, putting so much emphasis on the "our" that even I could hear its lead-penny ring.

Artie waddled after us, and when we had all got into the correct positions on the bed I picked one of the picture books from the pile on the bottom shelf of my bed table. "It's Cinderella!" I cried, pumping up my voice with delight. "Do you know Cinderella?"

"I don't know, maybe."

"Does he know Cinderella?" I pointed to Artie.

"No," Johnny replied.

"All right," I said, opening the book. "Once upon a time there were two brothers. One was a herring salesman, his name was Johnny—"

"Why was his name Johnny?"

"Why is your name Johnny?"

"I don't know."

"I don't know why his name was Johnny, too. Maybe his real name was Ashiepattle."

Artie tried to tear the book away from me and ripped part of a page. His brother slapped his hand, forcing me to have to make funny faces, blow out my cheeks, put my thumbs to my temples and wave my fingers to keep him from blubbering. At last I was able to continue, "And the other brother was a rent collector—"

"What was his name?"

I thought a moment. "Hartichoke. And they had a little, little brother"—I could see that Johnny was going to ask for the brother's name, so I provided it—"and his name was Shaftoe.

"Anyway, so the two brothers did nothing all day long. One of them sold herrings from a stinky barrel. The other one was the rent collector, the worst, 'cause he layed in the little, little brother's bed, which wasn't his. And they made the little, little brother do all the work and she had to sleep on the cinders—"

"I thought it was a he?" Johnny asked.

"It was."

"But you said she."

"I didn't."

"You did."

"No, I didn't."

"Yes, you did."

"Give me back my bottle cap I gave you today."

He got up to get it.

"No, don't give it back. I was only fooling. Do you want to hear the story?"

"Yes."

"All right, then you make like I'm Miss Diamond and you pay attention."

He climbed back on the bed.

"So he had to do all the work and he cleaned the dishes and he scrubbed the floors and he had to sit out all day on the top floor and clean the windows. And on Fridays he had to scrub the floor again and put down papers. And just as soon as he put down the papers his two brothers, the herring salesman and the rent collector, knocked on the door and said, 'Fee-fi-fo-fum, I smell the blood of an English man.' So little Bobby—"

"I thought you said his name was Shaftoe?"

"Shaftoe was his real name, like my real name is Robert Benjamin. His nickname was Bobby. All right?"

"All right."

"So little, little Shaftoe began to shiver and he hid in the iron stove. Then the two brothers came in and dirtied all the papers on the floor. The brother who was the rent collector told the brother who was the herring salesman to bring him his dinner. And he did. And he came back with two empty plates. 'Someone's been eating my porridge,' the rent collector growled. 'Someone's been eating my porridge,' the herring salesman growled in his middle voice. And little, little Shaftoe squeaked in his little voice, 'Someone's ate up all my porridge, too.'

"So the rent collector went to the stove where little, little, Shaftoe was hiding and said, 'I'll huff and I'll puff until I'll blow the stove in.' And the herring salesman stuck his big, fat head in the stove and said, 'Nibble, nibble like a mouse, who's been nibbling on my house.' Like a rotten witch he said it. So little, teeny Shaftoe said, 'I've run away from a little old woman, a little old man, and I can run away from you too.'

"So he jumped out of the stove and on the way met Henny-Penny. 'Where are you going, Henny-Penny?' he asked. 'The sky is falling,' said Henny-Penny. 'I must go tell the king.' 'I'll go with you and tell the king on my brothers, the herring salesman and the rent collector,' said little, little Shaftoe. So then they met Cocky-Locky and Ducky-Daddles and Goosey-Poosey and Turkey-Lurkey and Foxy-Woxy and Martha-Partha and Peter, Peter the Pumpkin-Eater and Mr. and Mrs. Fineshmecker. So they came to the king's castle and Henny-Penny told the king that the sky was falling. So the king sent Jack and the Beanstalk to plant some beans that would grow up so high it would hold up the sky from falling. And then little, little Shaftoe—he was so little that his real name was Hop o' My Thumb—told the king on his two brothers and he told the king how hard he had to work and he showed the king the big galoshes on his hands—"

"Galoshes are for feet," Johnny interrupted.

"No, these are different galoshes. You get them on your hands. My mother showed them to me. Just today she showed them to me."

"Gloves are for hands," he insisted.

"Come on," I said, scrambling off the bed, "I'll show you." But I stopped in the middle of the room. I didn't want him to see my mother's hands. I didn't want him to touch her hands. "Oh," I said, turning and feigning indifference, "they're only little bumps, maybe she washed them off already. Do you want to hear the rest of the

102

story?"

"All right."

"So the king sent out an 'extra' that if anybody should catch the two bad brothers he would make him a prince. So Shaftoe, little, little Shaftoe, went to the house where the brothers lived and he stole the golden harp and when he ran away with it, the harp cried, 'Master, master!' So they ran after him until he got to the beanstalk. And he climbed down and the bad brothers climbed down quick, too. But he got to the bottom first and chopped the beanstalk down so the rent collector fell down and broke his crown and the herring salesman came tumbling after.

"So the king made little, little Shaftoe a prince and he married Rose Red, whose real name was Snow White, and they lived happily ever after they threw everything from the two bad brothers' house out on the street. . . . Wasn't that good?" I asked.

"What happened to Cinderella?" Johnny asked.

"Her real name was Snow White," I said. But just then I heard Martha and Peter return and I rushed from the room.

I shared my chair with Johnny. My mother picked up Artie and set him in her lap, bringing back my earlier fear that they might live with us always. Now I could see that if that happened I would be replaced by Artie. He would be the youngest. He would come first. Everything would be for him, the special cakes, the answers to questions, even the sound of the nightingale, I realized, when my mother, playing with Artie's hands and rubbing his stomach, sang, "Patty-cake, patty-cake, patty-cake, who's going to get a bellyache." Then I remembered Johnny's mother and her bellyache and the baby and how wonderful I had felt, and I gave Johnny more chair space than I had.

"Where did you buy the delicatessen?" my mother asked, as my father emptied the contents of the paper bags on a platter.

"The usual place," said Martha.

"The usual place can expect a piece of my mind with ruffles on it tomorrow," my mother said. "I should have enough for six sand-wiches—if I make five, I'm lucky. Our delicatessen man figures that since there are less dollars for delicatessen, he'll give less delicatessen for the dollar. He'll be skipping rope with his knockwursts before he sees my money again."

Then, giving my father a just-between-us look, she asked, "Did you see what's on the corner of Union and Dawson?"

"No."

"Another one," she said, lowering her eyes.

My father shook his head.

"Another what?" I asked.

"Another plate for the handsome young man with the greedy, beady eyes."

"Whose real name is Rumpelstiltskin," my father added.

"You listened!"

"I didn't listen," he explained, "I heard."

"Don't you know these walls are thin as a landlord's promise?" my mother asked.

"In fact," my father said, "they're not even walls, just wallpaper."

The dumbwaiter buzzer rang.

"Peter," was all my father said, and my brother, his eyes lowered, put the garbage on the lift, rang the bell to signal he was through and meekly went to wash his hands.

"If these kids are sleeping here tonight, where's everybody going to sleep?" he asked when he returned to the table.

"That's the first sensible question I've heard all evening," my father remarked.

"I figured it out," my mother said. "You, Peter and Bobby will sleep in our bed. I'll sleep with Martha in the living room."

Peter yelled, "No!" Martha complained there wasn't enough room in her bed. I was too miserable to say anything. I cared less about sleeping with my brother and father than about having my bed taken from me and given to Johnny's brother . . . maybe forever. Peter threatened that even if he never slept a wink for the rest of his life, he wouldn't sleep in the same bed with me. Without warning, Johnny burst into wails for his mother. My mother hushed him and caressed the back of his head; this only set Artie off. Although my mother clasped him to her bosom, he was inconsolable.

Jealousy wormed its way outward.

"All right!" my mother announced. "We're going to have a grand parade!" Keeping Artie close to her and holding Johnny's hand, she began making drum sounds, "Bump-bee-dee-bump-bump . . . bump-bee-dee-bump-bump," and marched around the kitchen table into the living room.

Peter banged on his plate with a fork and bawled, "And the monkey wrapped its tail around the flagpole . . . around the flagpole . . . around the flagpole. . . ."

Even my father joined in and drummed the tabletop with his fingertips.

Parading back into the kitchen, my mother said, "Martha dear, take the milk out of the icebox, shake it up well, and pour half of it in that enamel pan, over a very low flame."

"I thought Lincoln freed the slaves," Martha said.

"Only the colored ones. Then take the sandwich bread out of the breadbox and put two slices in the warm milk and add about a quarter of an inch of butter—make it a half an inch. Watch it, stir it and don't let it boil."

While Martha went about following my mother's instructions, muttering through it all, my mother played a game with Artie. "Who's got the funny little button nose?" she sang and pressed his nose with her finger. "And who's got funny little twinkling toes?" she tweaked his toes.

I felt myself curl up into a tight ball and die in a dark corner.

"Bobby?" my father asked. "What's wrong with you?"

"Don't you feel well?" my mother asked, quickly. She stretched across the table trying to feel my forehead with the back of her hand.

I pulled away. "I'm not sick."

Artie broke into sobs again.

"You really want to see him laugh?" asked Martha. "Here, just watch." She took an aluminum frying pan, and hitting it with the wooden spoon, kicked first one leg, then the other, and sang as she danced, "Constantinople, C-o-s-t-n-s-p-i-t-n-l-e-p-e, Constantinople, it's so easy to sing if you know your A-B-C-. . ."

My mother clapped her hands to the rhythm, and told my father that while Martha might not take after her when it came to singing, she certainly did in spelling. Peter hit the empty seltzer bottle with the end of the fork. And my father was actually whistling. I was able to resist no longer. I grabbed a paper napkin, carrying it like a banner in a high wind. I ran in circles around Martha, shouting,

> "Minnie and a Minnie and a hot-cha-cha!
> Minnie kissed a fella in a trolley car.
> I'll tell ma, you'll tell pa.
> Minnie and a Minnie and a hot-cha-cha!"

Artie's tears dried on his face. Johnny slapped the table with his hands. My mother sang along with me and the noise grew louder and louder, until the doorbell rang and the milk boiled over at the same time.

My father went to the door.

"Who's getting married?" It was Mrs. Greneker's booming voice. She came into the kitchen, poked Peter and said, "Pascudniack, get up and give an older person a seat, like they teach you in school," and sat down in his chair.

For a few moments, she studied Johnny and his brother and then clasped the back of one hand in the palm of the other. "So young and already they know sorrow."

"Please, Greneker," my mother interrupted, "we're standing on our heads to make them laugh and you come in like Lon Chaney with a long face."

My mother bathed Artie, and then Johnny, and finally me "last on the list." Leading me through the living room, where Mrs. Jackson and Mrs. McCarthy had joined Mrs. Greneker ("The ladies auxiliary meets as usual in Hirshman Hall," she said), she asked my father to put me to bed.

He pulled back the blanket and sheet and ordered me in.

"Where's Mother?"

"She's putting Johnny and his brother to sleep."

"And not me?"

"I'm not good enough?"

"Yes, but . . ."

"But, what?"

"But why isn't she in here?"

"Let me ask you something. . . Suppose you got a new sled, what would be the first thing you'd want to do with it?"

"Sleigh-ride."

"What if it didn't snow?"

"I'd pray to make it snow."

"What if God was too busy just then to listen to your prayers?"

"I'd get even and I'd get mad on Him."

"When you get mad at your mother because she doesn't give you something you want, does it help?"

I considered it.

"I asked you a question," he said.

"No."

"No, what?"

"It doesn't help."

"Now let's go all the way back to the new sled and no snow. Don't you think you'd be better off if instead of praying and getting mad at God, you played some other game until there was snow?"

"What game?"

"Like cops and robbers, or any other game where you didn't need snow."

"Then what?"

"Then, when the snow came, you'd use your sled. In the meantime you'd be having fun anyway. Now if I could only get it across to you that the same thing applied to your mother's not being here the minute you wanted her, I'd be a genius."

"What's that?"

"Someone has to throw the ball before it can be caught."

I was going to ask what he meant, but I heard my mother singing my good-night song to Johnny and Artie.

"Connais-tu le pays"—her voice waved like a wide velvet ribbon in a gentle wind—*"où fleurit l'oranger, Le pays des fruits d'or et des roses vermeilles? Où la brise est plus douce et l'oiseau plus léger. . ."*

I didn't understand the words, but I felt they were filled with softness and sleep.

"Un éternel printemps sous un ciel toujours bleu? Hélas!"

It was at this part of the song that my mother's voice unfolded like a great feather-filled quilt and enveloped me in sound.

"C'est là,—c'est là que je voudrais vivre, Aimer, aimer et mourir! C'est là que je voudrais vivre, c'est là! oui, c'est là!"

It was *my* good-night song! *Mine!* Hadn't she told me that she sang this song with its strange words only to me; that she had sung "Rock-a-bye Baby on the Treetop" for Peter, and "Lullaby and Good-Night" for Martha? And hadn't she said that nobody ever had a good-night song like this before? Why was she singing it to them? Why? She was taking everything that was mine and giving it to them. Why?—if they're going to be with us for such a short time.

I punished myself with hate.

I heard Mrs. Greneker say, "When you hear what I've got to tell you, you'll bust."

"Is it bad?" Mrs. McCarthy asked.

"It's the worst," Mrs. Greneker assured her.

I knew then that it had to be about the rent collector. I didn't care.

Just outside the door my mother asked my father where Peter and Martha were.

"They went out."

"And the little one?"

"Inside," he said, and then added, "We better have a talk about it."

"You're telling me. I could see what's going on in that head with my eyes shut."

She peered into the room, came up to the bed and whispered, "Don't you want me to sing your good-night song?"

I wanted to say no, but thought it even greater revenge if I showed her I could fall asleep without her song. I kept my eyes shut. She tiptoed out, leaving the door slightly open in the event I called.

"How would a nice hot cup of coffee appeal to you ladies?" I heard her ask.

"Coffee we can have anytime," said Mrs. Greneker. "Just wait till you hear my news."

I heard my father excuse himself.

Mrs. Greneker began with relish. "Well, my friends, if you think we had tsores before, we'll soon be taking a bath in it."

"What's that mean?" asked Mrs. McCarthy.

"Tsores means trouble," Mrs. Jackson explained.

"I was down by Mrs. Fine this afternoon just to buy a few odds 'n' ends, when she adds up, I asked her, 'My dear Mrs. Fine, I am the first to agree that a person has to make a living, but why, tell me, why is everything up a penny on this and two cents on that?' So she tells me that she has to charge what she charges or close the doors. 'Why?' I ask her. So she tells me that they raised her rent. To make it short, the story is that people are so far behind in rent that the landlord—in order to stay alive, he says—has to get rid of those who can't pay and raise those who can pay. But I ask you, who is this landlord?"

"Mr. Fell, isn't he?" Mrs. McCarthy said.

"No more," said Mrs. Greneker. "From now on it's the Eichmir Realty."

"Acme," my mother corrected.

"And who is the Eichmir Realty, you ask?"

"Acme, Acme," my mother said.

"Please, Frances, what difference does it make as long as you understand me?"

"I just wanted to be sure that McCarthy understood," my mother explained.

"I just need the high points . . . just the high points," said Mrs. McCarthy.

"So, go on," Mrs. Jackson urged.

"First, if you remember," Mrs. Greneker said, "he called himself Feldman. But how could a Feldman give a dispossess to a Levine, a Horowitz, a Thomashevsky? So, all of a sudden the name on the rent receipts is Fell. And he already owns half this street and half from Dawson and almost half Prospect. So, a choleryah should take him. . ."

"That means . . ." Mrs. Jackson said, but Mrs. McCarthy answered, "That one, I know."

"But that isn't enough for Fell, so he makes a proposition to the other landlords that they should protect themselves and have an association. They figure that one skunk only doesn't smell so good, but four or five skunks can make a real big stink. So they got together and they said, 'I pledge allegiance,' and right away they're the Eichmir Realty Company. Now, it's not so expensive for them to go to court and get dispossesses. Now, if one wants to raise the rent, they all raise the rent. Now, if one wants to stop collecting garbage by the dumbwaiter, the dumbwaiters in all the buildings drop dead together. So, my dear ladies, if you're looking for a change of furniture there will be plenty on the street to choose from, very soon now."

"Does that mean every building on the block?" my mother asked.

"According to Mrs. Fine, each and every one. Like in a pogrom there are no exceptions."

"Even The Poorhouse?" My mother sounded as if she thought this impossible.

I sat up in bed. The Poorhouse was Johnny's house!

"What do you mean *even* The Poorhouse?" Mrs. Greneker asked.

"*Especially* The Poorhouse. I understand the landlord didn't collect a penny from that building for so long he couldn't afford a collector and was afraid to go by himself. But now he belongs to the Eichmir, they'll be thrown out like sins on Yom Kippur."

"I'd better put up the coffee," my mother said.

"Well," said Mrs. McCarthy, "it won't be too long before I'll be having words with the Akmir Company. If old McCarthy keeps on working one and two days a week, they're going to have a long wait for the rent. I feed my family first and the landlord's later."

"Amen," said Mrs. Greneker. "Did you see today on Dawson Street, already they decorated the sidewalk."

"I saw it," my mother said. "It was a pity to see."

"And it was a Jewish family too!" said Mrs. Greneker.

"How do you know?" Mrs. Jackson asked.

"They took the mezuzah off the door. I saw it on top of a chiffrobe."

"A mez——" Mrs. Jackson started to say when Mrs. McCarthy interrupted with, "I know . . . I know . . ."

"I should hope so," said Mrs. Greneker, "after living in this house already more than fifteen years."

There was the clattering of cups and then I heard my mother say, "This has really got me worried."

"Why should it worry you?" Mrs. Jackson asked. "Teachers and library people and civil service are on the safe side."

"I'm thinking about my friend, Jeanette," my mother replied, "the one I took to the hospital today. She already owes them two months' rent. What will they do to her now?"

"Is her husband out of work, too?" Mrs. Jackson asked.

"Her husband left her. It's been almost a month," my mother said.

"Isn't that a crying shame," said Mrs. McCarthy.

"It all depends who's doing the crying," Mrs. Greneker remarked. "If it was on his head it wouldn't be a shame."

"Doesn't he send her anything?" Mrs. Jackson asked.

"Crumbs," my mother replied. "He wants a divorce. She's not

fancy enough for him. After all, what woman could be good enough for a traveling salesman dealing in women's underwear?"

"She shouldn't have married him in the first place. Any man who sells women's underwear always has his eye for what's under the skirt," said Mrs. Greneker.

"Why should that be?" asked Mrs. Jackson.

"Because he's got to see if she's wearing what he's selling."

"Oh, Mrs. Greneker, go away with your jokes." There was a blush in Mrs. McCarthy's voice.

"Well, if it was me," said Mrs. Jackson, "I'd give him a divorce before he could say, 'Bella's bloomers,' and I'd take every last cent he had."

"You belong to my club," my mother said, "but not Jeanette. She told him she would never give him a divorce. When I asked her why, she told me that she was thinking of the children."

"With that I agree," said Mrs. Greneker. "When children see that other children have fathers, and they don't, they hang their heads with shame. After all, it's like being fifty per cent an orphan. And when they get old enough to understand that they have a father, but he has no use for them or their mother—this is like a pain in the heart for which there is no operation.

"Besides, what man wants to marry one and feed three? Especially these days when it's the other way around. By where my husband works, there is a finisher from cloaks. So, they laid him off. What do you think happens? He sits home and holds his stomach while his wife goes out scrubbing floors in the big offices by night. So, if she gives him a divorce, she'll find out soon enough that there won't be a lineup every night of men singing under her window with banjos."

"Besides," Mrs. McCarthy declared, "it's a sin."

"Meanwhile," my mother said, wearily, "she doesn't have a husband, the children don't have a father, and they count pennies as if they were diamonds. Poor Jeanette, she was a picker and chooser who turned out to be the all-time loser. You should have seen her when she was young. She was as beautiful as a child's dream. She dressed like every day was Saturday night and as if any minute Prince Charming would step out of an Auburn and hand her the glass slipper without even a try-on. Jeanette had platinum-lined hopes for herself. The man she was going to marry was not only going to be tall, dark and what-have-you, but he was going to have the key to the national treasury. She was going to dance with J. P. Morgan and chat with Mrs. Wilson and even the stars in the sky would throw kisses at her when she went out at night.

"So she sat up on her balcony complaining that this man couldn't touch her and that man shouldn't look at her, but there was one thing she couldn't keep from touching her and looking at her. Time. So she ended up with an underwear salesman, whom she admits she never loved, a bellyful of pain and an apartment on the top floor of The Poorhouse—and without enough money to even go see Dr. Reuben.

"I finally convinced her she should go this morning. He examined her and told her that she should be in a hospital at once. She said no, and he called me. It took almost blood to get her to go. So, we got her things together—things, what she had went into a shopping bag and there was still enough room to hold a full day's shopping—and I got her over to Morris View Hospital."

"Hirshman"—Libby's mother's voice was low and troubled—"you don't think it could be . . .?"

"God forbid and bite your tongue," Mrs. Greneker ordered.

"I asked Reuben," my mother said. "Of course, he doesn't know, but . . . well, we'll soon find out. Such news is never slow in coming."

chapter 5

The weather began to cool, bringing days that were ginger-sweet to the taste with a sharpness that lingered. The street relaxed, sighed as in relief that the heat of summer no longer lay on it so heavily. In the evenings, during those moments when the mothers were preparing dinners, when the children were called home, when the last sounds hung like the papery leaves on our two trees, and just before those fathers who still had jobs were to return from them, the sun would pour its gold over the buildings, softening their raggedness, gilding their pocked faces. A hush would fall. The street would hold its breath; beauty was walking through it. But she had to pick her way carefully around the lonely islands of evicted belongings that appeared with greater frequency. To all of us they were mute signs of mourning that were to be respectfully avoided. A pair of men would carry the furniture on their wide backs and dump it on the sidewalk, where no one ever seemed to stand watch over it, and it would disappear into the pockets of the night.

I felt a sense of sympathy. Hadn't I too been ousted—thrown out on the sidewalk of my world? And now that everything and everyone was concerned with the Schafers, there was no one, I felt, to "stand watch" over me. There always had to be someone to "mind" Artie. My mother visited theirs in the hospital at least once a day, sometimes twice. And I was being told constantly to "go play with Johnny."

He was taken to school with me, sat next to me in class, ate lunch with me, was taken home with me, followed me wherever I went, even in my search for bottle caps, got candy money when I did every day and my good-night song as well. And even when I sought escape by asking if I could play with Libby in her house, I was told to stay home and play with Johnny.

It was as if I were tied to him. And the bondage was made more unbearable by his eyes, which reflected a loneliness and hurt that no game, no toy, no invention of mine, could alter.

One evening, after my mother had left to visit his, I went to where my father sat reading and "minding" Artie, and as an excuse to talk asked why the furniture was being put out on the sidewalk. Without lifting his eyes from the page, he replied, "I'll tell you some other time. Why don't you play with Johnny?"

Angry, I returned to where Johnny was playing with my ball-in-the-cup toy. "Do you want to play a real game?" I asked.

"Sure."

"All right. Put this sissy toy away and do like I show you." Motioning to him to follow, I walked around one end of the dining-room table. "It's called Run-Me-Over and you're supposed to cross the street and I have to try and run you over." The "street" consisted of the perimeter of the table, with one end the safety zone.

"Are you ready?" I asked.

"Sure."

"Okay. Run! Run fast!"

He ran around the table while I twisted an imaginary wheel and made humming and honking noises. He thought I would chase him, but I reversed my "auto," and turning, with all my might and my head down, I ran into him. He fell backward and I heard the thud as his head hit the foot of the table.

"Ooh," was the only sound he made, but his eyes rolled up like a sleeping doll's.

My father was there in a second, and without asking what had happened, pulled Johnny into a sitting position, rubbed his head and asked how he felt.

"I was just playing Run-Me-Over," I explained.

"It sounded more to me as if you were playing steam-roller." He looked annoyed and asked me to come into my room. "Bring Johnny, too, and I'll show you a game I used to play."

He sat down, crossed his legs and told me to straddle the one that was outstretched. Then, taking my hands, he bounced me on his leg as he recited:

> "There was a man, he went mad,
> He jumped into a paper bag;
> The paper bag was too narrow,
> He jumped into a wheelbarrow;
> The wheelbarrow caught on fire,
> He jumped into the muck and mire;
> The muck and mire was too gooey,
> He jumped into something chewy;
> The something chewy was too sweet,
> He jumped into Union Street;
> Union Street was full of stones,
> He fell down and broke his bones."

When he came to "and broke his bones," he kicked his leg higher and let go of my hands. I sailed upward and backward and fell to the floor with a thump.

"Isn't that great?" he asked. "Now for Johnny."

The fall didn't hurt me as much as the thought that he had done it

to punish me for running into Johnny. I got up and as Johnny straddled his leg, I ran out of the apartment.

I sat on the steps and kicked the riser with my heels. I had to find
a way of revenging myself on him, my mother, on Johnny and his
brother, on the whole world.

I heard Libby singing. "Your mother'll give you a fishy, in a little
dishy, if you don't make pishy, till your daddy comes home." Since
she'd been shut out of the games I played with Johnny, she'd threatened to get even. There would be no use trying to enlist her help out
of my predicaments.

To make matters worse, I was sure my father was so indifferent to
my running out that he was still dandling Johnny. I went to the hall
window, which was diagonally opposite my bedroom, and stuck out my
head.

A paper bag whizzed by a few inches from my face. I pulled my
head in just in time to avoid the barrage of bags that followed.

A moment later I heard Mr. Sobieski, the janitor, rave angrily from
the yard below about sonzabitches and garbage. His cries were countered by voices from all directions.

"Hang up!"

"Close the hole!"

"Vehr geharget!"

"Pull the chain!"

"Sha!"

They fired Mr. Sobieski to louder and longer yells. It came to me
that what was happening was tied up with something that occurred
earlier that day.

We had just arrived home from school when Mrs. Greneker came
out of the building, angry and excited. "Did you see it? Did you see
it?"

"What?" my mother asked.

"It's right inside. The Eichmir Company has already started with
its monkey business. Come look for yourselves."

We followed her into the hall, and stopped in front of a large sheet of paper that had been tacked up on the wall.

My mother read aloud: "Notice to all tenants: Due to increased operational costs and continued dumbwaiter breakdowns, we are forced to introduce a more modern method of garbage collection and disposal. Effective as of twelve o'clock noon, this day, the dumbwaiter will be permanently out of commission. Tenants are required to bring the garbage to the basement, where they will find cans provided for their use. The BOARD OF HEALTH has been notified and has APPROVED this more sanitary method of garbage disposal. We request and appreciate the prompt cooperation of all tenants. Signed, The Acme Realty Company."

"I should come all the way down from the top floor to put garbage in the cellar?" Mrs. McCarthy asked, her eyes wide with the impossibility of the thought. "They have a fat nerve—and they've got a fat chance catching me do it."

"And you'll sooner find me doing a Russian kezatzki in the streets before you'll find me going down in that cellar with that Sobieski, who when he's had a schnappsel and he takes a look at a Jew, you can see it's pogrom time in his eyes," said Mrs. Greneker. "Besides, if I wanted an apartment without a dumbwaiter I could have stayed in my old neighborhood where I paid six dollars less a month for the same three rooms. So, all right, let's say it's worth three dollars to have your private bathroom inside your apartment and not in the hall, but what about the other three dollars?

"And for another thing, all of a sudden my new parnosseh is to be a garbage collector? In the old country where I came from, in our eyes the one who collected garbage was the same as the gravedigger— lower work you couldn't find."

"What can you do?" my mother asked. "If they don't run the dumbwaiter, you can't keep the garbage in the house."

"Don't worry," said Mrs. Greneker knowingly. "They'll run the dumbwaiter, even with thorns in their fingers they'll run the dumbwaiter."

"But how?" Mrs. McCarthy asked. "How can you force them to?"

As they walked back outside, Mrs. Greneker explained, "I have a good friend, from the old country yet, who lives downtown from here, who had the same situation in her building just a few years back. And the tenants took care of the problem in such a one-two-three that the landlord put the dumbwaiters back to work with a smile on his face."

"What did they do?" Mrs. McCarthy asked.

"First they complained to the Board of Health but the Board of Health was busy having its ears examined, it heard nothing. Then they went around like a bunch of greenhorns and signed petitions. When everybody in the building signed three and four different names, they took the petitions to the same Board of Health. This time it was having its eyes examined, it couldn't read the petitions. So then the neighbors got together and they thought. What did they think? They thought that windows are nice to let light in, to let air in, to look out from, to put up curtains, but also for something else—to throw garbage from."

"But that's terrible," my mother said.

"Of course, it's terrible," Mrs. Greneker agreed, "but after a few days, you know what they found out?"

"What?" asked Mrs. McCarthy.

"They found that the landlord had given someone at the Board of Health a nice few dollars he should keep quiet. But when the garbage came from the windows and even the deaf heard the complaints, then the upstairs from the Board of Health came to take a personal look at the situation. When they saw what they saw and heard what they heard, they gave the landlord a fine that he could have fixed the dumbwaiter one hundred times over and still have money to burn. And I tell you, take my word for it, it took a few days only."

"I still think it's terrible," my mother said.

"Listen, Frances," Mrs. Greneker said, "if the whole building goes with, you're not going against, are you?"

"What do you mean, against?"

"If the whole building should come to the decision that it's out the window, anyone who takes it to the cellar is going against."

"Please, Greneker," my mother said, "I can't even think about it."

As the day progressed, word spread that the dumbwaiter service had been suspended in all the buildings on the street except for The Poorhouse, which hadn't had it as long as anyone could remember.

Listening to Mr. Sobieski's curses now, I concluded that window garbage disposal was in operation.

I thought of telling my father of my discovery but decided that since he had as much as kicked me out he didn't deserve to know. Instead, I would tell Mrs. Greneker that her plan was already in work. I climbed the several flights of steps and knocked on her door.

"You came to see me?" she asked with what I thought was genuine surprise. "I never thought I would live to see the day when Bobby Hirshman would come all the way upstairs just to see poor old Mrs. Greneker. Come inside and say hello to Mr. Greneker for the same money."

I walked in. Mr. Greneker was sitting in the living room and peered over the top of his newspaper. "Come here, Bobbeleh gonif," he called. I went up to him and he patted my head. "Now go hock Mrs. Greneker a chinick."

"You know what?" I said to her. "I was in the hall and I looked out the window and somebody threw lots of bags of garbage in the yard, and Mr. Sobieski is yelling at them. So, they're doing what you told my mother today . . . already."

"Already I'm in jail," she said, clamping her hand over my mouth.

I pulled my head away. "Why?"

"Because if you go around telling everybody that it was Mrs. Greneker's idea to throw garbage from the window, then the police will come and arrest me and that will be the finish from Mrs. Greneker. Do you understand?"

"No."

"But everyone tells me that you're the smartest boy in the whole neighborhood, so why don't you understand? No one is supposed to throw garbage from the windows."

"So why did you tell them to do it?"

"So they should fix the dumbwaiter. Come here," she said, walking into her kitchen, "how would you like a nice slice of rye bread with some chicken fat?"

"No," I said. "I ate already."

"But if I asked how would you like a chocolate devil with marshmallow inside, it wouldn't make a difference that you ate already?"

"Do you have chocolate devil with marshmallow inside?"

"No."

"So why did you tell me?"

"I told you because if I had one I would give it to you. So help me."

"What else have you got?"

"Are you looking I should give you a bribe?" She thought a moment as if in deep reflection, then clapping her hands, said, "Ha! I got just the thing . . . *just the thing!* But you got to turn around and don't look until I tell you I'm ready."

I did as she instructed, heard rustling, and then she said, "You can look now."

I turned. She was holding a bottle cap as daintily and proudly as if it were a rare pearl. "It's a genuine, honest-to-goodness Dr. Brown's Celery Tonic bottle cap. It's one-of-a-kind. You won't find another one like it in a hundred and twenty years . . . maybe."

I held my hand out for it.

"Not so quick," she said. "First, you got to promise Mrs. Greneker that you won't go around telling everybody that people are throwing garbage out the window on her recommendation."

"I promise."

"All right. I take your word for it. But if I hear from someone that you are going around with a big mouth, I'll fix your wagon."

Just then I heard my mother calling me. She sounded worried.

"Go tell her where you are," said Mrs. Greneker.

122

"I'm up here," I shouted. "In Mrs. Greneker's house."

"Come down, right now."

"She's mad at me, I think," I whispered to Mrs. Greneker.

"Go make her glad," she urged, and nudged me gently out into the hall.

"Why didn't you tell your father where you were going?" my mother asked when I reached her.

" 'Cause he kicked me out of the house," I complained.

"He did not. He thought you went to Libby's." Taking my hand, she led me into the kitchen and sat down at the table. "What am I going to do with you?" she asked.

"Throw me out, like the furniture and garbage bags."

"If I could find a bag big enough, I would."

"You can put me in my coat and tie the sleeves around me."

"Well," she said, rising, "I can see that I'm getting nowhere very fast, so give my regards to the herring salesman and the rent collector."

"You don't care what happens to me."

"That's what you keep telling me, isn't it? That your father kicked you out, that I should throw you out . . . maybe you've finally convinced me that I don't care."

"You don't." I blubbered.

"Bobby," she said as she knelt and drew me to her, "don't you think I love you when you are at school or playing in the street, or when you're asleep? Why is it any different 'cause Johnny and his brother are here?"

She must have known that I had no reply, for she went on, "Do you remember that place in the country we went to this summer?"

I nodded.

"Tell me, if you found two little baby birds had fallen out of their nest, what would you do?"

"I'd put them back."

"But what if the nest were all the way near the top of the tree and you couldn't reach it, then what?"

"And they couldn't fly yet?"

"That's right."

"I'd put them in my hands, but I wouldn't make a fist, and then I'd bring them into the house and make a nest from a box and I'd put grass in it and maybe some leaves. Then I'd put it on the window-sill so their mothers could maybe find them and take them home."

"But when they grew strong enough to fly away, I'd bet you'd be a little sad, wouldn't you?"

I nodded.

"Well, if you'd go to all that trouble for two little birds, why can't you for two little boys? I don't think you'd feel at all sad if I told you they were going home, would you?"

I felt trapped and ashamed.

"I wonder how you would feel if you were in their shoes?"

"But you said you wouldn't go to the hospital," I blurted.

"But I might have to go and stay with your grandmother, or one of your aunts might need my help for a while . . ."

"So who would take care of me?"

"Your father."

"But when he works?"

"Martha."

"Martha?"

"Yes, what's wrong with Martha?"

"You said she doesn't know how to dry a dish."

"You'd be surprised what Martha does know."

"She does?"

"Yes, she knows a great deal about taking care of a family. She just doesn't like to show off about it. Then, there's Peter."

"What can Peter do?"

She looked away. "What *can* Peter do?" she asked herself. "Well, Peter can teach you to skate and to ride a bicycle and how to run fast and play stickball. Also, Mrs. Greneker could watch you, and in an absolute emergency there is always your Aunt Shirley."

"Is she married yet?"

"She couldn't get herself arrested."

"Could Mrs. Greneker?"

"Could Mrs. Greneker what?"

"Get herself arrested."

"What for?"

I whispered, "For throwing garbage out of the window."

"I see where the eyes and ears have been working overtime."

"Could she?"

"Yes, so you mustn't tell anyone about it."

"Could you?"

"Of course."

"Would you take me with you?"

"Yes, so you don't have to throw anything out on your own. Do you understand?"

"Yes."

"Under no circumstances are you to throw anything out of the window. Now, come take your bath and we'll wash away all your black thoughts and leave only the nice white ones."

"Before Artie and Johnny?"

"Yes, you're first."

She sang my good-night song and left me wrapped in a half-light of peace. It was strange. I was still in her room, Johnny and Artie were in mine; nothing had changed, but I felt a great soft contentment within me.

My father came, sat at the edge of the bed, passed his hand over my forehead.

"Are you awake?"

"Yes."

"I want you to know that I really thought I was playing with you and not punishing you. But I suspect you were right and I wasn't. I'm sorry."

I understood only the last words but they were sufficient.

chapter 6

On the way to school the next morning we met Libby and her mother, who pointed to some paper bags and bundles strewn in the gutter, and said, "It's catching on fast."

"So does an epidemic," my mother retorted.

"It can't hurt."

"It won't help."

Skipping to my side, Libby asked, "Did your mother throw some out?"

"No."

"Mine did."

"She's gonna be arrested."

"Maaaaa . . ." Libby bawled, "what he said!"

"Libby, I'm talking," Mrs. Jackson said.

Libby ran to my mother and walking backward, began, "Mrs. Hirshman, you know what Bobby said's going to happen to my . . ."

"Libby," my mother said, "if Bobby wanted me to know, he'd tell me himself. So it must be a secret, keep it that way."

Libby sulked, and gave me a look indicating she was adding this to her mountain-high collection of grievances.

In school we sang "Three Blind Mice," "Little Bo-Peep" and "Baa, Baa, Black Sheep."

The morning limped.

We cut small rounds of colored paper, pierced them; then snipped sipping straws into smaller lengths and beaded the two alternately on strings of raffia. Miss Diamond said that the girls should wear the ones they made and the boys should give theirs to the most beautiful girls they knew. Gerard Shuminsky walked up to Miss Diamond and presented her with the one he had made. I wondered why he hadn't kept it for his mother.

The afternoon lagged.

The bell finally rang and we found Mrs. Jackson waiting to take Johnny and me home.

"Where's my mother?" I asked.

She dismissed my anxiety with a wide look and, "You're going to get a big surprise."

"What kind?"

"The kind that if you ask me no questions, I'll tell you no lies, but all I can say it's the biggest surprise."

"Is it in my house?"

"Maybe yes, maybe no," she said, smiling mysteriously; then, taking Libby's hand and mine, and telling Johnny to hold fast, she said, "Let's go, gang."

Libby held back.

"What's the matter?" her mother asked.

"I don't wanna," she complained.

"You don't wanna, what?"

"I don't wanna you should take them home."

"I'll give you an I don't wanna with my pocketbook, you'll forget to get up forever."

"No. They stink on ice. They don't play with me."

"Libby!" her mother warned, and yanked her toward us.

"No!" Libby cried, and slipping her hand from her mother's grasp, she ran ahead.

"All right," Mrs. Jackson said decisively as she took Johnny's hand and mine, "she can go find herself another mother."

The idea was inconceivable. I looked up at her, "Could she?"

"What other mother would want her?" Mrs. Jackson replied.

It wasn't what I had wanted or expected to hear and I found myself once more floundering in a muddle of questions as to whether Libby or, more importantly, I ever might have to find another mother, and whether Johnny and his brother had already found another mother in mine. Could these beads that were so carefully folded in my pocket fit around the neck of any other mother?

I saw Johnny's beads hanging limply from his hand. "Who are you gonna give your beads to?"

"*My* mother!" he snapped as if expecting I wanted them for mine.

Up the street Libby was peeking out from behind a recess in the wall. As we passed, her mother said in a loud voice, "Just look at that poor, little girl. She has no one to take her home from school."

Libby flew out of her hiding place. "I don't need no mother to take me home from school. I'm old enough to do it myself. Besides, you're not their mother. Their mothers hate them so much they don't even care if they come home from school."

Johnny's neck stiffened and his eyes blinked; at the same time I felt the tighter clasp of Mrs. Jackson's hand.

"Just keep it up," she said, "as soon as we get home I'll sign the papers and you can start looking for another mother. And don't ask for any references from me."

"Ha-ha," Libby said, but she looked a little worried.

Without warning, a bag thrown from a window in Sonia's Hole skimmed our heads. Mrs. Jackson dropped my hand and quickly grabbed Libby to her side. "Look before you throw!" she shouted. Nudging us forward, she brought us to safety in front of our building and then called, "Now throw to your heart's content, yourself included."

Giggling and tittering at this, we scurried inside. I was grateful Libby had won her mother back so quickly; it meant she wouldn't have to come and ask for mine. But I remembered too that it was my hand her mother had dropped in that moment of danger.

I raced up the steps. Johnny followed.

I pounded on the door, and Mrs. Greneker, holding Artie, opened it.

"Is it here?" I shouted, darting into the apartment.

"If you're here, it's here," said Mrs. Greneker, taking Artie back into the bedroom.

"You're making funnies."

"So, if I'm making funnies, laugh."

"There's no surprise?"

"I'm no surprise?" she countered.

"No."

"Then good-bye, and give them my regards."

"But Mrs. Jackson said there would be a surprise," I insisted.

"Then that's her department." She disappeared into the kitchen.

"What kind of surprise?" Johnny asked.

"I don't know," I said. "Maybe it's hiding somewhere."

We went through cabinets, bureaus, tables, closets; under the beds; felt every inch of mattress and every pillow for suggestive bumps; climbed on chairs to search shelves we couldn't reach; went under tables; slithered arms under the couch and chairs; slid a stick under the bathtub; reached behind the toilet bowl; stepped into the tub, then to its rim, and with my knees on the edge of the sink, examined the medicine chest. Having searched the two bedrooms, living room and bathroom, we came into the kitchen.

"Just in time for some delicious milk," said Mrs. Greneker.

"With what?" I asked.

"With a glass, what else?"

"No cake?"

"How would you like some fluffy bread and butter?" she asked.

"No."

"No is no," she said flatly.

"No cake, no milk," I insisted, deciding that this would be an excellent opportunity to test the amount of authority Mrs. Greneker had over me and, at the same time, the extent of my control over her.

"Where is there a law that there's got to be milk with cake only?"

"My mother gives it to me all the time."

"Ah klug tsuh Columbus."

"What does that mean?"

"It means that if Columbus knew that in this country, today, there are certain people who won't drink their milk unless they have cake, he would be sorry he discovered America. So now you'll drink your milk without cake, maybe?"

"No."

"Let be, no." She put the glasses of milk on the table and busied herself with putting away the dishes, while singing, "Dum-dee-dye, diddle-diddle, dum-dye; milk makes bones and strong teeth. Dye-dye, diddle-dum dye. With milk the arches can't fall from the feet. Dum-dee-dye, diddle-diddle, dum-dye. Cake because it tastes so sweet. Dye-dye, diddle-dum dye. Cake makes big holes in the teeth. Dum-dee-dye, diddle-diddle, dum-dye. When the dentist looks in your mouth. Dye-dye, diddle-dum dye. He has to pull all the teeth out. Dum-dee-dye, diddle-diddle, dum-dye. When you got no teeth to chew. Dye-dye, diddle-dum dye. There is only one thing you can do. Dum-dee-dye, diddle-diddle, dum-dye. You have to drink milk the rest of your life. Dye-dye, diddle-dum dye. And a boy without teeth can't find a wife. Dye-dye, diddle-dum-dum dye."

Johnny made a gesture toward his glass. I silently signaled him not to.

Glancing over her shoulder, Mrs. Greneker remarked, "I see I got a strike on my hands." We were both silent, but Johnny couldn't suppress a smile. And I pressed my lips together. "Well," she continued, "as it just so happens, I have upstairs in my apartment some of the most delicious mandelbrodt in the world."

"What's that?" I asked.

"You never heard from mandelbrodt?" Clasping her hands, she looked upward and said, "America, what are you doing to our people." Then, pointing at us, "Go in and mind Artie until I come down. And don't let nobody in unless you are one hundred per cent sure who it is and then ask twice, at least."

As soon as the door had closed and the lock turned, I went to my bedroom, where I found Artie chewing at the edge of my Cinderella book. Johnny tore it away from him. But when Artie began to cry, I said, "Give it to him. He's only a baby."

"No, I can't." Johnny said.

"*Why?*"

"If he eats up words now he won't be able to read them later."

"Who told you that?"

"My mother."

"Oh."

A thick thud came from the back yard.

"They're throwing again," I said. We ran to the window.

"Who threw that bag of garbage?" a loud, angry voice demanded. It wasn't Mr. Sobieski. I wondered who it could be.

"If you tell me what type of garbage it is, maybe I could help you," a voice sang out. It sounded to me as if Mrs. Greneker were imitating my sister Martha.

"It's got eggs and a melon skin and carrot peelings . . . " the man's voice reported.

"What kind of melon?" the woman's voice asked.

"A muskmelon."

"A muskmelon, I can't help you," the woman's voice replied. "But if it was an Andrew Mellon, that would be another story."

The yard rang with the bells of women's laughter.

"You won't think it's so funny if I ever get my hands on you!" the man's voice threatened.

"He must be a cop." Johnny's whisper trembled. Just then there was the noise of a key in the door lock, and we ran out of the bedroom.

"All right, here's the mandelbrodt," said Mrs. Greneker. She was hurried and short of breath.

"Who's that man in the yard?" I asked.

"Could be it was the janitor."

"Not the janitor."

"Not the janitor, then I can't help you," she replied.

The doorbell rang and Mrs. Greneker opened it for Martha, who flew in as if she had been pushed. "Mother, we got to move from this crazy neighborhood at once. Everyone's insane. The street's full of health inspectors and the kids are throwing bags of water at them from the roofs. And the inspectors are chasing them from one roof to another. And that lunatic, Carmella, caught ahold of an inspector's coat and tried to hold him back from chasing a kid and she tore the coat right in two—"

She stopped and looked about her with surprise, her mouth slightly open as if the words had been snipped off. "Where's my mother?"

"She went out. She'll be back in a little while," Mrs. Greneker replied.

"What if I needed her for something?"

"That's why I'm here."

"You're not my mother."

"And you're not Clara Gimpel Young."

"Kimball . . . Kimball."

"You're not her, too."

Martha threw her head back and brushed past Mrs. Greneker into the kitchen. "Robert," she said, "I would like to leave a message for Mother. Tell her I won't be home for dinner because I am going to rehearse the part of Portia in *The Merchant of Venice* by William Shakespeare with Henrietta, at her home, and that I will have my dinner there. And I haven't the faintest idea when I'll be home; and please tell her not to send you or anybody to call for me there because it's a very long rehearsal; because first I have to rehearse Henrietta and then she has to rehearse me; and it's very important because starting the day after tomorrow the Dramatic Club is having tryouts and if I don't get the part I'll quit school and never go back again no matter what anyone does. Can you remember it all?"

Before I could answer, Mrs. Greneker said, "Why stop now, put on one more line and you got a book."

Martha gave her a 'I-didn't-even-hear-a-word-you-said' look. "Now don't forget to give her the message. And also give her this, I found it stuck in the letterbox in this stupid building." She put a folded sheet of paper on the table. "I'm going now," she announced.

"I'll clap after the door is closed," Mrs. Greneker said.

After the door slammed shut, Mrs. Greneker returned to the kitchen. "Well, what's the decision about Mrs. Greneker's mandelbrodt."

"It's good-good," Johnny declared.

"It's delicious-good," I added, privately thinking I liked my mother's cake better.

"That's all I want to hear." Then, eying the paper that Martha had left, she asked me, "Tell me, can you read yet?"

"Yes," I replied.

"That's marvelous. Let's see how good you can read," she said, unfolding the sheet.

I studied the rows of letters. "It's not a story," I said, returning the sheet.

"I see," she said, "if it's not a story you can't read. How about you Mr. Spinoza?" she asked Johnny.

"I can say the A-B-C," he offered.

"That's very good, but let's see why this not a story," she said as she resettled her glasses on her face.

She read to herself for a few moments, and then, her voice growing angry, read aloud: ". . . an offender will be fined up to $200 and will be subject to a maximum sentence of no more than one year in jail. The Department of Health of this city have been duly informed of the transgressions that have been taking place on these premises and have appointed special investigators equipped with police powers to remedy this situation. Any person found disposing of refuse in any other way than that provided by law will be prosecuted to the full extent of that law and will be subject to fine, imprisonment and immediate eviction. So, stop throwing garbage from the windows. Signed by The Acme Realty Company."

"What does it mean?" I asked.

"It means that this is the answer to your question about the man in the back yard who wasn't the janitor. He's an investigator from the Health Department. And another thing, you're right, it isn't a story and isn't worth reading."

We finished our milk and I asked Mrs. Greneker if Johnny and I could go out and hunt for bottle caps. She said no. "First of all, there's too much going on outside and you might, God forbid, get hurt. And next, if you go by your mother's window and look out you'll soon see the surprise you were looking for."

We dashed into the bedroom and looked out on the street. Everything was still, abnormally quiet. No children, no wild noises of play. A lone woman walked, stooped by her shopping bag. The windows of buildings mirrored the whiteness of a sun ready to set.

Two men came out of a cellar doorway, peered up and ambled slowly. Though they wore no uniforms, the leather thongs of their nightsticks hung out from under their jackets.

One stopped opposite the window. Craning, he shifted from one foot to the other. Suddenly a bag of water exploded at his feet. He jumped back, looked up and pointing a threatening finger, flew

135

into the building behind him.

A moment later, two older boys, their jackets streaming behind like pennants, dashed out of the adjoining building, disappeared up the steps of another. And then, once again, the quiet, the stillness.

We hugged the windowsills. Artie waddled into the room, and continued his painstaking destruction of my Cinderella book.

An event! An event! More important than anything else happening in the street.

A taxi pulled up in front of Johnny's building. Could it be? Why didn't the door open? Why didn't someone get out? We knew. Yes, we knew, but our eyes had to know too. All we needed was the top of a hat, any little signal. Why were they taking so long?

Then I saw that hat, that black hat, and my yells, my hurrays, punctured the sickly silence of the street.

She helped Johnny's mother out, carefully, slowly, gently as if she were a china doll. Then, together, Johnny and I whipped ourselves into a magnificent frenzy of wild delight.

"She's home!"

"Your mother's home!"

"*Your* mother's home!"

We waved. We whipped our arms about as if they were boneless.

They saw us! Johnny's mother, clutching something to her that looked like a shapeless paper sack, waved gently with her free hand.

"Ma-ma-ma-ma-ma-ma-MA!" he trumpeted.

Artie pummeled us to discover why our delirium. We tried to pick him up. He was too heavy. We pushed him onto a chair and slid it in front of the window. We pointed frantically to guide his eyes. He was stupid, he was crazy. He kept looking the wrong way.

Seeing Artie, Johnny's mother threw him a kiss. Johnny told his brother to, "Kiss back! Kiss back! Kiss back to Mommy!" while he hurled fistsful of kisses into the golden air.

My mother kissed her fingertips and blew. I could almost see the kiss, like a blue and ruby butterfly, leave her fingers and soar smoothly to me. I caught it carefully in the cups of my hands, and releasing it slowly, kissed it back to her.

We jumped, we ran, flew!

Mrs. Greneker shouted from the kitchen, "What's all that noise? Stop, already."

We refused to hear.

> "Marguerite,
> Go wash your feet;
> The Board of Health
> Is 'cross the street."

> "Fudge, fudge, tell the judge
> Momma has a new baby,
> It's not a girl and it's not a boy;
> It's not a boil and it's not a goy;
> So wrap it up in toilet paper
> And throw it down the elevator:
> First floor, bang;
> Second floor, smack;
> Third floor, whang;
> Fourth floor, crack
> Fifth floor,
> Kick it out the cellar door."

"What's with this hoo-ha?" Mrs. Greneker caught me as I tried to pass her.

"No-no-no-no," I protested, and tried wriggling loose. "They're here! They're home!" I shouted.

"So all right, so quiet. What's so special that your mother is home? She only left here a little more than half an hour. Why should you carry on like she hasn't been home for a year and a half?"

Her words stunned me to a stop. My hypocrisy stood naked and blue in the cold. I knew at once that I had been whirling on this carousel of joy only because his mother's return meant I would be finally free of Johnny and his brother.

"Come," said Mrs. Greneker, releasing me, untying her apron, "I'll make like Commissioner Whalen and you'll be my whole Coxey's Army." With her voice behind us warning, "Be careful, don't fall, wait for me in front of the house, don't cross the street without me," we flew down the steps, through the hall and out the front door.

I tried grabbing Johnny's arm and cried, "Wait!"—but as if nothing could stop him he ran across the street, up the steps to where his mother stood and flinging himself at her, buried his head furiously into the lap of her coat. When she tried lifting his face, he fought against it and dug his head more deeply. And I could tell by the lurching of his body that the tears had finally come.

With Artie in her arms, Mrs. Greneker reached for her handkerchief. "Everybody has something expert to say about a mother's heart, but to see into a child's only God has the eyeglasses. Come," she said, taking my hand, "let's go over. My heart tells me in a minute we'll have a real crying party."

I went with her, but reluctantly. And when we reached them, I dared not look up at my mother for fear she would see the guilt inscribed on my face.

Johnny's mother took Artie from Mrs. Greneker and pressed her mouth so hard on his cheek that the flesh pillowed up around it. "Mama, Mama," Artie mumbled, and then twisted and stretched his arms for Mrs. Greneker.

Without lifting his head, Johnny dug into his pocket, pulled out the beads and held them up for his mother. She said she had never seen such beautiful ones before, and my mother agreed with her, which of course made it impossible for me to give her mine.

My mother indicated something in the bundle. Johnny's mother reached into it and brought out a rose as large and tight-petaled as a young cabbage. She stroked Johnny's head, and when he looked up at her gave him the flower. He stared at it as if it were revelation, touched it as if it were a dream. And when my mother said, "I told you she was saving a rose for you," he pressed it to his lips, kissed and kissed it until the petals began to fall.

I knelt and collected some to return to him. When I looked up I saw the women weeping.

The petals were still in my hand when I had the thought.

It grew. Like the little Japanese toy clam-shell which, when dropped into water, opens and releases a violent pink paper peony that expands slowly until it more than triples in size.

Where was the baby?

Why wasn't there a baby?

There were for me, at the time, two general categories of the unknown: those that could be questioned, and mysteries. Though mysteries could be questioned, the answers were not expected to be understood. And topmost among the mysteries were God and babies. The only important question I had about the former was why it was a "He"; babies, more profoundly, "Why?"

I was never particularly interested in their origins until the day that Libby, in an attempt to involve me in one of her games, announced she knew and would tell me if I would play with her. And since I didn't want to forfeit my freedom, I went to my mother with the question.

Instead of being surprised, or even hesitant, she seemed pleased and replied, "The birds tell only the bees, the bees tell only the flowers, the flowers tell only the seeds, and only the seeds will tell you." And when I remonstrated, "You can't fool me, seeds don't talk," she replied, "Maybe not, but when it comes to seeds, actions speak louder than words."

Now I stood at the foot of the steps to Johnny's house, looking at her, wondering if I could ask her what had happened to the baby Martha told me about. But a glance at the tiny beads shimmering like quicksilver on the rims of her eyes was like a hand over my mouth.

Who else could I ask? Did I dare go for Martha at Henrietta's? No. Who, then?

My answer came out of her father's barbershop holding a huge orange, admiring it before she clamped a vise of even, white teeth into its flesh. I slipped away to meet her.

"Hello, Carmella," I said offhandedly.

Without lifting her eyes, she bit into the orange skin, ripped off the peel with her teeth and spat it on the sidewalk. "Phah." The bitter taste twisted her face. Then, peering back into the store, she rose quickly, retrieved the skin and threw it into the gutter.

"Hey greenie, you like-a this country?" she asked, waving the orange at me. "Stay another two weeks."

"But Carmella, I'm Bobby."

"Never saw you in my whole life. You musta just got off-a the boat. And if you wanna piece of orange, you got another big fat guess coming around the corner for you, you betcha sweet life."

"I don't want your orange. Why are you mad?"

"Mad?" she roared. "Ho boy, that's a good one! I'm so sore at you like you were excommunicated from now until His kingdom come."

"Why?"

"You know why? Remember you and your dopey sister was coming out of The Poorhouse and she was walking like she was Mrs. Sheik of Araby and not talking to nobody, and I asked you what you was carrying. Do you remember?"

"No." But I did.

"I asked you what you was carrying. And you said if I really wanted to know, 'cause it was a secret. And I swore to God—to God, I swore—that I wouldn't tell anybody if you told me. Right in front of everybody, I swore to God . . . in front of Mrs. Greneker and Mrs. Lundgren and Mrs. Kuritzky and that Mrs. What's-her-name whose husband's got a hunchback, and lots more, I swore to God. And you remember what you said?"

"No," weakly.

"You had the goddamned, dirty, stinking, rotten, lousy, enemy nerve after I swore to God in front of everybody—and I bet He heard, too—to tell me that you was carrying something for President Hoover and a midget. What kind of a minus answer is that to give me, your friend?" She bit viciously into the orange, and munched the pulp.

"Did I say it?" I asked unbelievingly.

"You can bet your rootie-patootie that it wasn't no saint up in the clouds who said it. It came out of your own loudspeaker."

"Maybe you didn't hear me right," I protested.

"Hear you right? I got twenty-twenty hearing. And do you know what kind of hearing is twenty-twenty?" She spat the orange pulp on the sidewalk, looked back guiltily, picked it up and threw it into the gutter.

Returning, she beckoned to me and with an impish smile said, "The other week, I was sitting here chewing polly seeds and throwing the outsides all over the front of the store, and my father came out and caught me. So you know what he went 'n' did?"

"What?"

"He gave me such a bang over my ear that I couldn't hear straight for three days, except it was ringing like a bell got busted inside. So he had to let my mother take me to the doctor. And the doctor cost three dollars and the ear drops cost seventy-five cents. So that smack he gave me cost him plenty of money. Ain't that something?"

I agreed.

"Well," she said, "so now we're friends again."

"Carmella," I began, "do you know about babies?"

"Do I know about babies? Do *I* know about *babies!* Listen, there isn't nothing in this world that I don't know about babies. Everything! I can diaper them and dress 'em and feed 'em and sing and rock-a-bye baby them. I know all about formulas. I even invented some myself. I can even talk the same language. And when I sit them down, they make and no waiting around for two or three days, either. When I get married—St. Agnes, please be on my side—I'm going to have more babies than in this whole neighborhood put together. You just stick around and watch. What else?"

"Where do they come from?"

"Why, your mother going to have a baby?"

"No."

"Then why you're asking?"

" 'Cause I have a friend . . ."

"You're sure your mother ain't going to have one?"

"Yes."

"Swear to God and hope to die."

I swore.

"So what do you want to know about getting babies?"

"How do they get them?"

"First they gotta be absolutely married. Then they gotta go to the priest and have an extra-long talk. And he makes up his mind if they should go to Saint Ursula's Hospital or call Doctor Sorrentino and have it in their own house, which they have to have blessed so the angels can be looking down when it happens. Saint Ursula's has its regular angels all the time so they don't need extra blessings if they go there."

"If it's in the hospital, when does the baby come home?"

"What d'ya mean, when does the baby come home?"

"I mean, can they keep the baby there?"

"You're gonna make me a little crazy with your questions. They don't keep the baby nowhere. The baby belongs to the mother. She takes the baby home with her."

"Always?"

"Sure, always."

"They don't keep the baby for a little bit after, maybe?"

She spat out orange pulp and addressed the street as if it were thronged with an audience. "You know what I'd do if they tried to keep my baby? I'd go down to the place where we used to live and I'd buy a box of vendetta powder and a box of hate powder an' a bag of sick-and-die powder. I'd go into that hospital and I'd spill the powders on every floor so the doctors and the nurses would begin to hate each other—then they'd fight each other with the knives they operate with, they'd choke and call for help and their eyes would fall out of their heads and their tongues would hang down to their shoes, and they'd die after they rolled over three times. Then, I'd get a broom and a garbage can with wheels like the street cleaner has and I'd walk down the halls and I'd sweep 'em up like dead rats. But just in case I missed even one, I'd take the biggest bomb I could get and I'd throw it right in the hospital and it would go WHOOM-BAM!"

"Shut up your crazy mouth, you strega, you," her father shouted from the doorway. And drawing his arm back, he roared, "Shut da mouth, or I give you such a whoom-bam I knock every tooth out of your crazy head."

Stepping beyond his reach, Carmella shouted, "You just try! You maybe just try! It'll soon cost you at least a hunnert and three dollars and seventy-five cents, at least."

Instead of letting his hand fly, he pointed his finger at her and they fell into a beautiful Italian opera for all to hear.

I returned to our building in answer to Mrs. Greneker's call, and as I climbed the steps I heard Mr. Calabrese threaten (in English by now), "I kill you one day. You see, I kill you." Carmella flung back, "So, you kill me. Big deal! You know what happens to you if you kill me. You get the 'lectric chair. And the Church don't bury you, so there."

Mrs. Greneker's rattle of dishes resounded through the apartment, suddenly empty where so recently it had been crammed with excitement, but not empty enough to house all my guilt.

Instead of going to wash and coming to eat, as Mrs. Greneker had told me to do, I went to my room and crept under my bed. Here in the half-gloom I pursued, like the farmer's wife, the three blind mice of my misfortune: Johnny, Artie and their mother; how they had come so recently yet so decisively into my world; how first they sped its whirling, then reversed its direction, and now helped send it off course; how they summoned up in me thoughts and feelings I had never before experienced; and how they raised questions so difficult I did not know whether I wanted the answers.

Even now, blowing the little dust ball around in front of me, I wondered what my mother was doing in their apartment. What *could* she be doing there? And why did I care that she was in their apartment? How many times had she gone to Libby's apartment and Mrs. Greneker's and Mrs. McCarthy's, or to the apartments of people whose names I hadn't known, and it hadn't been important. Why did it matter that she was in Johnny's mother's apartment? Why did everything that included them exclude me?

In self-debate, I asked myself what they had actually done to me. I imagined myself complaining to my mother about them—what would I say? The only evidence I had was my Cinderella book, and even I had helped destroy it, finally. Beyond that, I had, as my mother would say, no case in her court.

"Bobby, where are you? Bobby?" There was anxiety in Mrs. Greneker's voice.

"In my bedroom."

"I'm in your bedroom too, but I don't see you. Where are you hiding yourself?"

"Under the bed."

"What are you doing under there?"

"I'm thinking."

"For thinking you need strength—come eat your dinner."

"I'm not hungry."

"Save the 'not-hungry' for Yom Kippur. It will come in handy then."

"What's Yom Kippur?"

"It's enough to break the heart that a Jewish boy shouldn't know from Yom Kippur," she said to the world. Then, to me, "Yom Kippur is the day you don't eat because you are praying to God all day to forgive your sins."

"I don't have any sins."

"As it so happens, you're right, but only because until you're thirteen years old your father takes all the blame for your sins."

"He never told me that."

"Why should he? It will do him no good. For instance, it's a sin not to eat your dinner. If you knew that this sin would go on your father's head would you come out and eat dinner?"

"Sure."

"So what are you waiting for, an invitation?"

I scrambled out from under. "You're sure you're not fooling me," I asked.

"Listen to me, Bobby Hirshman," she said, taking my hand, "when it comes to God and His ways, Mrs. Greneker doesn't fool not with you, not with anybody. What God says, goes right down on the line with no bargains, no questions and no dancing on one foot and begging for favors with the hand." She led me to the bathroom, turned on the faucets and washed my hands.

"Who is God?"

"Something in my heart told me this would be the next question." Then, wiping my hands, she said, "I'll tell you all about it while you eat."

Seated on my telephone book, waiting to be served, I had the feeling that for the moment Mrs. Greneker and I were the only people in the entire world, and that she was going to tell me a great secret about God. However, just as she placed the plate of chopped liver in its curl of lettuce, topped with a great white onion ring, the door opened and my mother came in.

"Just in time to take the floor," said Mrs. Greneker.

"I can only be a minute," my mother said. I saw the perspiration on her forehead. She opened the cabinet beneath the sink and took out two shopping bags.

"When are you coming back?" I asked.

She looked at me, sadly I thought, and said, "All I have to do is take the children's things to them, just fix a little dinner and I'll be back in less than an hour."

"Promise?"

"I promise."

"Swear to God?"

"No, that I won't do, I'm sorry. God may not let me keep that promise. I can only tell you that, God willing, I'll be back in an hour, maybe before." She hurried into my bedroom while I sat and miserably contemplated God, my mother, the chopped liver and my misery.

After she had left, Mrs. Greneker lowered herself slowly to a chair beside me. "Aren't you going to eat? I chopped this liver for you with my own two hands."

"No," I said, pushing the plate away. "I'm not hungry."

"We are back to the beginning again? I thought you wanted me to tell you about God."

"No I don't. I don't want to hear about Him, never."

"Why not?"

"Because He might not let my mother keep her promise."

"I see," she said. "From where you sit, everybody should stop doing whatever they are doing and do everything the way you want it?"

"Yes."

"So you are a bigger schlemiel than I thought. Just think, if everybody should stop doing whatever they are doing and do everything the way you want it, then you have to be God."

"So?"

"Anybody who wants God's job is either a schlemiel or meshugeh."

"So, why does God want the job?"

"Eat and I'll tell you. First of all, He didn't want the job. For thousands and thousands of years, He was sitting around with His hands in His pockets living the life of Riley. He didn't make anything. He didn't need anything. He didn't want anything. He was living on Easy Street."

"Why didn't He want to make anything?"

"Because He didn't want the headaches. There were no stars he should have to polish so they should shine up in the sky. There was no earth He should have to water; no sun He should have to put out in the morning and take in by night; no clouds He should have to push away from in front of Him so He should be able to see. And, as it so happens, there was nothing to see."

"Why don't you eat with bread?"

"I don't want any bread."

"Who ever heard of chopped chicken liver without bread?"

"All right, but I won't eat the onion. What happened to God?"

"Don't talk with your mouth full. So God was enjoying Himself doing nothing, until one day His wife, Torah, says to Him, 'To tell You the truth,' She says, 'I'm getting very tired from doing nothing.' So He says to Her, 'Please leave Me alone, I'm resting.' 'You're resting?' She says. 'You haven't lifted Your little finger in a million years, so from what are You resting?' So He says, 'If You can be tired from doing nothing, then I can be exhausted from the same reason.' Intermission for one minute while I get the soup." She ladled the soup into a plate and returned.

"Here," she said, "eat, it's one hundred per cent pure gold. It's real fourteen-carat kosher chicken soup."

"It's hot," I complained.

"I'm sorry, with ice I don't know how to cook."

"Are you going to tell me more about God?"

"If you eat nicely and don't slup the soup. So Torah says to Him,

'What's the use of being God if there's nobody and nothing to be God over?' So He stops and thinks for a second. And that's where He made His mistake."

"Where?"

"Because as soon as Torah saw that He didn't have a ready-made answer, She quick got in her two cents and said, 'Come on, be a sport, let's have a little life around here. At least make some angels.' 'Angels,' He says, 'are out of the question.' 'Why?' She asks. 'Because,' He says, 'they're always going around losing their feathers, and feathers make Me sneeze.' 'So,' She says, 'make little ones, baby angels. And give them violins so they can fly around and make music.'

"Here, wipe your mouth. But God said, 'Baby angels, maybe, but no violins. If I have to listen to them practicing all day long, it will drive Me out of My mind.' So Torah says, 'All right, give them violins but don't give them bows. Without bows they'll only be able to plink on the strings and that doesn't make too much noise.' Another intermission while I get chicken."

"Don't give me such a big piece."

"It's a small piece on a big bone. Let me see, where was I?"

"The baby angels should only plink on the strings."

"That's right. So He made the baby angels; and He gave them violins; and right away He knew He was on the spot."

"Why?"

"Because whoever heard of baby angels without mother angels? After all, who was going to take care of them if there was no mother angels? And then He quick also had to make father angels."

"Why?"

"Because somebody had to support the baby angels and the mother angels. They had to have from what to eat. Why aren't you eating the skin from the chicken? Chicken skin is good for you, and if you eat it with a piece of bread it will slide down easier."

"What happened then?"

"God knows."

"Huh?"

"So, then, the baby angels were flying around plinking on the violins, the mother angels were flying around taking care of them, and the father angels were flying around trying to make a living. And except maybe for the feathers, God didn't mind it too much."

"And after that?"

"If you used your mouth more to eat than to ask questions, the dinner and the story would come out even."

"Is that the end of it?"

"Let me see," she said reflectively, and then, "Oh yes, one day Torah says to God, 'I have an idea.' So God says, 'Ideas I got plenty of My own right now. When I need one I'll come to You.' So Torah says, 'All right,' she says, 'You're the Chief. What You say goes. But maybe will You do Me a favor?' 'A favor,' God says, 'is still something different. Let me hear.' 'The angels,' says Torah, 'are the most beautiful things You ever made. They are so good, so kind, so sweet . . . like sugar they are sweet. But who can live on sugar alone?' 'So?' says God, ready to make with a big no, regardless what She should ask. 'So,' says Torah, 'I would consider it a big favor to Me if you would make, for a change, just one bad angel.' 'What!' God asks. And it was such a *big* what it almost blew Torah away. 'Why do You want to start trouble?' He asks. 'It's no good that everything is quiet and nice and peaceful? What for do You need a bad angel? What for, I ask You?' So Torah, who was quick with the ready-made answers, said, 'So Me and the angels should have somebody to talk about.' "

Someone knocked impatiently on the door.

"Hold your horses," said Mrs. Greneker as she got up to answer. "Who is it?"

"It's me," Martha snapped. Mrs. Greneker gave the door a vanishing look and opened it.

"I thought you were going to be very late," I said joyfully.

"Don't talk to me," Martha muttered, and flounced into the living room.

"Gee," I said, "am I glad you came home."

"I said not to talk to me, didn't I?"

"But I have to talk to you!"

"How would you like what I just gave rotten, stupid Henrietta?"

"What was that?"

"I gave her such a slap in her ugly face that it wouldn't surprise me if she didn't remember her stupid name for at least three days."

"Martha," Mrs. Greneker called from the kitchen, "would you like some tea?"

"What do you think I am, a communist?"

"If I told you what I think you are," Mrs. Greneker called back, "I wouldn't be allowed to put a foot in this house even if I should live to be one hundred and twenty."

Suddenly and unexpectedly Martha burst into tears. "Everybody's against me," and wailed, and flung herself the length of the couch.

"Your bloomers are sticking out," I whispered to her.

"Get away from me!" she screamed as she pulled down the back of her skirt. "I'll kill you!" Then, burying her head in the pillows, she mourned, "Everybody hates me . . . everybody."

"What's happening here?" Mrs. Greneker looked alarmed as she rushed in from the kitchen. "What did you do to her?" she asked accusingly.

"I didn't do anything."

"Go 'way! Go 'way! *Go 'way!*" Martha screamed into the pillow. "Where's my mother? *Where is she?*"

Martha's crying tantrums were nothing new. Until now, they had failed to touch me. They were elaborate, noisy and often funny and they only helped reopen an old question: How could she and I belong to the same family? I didn't openly doubt this, but I was secretly convinced that one of us belonged and one didn't. The problem, as always, was to prove she didn't and I did.

I reasoned this way: Martha was different. She was a *one* person. She had one friend, Henrietta; one interest, movies; one purpose, to be an actress; one world, the vanity mirror in my mother's bedroom. There she would sit for hours, examining her face—its planes, angles and contours, its shading, lights and shadows. When she thought she was alone in the apartment, she would play-act: "Rodney, just look at the size of this diamond . . . and for me. For *me!* Ah, no, alas I can't accept it. 'Twould be folly . . . folly, I tell you. To what occasion would I wear it, especially because no one is supposed to know that you gave it to me as a token of your affection. And your wife, my best friend, dearest, dearest Daphne, what would she say if she ever found out? I can hear her heart now, breaking in bits and pieces. No, Rodney, you must take it and go. And please, my darling, don't turn around. I couldn't bear it if you turned around. Help me be brave. You dasn't come here again. What would my dear husband say, should he return and find you?" At which Peter, who had been hiding with me in the closet and waiting for the right moment, would open the door, and mimicking her voice, would shout, "Your husband'd say you ought to have your head examined."

Martha would scream, accuse, threaten and finally subside into a state of icy scorn and announce, "You stink!"

I noticed that my father was nice to Martha, although he never paid too much attention to her or her world. This was significant only because it was the attitude my mother recommended I take with people I didn't like. "Just be nice to them. Don't pay any attention to them. Let them go their ways and you go yours," she would say.

She, on the other hand, paid a great deal of attention to my sister. She called it "putting up" with her. And I once overheard her tell my Aunt Shirley that Martha had reached *that* time of her life. When I asked what *that* time meant, my mother replied, "Thirteen o'clock," which in its cryptic way I took as proof that Martha functioned even on different time than the rest of the world.

Peter paid just about the same amount of attention to her as he did to air, water, skies and algebra.

Now, here was Martha weeping, unable to restrain her tears, not posing, not dabbing her eyes affectedly, not glancing out of their corners to check the effect of her performance, just crying. And for once I cared, and I rummaged through my mind for something I might say or do to stop her tears. I thought of openly admitting her to the family, but then realized she had never known of her exclusion. So I stood and watched her and helplessly accepted her as my sister.

"Listen Martha," Mrs. Greneker said, "you must stop crying. With every tear you are losing an ounce from your beauty."

Where Mrs. Greneker and I failed, my father's appearance effected the miracle. At the sound of his voice her tears dammed up; she wiped her eyes on her sleeve and fled to the bathroom.

He asked Mrs. Greneker if she knew what was wrong, but she could only shrug her shoulders. "Maybe she reached *that* time of life," I offered, whereupon Mrs. Greneker called me "a regular talking machine, a parrot without feathers and a big noise in a little pot," and excused herself, saying that if she didn't go and make her husband's dinner he would give her a double divorce.

My mother and Peter came home at the same time, and although the things she said—"At last our home is our own," "Thank God that's over with," "Bless Mrs. Greneker, she went to all the trouble of making a real Friday night dinner and it's only the middle of the week"—lit the gloomiest corners of my mind, there was no mistaking the weariness and worry in her words. And when Martha was finally dislodged from the bathroom and my mother saw her eyes and bleary mouth, instead of saying something offhand as she usually did after one of Martha's dramatic excursions, she took her face between her hands and asked, "Martha, dear, what's wrong? Why are you so unhappy? Tell me."

Perhaps it was the sound of tenderness, for Martha's tears came back in a rush, and falling on my mother's neck, she blubbered how

Henrietta had refused to keep her part of the bargain and give her the cue lines as she had done for her all afternoon; that Henrietta had accused her of reading Portia with a Jewish accent; that when she had slapped Henrietta for saying something so terrible, Henrietta had thrown her whole Shakespeare book at her; and that when she had come home Mrs. Greneker had said something rotten to her.

I interrupted to say that the last was not true, but was told by my mother not to meddle when women were talking.

Martha continued building her house of woe: Now that she was never talking to Henrietta again, she had no one to help her, and with tryouts in a couple of days she was sure she wouldn't get the part and would just die. "I'll just die. I'll just die. I'll *just* die," she wailed, to which my mother said, "You can't. You owe it to your public to live." Whereupon my father offered to help her study the part. She "came to life," kissed my father, my mother, even me, but stopped short of Peter, who held his hands in front of his face and cried, "Don't, you'll give me pimples."

"All right, let's get to the table before everything on the stove turns as cold as good advice," my mother said. She took off her hat, her coat, hanging the coat in the closet, putting the hat carefully on the shelf. As she did I found myself praying both to God and to Torah that she would never have to wear that hat again.

After dinner my father rose, saying to Martha, "Come, let's torture poor Portia," and Peter said, "I'm going over to Buddy Jackson's to study," at which my mother put in, "You don't have to study open poker, you're a genius at it already. And don't forget, if you lose your allowance money there'll be no advances."

I sat and silently basked in the privilege of being able once again to be alone with my mother and watch her do the things she had always done: stack and rinse the dishes, the glasses and the Community Plate silver; give the seltzer bottle an extra squirt in the sink to make sure it was empty; shake each napkin over the tablecloth;

and then, after opening the window, gathering the four ends of the cloth and bearing it like a crumb-filled cloud, empty it out the window. "The birds have to eat, too," she explained.

This time, however, instead of going back to the sink, she returned to the table, sat and, folding her arms on the bare enamel top, rested her forehead on them.

"Are you tired?" I asked.

"A little."

"Can I help you wash the dishes?"

"When you've grown enough to reach the sink."

"Am I grown enough to have an allowance?"

"Not yet. But why rush it? The time will come soon enough. And then you'll find that all the allowances in the world won't be enough to buy back even so much as a minute of today."

"Will I have to wait until I'm thirteen before I get an allowance?"

"Why until then?"

"Because Mrs. Greneker said that until I'm thirteen, Daddy has to pay for all my sins. So, when I get my allowance, I'll pay for my own."

"You know something?" she whispered confidentially.

"What?" I whispered in return.

"Your eyes are mine, your nose is mine, your mouth is your father's and so are your ears, but where that head came from I just can't figure out."

"Didn't it come with me?"

"Of course."

"Were there angels looking when you took me from the hospital?"

"What kind of angels?"

"Carmella told me that St. Ursula's Hospital has regular angels for when babies are born there. Did I come from St. Ursula's?"

"How come you and Carmella were having a conference on babies?"

"Why do you always answer a question with a question?"

"It's a gift from my mother. What else did Carmella tell you?"

"You didn't answer my question, first. Was I born in St. Ursula's?"

"No, you were born at Morris View Hospital."

"Do they have regular angels there?"

"Yes, they fly around with bedpans day and night. Wipe your nose—with a handkerchief."

I did. "Did you take me home with you when I was born?"

"Yes."

"Then why didn't Johnny's mother take the baby home today?"

Her eyes widened, tiredness fell away from her. "Who told you that Johnny's mother had a baby?"

"Do I have to tell?"

"I think so."

"Would you punish her?"

"No, I wouldn't punish Martha," she said, standing and leaving me awed in the face of her omniscience. She went to the sink, turned the faucets and stood with her hands motionless beneath the flow of water. "No, Johnny's mother didn't have a baby," she said at last.

"Why?"

She lifted her head and without turning said, "Maybe the right angels weren't looking."

"Will she have to go back to get another one?" I dreaded the answer.

She shrugged her shoulders and I realized she was weeping.

I slipped off the chair and went to her. "Did I make you cry?"

"No," she said, drying her hands on her apron.

"Then why are you crying?"

"I'm crying for the world."

"What's that mean?"

"Your grandmother would say that I'm crying into the ground so that the sorrows of yesterday will sink into the wet sands and be forgotten; and that the suffering of tomorrow will never take root in an earth made salty with tears."

"Would it help if I cried, too?"

"No, only mothers can cry that way. Besides, if you cry you'll spoil my fun. Now, let me finish the dishes."

I went back to the table, sat and watched her.

From my mother's bedroom, I heard Martha declaim, "By my troth, Nerissa, my little body is aweary of this great world."

"Let's understand one thing—we're not trying to kill Portia, we want to bring her to life, Martha," my father interrupted.

"Bobby," my mother said suddenly, "go see if the door to my room is shut, but do it softly."

Struck by her change of mood, I left the kitchen and was back in a moment to tell her that the door was mostly closed. She signaled for me to be very quiet, put on the hall light and switched off the one in the kitchen, then lifted the kitchen window a little higher. "I'm going to show you a new game." Her voice, her eyes, her movements, were all excitement.

I stood on the tightrope of wonder.

She picked up a small bag from under the sink, held it up and taking the hem of her skirt in her other hand, she began to dance and sing:

> "I'm Sally the ballet dancer,
> I dance on the tips of my toes.
> And when I kick so high,
> That I reach the sky,
> Then, out the little bag goes."

On the last word she sent the bag sailing gracefully through the window.

"Mrs. Greneker left me quite a collection today," she remarked as she stooped and got another bag. "Want to see another one?"

"Sure," I said, suddenly realizing that this was how the garbage had been removed ever since the dumbwaiter trouble.

Taking up the hem of her skirt she sang:

"I'm Bertha the sewing machine girl.
I make the fanciest clothes.
I'm as quick with my needle
As Mischa with his feedle.
And out the little bag goes."

And the bag flew neatly through the window.

"Can I do one?" I asked.

"Yes, but only when I'm with you," she said, and gave me a well-stuffed bag.

Trying to imitate her, I held it up and waltzed as she sang:

"He's Bobby, the biggest of gonifs;
He can steal from under your nose.
He steals all the girls' kisses,
Won't make any his missus,
And out the little bag goes."

Just as the bag left my hand the kitchen light came on. My father in the doorway, Martha behind him—his face, the mirror of the incredible; hers, snickering.

My mother covered her face with her hands and peeped through her fingers.

My father, sternly: "Fran, if what you're doing isn't bad enough, you have to make a henchman out of him?"

My mother laughed. Her laughter skittered up the walls, bounced against the ceiling, bubbled, puffed, echoed, filling us as if with rich holiday wine until we became tipsy and we laughed. We laughed and pointed at the floor beneath the window where the lonely chicken bones, empty eggshells, curling carrot peelings and the broken bag lay without shame.

I was given my bath, good-night song, finally, my bed.

My bed!

I explored the memory of it to be sure it was the same. I tested the warm side, the cold side; they were there. I searched for the little lump; I slid under and felt for the two places where the buttons were missing from their tuftings. I turned to the pillow, kneaded the down inside the case and the ticking, cracked the fragile feather needles, punched it, mashed it, crushed it against me, sniffed its corners, smoothed it, cuddled it, babied it, kissed it and finally let my head fall on it to see if it felt as before. Almost . . . almost. I shook it from one end, from the other end, whipped it around four times one way, four times the other, pummeled it back into shape, punched its middle, punched its sides, threw it to the other end of the bed, kicked it soft with my heels, pulled it back to the middle of the bed, steam-rolled it ten times, said hello to it, hugged it, smoothed it again and again and once more let my head fall on it.

I had won back my bed.

chapter 7

For days my world wore white with jelly-apple stains. Everyone had his mother who took him to school and called for him. The sun sang, the wind danced, the number of health inspectors was doubled, the street cleaners shuffled along the curbs removing the little brown-paper coffins that littered the street.

I never for once doubted that the women would win—weren't they mothers! And the appearance of evicted belongings that sat on the street like gypsies waiting for the nightly caravan to take them away only incited them to greater boldness.

The rebellion was carried on practically in the open. Women living in The White House were now on "talking terms" with those of The Poorhouse; everything became "honey-dearie." And it became customary for a woman making introductions to say, "Mrs. Jesse James Zaretsky, I would like you to meet my friend, Mrs. Al Capone Ganz."

Arriving from school one afternoon, we saw that a wooden platform had been built at one end of the street, and decorated with red, white and blue bunting and American flags. A large sign tacked to its rough unpainted boards read, "Gala Meeting at 4:30 Today! Be Sure to Attend!"

We ran to get the "best seats"—even though there weren't any—and once again I found myself sandwiched between Johnny and Libby.

Crowds grew thicker around us. We learned that the meeting had been called by the Department of Health in another attempt to end garbage-throwing. Sensing the prevailing sentiment, we were immediately *opposed*, with Libby going so far as to sit on the steps leading to the platform. Her daring surprised me. I was certain she was not as involved with the situation as I, and I had taken her indifference as a sign of my greater maturity.

The chimes of a glockenspiel were heard, followed by the pulse of a drum and the neigh of a trumpet. Three members of the Sanitation Department Band stepped smartly around the corner and heralded the approach of a shining black car draped with flags. It stopped at the edge of the crowd. The driver, in a crisp white cap with shining black visor, got out, straightened his jacket and ran around to open the door for a man in a royal blue cap with a purple band, who allowed white cap to make way before him as he walked through the crowd, bowing from left to right and smiling like a toothpaste advertisement—for which he received stone-cold staring silence.

White cap arrived at the foot of the steps, where Libby now sat with arms and legs outspread, her hands holding onto the wooden side slats.

"Come on, Dolly," white cap said, "you have to let us pass."

"No," said Libby, gripping the posts.

"But the man has to make an important speech, Dolly," he insisted.

"No," said Libby.

By this time navy blue cap with purple band had come up and asked what was wrong. White cap explained. So navy blue cap gave him a get-out-of-my-way look, and kneeling, said, "Aren't you a pretty little girl?"

"Yes," Libby agreed.

"Is the pretty little girl going to let the nice man up the steps?"

"No."

"Why?"

" 'Cause."

"Why 'cause?"

"Why 'cause you dropped your drawers."

Those who heard, tittered. And I thought Libby was just like a real princess.

"Would you let the nice man up if he gave you a penny?"

"No."

"A nickel?"

"Maybe."

He drew out some change, selected a nickel and held it out to her. "Here's a shiny new nickel."

"It's not shiny."

"All right," he said, examining the rest of the change, "let's see if I have a shiny new one for you." Then, turning to white cap, he asked, "Hey, capo grasso, you got any nickels?"

White cap shrugged, so blue cap said, "As it so happens, the nice man doesn't have any shiny new nickels, but how would you like a shiny new dime?"

"Let me see," Libby bargained.

He held the dime between thumb and forefinger. She examined and then decided, "No."

"Why?"

"Because."

"Why because?"

"Because you gotta play grocery store with me first."

"But I have to make a speech," he argued.

" 'Bout what?"

"About no throwing garbage, that's what!" His voice was louder, his smile thinner. Then, turning to white cap, he muttered, "See if you can find out who the brat belongs to."

"I'm not a brat," Libby insisted.

"I didn't say you were, I said you were a very pretty girl."

"No you didn't, you called me a brat. I heard you."

"What if I give you two dimes?"

Meanwhile, white cap wandered back into the crowd asking if anyone knew to whom the little girl on the steps belonged.

"Two dollars," Libby replied.

"Two *dollars*?" he asked. "Now what would a little girl like you do with two dollars?"

"I'd buy a doll with sleepy eyes."

"All right now," he said, straightening the hem of his jacket nervously. "Fun's over. Let me pass."

"No!"

"Come on, girlie," blue cap said, and he knelt with arms outstretched to pick her up.

The mood changed at once.

"Don't touch her," came a voice from the crowd.

"Who is she?" blue cap demanded, backing away from Libby. "Who does she belong to?"

"Don't touch her," another voice from another part of the crowd.

"What do you mean?" Blue cap's jaw tightened.

"Don't touch her," another voice, another direction.

Attention suddenly swerved from blue cap to a woman who had a small American flag pinned to her bosom and carried a large sign which read, SRETIAWBMUD EHT XIF.

It was Marcia Weissbaum's mother, and the carefully colored lettering had undoubtedly been done by Mr. Weissbaum, who, when he worked, was a sign "paintner."

Blue cap and white cap looked at the sign and then at each other, making a dumb show of ignorance, while Mrs. Weissbaum walked solemnly toward them, winking now and then at faces she knew.

"What does it say?" blue cap asked as she drew near.

"You should know," she replied, did an about-face and marched away. Then she turned and came toward the pair again.

"What's it say, lady?" blue cap asked again.

"You're from the Department of Health?" she asked.

"Yes."

"Well, it seems to me that in your department everything is backwards forwards. You should be able to read this sign like A-B-C." She marched away again.

"It says, 'Fix the dumbwaiters,' " someone shouted.

The crowd hooted and whooped as the two caps disappeared into the car and rode off leaving the three musicians looking miserable and the four flags fluttering smartly.

Libby was heroine of the day. Her brother swept her up on his shoulders and marched her around. People applauded and cheered hurray while she complained she wanted to be put down. The moment he did, she wanted to be up again. But by this time the crowd was breaking up, and—no longer famous—she threw a pocketful of pebbles at Johnny and me.

"I understand everybody thought your girl friend was pretty wonderful," my father said when dinner was over.

"She's not my girl friend."

"Did you think she was wonderful?" he asked.

"Sure. She didn't let the man go up."

"What if the man had a right to go up?"

"But he was going to say not to throw garbage, and still not to fix the dumbwaiters," I protested, and wondered at his reasoning.

"But he had a right to ask anything he pleased," my father said, at the same time shooting a glance of desperation at my mother. She returned a weak smile.

"And," he continued, "Libby was very naughty to interfere in

163

business that belongs to older people. How would you like it if you were playing Hide and Seek and I came along and wanted to play, too?"

"I'd like it a lot," I confessed.

He looked at my mother once again. "How do you get things across to him? I'm always running into a blank wall."

"I don't know. Maybe I just tackle the easy ones. But why hurry it? One of these days it will be Father's Day for you, and I'll have the baby curls in the cigar box to keep me company."

"I'm trying to remember if I had the same trouble with Peter."

"I remember," she said, "and it was worse. Until Peter started school he thought you were part of the furniture. But one day you took him out to play catch and I became a picture on the wall. That's the way it goes." Then, drawing me to her, she said, "Remember what Mrs. Greneker told you about your father having to carry all your sins until you're thirteen?"

"Yes."

"Well, what Libby did was a sin. Because of her stubbornness there could have been a terrible fight."

"But you're having a fight anyway," I argued, "and maybe you can win faster."

"Maybe we can lose faster, too."

"But you can't . . . Besides, why did everybody say hurray for her?"

"Because they forgot for a moment that Libby was only doing it to show off. And that's why when her father gets home tonight he'll give her a hurray, she won't be in such a hurry to sit on anything, including steps.

"I'm going to see Johnny's mother, do you want to come?" she asked without changing the expression in her voice or on her face.

"No."

"No?" she asked with mock surprise. "Are you feeling all right? Do you think I can cross the street without my escort?"

"I have to look at my bottle caps," I said, but the truth was I didn't want to have to see Johnny's mother or hear her voice. Her face had become as yellow as the dusty dried corncobs that hung on the side of the window in the vegetable store. Her voice had the crunch of crumpling tissue paper. And her smile was nothing more than her lips trembling. Everything she did was an effort, starting with a gasp and ending with a sigh. And haunting the sharp smell of disinfectant in their apartment was another that surrounded her and reminded me of wet rags decaying in a dark corner.

"All right," she said, "I'll give them your best regards," and she stood and stacked the dishes.

I went to my room and under my bed to wonder at the possibility that the mothers could ever lose.

They couldn't! I willed them to win! Their winning was somehow my winning—irrefutable proof of my belief in their omnipotence. Another thread of thought wound through: that this fight was more than a game and so excluded me and, it seemed, even Libby. But I knew that someday Libby would be part of such things, while I wouldn't be, ever.

I pondered the differences: that Libby had to sit when she did number one and I could do it standing, that I could read better, run faster, jump higher, fight better. Yet with all my superiorities, I, like my father, like all the men, had nothing to do with this fight. It belonged only to the women, the mothers. They alone could win it.

My mother returned and told me to get ready for my bath. I was in my robe and slippers and having my milk when Mrs. Greneker arrived with "news."

She had received a visit from Mrs. Fell, in person, in her two-toned wig, "orange marmalade in front, raspberry flavor in back." Mrs. Fell had come in her husband's behalf to seek arbitration in the garbage dispute and wanted Mrs. Greneker to get the tenants to agree to abide by any decision made by the rabbi. And Mrs. Greneker could even choose between the old, old rabbi or the old, young rabbi.

"So what do you think?" she asked my mother.

"I think the sooner this whole business is over with, the better," my mother said. "It's already gone too far. If that man had put a finger on Libby today, there would have been blood. It would have meant the police. And these days, the police use their sticks first and ask questions later. Besides, even if the rabbi's decision should go against us it gives us an opportunity to say we lost without giving up the fight."

"That's what I was thinking," said Mrs. Greneker, "but I was also wondering maybe I shouldn't ask Mr. Hirshman, too."

A gulp of milk stopped on its way down my throat. I could no more imagine Mrs. Greneker asking my father's opinion than mine.

"He's in our room talking to the wall," my mother said.

Mrs. Greneker looked alarmed.

"He's trying to drum Shakespeare into Martha's head, it's the same thing. I'll get him."

She returned and told Mrs. Greneker he would be with her in a minute. I was dragged to the bathroom protesting that I wanted to hear, to which my mother replied that was all the more reason to clean my ears. But I knew she meant that since the subject was the dumbwaiters, it was no concern of mine.

chapter 8

I was awakened the next morning by the ringing of the doorbell. It was Mrs. Jackson. In a voice that wore a "cold compress" she asked my mother if she would take Libby to school; and explained that every time her husband punished one of her children, she was the one who got the splitting head.

I had just finished breakfast when the doorbell rang again. Certain it was Libby, I went to the door, and putting my mouth to the crack, I whispered, "You can't go to school if you got a mustard plaster on your behind."

"It's me! It's me!" came Johnny's voice. "I need your mother. I need her!"

I opened the door. He rushed in, his face white, frightened; his eyes desperate, hunting. "Where is she?" he begged.

"What's the matter?" I caught his arm.

He shook me off. "No! Not you! I need her!"

"Mother," I shouted, "come out quick, quick!"

"Just a second, let me finish dressing," she called from her room.

Peter came from our room, Martha from the bathroom. Seeing Johnny, Peter shouted, "Ma, you better come out, he looks like trouble."

Martha went up to Johnny. "What's wrong?" "I need your mother, only your mother," he muttered fiercely. "Mother, can't you hurry up?" she called.

Johnny, his elbows pressed to his sides, stood opening and closing his fists to hasten time, to pull my mother from her room.

She came out fumbling with her belt, threw back her uncombed hair. "What's the matter?" she asked.

"My mother needs you, she said—" Before he could say more, she dropped the two ends of the belt and catching Johnny's hand, flew out of the apartment.

"Gee," said Martha, and the word floated.

My father, crackle-eyed with sleep, asked what had happened. Martha told him. He returned to his room without a word. Peter wandered around the room with one shoe on, the other in his hand, then went back to the bedroom. Martha stared, her lower lip sucked between her teeth, her eyes like unanswered questions. She finally went back to the bathroom.

The apartment door was slightly ajar. I wondered if I should follow to see why everybody needed my mother, and why their needs were more important than mine. Then I heard a door in the hallway slam shut, quick little tapping footsteps, and Libby was at the door.

"Mrs. Hirshman, I'm here."

"Go home, we can't go to school," I said.

"Why not?"

"My mother won't take us."

I was about to push her out of the apartment when my father appeared and said, "All right, Libby, wait a second." He went to the bathroom door and knocked. "Martha, hurry, you'll have to take the kids to school."

The door flew open and Martha, her mouth globbed with toothpaste, emerged making protesting noises as she jabbed the air with her toothbrush.

"That's enough, Martha."

She turned back to the sink, hastily rinsed her mouth and was out in a second with, "What's the matter with Peter?"

From the bedroom came Peter's mocking singsong, "What's the matter with Peter? He's all right." Then raising his voice to a shout, "There's nothing the matter with Peter that would keep him from pushing your nose into your face so far you'll be able to smell comin' and goin'."

"Quit it, Peter," my father ordered.

"When is she going to grow up and learn there's a difference between men and girls?" came Peter's voice.

"Man, hah!" said Martha. "Just because he's two years older'n me, he thinks he's a man. Ha-ha, ha-ha. If I was wearing a sleeve, I'd larf right up it." Then, more seriously, "Besides, if you had any brains you'd know that girls mature more quicker'n boys. And I bet I'm at least five years older'n you in my emotions."

"Your mother's a few years older than you in every way," my father said, "yet she doesn't think anything of taking Bobby to school."

Martha became embarrassed and flew back to the bathroom with a reluctant, "Oh, all right."

Libby ran out of the apartment saying she'd have to get her mother's permission if Martha was going to take her. She was back in a few moments, with her mother immediately behind, a wet towel on her head and an inquiring look on her face.

"What happened?" she asked my father.

"They came to call her from across the street," he replied.

She lowered her eyelids but not quickly enough to mask the sorrow. Then, turning to Libby, she said, "In a few years you'll be telling everybody how that great actress Martha Hirshman once took you to school."

"Maybelline Hotchkiss is my stage name," said Martha.

"It has a nice ring to it," Mrs. Jackson admitted.

"That's because the first name is refined and the second one is sultry," Martha explained.

"Sultry?" my father asked with surprise.

"Isn't that a word," Mrs. Jackson remarked. "I always said, God bless American education. The kids today got it all over their parents." She left.

When we were ready to go, my father thanked Martha and told me my mother would probably call for me after school.

To myself I said, "I don't care."

Johnny was not in class.

I didn't care.

Miss Diamond told me not to slump in my seat.

I didn't care.

She read us, " 'Dicky Dare went to school. On the way he met a cow . . .' "

During rest period, Libby, wrapped in the burnoose of her blanket, lay next to me, batting her eyelashes, touching the end of her nose with the tip of her tongue. "Mezzle, bezzle, ippity beezles," she finally whispered, "please give Bobby the German measles." She continued, "Mezzle, bezzle, ippity loop, Please give Bobby the rotten croup."

I didn't care. In fact, I wished I had both the German measles and the croup. I prayed to be sick, to be in bed with hot-water bags at my feet, a cold towel around my head, a mustard plaster on my chest, a heating pad under my back, and Dr. Reuben exploring my throat and listening to my chest with his private telephone and shaking his head; and everyone crying and praying and crying, especially my mother. I was dying. I could feel the wings beginning to push through my shoulder blades. And nothing would help—neither my mother's pleas, nor Mrs. Greneker's holding a plateful of chopped chicken liver under my nose, nor Martha's singing and dancing, nor the regular angels at St. Ursula's or those at Morris View, or even Mrs. Greneker's father and mother angels and their baby angels plinking violins. And everyone cried, even my father, even my brother.

But even if all their tears were caught in a bowl and were made into crying soup, which Mrs. Greneker had once said could cure the sickest person in the world, it would not help.

Miss Diamond brought me back with the announcement that rest period was over. I spent the remainder of the school day swinging from hatred to plotting, from I don't care to I hope I die, from blaming Johnny to blaming my mother . . . a swinging that I knew would only end with the ringing of the schoolbell.

It seemed my life was regulated by the ringing of bells. The bell in the clock woke me. The chimes on the radio were time signals. Bells began class; they rang for recess, they rang to end it; they began class again and ended class for the day. Three bells announced fire drill; five, that the school doors were being closed for the day.

There were the bells with the terrible throats: fire engine's red bells, ambulance's white bells. There were bells that promised: the merry-go-round, the ices wagon, the one-man orchestra with his bell-studded strap. There were the bells that begged business: the old-clothes man, the knife-and-scissors grinder, the hot-dog, sauerkraut and lemonade man. There were the bells that demanded answers: the downstairs bell, the upstairs bell, the dumbwaiter bell (would it ever sound again?), the bell that Melvin and Irwin's mother rang to call them home because she didn't have the strength to shout. And then there were the church bells that called and called and to which I had no answer.

The gong rang.

"Class dismissed," said Miss Diamond.

Gerard Shuminsky, bolted to iron, went stiff-legged to the door; the class followed him, formed a double line behind him. Then, and only after checking to see if the lines were even, Gerard Shuminsky opened the door and we filed out, leaving Miss Diamond behind her veil of chalk dust.

The mothers were there holding their dark dripping umbrellas uncomfortably away from them, clutching the yellow and green slickers, the rain hats and the rubbers. I looked for my mother. Libby looked, too. She wasn't there. And I knew it. I knew she wouldn't be. Hadn't I almost told myself she wouldn't, all during the day? And I didn't care!

The mothers swooped down on the children; the children rushed up to the mothers; they fussed and fidgeted, the children rustling, struggling into their raincoats, the mothers grunting, bending, kneeling, fighting to get the rubbers onto their shoes, then decorating their heads with rain hats as if every child were a kewpie doll, a special prize; they rushed to the doors, opening the umbrellas while still inside, everything blending into black blur.

Libby and I watched. The schoolyard grew larger as it became emptier, darker as it was drained of sound. We sat on the bench near the doorway. My eyes darted from windows to doorways to hallways, to stairs. Did something stir in the steel ribbing overhead? Did someone slip behind one of the giant columns?

A gong sounded. We jumped. Three gongs.

"Maybe it's a fire?" Libby gasped.

"No it isn't," I assured her but not myself.

"I don't like it here."

"We have to wait for my mother."

"Maybe she won't come 'cause it's raining."

"She'll come 'specially 'cause it's raining."

"Maybe she's sleeping."

"No, she isn't."

"How do you know?"

"Because she once said she can only sleep when it's night outside."

"My mother sleeps anytime. Sometimes she takes my afternoon nap with me."

"I'm too old for afternoon naps."

"Girls have to have beauty naps."

I gave her a "rotten" look. She returned a "go-to-hell" look.

"I know why your mother isn't here," she said, her voice all wisdom.

"No you don't."

"Yes I do. And I know where she is, too."

"No you don't."

"Oh y-e-e-s I do. Why did your sister have to take us to school this morning? Hah? So's your mother could go to Johnny's house."

"No it's not," I insisted, but weakly.

"Oh yes it is. And I know what they're doing. They're baking patty cakes. And your mother is making an extra one for Johnny and one for his stupid brother. And none for you, 'cause she likes them better'n you. And she isn't going to come for us even though it's raining."

"You're lying," I shouted.

"I'm not. It's the God's honest truth, so help me. I swear."

"You don't know what the truth is! You're crazy like a daisy, Fifi la-la Libby. You got a bellyful of jelly beans and a headful of nits. And I'm going home right now without you." I ran to the door.

"You'll feel sorry for what you said. Just wait and see what's going to happen to you. You're full of cockamamies. And I'll never talk to you again as long as I live, so help me God." Libby and her voice followed me out of the playground and into a wind-driven rain that almost swept us down the steps.

I ran up the empty street, pushing against the wind. The rain seeped through my hair and down the sides of my face. I could hear Libby calling me names. I didn't answer. I had to find out if my mother had not come for me because of Johnny.

I flew up the steps of our apartment house, and when I got to our door I turned my back and kicked with the heel of my shoe. I waited to hear my mother say something about knocking the way I had been taught, but I heard nothing. I made scratching noises on the door. No answer. I made kissing noises into the crack of the door. No answer. Finally, I knocked the way I had been taught. Still, no answer.

"Open the door," I called. I pounded it with my fist. "Mother, please open the door. I'll be very good. I'll be one hundred per cent good if you'll open the door."

In angry desperation I pounded and kicked, yelling, "Open it! Open the door! *Open the door!*"

"Bobby! Stop that! What are you doing?" It was Libby's mother. She stood in the doorway to her apartment, clutching her faded blue bathrobe with one hand and keeping Libby from coming out into the hall with the other.

"My mother doesn't want to let me in."

"Maybe she isn't home," Mrs. Jackson said.

"She *is* home. She just doesn't want to let me in," I insisted.

"Don't be silly," said Mrs. Jackson. "She must have gone shopping and got caught in the rain. Come, wait for her here." She beckoned to me, then quickly caught her bathrobe before it fell open.

"No. I've got to find her. I'm going to look for her." I started down the steps.

"Bobby, come back," Mrs. Jackson called. "It's raining rivers."

I headed for Mr. Fisher's tailorshop. "Is my mother here?" "Hello, Bobbeleh-bubeleh," Mr. Fisher said. "Yes, she's hiding under the pressing machine."

I ran across the street to the grocery on the corner. "What's the excitement?" asked Mrs. Fine. "Did you see my mother?" "No. Was I supposed to?" "She's not home. I don't know where she is." "Isn't that a shame," said Mrs. Fine. "Here, come inside and dry off a little. You're wet like a sponge. Come on, I'll give you a coconut marshmallow puff." "No. I've got to find her." I ran to the next corner and opened the door to Joe's vegetable store. "Was my mother here?" "Not today, bambino." I flew across the street to Herman's pickle store. From there I ran back to Mr. Goodman's candy store, Mrs. Spector's candy store, the Dawson meat and fish market.

Mrs. Greneker was behind a counter flicking a chicken she had bought.

"Mrs. Greneker, did you see my mother?"

"A choleryah should take my enemies," Mrs. Greneker said as she came toward me. "Look at this child. Like a drowned rat he looks." She wiped my head with the apron she wore.

174

"I can't find my mother. I looked everywhere. She isn't home. She doesn't answer the door. I don't know where she is."

"Sh-sh," said Mrs. Greneker as she sank to one knee and clasped me to her soft, floury bosom.

"Maybe she's sick and can't answer the bell?" I asked fearfully.

"Don't talk foolishness. You know what I think? Maybe she went to your friend's house across the street. Did you look there?"

The one place . . . the right place . . . why had I forgotten?

Could the thought of finding her there, in that apartment, in his house, have been more unbearable than the agony of looking for her?

My feet started. Mrs. Greneker caught me. "Just a minute, Mr. Fast-like-lightning, if she's not there, I want you should come right back to Mrs. Greneker and let me know. Promise?"

Nodding, I ran, fought against the wind, crossed the street and raced up the steps of *that* house.

The stairs were up, up, endlessly up. I wished she would be there. I wished she wouldn't. Which did I wish more? I didn't know.

And there was the door. The dirty brown door. I knocked and wiped the knuckle on my pants.

Silence. I waited. Something like an insect climbed inside my throat. My ear itched. I knocked again.

A man's voice: "Yes?"

"Is my mother there?"

"Who is it?"

I knew the voice now. Dr. Reuben's. Why hadn't he recognized mine?

"Bobby Hirshman."

"No, she isn't . . ."

Glad! I was glad! I flew down the steps, not listening, not caring what Dr. Reuben was saying and saying.

I was in the street. But where was she? Where could she be? Where else was there to look?

She was home. I knew she was home. She just couldn't answer the door. Something kept her from opening it, from calling out, from letting me know she was inside. What?

I thought of going back to Mrs. Greneker. Another thought kicked it out of the way: Peter had a key! But where was Peter? In school. Where was his school? Martha knew. Where was Martha? I ran to Henrietta's.

Once in the hallway, I realized I still didn't know her family name or her apartment. I looked desperately at the doorway out of which the old lady with the white scarf and the yellow fingers had appeared the last time. There was no other way. I cupped my hands around my mouth and shouted, "Calling Martha Hirshman in Henrietta's apartment!"

The door to my right flew open as if the old woman had been waiting for me to come back all this time.

"Enough already, you crazy. I'm calling the police this second. Go away, or I'll give you over the head with a broomstick, you crazy, you," she threatened, shaking her finger at me.

"I can't help it. I have to find my mother."

"What's with your mother?" She spoke more kindly now.

"I can't find her."

"Maybe she's up by Zipke, the Hungarian pig-woman who smokes cigarettes in her window so men should see her from the street and pay her a visit."

I shook my head uncomprehendingly and began to climb the steps. Suddenly I heard Henrietta call, "She ain't here!"

"Henrietta—Henrietta, help me!" I ran up.

The old woman shouted after me, "I'll help you. . . . Over the head I'll help you with a sewing machine. Get out from this house, you crazy, you!"

"Henrietta," I called. "Henrietta."

She didn't answer. I burst into tears.

"What are you crying about, you big baby?" Henrietta crouched on the steps just above me. "What's the matter?"

I explained through sobs, "I can't find my mother. I looked all over. I asked everybody. Nobody knows where she went. I have to find my sister so we can find Peter. Peter has the key. I can't find my mother." I repeated this last sentence over and over while Henrietta flew up the steps and returned a moment later with her beret and coat.

"Come on," she said, catching my hand. "Martha's at the Dramatic Club meeting. I'm supposed to be there, too, but I'm not talking to her, forever."

The old woman was at the foot of the stairs brandishing a broom. "I'll give you. I'll show you, you crazy, you."

"Go tell it to the marines, old fruity toot," Henrietta said, brushing her aside. I was amazed at Henrietta's disrespect and would have apologized to the old woman for her but she pulled me away too quickly.

We reached the school steps with water swooshing out of our shoes, and after what seemed to be endless running through wide, silent hallways, found ourselves in a huge auditorium. A girl about Martha's age and height stood on the stage. She recited:

> "The quality of mercy is not strain'd,
> It droppeth as the gentle rain from heaven
> Upon the place beneath. It is twice bless'd . . ."

I turned to ask Henrietta where Martha was, but she held my shoulder with one hand and signaled me to keep quiet with the other.

Suddenly I spied Martha sitting at the far end, watching the stage with intense disinterest. "Martha!" I cried.

Her head snapped in my direction. The girl on stage stopped reading. I ran toward my sister, and in a moment the auditorium was in a turmoil of girls wondering aloud about who I was and what had happened, and the teacher calling for order from the balcony. Once I had gotten through to Martha why I had to find her, she immediately blamed Henrietta for scheming the "whole thing so I won't get a chance to play the part." Whereupon Henrietta called her a pickle with pimples, and the fight was on. Slapping gave way to kicking, then scratching, and by the time the teacher arrived, they were deadlocked in a bout of hair-pulling.

"You should have heard what she called me," Martha complained when the teacher had finally forced them apart.

"I'm not interested," the teacher said.

"I can't find my mother," I interrupted.

"First stop crying," the teacher ordered.

"I can't."

"Try."

"I'm trying very hard."

"Martha," the teacher asked, "what do you know about this?"

"She made it all up. She schemed it because she's jealous on me." Martha's accusing finger went to within a hair of Henrietta's nose.

"I'm jealous on you?" cried Henrietta. "You ain't even frying size yet."

"All right, you two," the teacher intervened. "Martha, why don't you take your brother home now?"

"I don't want to. Besides, there's nothing wrong."

"But," the teacher argued, "you won't be reading until late tomorrow or the day after."

"I don't care—I want to listen to how bad the others are doing it."

"But if by some chance there is trouble at home, wouldn't you want to see to that first?"

"I know there's nothing wrong. She told him to say there was."

"She didn't! She didn't!" I shouted, and listed all the places I had been, all the people I had seen, in my search for my mother.

From her purse, the teacher took a small white handkerchief with a little blue flower on one corner and dabbed my face while I continued, ". . . and I don't know where Daddy's liberry is and Peter has a key and I have to find him, but I don't know where he goes to school . . ."

The fact that I was trying to find Peter and not her apparently convinced Martha. "Come on, quick!" she said, and ran from the auditorium. Henrietta and I followed. We burst from the building. Faces blurred, places smudged as I ran. I became the motion of my feet. A ball inside my chest grew . . . grew . . . grew . . . grew until it felt as if it were going to explode and shatter me to fragments as fine as the rain.

I kept running. I had to reach the next gutter, the next sidewalk. As I began to fall behind, Martha took my left hand, Henrietta my right. They pulled me with them, hoisted me over puddles and broken pavements.

"I can't," I complained.

"It's just one more block," Martha promised.

Three more gutters, three more sidewalks; we ran.

"I can't . . . no more," I gasped.

"There it is. Look," Henrietta announced, pointing at a mountain of cold gray granite rising aloof from the buildings around it.

There were steps, more steps, until we fell onto the main floor. An arrow-shaped sign read "Visitors"; we followed it into a room where a tall boney-nosed woman stood behind the high counter. She had a pencil over her ear, paper clips between her lips, and every now and then would slap down a sheaf of papers as if crushing bugs.

Martha cleared her throat several times. Henrietta raised her hand and waved it timidly.

Wham! The file drawer slammed shut. She leaned over the counter and peered down at us. Then, removing the clips from between her teeth, she said, "Yerss?"

"Can you tell me how I can find Peter Hirshman, please?" Martha asked shyly.

"Who?" An owl called from above. Henrietta tittered nervously.

"My brother," I said.

"What about him?" the woman asked.

"He goes to this school and we're trying to find him," Martha explained.

"Now I've heard everything," she declared, and slapped the top of the counter with the flats of her palms.

Turning her back to us, she addressed the equipment against the wall. "First, it's Miss Schwartz, we're doubling up this term as part of the economy effort. So, Miss Schwartz, you will teach Ancient History, History of the Middle Ages, and History from the Reformation to Napoleon. Also, Miss Schwartz, you will take Civics one and Economics two and three.

"Naturally, Miss Schwartz, you will continue to act as staff supervisor for the History Club, and this term we would like you to attend the meetings of the Bull and Bear Club, to acquaint yourself with the way Mr. Ellenbogan runs it in the event you should have to take over for him from time to time.

"Miss Schwartz, I'm sure you've heard the rumor that there has been some cutting back of clerical help. Well, Miss Schwartz, it isn't a rumor and we know you will be glad to pitch in at the desk when needed. So in addition to your daily agendas, weekly syllabi and monthly reports, Miss Schwartz, you will not only be giving out papers, taking back papers and grading papers, you'll also be classifying papers, departmentalizing papers, coding papers, filing papers, and, Miss Schwartz, if you ever get time to read a paper you'll be the cockeyed wonder of the world.

"And now, Miss Schwartz, if you'll just tear yourself away from your beloved papers, you can take over the lost and found department and help find a Peter Hirshman. His family needs him."

"Please, miss," Martha jigged with impatience, "it's important— it's because we can't find our mother."

"What do you mean you can't find your mother?" she asked quickly.

"She didn't call for my brother at school and she isn't home."

"It should happen to me," she said, and then added, "How will finding your brother help you?"

"He has a key and my little brother says he thinks our mother is inside the house but she can't answer the door because maybe something happened." Martha couldn't rush the words fast enough.

"Well, why didn't you say so in the first place?" she demanded. "You know school's out for the day. What makes you think he's here?"

"Because he's on the swimming team and he's always practicing after school."

"Let me see," she said, ruffling through a flounce of papers on a clipboard. "As it so happens, the swimming team is meeting this afternoon, but it's downstairs in the lower gymnasium. And girls aren't allowed—not even me."

"I could go," Henrietta said bravely.

"Since when aren't you a girl?" the woman asked.

"Couldn't he go?" Martha pointed at me.

The woman leaned over the counter and looked down at me. "No. He's too small and the steps are circular and steep. They're made of iron or something. And if he fell, I could see Miss Schwartz selling papers for a living."

"Please," I begged. "I won't fall."

"Just a second," she said. "Boy-hoys," she called. "Are there any boy-hoys around?" She waited a moment, then: "The card game must've moved down to the lunchroom." Kneeling in front of me, she said, "Listen to me, young fellow, I'm going to take a chance on you to go down there but you must be very, very careful. Go very slowly. Remember, if anything happens to you, Miss Schwartz will not only have to answer to the principal and the State Board, but God help her, to her own mother."

Peter was less easily convinced than Henrietta and Martha had been, but our presence in his school seemed to embarrass him and he hurried into his clothes. As we came up to Martha and Henrietta, the woman put her head out the door, "Did you find him, all right?"

"Yes," I said eagerly, holding Peter's hand, "this is my brother."

She looked at Peter and asked, "Aren't you in one of my classes?" He nodded. "The conqueror of Peru was Pizarro not Pierce Arrow," she commented acidly; then turning to me, "Don't be so proud."

We hurried away.

"Why did she say that?" Martha asked when we were outside.

"Oh, her," Peter replied indifferently, "she's fluffed her duff and lost her muff."

The rain had stopped. The cold wind nettled my eyes. At the corner, I sank to my knees.

"What's the matter with you?" Peter asked.

I shook my head. My bones had become gelatin.

"Well, look where he's been today," said Martha. "He's been running at least a thousand miles."

Peter looked doubtful. "All right," he said finally, "we'll make a monkey's cradle."

He and Martha crossed arms, took each other's hands and scooped me up. I put one arm around his neck, the other around Martha's, and in a moment I was cloud, weightless. Air cushioned me, winds carried me. Fear and exhaustion drifted out of me. I was sure my mother would be home and waiting for me. At first, she would make believe she was angry with me. She would make me change my wet clothes and give me a scalding bath, but then she would give me hot cocoa and cake and perhaps, if I asked her, even sing for me.

Just before turning the corner to our street, Henrietta said, "I got to go home now."

We stopped.

"I'm sorry I pulled your hair, Henrietta," said Martha.

"Well," Henrietta drawled, "in the beauty magazine it says that pulling your hair makes it stronger."

"And thanks for the favor you did me," said Martha. "If you want me to, I'll come to your house in a little while."

"Sure, if you want," Henrietta said.

Peter and Martha deposited me in front of our building.

"If you made this whole thing up," he warned, "I'll make a basket-ball out of your head."

"I'll lynch him from top to bottom," Martha added.

We were at the door. Peter reached into his pocket, fished out his key, couldn't seem to slip it into the lock.

"Hurry up!" I begged.

I ran through first, turned at once for the kitchen. . . . There she was! At the sink, about to jab a hypodermic needle into an orange! She stared at us. We stared at her hands.

"What are you doing?" Martha asked.

"This?" my mother asked innocently. "It's a new gadget . . . a new way to get orange juice without squeezing. I'm just trying it." She quickly put the needle on the windowsill behind her and dropped the orange into the sink.

"You lied!" Peter shouted, and his slap to the back of my head sent me stumbling toward my mother.

"I'll murder him to death," Martha shrieked.

"Peter, don't!" my mother cried, and caught me. "You're drenched!" She felt my clothes, my head, my shoes. "Where've you been?"

"I didn't lie," I shouted back at Peter. To my mother I said, "I went to save you." But she seemed too lost in the effort to undo the buttons on my clothes.

"Just tell me one thing before I commit suicide on him," Martha insisted. "Did you take him home from school?"

"Martha," my mother replied, "put your finger back in your pocket and your tongue back in your head."

"Well, *did* you?" Martha demanded.

"Keep talking to me that way, and I'm liable to forget I'm your mother."

"There she goes," said Peter, "covering up for him. Now she'll say she didn't take him home, and give him an alibi. That's what she'll do."

"I'm not covering up for anyone," my mother said as she peeled my clothes from me. "As it happens, I did go for him, but I was too late. I was very late."

I tore away from her, pushed past Peter and Martha, ran to my bedroom, where I kicked off my shoes, ripped off my socks and threw myself into bed, twisting the covers around me until I had cocooned myself from everyone, especially her.

She had admitted it. Right in front of my brother and sister, she had admitted she was very late! But she hadn't said why. I knew it was because she was in Johnny's house. Maybe she was baking Johnny a patty cake . . . and Artie, too. And she had forgotten me until it was too late. Too late!

Someone tried to pull the covers from around my head. "G'way!" I yelled.

"At least you can give a fellow a decent trial," she said, using Peter's favorite phrase when his allowance was in danger of being forfeited as punishment.

"No," I said quickly, and was sorry I had.

"Well, do you want to tell me how you saved me?"

That was just what I did want and I recited it with many "ands," "thens" and "sos," ballooning it until she couldn't possibly miss the difference between all I had done for her when she couldn't even do a little thing like calling for me on time.

When I had finished, she asked, "Now, do you want to hear what kept me from calling for you?"

I was afraid to. What if it were only baking patty cakes? Yet I wanted to at the same time. She took advantage of my silence to ask, "Or would you believe me if I told you I just couldn't help it, and that I'm very sorry?"

She sat at my side, looking beyond me, my pillow, the room, waiting, waiting, her hand lightly holding my ankle under the bed-clothes, as if holding me to an answer.

If I had no answer, I might have a question. But what?

If only I could have taken words, like the paper beads, and have strung them on a string of raffia to make a question. The beads . . . the paper beads . . . I had my question!

"Why didn't Johnny come to school today?"

"He had no one to take him," she said; and patting my leg, "Try and nap. You've done a great deal of traveling today."

The doorbell rang. "Hirshman! Wait till you hear!" And Mrs. Greneker burst into the room. Seeing me, she asked, "So you found her?"

"Yes," my mother said, "he found me, but in the meantime I lost him."

"So you'll kiss and make up," Mrs. Greneker said. "But after what happened today there will be no kissing with the Eichmir Realty Company. When the neighborhood finds out, it will be *war!*"

My mother glanced at her and then at me. "He can listen, it's all right," Mrs. Greneker assured her. "Remember I told you how Mrs. Fell, it should happen to her, came to me to ask for arbitration with the rabbi?"

"Yes," my mother replied.

"I just came from there as fast as my feet could carry me. Listen to me," she said, touching my mother's knee daintily with the tips of her fingers. "About an hour and a half ago, I'm just putting the salt on the chicken when the bell rings. Who is it? A messenger from the Eichmir Realty Company. They want I should come right away to the synagogue, the rabbi is going to give them a few minutes from his time. So I leave everything in the middle and I quick get into my black dress with the black lace shawl and make myself beautiful, considering—and I run.

"I come there and there is a crowd like it was the movies and they are giving away, not one dish to a customer, but a setting for twelve free to everyone. There was the Health Department and the Street Cleaning Department and the Park Department and a hundred other departments. There was the landlord department with their great leader, Mr. Fell, it should happen to him. And then there was also the rabbi's department with his assistants and the agents for their assistants. And in the whole ocean is one girl fish. Me!

"Finally, the shamas opens the doors. From whatever crazy house they found him, they should send him back. He bowed and he clapped his hands and he kissed the air and he reminded everybody they should kiss the mezuzah on the door and they shouldn't take their hats off. Then he takes one look at me and says, 'You can't come in downstairs, missus. You have to go upstairs to the ezras noshim where the women sit.' So I gave him a look, I was surprised he was still standing, and I said that if the arbitration was going to take place downstairs and I was going to be sitting upstairs, is good-bye arbitration. And just to put him in his place, under the ground, I reminded him that on the big holidays, I'm the zogerkeh . . ."

"That, I don't know," my mother said, as she slipped her hand under the covers and gently rubbed my back.

"Oy, Frances, what kind of a Jew are you?" Mrs. Greneker asked, and then added, "You see, most women don't know how to read Hebrew, so during the holidays they follow me. I tell them what to say, when to cry, when to stop crying, and they follow me. But the rest of the year, when they see me on the street, they turn up their noses and look the other way.

"So, naturally there is a whole hoo-ha and I'm standing there like Beauty at the ball, while they're all fighting over me. Finally, the old, old rabbi says that because of me, God forbid I should make the synagogue treyf, he will give his opinion in his office. Good. Mr. Fell presents his side of the situation. The Department of Health has his say and I speak my piece. And the rabbi sits there and he combs his beautiful white beard with his left hand and he tests the material from his caftan with his other hand.

"Then when everybody said something, the rabbi lifted up his little finger and he talked. Hirshman, did he talk!"

"What did he say?" my mother asked.

"Who knows? It was such deep Hebrew I was lucky I could catch here a word, there a word. But I tell you, he left nobody out of the picture . . . not Adam, or Noah, or Abraham, or Sarah, or Isaac, or Esau, or Jacob and Rachel, and, of course, Joseph. And when he came to Moses, it was like he had just started all over from the beginning again. Mommeh, did he talk! Like tomorrow was coming on one foot. I thought he would never finish. And, who knows? Maybe he didn't.

It could be he stopped because he got plain tired.

"But you should have seen Mr. Fell while the rabbi was giving his opinion. He stood first on pins, then on needles, then on fire and then on flames. He could hardly wait for the finish, when he jumped right in with, 'So, Rabbi, what does it mean? What does it have to do with their throwing garbage?'

"The rabbi closed his eyes for a second and then he began to shake back and forth, not too much, but just enough, and he said, 'It means, the landlords got to fix the dumbwaiters,' and he points with his little finger to the table and says, 'Leave the donation here,' gets up and good-bye."

"Wonderful!" my mother exclaimed.

"Hold your horses, my neighbor," said Mrs. Greneker. "So everybody goes out the front way except Mrs. Greneker, who has to use the back. When I come out there is Mr. Fell, so I took a chance and said, 'Well, all's fair in love and war, Mr. Fell. When are you going to put back the dumbwaiter service?' And he says, 'I'm not.' So out of the argument comes this information: First of all, that the arbitration idea was not his, but his wife's, it should happen to her. Next of all, that his wife asked me I should help convince the neighbors that they should abide by any decision the rabbi should make; that she didn't tell me that the landlords would also promise to do the same. In other words, it was a one-way street."

My mother shook her head, and then glancing sidewise at me, she sang:

"I'm Rudy the Valentino.
I have the perfect nose.
But, when I pose
I have to dispose,
So out the little bag goes."

"Right," said Mrs. Greneker. "I have to go spread the extra. We'll talk more when little eyes are looking at the moon."

The hall door opened, followed by Mrs. Jackson's excited, "They caught someone. They caught—"

My mother, "Who?"

Without a word, Mrs. Greneker was out of my room. My mother following immediately with, "No, no, Greneker, don't go out there."

Mrs. Jackson shouted, "Libby, come here!" The door slammed shut.

"Hirshman, you're not going, too?" Libby's mother asked.

"No," my mother replied, "I'm just going to listen at the door."

I heard steps coming toward my room and closed my eyes. Suddenly, a voice close nearby: "Are you sleeping?" Libby asked mysteriously.

I didn't answer.

"Are you sick?"

No answer.

"Are you dead in bed from your toes to your head?"

No answer.

"Maybe you got the worst and—"

"What's the worst?" I asked, trying to sound asleep.

"It's like what Johnny's mother got and it makes you die before you know it."

Anger tore open my eyes. She was lying! She was making it up! How could *she* know? How could that crazy Fifi la-la Libby know? She didn't know. Mothers didn't die! I knew! I had proof!

"How do you know?" I asked, forgetting my sleeper's voice.

"I heard my mother tell Leatrice's mother on the telephone when she thought I was still sitting on the terlet."

"I got mumps, measles 'n' chicken pox," I screamed at her, and throwing over the covers, blew in her face.

She quickly pulled the little muslin camphor bag from under her collar and waving it like an amulet to ward off evil, ran screaming from the room. I heard her babble to her mother, my mother. I pulled the covers up again, shivering at what she had told me.

I heard my mother's footsteps. "Stop trying to frighten people," she said, pulled the covers from my face, felt my forehead with the back of her hand, and saying, "You're sound as a dollar, whatever that's worth these days," left.

The bell rang. Mrs. Greneker was back again. "Give me a glass water, before I faint on the spot."

"Here, sit down," my mother ordered. "I'll get it."

"Maybe you want some spirits of pneumonia," Mrs. Jackson asked.

"No, no, the water is fine. It rescued me. Aah . . ."

"Who was it?" My mother's voice was hushed.

"If I asked you who was elected Miss Bad Luck from this year, and the year before and for ten years before, and who lives on my floor, who would you say?"

"Don't tell me it was Miss Lefkowitz?" my mother asked.

"Who else? I tell you that woman is such a schlemazel that if she would fall down and break a leg, it would only be on her own property."

"How did they catch her?" Mrs. Jackson asked.

"How? Because if you took her brains and put them in a little thimble your finger would still feel nothing. Like everybody, she was told, to put the garbage in little bags . . . not to save it up until it made a big bundle. But she isn't Miss Lefkowitz for nothing, so she saved up from three days' worth and wrapped it up nice and neat in the paper that the laundry sends her brother's shirts. And she tied it with a string so it was good enough to go to the post office. Then she waited and waited for the right time, and when it came, out it went. And back it came in no time, because you know what Miss Brilliant-like-a bagel did?"

"What?" Mrs. Jackson asked.

"She forgot that the laundryman wrote down, 'Lefkowitz, fourth floor,' and the address. So, if she stuck her head out and called, 'Yoo-hoo, Mr. Health Inspector, look, I'm throwing out garbage,' she couldn't have made it plainer."

"So what are they going to do?" my mother asked.

"They already did it," Mrs. Greneker said. "They arrested her."

"Couldn't you stop them?" Mrs. Jackson asked.

"I did everything but lay down on the floor, they should dare cross my body with her. Nothing helped. But wait until her brother, Mr. Big-Bum the strikebreaker, comes home. He's always talking that he's got connections. Meanwhile I think we should hold up a little bit with the garbage. Maybe, when they see we're not throwing so much, they won't be so hard on her."

My mother and Mrs. Jackson murmured agreement and lapsed into silence while I murdered Libby's ears for hearing wrong and her mouth for telling wrong about Johnny's mother.

I made a special effort to appear indifferent when my mother didn't say much to me during my dinner. And when she said nothing about my leaving most of my food untouched as I returned to my room. And when my father arrived home and didn't come to see me. And even when my mother said that dinner was ready, and that she had to go out, would they serve themselves?

Hurriedly I went into the living room so she couldn't miss seeing my hurt and anger. She crossed to her room, and when she returned I noticed she had slipped a narrow black-leather case into her coat pocket.

"I'll be back," she said. "Be good."

I know where you're going, I said to myself, and I don't care. And I won't be good.

It was painful enjoyment listening to Martha tell my father what had happened during the day. When she got to the part about my mother extracting orange juice with a funny needle, Peter interjected with, "It's the kind the doctors use in school for giving shots, and it's not for squeezing orange juice."

Martha responded with a prolonged, "That's right," which was followed only by the sounds of eating.

"Well, you saw quite a bit of the world today," my father said to me as he came into the living room.

"I did?"

"Weren't you in places you'd never been before?"

I nodded. How could I tell him that they weren't places, only stations on the way to my mother.

"Did you like Peter's school?"

"There was a lady there who said a lot."

"Didn't you like her?"

"I like Miss Lefkowitz better."

"Who's Miss Lefkowitz?"

"She's got brains in a thimble and you can't feel it so she got arrested for throwing garbage, but maybe her brother, the bum, will save her."

"Do you have brains?"

"Sure."

"What do you do with them?"

"I use them."

"For what?"

"To make things think."

"Now we're getting somewhere," he said, apparently pleased with my replies.

"Where are we getting?"

"We're getting to the point where I have learned not to say we're getting somewhere, when we are."

"We are?"

"I thought so for a moment." He paused, looked up at the ceiling. "Were you disappointed that your mother didn't call for you at school?"

I wondered what he wanted me to answer, and finally said, "No."

He didn't hide his surprise.

"I didn't care."

"You certainly went to a lot of trouble for someone who didn't care."

"I thought something bad had happened to her."

"You didn't have to worry about that. If anything had happened you would have known about it right away."

"How?"

"Who told you about Miss Lefkowitz?"

"Mrs. Greneker told Mother."

"You see, you knew about it even before I did."

"Do you know something before me?"

"What?"

"Do you know why Mother went over there today and didn't come for me until it was too late?

"Didn't she tell you?"

"No."

"She will just as soon as she gets the chance."

"She had the chance, but she didn't tell me."

"Maybe she'll get another chance."

I kept from saying it, but I could hardly keep from thinking that I wouldn't give her another chance.

"How would you like to make a plan with me?" he said.

I didn't want to agree without knowing what it was. I watched as he went to the secretary, took an envelope from the drawer, scribbled something on the face of it. Reaching into his pocket, he drew out a coin and slipped it into the envelope, which he then folded over and over until I thought it was going to disappear.

Returning to me, he said, "If by some chance it should ever happen again that your mother is late in calling for you, or if you find she isn't home, I want you to take this to Mr. Goodman and ask him to telephone me. There's a nickel in the envelope and my telephone number is on the outside. What do you think of that as a plan?"

The exalted privilege I first felt disappeared the moment I realized that there might be other times when she would not call for me or not be home.

I could be inspired to no more than a sulky admission that it was a good plan. And then Martha's sudden announcement that she had rinsed and stacked the dishes and was ready to read Portia severed the slim web of words and gestures that had been woven between my father and me.

They went into his room and I sat and waited.

I studied the folded paper, wondering if it was all I would have to help me at such times when she failed me. Then I jammed it into my pocket, buried it with bottle caps, a key I once found and thought would open something important someday, several metal nuts, a lucky button, a pointless pencil stub, a fountain-pen cap, a cork and dry gray fluff.

What was I doing? I asked myself. I was waiting. For what? For her. Why wasn't I doing something while I waited? Why was waiting the only thing I could do? Without realizing, I was learning that time was not what the clock or bells said, but what I did between the ticking and the ringing. A miserable little hand fisted inside me. I heard Libby's voice singing, taunting: "Patty cake, patty cake, baker's man, Pat it 'n' pat it, fast as you can, Pat it 'n' pinch it 'n' mark it with B, And throw it in the oven for baby and me."

Steps walked through Libby's singing. *Her* steps, the private beat of my mother's feet on the hallway tiles. A key whispered into the ear of the lock, giving it the secret password to open.

She was here!

How could I tell her I *did* want to know why she had been late calling for me? How could I tell her I *would* give her another chance?

"I'm back," she said.

I responded with a turbulent silence and, I don't care.

We went through the routine of my bath. She sang my good-night song while I thought that it was no longer mine; that I didn't want it, didn't need it. And after she left I lay staring, giving the night the torments of the day.

My father helped Martha for what seemed many hours. No one helped me.

Peter came home, undressed, left for his bath, returned and went to sleep.

I imagined faces in the shadows. They were on the world's side. No one was on mine, except maybe for Miss Lefkowitz, who I imagined as cowering in the corner of a black cell trying to keep from sinking into a morass of cockroaches.

The door to my parents' room opened. I heard my father tell Martha she was doing much better and her, "Gee, thanks." My mother remarked that she wished she could say the same about Martha's dishwashing, to which Martha said that when she became a famous actress she would have a maid to do the dishes; to which my mother said she already had one.

There were the sounds made by those still awake in deference to those they thought asleep: tinklings, patterings, steps going, steps returning, the switch of light in the living room, the creaking of the door to my mother's room, left always half-closed in case I had to call.

To call. If I wanted to call I would have to go to Mr. Goodman's and give him the envelope with its message and nickel and ask him to call . . . my father.

Then, through the silence, I heard their voices, first whispers only, then gaining volume until I clearly heard my father's, "But at least you might have tried to explain it to him."

"What?" my mother's voice asked. "What could I explain— that when I got there this morning, Jeanette was beating her head against the bathroom floor and screaming to her mother in heaven not to let them take her from her children; that I had to run down those broken steps to call Reuben and then up again; that by the time Reuben came I thought I would go insane with her screaming, her pain; and those children shivering in the bedroom.

"And then finally the needle took. While she slept Reuben told me what I had known all along, but wouldn't admit—that I could count her days on my fingers . . . my fingers."

"Did he have any suggestions?" my father asked.

"What could he suggest? Miracles? Even if they would take her at Morris View, she wouldn't go because . . . well, you know what would happen to the children."

Would they have to come to live with us again? No!

"Even if she would go, before social service would come creeping like molasses in January, it would be too late. Besides, that would bring her husband into it, and just the sight of him would be her end. A private day and night nurse is out of the question, so is a visiting nurse—besides, they're never around when they're needed. But we were talking in circles; everything always came back to me."

"Why only you? There are plenty of other women around, aren't there?"

"Other women? Most of them, if they just heard what was wrong with her, would run in the opposite direction. What's the use of talking? Who does she have, besides me? And she doesn't want a stranger to see her in her condition."

My father began to say—

She overrode him with, "Oh, I know how she feels. It was like the time I was giving birth to Bobby and the doctors told me to scream, and I'm looking at the strange nurse and feeling embarrassed—I couldn't scream in front of her. And it's even harder for Jeanette. She still has that dream, that she's Miss Baby Blue Eyes of nineteen-twelve."

"And you cater to that kind of nonsense?"

"To a woman in her condition, you don't cater. You give as if time were air and money water—and you ran on horsepower. Anyway, Reuben agreed that even though it wasn't kosher, he'd teach me how to give her a needle. He didn't have time right then, and when he did it had to turn out to be the time I usually go for Bobby. I met him up there and he showed me the ropes . . . some ropes, I'll hang myself before I'll learn how to use that damned thing . . . so he suggested I get a navel orange to practice with.

"Then when I thought I was through and ready to leave, he told me I'd have to get two prescriptions filled at once so he could show me how to measure the doses. So, for the thousandth time I ran down those steps, and when I got back he said that Bobby had been there looking for me and that he had told him I wasn't there but that I'd be back in a minute."

Dr. Reuben had lied! lied! I protested inwardly, at the same time remembering dimly that he had kept on talking after I had run down the steps.

"So I came home again, and on the way up I heard Libby playing some game and took it for granted he was with her. Since I wanted to practice on that orange, I slipped into the apartment—and there's the whole story. What part of it do you think I ought to tell him?"

"Why not tell him that she's sick and that you had to help her?"

"You think it's as simple as all that? It's no wonder you keep asking why you find it so hard to get through to him. You never heard of the diabetes that became diet beetles and then became dried beets. You forget that he goes to school with Johnny—that he could get a worm to come out of its apple just by asking questions. And all he has to find out is that she's dying—"

"Frances!" His voice was like a hand against her mouth.

I threw protests and denials like rocks. I wrestled against her words as if they were chains. And when I had broken out of them my fury welled up into a triumphant, Hurray for me!

I was the smart one! Hadn't she herself said I was as smart as people who were already married? I had been the smart one not to believe her, not to ask why she had been late.

Now she was lying again. She knew mothers didn't die—they couldn't! She had said it only for me to hear—knowing that I wasn't asleep, the way she knew everything despite walls, space and night. She couldn't fool me anymore. I wouldn't care if she went to Johnny's house every day—even to live there, forever; even to be like his other mother. I didn't need her. I didn't need anybody. And I'd show everybody—*everybody*.

When my mind became frightened of what it was doing to her, I fled into the sanctuary of sleep—out of which I was flung by my screams. And her cool hand on my cheek, her voice restoring me with, "It was only a dream, only a bad dream."

chapter 9

The morning was a flurry of hands. Her hands as she dressed me, the quick twist of the fingers on buttons, the knowing flip of the wrist in knotting the knitted red tie. Her hands as she combed and recombed my hair, her palms persuading a rebellious tuft to take its place with the others, her hands as she served the breakfast. Hands became the blur of bird's wings. I saw her hands, but not her face.

On the way to school: "What are you going to do today in class?" "I don't know." "What did you do yesterday?" "Nothing." "That's nice."

She talked to a woman. The woman talked to her. They talked, talked, talked, talked about Miss Lefkowitz.

Miss Lefkowitz was still in jail . . . her brother couldn't do a thing. . . . What kind of connections could a strikebreaker have these days, there hasn't been a strike to break around here in God knows how long? . . . Where will she get the money to pay the fine? . . . Who knows, but maybe since we haven't been throwing, they won't be so hard on her. . . .

The class line had begun to form. No Johnny!

She patted my cheek. "Be good," she said and hurried off, her hair bouncing with the spring of her steps, pushing the pavement behind her.

The line began to move, and we marched into class. The seat next to mine was empty.

We said our good-mornings and sat. Miss Diamond licked her lips and was about to speak when the door opened, just wide enough for Johnny to come through with the help of a woman's urging hand.

I knew it was *hers!*

He sat. I glanced at him, but he didn't respond, stared ahead. How did he know I wasn't his friend anymore?

Miss Diamond asked if he was feeling better. He nodded. Why didn't Miss Diamond know he hadn't been in school the day before because there had been no one to take him?

Miss Diamond asked us all to report on our collecting.

Libby boasted she had five zillion stones and more. I said I had lots of bottle caps. Johnny mumbled his reply. Miss Diamond asked him to speak more loudly. He stood and almost shouted defiantly that he had "like ten bottle caps."

Knowing he had more, I said, "No, you got ten hundred." He looked at me. And I saw the emptiness in his eyes.

Miss Diamond cautioned me not to speak for anyone else, but her words couldn't pull me away from wondering about his eyes. They were without speech or feeling. I had seen him look that way only once before: that afternoon, on the steps of his building, just before he buried his face in the rose his mother brought from the hospital. I tried to give him a private smile, but he turned his head away. And in that instant I hated and loved him for somehow being the cause of my misery and at the same time being more miserable than I.

The sight of Mrs. Greneker waiting to take me home from school only confirmed a suspicion I had been feeding on since my mother left me that morning. But she had also come for Libby, and it was Libby who voiced my feelings when she demanded to know where her mother was.

"She's laying down," Mrs. Greneker said.

"Why is she laying down?" Libby insisted.

"Because she isn't standing up. And stop with the questions."

Seeing a strange woman take Johnny's hand and lead him toward the exit, I quickly pulled Mrs. Greneker's sleeve and asked, "Who's she?"

"A next-door neighbor," she replied. Grudgingly, I had to admit I was better off than he—at least I knew Mrs. Greneker.

After Libby left us, Mrs. Greneker confided that there was a special surprise for me in our apartment.

"If he's in my bed," I shouted, "I'm not going inside."

"Turn down the radio. There's nobody in your bed. Not even a bedbug would go in your bed."

She unlocked the door and I entered on the toes of suspicion. "Look who's here," Mrs. Greneker announced.

I saw my Grandmother Hirshman sitting in the kitchen like a black cloud.

Grandmother Hirshman exhibited only three points of white: her face under mountains of black hair; her fragile-fingered hands emerging from stuffed sleeves drawn tight at the cuffs. She had two pairs of black-rimmed glasses, one for reading, the other for looking. She rarely looked. A tiny gold watch was pinned to the balcony of her bosom. Each time she consulted it, which was often, as if she were marking time until a certain inevitability, she would have to unpin the watch, hold it close to her face and then repin it with a sigh.

Whenever we went to see her, her greeting for me was always accompanied by a trickle of tears. I thought the sight of me must pain her; actually, the reason was that I had been named in honor of her husband.

Now she sat, her hat on, with her customary look of being prepared to leave. "Nu?" she said.

"Go and kiss the bubbeh," Mrs. Greneker said, and nudged me forward.

"You know who I am?" my grandmother asked.

"Yes."

"Thank God there's something you know." She unpinned her watch, peered at it and repinned it, opened her prayer book and rocked.

"Aren't you glad your grandmother is going to stay a few days here?" Mrs. Greneker prompted.

"She is?"

My grandmother peered over her glasses at me, waiting for my answer. I nodded feebly. "My enemies should be so glad," she remarked.

Mrs. Greneker left and I soon heard her slapping pillows and flapping sheets. I stared at my grandmother. She looked up slowly and studied me. "When your father was your age, he was beautiful."

"Only girls are beautiful," I countered.

"Boys are beautiful also."

"No, boys are only smart."

"Maybe there will be something from you yet," she said, but doubtfully.

"Are you going to sleep here?" I asked.

"Who knows?"

"Are you going to make the dinner?"

"If I knew where to start."

"Is my mother coming home?"

"I thought you said boys were smart, didn't you?"

"Yes," I replied.

"Smart boys don't ask so many questions."

"Can I ask you just one more?"

"What does this child want from my life?" she asked the ceiling.

"Just one more . . . please?"

"All right, but just one."

"Is Grandma Kirchner coming?"

"Mrs. Greneker!" my grandmother called. "Take this flea from me. He's eating me up alive with his questions."

Mrs. Greneker's voice called from inside. I turned my back to my grandmother to signify my disappointment. "Go, go," she said as I walked away, "take a little nap for yourself. It's good for the inner eyes."

Inner eyes?

Mrs. Greneker unbuttoned my coat, helped me change to my play clothes.

"Where are my inner eyes?" I asked as she tied the laces on my shoes.

"In your keppeleh," she replied, patting the top of my head.

"Can I see with them?"

"More than with the other eyes."

I shut my eyes and immediately thought of my mother. I opened them quickly. "Why is Grandmother Hirshman staying here?"

"Because when you need a little help in the house, the first one you ask is the grandmother."

"What kind of help?"

"To clean a little, to cook a little, to shop a little, everything a little."

"Can't my mother do it?"

"She is doing it, but across the street."

"All the time?"

"Just regular time—no overtime and no double time. And now it's time for you to go out and play. To ask questions you have to have strong lungs, and for strong lungs you must have fresh air."

It was always the same. Whenever I had a question that promised to untwist the world, there was never an answer. There were words but no answers.

I went to the window in my mother's room and, as if unintentionally, let my eyes climb the walls of Johnny's building to one of the windows of his apartment. There they stopped, and I allowed my inner eyes to see through the windowshade, through the room, to a kitchen where my mother stood, washing a little, cooking a little, baking a little patty cake. . . . Anguish wiped out the picture. In its place I saw Johnny's eyes and I knew it would take something more than a million patty cakes to rekindle them to life.

No, she wasn't making patty cakes. It was something different. Memory squirmed, like a worm in an apple. Where had I heard about a worm in an apple? I knew it had to be something to do with my mother being up there behind that window, but all I could come up with was diet beetles and that, I knew, was wrong.

My grandmother coughed and called out something to Mrs. Greneker.

Wrong, wrong, I thought. My answers were wrong, my guesses, wrong. Everything was wrong. It had even brought the wrong grandmother.

Grandma Kirchner was tiny and soft and smelled of vanilla. Whenever she came, she brought a present for each of us and a fund of stories in which right always succeeded over wrong, truth over lies. And she liked answering questions, or so it seemed. Secretly I believed that there were two little white-feathered wings folded against her back.

I decided to ask Mrs. Greneker why Grandma Kirchner hadn't come, and found her in the kitchen sitting where my grandmother had been, reading a newspaper instead of a prayer book.

"Where is she?" I asked.

"The bubbeh went home."

"Why?"

Mrs. Greneker gave a long, penetrating look. "Because in keeping house one foot is better than two crutches."

I didn't understand but was more interested to know if now my Grandma Kirchner would come. Mrs. Greneker assured me that she had wanted to but was already occupied helping to care for my cousins Harvey and Beryl, both of whom had measles. That too was wrong; and I went to the window to watch.

The days that followed were without time; they were marked by the opening and closing of doors. I saw less and less of my mother. At times she would rush in for a moment to "see if everything was all right," and lest I might miss her on these rare occasions I clung to the apartment.

Neighbors continued to visit, if only to keep Mrs. Greneker "up to the minute" on what was happening. It was from them I learned that Miss Lefkowitz had been given an "excuse for a trial" at which the head of the Board of Health spoke for three hours and the head of the Department of Sanitation spoke for two and one half hours; and that all Miss Lefkowitz said in her defense was, "If you made the landlord fix the dumbwaiter, I wouldn't have done it." The punishment was a five-dollar fine and a thirty-day jail sentence. The latter was immediately suspended.

Miss Lefkowitz returned, slightly a heroine, to a neighborhood that praised her defiance of authority. But the landlord carried out his threat. She and her brother were dispossessed. So, early in her brief engagement with fame, she became homeless.

From what the women told Mrs. Greneker, I learned that they had protested fiercely against the Lefkowitz eviction. They appealed to Mrs. Fell and even Mr. Fell. They even tried to return the ousted possessions to the Lefkowitz apartment, but a new lock had been put on the door. Failing in this, they soon began to realize that if they continued to throw garbage from the windows they might end as Miss Lefkowitz had. And when it came to a choice of taking garbage to the basement or risking eviction, the former was easily preferable.

So garbage no longer flew from the windows; the inspectors withdrew; fathers and older children complainingly carried bags and pails to the cellar; and Mrs. Greneker blamed the entire affair for causing a return of her "arthuritis."

But while the women were disgruntled at their failure, I was miserably glad. Their defeat enabled me to conclude that mothers couldn't win always; that they were not all-powerful—my mother included; that here at least was one instance where the men had won against them; and it made no difference that those men were the enemy, for there was no doubt—as in Grandma Kirchner's stories—that the right men would beat down the wrong if they chose to. And I dreamt of the day when I and the good men would fight together and win the battle the women had lost—just to show *her!*

The passing days, however, brought no signs of renewed conflict. Instead, evictions grew, those gypsy belongings that stole away in the night. And as they appeared increasingly on the street, so did the steadily expanding groups of men—the jobless, who had heretofore hidden themselves behind their papers and curtained windows, but were now of sufficient numbers to seek one another's company in the street to talk, to argue, and, fumbling, roll their own cigarettes.

I passed them on the way from school. I didn't know them, but some seemed to know me. They tousled my head, called me by name, asked me what I was going to be when I grew up.

I asked Mrs. Greneker who they were.

"The fathers," she replied.

I stopped and looked at them. "Don't they go to work like my father?"

Without looking at me she replied, "They're working very hard. To keep your self-respect is a full-time job."

Her words attached themselves to my mind. I too had a full-time job, not only watching that window across the street but the men as well. I had to know how they looked and moved so that when the day came to fight, I would know how to act exactly as they did.

I was occupied at this one afternoon, my knees on the chair, my elbows on the sill, my inner eyes looking at the window, my outer eyes studying the men, when Mrs. Greneker came into the room.

"It's still there?" she asked.

"What?"

"The building didn't run away yet?"

The words bruised; I didn't reply.

"Come," she said, prodding my shoulder, "be a mensch, stand up and give an old lady a seat."

I got off the chair and was about to leave when she caught me around the waist and hoisted me onto her lap. The gesture was unusual

204

and surprised me.

"Tell me something," she said, "you think you have been fooling Mrs. Greneker? You think Mrs. Greneker hasn't seen you go around with such a long face that it's a big wonder you didn't trip over it already? Tell me, what is wrong with you?"

Any answer would have been in tears, not words.

"Why are you sitting like a little puppy looking at the moon?" she asked. "Do you know why puppies look at the moon?"

"No."

"Because they think that the moon is made from cream cheese. But if they asked me, I would tell them different. I would tell them that in order for there to be cream cheese there has to be a man who makes it. And there isn't a man from the moon."

"There isn't? How do you know?"

"I know because I went to night school."

"What's night school?"

"Night school is where you learn how to complain in English."

"Complain about what?"

"It depends on which department the complaint is sitting. And the way I see it, your complaint is sitting on your heart and it's already the size of a cantaloupe. And if you don't talk it out, it will blow up like a watermelon. So let's hear a few words."

I hesitated.

"I guarantee you'll feel one hundred per cent better if you tell me."

"My mother . . ." I began, and immediately wanted to catch the words back behind my teeth.

"This," she said, "I could have told *you!*"

"How?"

"Because ever since the world began, the first to blame is the mother. Even in the Bible it says that Cain gave his brother Abel a klob. Why? Because his mother gave his father a bite from an apple."

A thought came: Could Mrs. Greneker possibly know about the worm in the apple?

She went on, "So, tell me, what did your mother do that was so terrible?"

What had my mother done? Could I possibly complain that for some reason she was spending most of her time in Johnny's home? It was only across the way. Why couldn't I just go over there myself? I hadn't been told not to, yet something kept me back. It sounded too unimportant to cause a cantaloupe.

There was more, but how could I tell her that I felt as if my mother had slipped her hand out of mine, that she had gone away as if forever, and even though she came back from time to time it was only to go away again?

How could I possibly explain the little hand that kept fisting inside me, one moment grabbing for her and the next pushing her away. And how was I to explain the emptiness?

I found an escape hole. I told her about the time I had expected my mother to call for me at school and how she hadn't.

"So that's the whole story?" she asked when I had finished.

"Yes."

"I see," she said, removing her spectacles and folding them into her apron pocket. Then she hummed and hemmed and buzzed to herself, until she asked, "Do you know from Columbus?"

"I know his name."

"Then, if you know his name, you know Columbus discovered America in 1492."

I nodded.

"Now, make believe you're on the ship with Columbus in 1492. And let's say it's about two o'clock in the afternoon and Mr. Columbus, himself, comes up to you and says that because you're such a good boy, he's going to give you something extra-extra special for dinner. So you ask him what is going to be so special? And he says that extra-extra special for dinner is going to be chicken noodle soup. Do you understand so far?"

I nodded.

"Now, remember, that was two o'clock in the afternoon. So what do you think happens? All of a sudden, completely unexpected, by four o'clock in the afternoon he discovers America. Imagine! So in all the excitement, the noise and the big hoo-hah—because after all you don't discover America every day in the week—he forgets to make the chicken noodle soup. Do you understand?"

"Yes."

"After all, it stands to rights, who can remember about chicken noodle soup when you are discovering America? So you wouldn't exactly say that Columbus broke his promise, would you?"

'No," I admitted.

"But the promise he didn't keep either, did he?"

"No."

"But in the case of discovering America, you have to forgive and forget, right?"

"Right."

"Well, I'm thinking that this is the exact same thing that happened to your mother. She told you she would come and get you from school, then all of a sudden something so important happened that, just like Columbus, she forgot all about her promise."

"What so important happened?"

"How should I know? I wasn't there and she didn't give me a first-hand report, but I'm sure it was important like Columbus discovered America."

I couldn't make the connection between Columbus and my mother without knowing the important thing that had happened to her. I was about to question Mrs. Greneker further when the bell rang.

"Come," said Mrs. Greneker, "let's see who it is. Maybe, for a change, it will be good news."

She went to the door. "Who is it?"

A leaden, cracked voice asked, "Can you spare me something to eat, lady, please?"

Mrs. Greneker's hand went automatically to her breast. She closed her eyes slowly and after taking a deep breath, said, "Yes. Certainly. Just one minute, please. Just one minute and I'll be right with you."

She took my arm and hurried me to my room. "Here, you stay inside like a good boy and don't come out until I call you."

"Why?"

"Because when a poor man is hungry, so hungry he has to knock on someone's door for something to eat, it isn't nice to sit and watch him. Stay!" She shut the door.

I heard her hurry across the living room and just as she said, "Come in, good man. Don't be bashful," I opened the door and peeked out.

A man gray as granite came humbly in. And his eyes, so like Johnny's. I quickly closed the door, pressed myself against it to listen.

"Come in . . . come in," Mrs. Greneker said. "Wash your hands in here, I'll get you a fresh towel."

The man mumbled.

"No trouble, not a bit of trouble, I assure you."

I heard the sounds of water, plates, the scraping of a chair.

"Now I want you to make yourself comfortable and make believe you're eating in your own home," said Mrs. Greneker.

I heard the icebox open. "To start with, which would you like better, chopped herring on crisp lettuce or half a grapefruit with a red cherry?"

"Anything . . . anything's all right," the man said.

"I think maybe you'll enjoy the grapefruit more."

"Thanks, lady."

"It's nothing. And for course number two, how would you like me to heat up some nice mushroom and barley soup. Homemade?"

"Thanks, lady."

"Please, don't thank me so much. It's me who should thank you for giving me the chance to give. So, also how would you like some veal cutlets? And before I forget, excuse me a minute and I'll go turn on some music."

The radio noised out other sounds, but I imagined him stuffing the food into his mouth, cramming it, gulping it without chewing, washing it down with glasses of seltzer, as if nothing could satisfy a hunger that had begun many years ago when his mother had stopped caring for him.

chapter 10

It was the morning of the day Martha was to read for the role of Portia. She was up much earlier than usual and spent most of her time running around the apartment, banging into furniture. She ran into our room just as Peter got out of bed—he flew back in—and asked us to wish her luck.

I did, but niggardly because I only wanted someone on my side. Peter said he needed all the luck he had for lacrosse on Saturday. Her neck grew long with haughtiness as she said, "I don't need your luck anyway. I got talent," and ran out.

I heard Mrs. Greneker call, "Stop running around like Queen Kvetch from Biala Podlaska!" And then talk to someone. Who could it be? I ran from my bedroom. *She* was there!

She stood beside the kitchen table filling a shopping bag with cans of food.

At the sight of me she stopped and her face showed surprise, but it could not mask the tiredness that had seeped under her skin. The base of her throat and its adjoining wells were bruised with shadows. She licked the white dryness from her lips. "Well, if it isn't the apple of his mother's eye."

"It's got a worm in it," I said, and again I heard her voice as it talked that night about diet beetles and the worm in the apple, and then: "All he has to find out is that she's dying. . . ." *That lie!*

"What are you doing?" I asked.

"Getting some food together."

"For poor people?"

"No, for my family across the street."

It is not easy to die so soon after waking. I left the kitchen.

She called, "Bobby, Bobby."

"What do you want?"

"Come back. I want to talk to you."

"About what?" I stopped in the middle of the living room. Her fingers under my chin forced me to look up at her. "So you're still mad at me," she said. I jerked my face away. She was silent for a moment and then said, "I wanted to tell you that Mrs. Greneker has something very important to do this morning so Libby's mother will take you to school."

I walked away, thinking that first it was she who had something very important to do and now Mrs. Greneker and soon it would be Libby's mother until there would be no one to take me at all.

Mrs. Greneker found me sitting at the edge of my bed. "Why are you looking like yesterday's appetite?" she asked, and began to dress me. I heard the apartment door close with the sound of forever.

"Pray for me, everyone," Martha shouted as she left.

"God has nothing better to listen to," Mrs. Greneker half-spoke in reply.

Peter left, but not before imitating Martha with, "Pray for me, everyone, my bloomers shouldn't fall right in the middle of the stage."

"Oy, are they a pair," Mrs. Greneker said, sighing.

I rang the doorbell of Libby's apartment.

"Who is it?" Libby's voice sang out, too cheerfully.

"Never mind who it is," I heard her mother say, "just open the door."

"Who is it?" Libby whispered now.

"It's me."

"Me, who?"

"Bobby."

"Bobby what?"

"Bobby Hirshman," I said, going along with her game.

"We don't have no old clothes today. Come back in another two weeks."

"Your mother is supposed to take me to school."

The door opened and Libby slipped out. "Oh no she's not. I heard her say that she wasn't going to take you to school."

I knew from her tone and exaggerated gestures that she was making it all up, but since it confirmed my feeling that nobody cared about me anymore, I asked, "Why?"

" 'Cause you're not my friend, no more. I have a new friend, but it's a secret so I can't tell you his name. I like him instead of you. And nobody likes you. Not even your mother, 'cause she won't take you to school or even call for you no more. So why should my mother, if your mother don't? She even once made your sister take us, so that proves she doesn't want anybody to know she's your mother. And we're not friends no more so go peddle your stinking old fish some-place else, you cockaloomyfoo."

A clot of tears between my eyes, I went back to the apartment.

"Aren't you going with Libby's mother to school?" Mrs. Greneker asked.

I slipped past her, went to my room. Without removing my coat, I climbed into my bed, buried my face in the pillow. Deep. Deeper.

The doorbell rang. Libby's mother had come for me. Mrs. Greneker mumbled something to her and the door closed.

I waited. No one came.

"I'll take you home from school today," Mrs. Greneker announced from the living room. And after a moment, "On my word of honor. So wait for me." The door shut. I was alone. All alone.

The fear of having been completely abandoned was just setting in when the door of my room was opened. "Come on, Bobby," my father said, "I'll take you to school."

Amazement spiraled up in me; I slipped off the bed. "You can't take me to school."

"Why not?"

"Because only mothers take children to school."

"No one else?"

"Maybe sometimes, big sisters."

"In that case, today you are going to be different from everyone else in your class, because I'm taking you."

Would people think it funny seeing him take me? Would the children laugh?

"Let's go," he said. I followed him out of the apartment.

But as we reached the street another problem bubbled up. What would I talk to him about? For the extraordinary length of two whole blocks what would we say? I tried, "Don't you want me to tell you why I didn't go to school with Libby's mother?"

"Only if you want to."

I thought, and found myself floundering in the quicksands of groundless explanations. "Can I tell you some other time?"

"Sure."

Carmella came up like an escorting barge, loaded with two piles of books. "Hello, Mr. Hirshman," she said, "look at all the books I got."

"Hello, Carmella," he replied. "You've got almost as many as we have in the library."

I was astonished that he knew her, even her name!

"You bet," she said proudly, as if they were the exact words she had expected him to say. "And I study every single one of them."

"They'll help make a smart girl of you."

"You wanna know how smart I am?"

"Yes, I'd like to know, Carmella."

"I made up my mind, all by myself, that when I get married I'm gonna have books all over my apartment. Every single room is gonna be filled with lots of books. And if my kids don't read every one of those books, I'll knock their goddamned blocks off, excuse me for cursing."

"That's all right, Carmella," he said, and as she started away he added, "Be careful how you cross the street."

"Don't worry about me, Mr. Hirshman," she crowed, "I got eyes in the back of my head. Good-bye."

My father had barely returned the farewell when Mr. Fisher called from behind his sewing machine, "Hello, Mr. Hirshman," as if he and my father were old, close friends. Coming out of his shop, he shook my father's hand warmly. "How is it with you, Mr. Hirshman?" he asked, not in the offhand way with which I was used to hearing older people talk, but as if he really wanted to know.

"Fine, Mr. Fisher," he replied. "It's getting a little harder to collect fines on overdue books, but otherwise the library business hasn't been hit."

"Thank God," said Mr. Fisher earnestly, "because when people stop reading books we can all go back with the apes."

"How's your business doing?" my father asked.

"Business? What business? I sit by my machine to keep in practice. And I keep the store open, the landlord should have something to eat."

"Things will be better," my father assured him.

"From your mouth to God's ear," Mr. Fisher said prayerfully.

As we passed the barbershop, Mr. Calabrese, who was shaving Mr. McClure the policeman, waved the open razor over his head. "Come sta, Mr. Hirshman," he roared.

"Fine, and you, Mr. Calabrese?"

"How are you, Mr. Hirshman?" Mr. McClure called.

"Fine, thank you. How are you, officer?"

Passing the shops, we bumped into Marcia Weissbaum's mother, who walked right up to my father, saying, "Oh, Mr. Hirshman, I am so glad I ran into you."

"How are you, Mrs. Weissbaum."

"I'm just grand, considering, but I've been so hoping that I'd see you one of these days. I have something really nice to tell you."

"You do?"

"Yes," she said, wetting her lips. "My oldest daughter, Shari, told me that she had personally been to your library. You know, she's in college. And has that girl got a head on her shoulders! She's a girl from the books, the absolute original. What she hasn't read, hasn't been written. Last term, all A's. Frankly, I don't know where she gets it from. Not from my family, and certainly not my husband's. And, as you can well imagine, when that girl does research on a subject it's with a capital R. She leaves no stone unturned. She has been, without doubt, in every library in this city, bar none. And she told me—and this is what I've been wanting to tell you—that of every library she has ever been to, yours is the best. She said that it might not be the biggest, but without doubt it was the best. She couldn't say enough about it." Holding a restraining forefinger up, she said, "Let me think. Oh yes, now I recall. She said everything was so compartmentalized; that all the references had all the cross-references and everything else. I tell you, Mr. Hirshman, the girl couldn't say enough about your library.

"Here," she interrupted herself, "she said something that sounded so extra that I actually copied it down."

While she explored her purse, I nudged my father's leg with the back of my hand. With an almost imperceptible flicker of his finger he ordered me to be patient.

"Here it is . . . No . . . no . . . it's the light bill. I tell you, when you have a daughter who spends the better part of her life reading, the light bill can go sky high. Ah, here it is. Talking about your library, she said, 'It combines the best aspects of the Dewey Decimel System and the Cutler Catalog.' "

"Cutter," my father said.

"Cutter? Not Cutler?" she asked with surprise.

"Yes."

"Leave it to me"—she gave a brief chirping laugh—"I don't even have enough brains to cross my t's, and I'm the mother of a girl who's practically an Einstein."

As she talked, several women passed and greeted my father; he nodded in return. I heard Mrs. Weissbaum ask, "Tell me, Mr. Hirshman, do lots of college students use your library?"

"Not too many," he replied, "we're not close to any of the colleges so we get mostly local residents."

"I'll tell you why I ask," she said, moving closer and shading her voice. "My Shari is such a really exceptional girl that I would like her to meet a young man with the same qualities. I mean someone who can really appreciate her for her superior mental endowments. And it just crossed my mind that perhaps you might know of such a young man, a college student, studying for a profession, who might be interested in such a girl."

"Offhand, I don't, Mrs. Weissbaum," my father said with a touch of remoteness that indicated he was checking to see if he knew of such a person, "but should I meet anyone who fits the description, I'll certainly be alert to the possibilities."

"Thank you. Thank you so much, Mr. Hirshman. You don't know how indebted I'd be to you for any small favor."

"It's quite all right, think nothing of it, Mrs. Weissbaum, I'll be glad to help if I can." They exchanged good-byes.

"School will be over by the time I get there," I protested.

"No it won't," he said, "and even if it were, you can't be impolite and walk away when someone is talking to you."

"Did you ever see Shari?" I asked.

"No."

"Peter says that she looks like a garbage can with glasses."

"Peter is probably jealous of her."

"Why?"

"Because she is probably a very bright girl."

After one more delay caused by Mr. Goodman, who wanted to know if my father had any figures on how many more people were reading books instead of going to moving pictures because of the Depression, we finally reached school.

I had been expecting him to leave me at the foot of the main staircase, but he took me to the door of the room, knocked, and when Miss Diamond said, "Come in," he led me to her desk.

Not a snicker, not a whisper from the class. I kept my head down.

"I'm his father," he said. "It's my fault he's late."

"Oh, how do you do, Mr. Hirshman," Miss Diamond said, standing, offering her hand. He shook it.

"I know you," she said. "You see, I borrow regularly from your library. I've often seen you sitting behind that glass partition, and I've been tempted more than once to come in and introduce myself."

"I wish you had," my father said. "I'm sorry to have interrupted your class."

"Not at all . . . not at all." Miss Diamond removed her glasses and smiled like the Star Spangled Banner. He left.

I raised my head as I went toward my seat. The class was an awe-filled gape except for Libby and Johnny. One side of Libby's mouth was sewn up in a smirk. Johnny's face was like a blackboard from which everything had been erased. I sat, beyond the reach of Miss Diamond and the rest of the world.

My father was important! People trumpeted their "hellos" to him; asked him what *he* thought; waited, like Mrs. Weissbaum, a long time to see him; and Miss Diamond spoke of going to his library, *his!* And he had brought *me* to school! But what was even more important: he knew the tailor, the barber, the policeman, and Mr. Goodman, and even Carmella! He knew my street and Mrs. Weissbaum! I bet if I told him about the twins, he would know who they were, and the rest of my friends, and their brothers and sisters, and their fathers and mothers; and that they all came to him, as Mrs. Greneker would say, "for an advise." And all this meant that I could talk to him about everything, and he would know. He would know!

I dimly heard Miss Diamond announce that our collections were due tomorrow, and then she held up a packet and rattled it, saying it contained seeds from which, she said, everything grew.

I could hear my mother's voice saying, "The birds tell the bees; the bees tell the flowers; the flowers tell the seeds; and only the seeds will tell it to you," when I had asked her about babies.

Babies!

My mind turned like the handle of a door. It turned back to that night, the night *she* lied about Johnny's mother.

My mother's voice: "It was like the time I was giving birth to Bobby and the doctor is telling me to scream, to scream . . ." And I knew! Martha had been right all the time. Johnny's mother was going to have a baby. It explained everything . . . everything.

Immediately. I had to tell Johnny immediately. I had to!

I inched my chair closer to his. Almost imperceptibly, he moved away from me. But he wouldn't if he knew what I had to tell him.

I writhed in the ecstasy of knowing something important, something that might even bring the lights back to his eyes, if he would only listen. Why didn't the lunch bell ring?

When it did, there were still the lunchroom rules: the first part of luncheon, eating; the second part, during which the milk was distributed, talking.

I tried muttering to Johnny with my mouth full. He ignored me.

The milk wagon meandered between the tables like a blind beggar.

At last! Milk bottle in one hand, cookie and straw in the other, I jumped up, whispered a furious, "Come quick" to Johnny and ran to a far corner of the room, where I slid to the floor. But he didn't follow.

The kids scattered like beads from a torn necklace, and I couldn't even see him. I stood, hunted, and collided with Libby.

"Who you looking for?" she asked.

"No one."

"Then why're you looking?"

I walked away. She followed. "Do you wanna know the name of my new friend?"

"No."

"Go to hell."

I was going to reply when I saw Johnny near the window. I ran around the edge of the room. "Aren't you going to drink your milk?" I asked him when I reached him.

He looked away.

"Do you want my marshmallow puff cookie?"

He shook his head.

"Don't you have a cookie?"

He opened his hand to show me a crumbled fig newton.

"Do you know what I know? I know a big something."

He looked out the window.

"If you knew what I know, you'd be glad."

Silence.

"If you knew what I know, you'd be so glad like the time when your mother came home from the hospital and we waved and yelled and ran. That glad."

He glanced at me, then looked back quickly.

"If you knew what I know, I'd be your best friend in the whole world, over everybody."

Silence, but I was certain he was about to turn his head toward me when Libby came up.

"What are you talking about?" she asked.

"Oh, you Fifi la-la Libby, you," I shouted, "why don't you play with girls instead of boys all the time?"

She looked vaguely surprised and said, "You're not a boy. You're a nothing."

"Good-bye, Miss Toilet-face," I jeered.

A snicker like a hiccup escaped Johnny's lips. Snatching my advantage, I continued with, "Good-bye Miss Tillie Toilet-face and tell them I sent you."

Johnny turned around. He looked at me first, then at Libby. A slight and shy smile.

Libby raised her eyebrows, lowered her lids, raised them slowly, looked at me from the corners of her eyes, batted her lashes and without threat or omen in her voice, said, "Just . . . you . . . wait." She winked at me and walked proudly away.

Johnny turned back to facing the window.

I had to be funny, I thought. I had to make him laugh. Remembering what Peter had said to Martha, I ventured with, "That Fifi la-la Libby has such a pushed-in face she smells coming and going."

It failed. I failed. The marshmallow puff was glued to my palm. I walked away to the far corner and slid to the floor again, muttering that Fifi la-la Libby had spoiled it all.

I sat blowing a froth of bubbles in the milk. A pair of Mary Janes stopped and stood in front of me. I looked up slowly.

Libby batted her eyes at me and said, as before, "Just . . . you . . . wait." She winked and sauntered away.

I went back to bubbling. Another pair of shoes in front of me. Girl's. I looked up at Leatrice Aronowitz.

"Do you love me?" she asked without enthusiasm.

I looked to see if Libby was nearby, thinking that if she were I would say very loudly, "Yes, I love you very much, Leatrice," but since she wasn't, I let the straw slip and pinching the end of my nose, I said, "Phew!"

"Phew on you," she said, and left.

Back to bubbling. Brown shoes. Boy's. Polished but worn, one toe shyly covering the other. I looked up slowly. "You want to tell me?" he asked.

I picked my marshmallow puff from the floor to make room for him. "Wait till you hear," I began with a rush, "but it's such a big, big secret, you got to do two things."

"What things?"

"You got to tell me something first."

"What thing first?"

"What does my mother do in your house?"

He wondered at the question, and then answered, "She cleans."

"That's all?"

"She cooks."

"Nothing else?"

He lowered his head, ran the tip of a fingernail between the floorboards. "She . . . she takes care of . . . of my mother."

"How?"

"I don't know."

"Don't you see?"

"Only when she gives my mother asspins."

I didn't bother to correct him. "That's all?"

"No, maybe. But when sometimes my mother screams very loud"— his face twitched—"she takes something from what's like cooking on the stove, and she covers it over with a towel so I can't see it, and she closes my mother's door, and she don't come out until my mother isn't screaming anymore, and she puts the thing back on the stove, in the pot."

"It's good that your mother screams," I said with satisfaction.

His look darted, questioning my seriousness. "It is?"

"Sure."

"How do you know?"

"I'll tell you, but first you got to do something else. You got to swear to God and to Torah that you will never tell it to anyone."

"Who's Torah?"

"She's His wife."

"I swear."

"No. You got to say the whole thing."

"I swear to God and Torah that I won't tell nobody, nothing."

"Now you give me your fig newton for my marshmallow puff."

We exchanged.

"There's only one more thing—"

"You said there were only two."

"But this is not a real thing. It's to drink your milk while I'm telling you so it won't look like I'm telling you an extra-special secret."

He sucked the straw into his mouth and I watched the white line rise. Then, taking my own straw between my lips to make believe I was sipping, I said, "All right. I think that my mother discovered something about your mother that's like Columbus discovering America."

He let go of the straw. "What?"

"I think she discovered something about your mother that's like Columbus discovering America, like your mother's getting something very soon."

"Something, what?"

"Don't talk!" I warned. "Drink your milk."

He caught the straw with his tongue and pulled it into his mouth.

"I think your mother's getting something . . . something like a . . . like a baby!"

"A baby?" he cried, the milk splattering.

"Sh. It's a secret, an extra-special one."

"How do you know?" His voice was impatient, eager.

"Remember you swore to God and His wife you'd never tell anyone."

"Sure! Sure!"

"My sister Martha told me," I said with great conviction. But even as the words came out I knew that they lacked the necessary weight of adult authority. He looked disappointed.

"And," I continued, "Carmella told me."

"Who's she?"

"She's the barber's daughter and she's the baby expert in the whole neighborhood."

"How old is she?" he asked suspiciously.

"I don't know, but she's almost going to get married any day now, like my Aunt Shirley who's older than my mother, I think."

I could see he was not easily convinced. "And," I added, as triumphant proof, "Mrs. Greneker!" I winced under the load of the lie. But since he was sworn to secrecy, I thought I could afford to take the liberty.

"Mrs. Greneker told *you?*" he asked unbelievingly.

"Not right to me," I said, "but once when she thought I was asleep, she called somebody up on the telephone—I think it was Libby's mother—and I heard her tell it."

"Do you think it's true?" he whispered.

"Of course! Didn't three people tell me, and one of them is old like my grandmother?" Then as if it were an unbidden question, I asked, "Did your grandmother come to take care of you before my mother did?"

"She couldn't."

"Why not?"

" 'Cause she's dead."

My tongue leaped in my throat.

"What's the matter?" Johnny asked.

I couldn't answer.

"What's the matter, are you sick?"

"Huh? No. I don't know."

"When do you think they're going to bring the baby?"

"The baby . . ." I repeated mechanically, feeling something colder than milk sink brutally down my throat and end as a frozen lump in my stomach.

"Did you just make it all up?" he asked bitterly.

The drop of his face forced me to blurt, "No! Honest! I swear! I *swear!*"

He threw back his head and laughter gurgled up out of the fountain of his throat. I knew at once that if I wanted him to believe me I would have to laugh too. I pushed my hands into my face and forced, "Ha-ha, ha-ha . . ."

He threw his arms around my shoulders and pulling my face close to his, "A baby . . . a baby . . ." he whispered, and giggled. Then, holding up his thumb and forefinger to show how small it was, he babbled, "Teeny . . . teeny . . . teeny . . . teeny." Suddenly, and as if beyond my will, I found myself reacting to him. "Teeny-weeny, teeny-weeny, teeny-weeny." Then, caught up in the madness of our own sounds, we gave ourselves up to uncontrollable laughter.

In a paroxysm Johnny slapped his hands together, squashing the marshmallow puff into a sticky ooze. Kicking my foot out, I overturned the milk bottle. Johnny fell on his stomach, pounded the floor with his fists. I was convulsed at the sight of my belly bouncing to the rhythm of my laughter.

Others began to gather around us, but nothing could stop us. Our laughs strutted, bounced, kicked each other out of the way; they spouted, spurted and sprayed. My eyes were tearing. One moment I could see Libby standing in front of me, her hands on her hips, her face tight with anger; another moment I saw the lunchroom teacher trying to stifle her snickers.

Everyone but Libby began to whoop and yowl, until sound erupted all around us. It was deafening, ear-searing, but it couldn't keep the teacher's, "Stop now, children. Enough! Enough!" from penetrating. The roar subsided to a rumble, to a murmur, a whisper, a hum, a sigh. . . .

Back in class and after rest period, Miss Diamond remarked how disheveled and disorderly Johnny and I looked, but she seemed pleased in Johnny's case and gave him her special smile. Then she told us the story of Johnny Appleseed, I thought, particularly for Johnny.

223

He sat, elbows on knees, chin on the heels of his palms and eyes enraptured, as he listened to how Johnny Appleseed walked the land strewing apple seeds for all.

I remembered his jelly beans and later his gumdrops—how he dreamt of giving them away—and that strange little hand inside me felt as if it were trying to open its fingers.

If Johnny's mother was going to have a baby, then I knew why my mother had to be there all the time. She was the angel, like the ones at St. Ursula's and Morris View, flying around with the bedpans.

Libby raised her hand and waved it as if she had something very important to tell Miss Diamond.

Removing her glasses, Miss Diamond said with a sigh, "Yes, Libby? And I hope it's important to interrupt such an interesting story."

"It is, Miss Diamond," Libby assured her. Leaning forward as if telling a secret, she said, "I smell something. It smells funny like I think Bobby Hirshman peed in his pants."

Shocked, my hand flew to my lap. It was dry. She was crazy!

The class's guffaws overtook its snickers. Miss Diamond rapped the desk with her pencil. Throwing the pencil down, she picked up the ruler and angrily slapped the desk with it.

Even Gerard Shuminsky laughed. He, who was famous for wetting himself every day. He, who was the monitor and was never, never allowed to be disorderly.

"Gerard! Gerard!" Miss Diamond's lips parted with astonishment. "If I hadn't seen it with my *own* eyes—heard it with my *own* ears—I would never have believed it. Absolutely *never!* Well! You'll never know how you have disappointed me. There is no doubt in my mind that we need a new, a better-behaved monitor."

Gerard Shuminsky's world crumbled and so did he. He slumped in his seat. It was as if the invisible ironing board that had been strapped to his back had suddenly collapsed.

"Sit up, straight!" Miss Diamond ordered. "Now Libby, stand up, please."

Libby jumped up eagerly.

"Suppose what you have just accused Bobby of is true—"

"It's not!" I interjected.

"Quiet, Bobby, please. I'll handle this. As I asked you, Libby, suppose it were true, what would you suggest I do about it?"

Libby had an immediate answer, "I would take him by his ear and throw him out of the room and not let him come back without his mother—and then he wouldn't be able to come back for at least a year, 'cause his mother isn't home anyway."

"Thank you for the suggestion, Libby. Now, in the event that what you said is not true, what would you suggest doing then?"

Libby nibbled the edge of her finger for a moment, and then protested, "But it *is* true, Miss Diamond. I swear. I can smell it. If you came over here and smelled it you'd right away put his stupid head in a toilet bowl and pull the chain."

"All right," Miss Diamond said, "I will come over." She sidled her way through our aisle until she reached Libby. "You have done the naughtiest thing ever," she said from between clenched teeth, and grabbing Libby's ear, she tugged her out of the aisle.

"Leggo," Libby yelled, "you're tearing off my ear!"

"That's not half of what I'd like to do to you."

"Leggo—that's my *bad* ear—LEGGO!" Libby shouted.

"The only thing that's bad is your tongue!" Miss Diamond pulled Libby to the corner between the blackboard and the clothes closet. "Now you will stand here with your face to the wall until the end of class. And following your own suggestion, you may not come back tomorrow unless your mother comes with you. Understand?" Her back to us, Libby wept soupily. Miss Diamond told her that if she didn't keep quiet the punishment would be worse.

It was strange, very strange. I knew that this was what Libby had meant by her "Just . . . you . . . wait." But I didn't know why she had done it; she could only hurt herself. And stranger than all else: Why wasn't I angry with her? Why did I feel sorry for her?

I decided, if I could find words, to ask my father about it.

That night after dinner, Martha went to Henrietta's. Peter left saying that he had to study someplace else because my father wouldn't let him do his homework and listen to the radio at the same time. Just as my father came into the living room, I heard Libby yell from her apartment, "Stop! Don't hit me! I didn't mean it! I said it for a joke! I promise, I swear! That's my bad arm! It's sore already! You're not supposed to hit me no more, 'cause I'm in school! Ma! Don't let him!" I heard her mother shout, "Not over the head, she's dumb enough already . . ."

My father went to his chair as if he heard nothing. "Did anything happen in school today?" he asked.

"No," I replied.

"Sounds like the end of the world," he said to himself, and opened his newspaper.

The bell rang and I opened the door. Mrs. Jackson dragged in a simpering bundle. Libby was all defeat except her eyes. Her look clearly said that despite cries and protests, it didn't hurt.

Mrs. Jackson stopped in the middle of the living room, flipped Libby around, and said, "Now, say you're sorry—and mean it!"

Libby put the tip of her forefinger between her lips and muttered a fainting, "I'm sorry."

Her mother ordered, "Take your finger out of your mouth and say it like, I pledge allegiance."

Libby sniffled, became kitten-eyed, removed the finger and recited, "I am sorry."

"I am sorry who?" her mother demanded.

"I am sorry, Bobby."

Turning to me, Mrs. Jackson said, "And as for you, Sir Walter Raleigh, don't be such a gentleman in the future. School or no school,

226

the next time she tries anything like that give her a swift kick in the bloomer department."

To my father she said, "If I could marry her off tomorrow, I'd sign the papers today." Then, taking Libby's hand, she pulled her out of the apartment.

"So," my father said, "nothing happened in school today?"

"I didn't want you to think I was telling on Libby." And I told him what had happened, ending with, "Do you know why she did it?"

He listened carefully. "It brings to mind a similar case," he said. "It was a long, long time ago when I was either in 1B or 2A—the same school you go to—"

"You went to my school?"

"Sure. Does it sound impossible?"

"Was Miss Diamond your teacher, too?"

"No, I had another jewel. But anyway, when I was in 1B or 2A I also knew a little girl."

"How little?"

"As little as Libby and just as pretty."

"Libby isn't pretty. She has a face like . . ."

"Never mind. Do you want to hear the story, or don't you?"

"Tell me."

"Well, this little girl followed me everywhere . . . upstairs, down-stairs, in the street, in my apartment, in school, out of school . . . everywhere."

"Why did she do that?"

"She was in love with me."

"She was?"

"Like crazy."

"So what did you do to make her better?"

"I couldn't make her better because I spent all my time trying to hide from her."

"Why didn't you kick her in her bloo-boos?"

"What's her bloo-boos?"

"Her bloomers."

"By the way, no matter what Mrs. Jackson said, I never want you to kick Libby anywhere. Do you understand?"

"I know—her mother was only making fun."

"Good, now let's get on with the little girl who was in love with me. As it happened, she was in my class, too. And one day the teacher called on her and asked her to hand in her homework. But she didn't have her homework."

"Why?"

"Because she hadn't done it."

"So what happened?"

"The teacher asked her why she hadn't done her homework."

"What did she say?"

"Here's the payoff. She gave as her excuse that I had stolen her pencil box and she couldn't do her homework."

"Did you?"

"Of course not. How could I? I spent all my time trying to hide from her, remember?"

I nodded.

"Anyway, the teacher knew it was a lame excuse."

"What's a lame excuse?"

"It didn't have a leg to stand on."

"Then what happened?"

"The teacher told me to stand up and she asked me if I had stolen the little girl's pencil box."

"What did you say?"

"What do you think I said?"

"You said yes."

"Why *yes?*"

"Because you were sorry for her, she told such a big lie on account of you."

"You're wrong."

"I am?"

"Of course you are. No one should be sorry for liars."

"Never?" My mother came immediately to mind.

"Well, most of the time. Anyway, I told the teacher that I hadn't stolen her pencil box. And the little girl called me a thief and a liar and just about everything else you could think of."

"Did she call you cockakazoo and nuts to you?"

"No, that wasn't around at the time. Then the teacher ordered the little girl to be quiet, which wasn't easy, and she asked her if the pencils in her box were the only ones in the world, and also if no one else in her whole family had another pencil."

"What did she say?"

"What could she say? That's why it was a lame excuse."

"So then?"

"So then the teacher made her sit in the corner on the dunce stool."

"Not stand?"

"No, in those days we sat."

"So then?"

"After class the teacher made us both stay late. And she asked her to bring her school-bag to the desk and to open it and to turn it upside down."

"Did she?"

"With tears, but she did. And out fell the pencil box, among other things."

"What did the teacher do?"

"She made the little girl bring her mother to school."

"She did?"

"Yes sir, she did."

"Then did she leave you alone and not follow you upstairs and everywhere?"

"Yes, but I fell in love with her. But she didn't love me anymore."

" 'Cause you told on her in class?"

"I suppose so. But then she fell in love with me. But I didn't care for her by that time. And so it went on. I fell in love with her. She fell in love with me until—you know what happened?"

229

"What?"

"We married."

"You did?"

"Yes we did."

"Then what did you do?"

"We had a little boy named Peter, a little girl called Martha, and a little boy, Robert Benjamin Hirshman, who had exactly the same trouble with a little girl named Libby Jackson."

"He did?"

We were interrupted by Mrs. Greneker. "Go make like the Ziegfeld Follies while I turn on the bathtub," she said to me.

During the bath I pondered my father's story, fitting the pieces together until I discovered that the little girl he knew was my mother and that in a way he was saying that Libby and I would get married. Passing him on the way to my bedroom, I said, "She loves me like poison." He buried his head in his newspaper and laughed.

Mrs. Greneker made sure that the blanket corners would not easily be pulled out, and then asked, shyly, "How would you like me to sing you to sleep?"

Surprised, I asked, "Can you sing?"

"Like Caruso's mother."

"A good-night song?" I hoped it wouldn't be the one my mother sang to me.

"Not exactly. It's more like a cradle song." Then, with mock impatience, "Do you want I should give you a written guarantee or I should sing you a song?"

I asked her to sing.

"First, I got to know your Jewish name. It's part of the song."

"I don't know it," I admitted.

"But that you're a Jew, that you know?"

"Yes."

"Good. That's the main thing." Turning, she called, "Hirshman, what's his name in Jewish?"

"Berel," he replied.

"Berel," she said as if sampling the taste of it on her tongue. "Ah, that's beautiful." She hummed a bit to herself and sang:

> "Unter Bereleh's vigele
> Shteyt a klor veis tzigele.
> Dos tzigele is geforen handlen—
> Dos vet zein dein beruf:
> Roszinkes mit mandlen.
> Shlof-zhe, Bereleh, shlof."

It was as soft as shadow. "What does it mean?" I asked.

"It means you should be asleep by the time I finish singing it."

She sang it again. I shut my eyes, but as soon as I did, my mind traveled to the things my father had told me earlier that evening and I knew I should have to think them over and over before I slept.

Turning off the light, Mrs. Greneker stepped lightly from the room and half-closed the door. "Sh," she said to my father, "he's sleeping like he was born this morning. "Ah," she went on, and I could hear the couch complain under her weight, "I've been waiting a long, long time to sing that song and it was worth it. It took a heaviness from my heart. Now, I have to have a little talk with you."

"Of course, Mrs. Greneker." I heard the rustle of my father's paper. "Would you like some coffee, or tea?"

"No, thank you. Nothing can sweeten what I have to tell you."

"Is anything wrong?"

"The answer, I'm afraid, is yes. I'm sorry I have to tell you, but I must give up the job. I don't want to, but facts are facts and one fact is that I'm not a chicken anymore."

"But why didn't you say something sooner?" my father asked. "As it is, we wouldn't know how to repay you for all you've done."

"What did I do? Compared to what your wife is doing over there, I've done next to nothing. But I want you to understand, I'm not giving up because I want to, or even because my huband wants me to. But, the doctor gave me this morning what he called an 'ultimatum.' He said, 'Mrs. Greneker, stop or you won't have to.' So, go argue. I didn't have the heart to tell your wife today. This is Thursday, so I'll be here already tomorrow. Then for the weekend you can maybe manage. But I'm wondering who is going to fill my shoes?"

"Don't you worry about that. It's my problem. The important thing is that you take care of yourself."

"What's there to take care of? Till a hundred and twenty I won't live. But here there are children, and especially that one in there. Don't I see in his eyes what's going on in his heart? Don't I know? So, who's going to look after him?"

"Please, Mrs. Greneker, don't worry. I'll have someone in my family or maybe someone in Frances' family can come over."

"Please, family is all the same. When they need you, they know exactly where the telephone is—they know how to find your number, they even know where the nickel is to put in. But when you need them, all of a sudden the telephone wasn't invented yet. And it's no different with the neighbors. Everybody loves your wife. Frances is everybody's favorite. But when it comes that one of them should go up there and give her a helping hand, there's nobody home. Jackson quick puts on a cold compress, and McCarthy—as soon as she heard what was wrong with that poor woman, she went to church and for all I know she's still there. So who is there to turn to?"

"I have all weekend to find someone. Don't worry about it, please."

There was a groaning sigh and the twang of the couch springs.

"Do you want me to help you to your apartment?" my father asked.

"No thanks. A cripple yet, I'm not."

"And Mrs. Greneker"—my father's voice was awkward—"I wish I knew of some way to show you how grateful I am and always will be for what you have done for us."

"Please, you shouldn't even say such a thing. It was my privilege. Don't forget, where I come from, God doesn't help those what help themselves. He only helps those what help others."

The door closed and I was overcome by a frantic desire to keep Mrs. Greneker from going, to keep the world from going away and leaving me behind.

chapter 11

The next morning Libby arrived early to say that her mother was in a very "crical" condition and would Mrs. Greneker take her to school along with me. Mrs. Greneker agreed and when Libby left, added, "Critical, my eye. If she wants to see a real, genuine critical condition, she should take a good look on me. The way I feel, I don't know why I said yes in the first place."

When Martha came into the kitchen, Mrs. Greneker asked, "Martheleh, will you be a good girl and do Mrs. Greneker a big favor?"

"What?" Martha asked suspiciously.

"Will you take your brother and Libby to school today?"

Martha staged what my mother would describe as a holy Roman fit until my father called, "Martha," whereupon she said, begrudgingly, "All right, but it's the last time. After all, they picked me to be Portia." Then, with a toss of her head, "And who ever heard of a star taking kids to school!"

It was the first I knew she had got the part, and I wondered why she had not made more of it, but I couldn't pursue it because Libby returned with two shoeboxes filled with her precious stones, reminding me that this was the day to show our collections. I got the bag of bottle caps from its hiding place.

Johnny was not on the line when we arrived.

I looked for him, searched up the street, craned in the hope of seeing him.

"Who're you looking for?" Libby asked as the line began to move. I was going to tell her to mind her own business, but remembering my father's story last night, I replied, "Johnny."

A shadow of disappointment on her face. "Why're you looking for him?"

" 'Cause he's my friend."

"Can't you have more than only one friend?" I wondered. "Can't you have two friends?" she went on. "Can't one friend be a girl and the other one a boy? Can't they?"

Leatrice Aronowitz, who was running up and down the line like an epidemic, told Libby to shut up. Libby ignored her. "Can't they?" she repeated with pleading insistence.

I continued to wonder.

"Do you have more than one friend?" I asked.

"Sure."

"What's the other friend's name?"

She pondered. It brought forth, "Selma."

"Selma, who?"

More pondering. "Selma Quiet."

"I don't know her."

"Why don't you know her?"

" 'Cause I never saw her."

"Maybe you never saw her because she has double ammonia and is dying from a cold."

"You just made her up," I accused.

"Yes," she admitted, "but she's the best friend in the whole world."

Once in class, Miss Diamond asked Libby what she was doing there without her mother. Unruffled, Libby opened her schoolbag and took out an envelope. "Here she is," she announced, and running up to Miss Diamond, presented it to her and made a little curtsy before returning to her chair.

Miss Diamond went to her desk, opened a drawer, took out a letter opener, closed the drawer, slowly slit open the envelope, reopened the drawer, returned the opener, drew a paper from the envelope, carefully unfolded it, resettled her glasses on her face and finally read.

After a time she refolded the paper, re-inserted it in its envelope. "Libby, I am afraid this won't do."

"What won't it do?" Libby inquired.

"It won't take the place of your mother coming to see me."

"It won't?" Libby was unbelieving.

"No, it won't."

"Ooooh," Libby gasped.

Miss Diamond returned the envelope and said, "Come with me, please."

"Where?" Libby asked anxiously.

"Mr. Pierce has to know about this."

A shiver rustled the class. Mr. Pierce was the principal; being taken to him was the ultimate punishment.

"I don't wanna go," Libby began to blubber.

"It is not for you to decide." Miss Diamond sounded like God's mother.

Libby looked at me imploringly. I took the chance, raised my hand. Miss Diamond looked down at me. "I hope you are not going to meddle in this, Bobby."

I stood. "No, Miss Diamond. I'm not going to meddle, but Libby's mother is wearing her cold compress and her 'crical' condition is worse than even Mrs. Greneker's. And that's why my sister Martha had to take Libby and me to school. And she's not a mother."

"You *are* meddling," Miss Diamond said. She folded her arms and to the rhythm of her tapping toe, looked from me to Libby, from Libby to me, while Libby tearfully complained to some invisible being whose head came up to Miss Diamond's hip, "I didn't do anything bad, but I get all the blame for nothing . . . and I told my mother . . . and my father hurt my sore arm . . . and my mother gave me the letter 'cause she's so sick . . . and I already stood in the corner yesterday . . . and my mother made me 'pologize to him even . . . 'snot fair . . . that's why I have to cry my eyes out . . ."

Miss Diamond left from foot-tapping and, kneeling in front of Libby, said, "All right, stop crying. We won't go to Mr. Pierce today."

"When will we go?" Libby asked untrustingly.

"The next time you are a bad girl."

"I won't be a bad girl." Libby became angelic, with tears.

"I hope not." Miss Diamond stood, returned to her desk and pulling down the sides of something under her dress, announced brightly, "Now let us have our collection show."

The unhappy wonder returned: Where was Johnny?

We were told to spread our collections out on our seats and if there wasn't enough room, on the floor.

We started with Leatrice Aronowitz's buttons, which were plain except for one she said her uncle had taken from a dead German during the war.

From there we went to Marcia Weissbaum's: straight pins, diaper pins, bobby pins, hairpins, needles of all lengths and her grandmother's cameo brooch, which she wouldn't let anyone but Miss Diamond touch.

Gazella Caccialanza brought a collection of pasta, uncooked. Each item was accompanied by a small card on which someone had written the name. Miss Diamond read them: "Occhi di lupo, ziti, mezzani, mostaccioli rigati, tufoli, fidelini, bucatini, gnocchi," but when she came to the one which she read as "farfalle," she picked up the little bow-shaped macaroni and asked Gazella if she was sure she had the correct name. Gazella replied that her father said it was and her father was always right.

From there we went to the match boxes, the rubber bands. Solly Mink couldn't spread out his collection. He had gathered leaves, but all he had now was a bagful of dried dust.

I lost interest in the collections and just tagged along as Miss Diamond crowed over the originality of Honora Wasserman's collection: chicken feathers.

Gerard Shuminsky could hardly keep his lower lip from quivering when Miss Diamond looked at his hundreds of gum wrappers and snorted that they were mostly from bubble gum.

About the only other specific comment she made was in reference to a black, twisted object in Libby's display of stones. Pointing to it, but from a distance, she asked Libby where she had found it.

"On the lots."

"I see," said Miss Diamond with a grimace of distaste. "Well, in the future, Libby, remember that everything hard is not necessarily stone." Libby said she would remember but her look stuck out its tongue.

I realized, after it was over, that there was no prize, not even a special prize. But I thought it useless to remind Miss Diamond; even if I had won, to whom would I show it?

After rest period, Miss Diamond waved the packet of seeds about as she explained the next project, but I was too busy listing the hazards that might have befallen Johnny. I went through all the home-confining illnesses, as well as falling down the steps, being hit by a car, bitten by a dog, kicked by the fruit peddler's horse, scratched by a rusty nail with resultant blood-poisoning, cut between thumb and forefinger and therefore lockjaw, falling where a cat had peed so his hand was burned off, falling down the coal chute, being kidnaped, caught by some kids and made to kiss the cross so that he could never talk again, breaking the Ten Commandments and falling in the sewer—

237

the possibilities were endless. The dismissal bell brought them to an end.

Mrs. Greneker was waiting for me, Mrs. Jackson for Libby.

Descending the steps—Libby and her mother had gone ahead—Mrs. Greneker said, "I'll tell you something very confidential. From climbing up and down steps, there are only two things can happen. One, I'll get a beautiful figure from the exercise, which is way out of the question. Or two, I'll get apoplexy and that will be the finish."

"The finish of what?" I asked.

"My finish. Whose finish did you think? Mrs. President Hoover's finish? I'll go caput, good-bye Mrs. Greneker, one, two, three."

I thought of her conversation with my father the night before. "Don't talk like that," I said.

"What shouldn't I talk like?"

"You're talking funnies."

"Listen to me, from apoplexy there's nothing funny."

"Do you die when you get it?"

She paused before answering, "Not always."

"Do men get it, too?"

"On apoplexy there is no exclusive. It's like voting in America, everybody has the opportunity."

"Me, too?"

"You got a long wait yet."

"How long?"

"Years and years and years and still more years." She waved her hand as if saying a regretful good-bye to time.

That evening my father asked if anything had happened at school.

I said the first thing that lurched into mind. "Johnny wasn't there. And I don't know why. Maybe something happened to him."

"You don't have to worry. He's all right."

"You know?"

He nodded. He went into the kitchen and came back holding a crumpled brown-paper bag. "Here," he said offering the bag to me, "it's yours."

I took it, opened its twisted top. Bottle caps!

But where had these come from? My mind had already begun to weave a dark answer.

I stared at them, didn't dare look up. I studied the fluted rims, the cork bellies, the specks and spots of color, and one that lay face upward, its paint rubbed off, empty.

"It's a present from Johnny," my father said.

"Don't he want them?" I asked, not needing an answer.

"Doesn't."

"Doesn't. Why didn't he give them to me?"

"He had to go somewhere."

"Where?"

"To a home."

"Whose home?"

"A home for children."

"Why couldn't he stay in his own home with his brother?"

"His brother went with him."

"He did?"

"Yes."

"Why did he have to go there with his brother?"

"Because their mother is sick."

"But isn't Mother making her better?"

"Yes. But until she is, Johnny and his brother are much better off in this children's home."

"They are?"

"Yes."

"Why didn't they come stay here like last time?"

"Because Mrs. Greneker isn't strong enough to take care of them."

"Did Peter and Martha have to go to a children's home when Mother went to Morris View to get me?"

"No."

"Why?"

"Because your grandmothers were here to take care of them."

"Both?"

"Yes."

"Why can't Johnny's grandmothers . . ." I didn't want to ask that question. I replaced it with, "Can I go to see Johnny in his new home?"

"Of course."

"Tomorrow?"

"Tomorrow is Saturday and the home is very religious. They don't allow visitors on Saturday."

"The next day, then?"

"Sure."

"Sure," I repeated. The word trickled away, leaving ache.

Mrs. Greneker came to bathe me. I thought she sloshed the water, rubbed the soap into the blue rubber sponge, more vigorously than before. When she stood me to wash my body, telling me to hold onto her shoulders so that I wouldn't slip, I saw the tears in her eyes.

"Why are you crying?"

"Who is crying?" She turned her head away slightly.

"You are."

"It's not so."

"Then why are your eyes wet like water?"

"Because I'm thinking."

"What?"

"I'm thinking that like everyone else, Mrs. Greneker is losing a job."

"What kind of a job?"

"The best job Mrs. Greneker ever had in her whole life. The best."

chapter 12

Usually Saturdays had a flavor all their own. With no school, with my father—more often than not—home, things happened at a deliciously slow pace.

This Saturday was different. Peter was already out of the room when I awoke. From another room came the sounds of housekeeping: a pillow being slapped back into shape; the trippity-tap of someone walking quickly, purposefully; the brittle clatter of a pan dropped; the faucet opened, the prattle of water, the faucet shut.

I wondered if one of my aunts had already come, or a neighbor. The possibility of its being a stranger made me take the precaution of robe and slippers.

The living room provided further evidence that this was no ordinary Saturday. Martha's bed had not only been made, but covered. There were no signs of my father's newspaper. His magazines had been neatly stacked on the shelf of the table next to his chair. Someone with an orderly hand had been through the room, and whoever it was, was now performing similar operations in the kitchen.

I went in, and found Martha.

"Well, if it isn't Mr. Rip Van Winkle himself," she said.

Her greeting was as surprising as her presence.

She stood in front of the drainboard, next to the sink, an orange . . . half an orange . . . in her hand, looking—for the first time to me—like my mother, and reminded me of that afternoon when we had all rushed in and found her there with an orange and that needle. . . .

"What are you doing?"

"What do you think I'm doing?" she replied, giving the orange-half an extra-hard twist on the glass reamer.

"Where's Peter?"

"In the bathroom . . . where he thinks he's going to spend the rest of his life." Then, shouting, "Peter, you're not fooling me. I know what you're doing in there. You're reading dirty books. And if you don't come out this minute, I'm going to bust!"

"Go ahead and bust," came Peter's unconcerned voice.

"Where's Daddy?" I asked.

"He went out. And don't ask me where, because I didn't ask him and he didn't tell me. But he's coming right back."

I noted that she took care of three questions with one stroke.

"You better tell Peter to get out of there," she said, "because I'm squeezing this for you. And you're not getting it till you brush your teeth and wash; and the longer it waits, the more vitamins and minerals it will lose." She poured the juice into a measuring cup.

"Why are you measuring it?"

"Because you're supposed to have six ounces."

"How do you know?"

"Because it says so in my domestic science class."

Peter came out smelling of Lilac Vegetal. "How does it look?" He beamed.

"What?" I asked.

Turning to Martha, he demanded, "Do you see any difference?"

"You look just as ugly as when you went in there twenty hours ago."

"I'm not kidding," Peter said earnestly, "don't you see anything different?"

Martha and I examined him carefully and shook our heads.

"You're both blind as bats. I just shaved!"

"With Daddy's razor?" Martha said with astonishment.

"What do you care with what? Don't you see the difference?"

"The same difference as if you shaved a watermelon," Martha declared, sounding, I thought, very much like my mother.

"I thought you were busting to get inside here," Peter shouted.

"You don't have to yell," Martha admonished. "The whole neighborhood doesn't have to know our business. Bobby," she said, "go ahead and wash yourself."

When I returned Martha asked me how I wanted my eggs.

"With their faces down," I said, thinking that having to turn the yolks without breaking them would be the most difficult test of her ability.

After serving the orange juice, which she had kept in the icebox, Martha took the frying pan, examined it for cleanliness, set it on the stove, turned on the flame, which she very carefully lowered, took out the large round butter dish, sneered at the large block in it and said, "I wish mother would stop being old-fashioned and would buy butter in cubes."

"Why?"

"They're easier to measure," she said, and digging out some butter the size of a walnut, popped it into the pan. She swished it around until it melted, and when it began to bubble she neatly broke in one egg, quickly took a fork and pulled the white immediately around it away from the yoke, repeated the procedure with the other egg, then taking the spatula in one hand and the pan handle in the other, she said, "One, two, three," and deftly flipped the eggs over and covered the pan with a plate.

Since my mother never covered eggs cooking in a pan, I questioned it.

"If the light gets at them while they cook," she said with assurance, "they can lose as much as, I think, forty-eight per cent of their Vitamin B$_2$."

"So, what's Vitamin B$_2$ good for?" Peter asked.

"I don't know," she said.

"So, you might as well lose it and save washing a plate."

"I don't have to worry about washing a plate because you're going to do the dishes," Martha announced.

"That'll be the big fat day—"

"That'll be this morning."

"Who said so?"

"Me—and Daddy."

"Since when?"

"Since last night when I told him that I would run the house for today and tomorrow."

"You're going to run *this* house?" he asked.

"You heard."

"I could run for president easier than you can run this house," Peter said. "Why, you don't even know . . . you don't even know how to get a run in your stocking. Not even that, you don't even know . . ."

During all this Martha hummed gaily, set up the metal toaster on the stove and placed a piece of toast against each of its sides.

They were still wrangling when my father arrived and settled the matter by saying that he and Martha had agreed last night that Peter would *help* with the dishes, but that if Peter didn't want to he would help himself. Peter's final disgruntled words to Martha as he took the towel were, "Well, at least you didn't win all the way."

As I left the building later that morning, I found Libby sitting on the stoop talking to a remnant of a doll.

"You got a face only a mother could love," she said, slapping the battered head. "And you wanna know where you were when God gave brains out? You were last in line, that's where. And just because you were so bad last night and ate so much radishes, you're so full of cockamamies and gas I'm gonna put you on your belly and bounce it out of you." She twisted the doll around and slapped it against her knees.

I continued down the steps. She called out teasingly, "I know something I bet you don't."

I kept walking.

She ran after me. "If I tell you what I know, will you play vegetable store with me?"

"No."

"Why?"

"Vegetable store's for girls."

"No it's not. Besides, it's about Johnny."

"What about him?"

"I'll tell you only if it's vegetable store."

The bait was too beautiful. "I don't want to play vegetable store."

"What will you play then?" She swung the doll by one leg.

"Nothing."

"I'm not telling nothing for nothing." She skipped back to the stoop.

It was tantalizing. Here, she knew something about Johnny, something perhaps very important. How could I find out without becoming enmeshed in her game? I didn't want to play games. But I had to find a way of learning what she knew. How?

The answer was back in our apartment. As I returned, I heard my father ask through the closed bathroom door, "Has someone been using my razor?"

"If you snitch, I'll break this plate on your head," Peter muttered to Martha.

I couldn't resist the impulse. "Not me, said the little bear."

"Shut up!" Peter hissed.

"I'm only playing the three bears," I said.

"Shut up, anyway."

I knocked on the bathroom door. My father asked, "Who is it?" and Peter whispered, "Are you going to tell him?" at the same time.

I replied, "It's me," to my father, and "No," to Peter.

"What do you want?"

"Can I ask you an important question?"

"Can't it wait?"

"Not too long."

He opened the door.

Peter gritted his teeth and made fists at me as I started to enter. I looked up. My father, his face lathered, was undressed. I stopped. I had never seen him before, I thought, without clothing. It was as if I had made a great mistake.

"Are you coming in? I can't keep the door open, come on."

I looked down and stepped into the room. It was difficult, strange, and I didn't want him to know I was ashamed. I turned and faced the window, studying it as if the pattern cut into the glass was of extreme interest.

Scritch-scratch went the sounds of his shaving. "I felt the same way when I first saw my father without clothes," he said.

My face grew warm, warmer.

"It's about time you realized that I'm human and not made out of salt water taffy. Turn around and sit down. You can watch me shave. It won't be as good a show as usual because someone's been fiddling around with my razor, but it's worth watching. Or if it bothers you too much, you can wait for me to come out."

I sat on the lowered toilet lid and concentrated on the furrows the razor plowed on the plains of his face, as I told him about myself and Libby, concluding with, "What shall I do?"

"What would you have done if I weren't home?"

"I would have thought very hard."

"And . . .?"

"And I would make her tell me."

"How?"

"I would play something but it wouldn't be vegetable store."

"I see," he said, scraping under his nose. "In other words, you would have given in."

"Yes," I was forced to admit.

"You don't sound as if you'd be happy about it, though."

"No."

"Well, don't you think before playing anything, you ought to try and determine whether what Libby has to tell you is that valuable?"

"Valuable like what?"

"Let me put it this way . . ." He took time to rinse his face. "What could Libby know about Johnny that you don't already know? For instance, you know that he and his brother are in a children's home. You know he is there because his mother is sick. You know that you are his best friend, because he gave you his bottle tops. And anything you don't know, you can ask him when you go to see him."

"But that's not until tomorrow and I want to know what she knows today."

"Then go play vegetable store," he said emphatically and stepped into the tub, pulling the shower curtain around him.

I left.

Libby was still on the stoop. "Listen here, you Selma you, when I say close your eyes and go to sleep, I mean it," she said, and smacked the doll's lolling head.

She looked up, started to speak, but I covered my ears with my hands and ran down the street shouting, "No! No! No!" and stopped only when I thought I had gotten away from her. But she was right behind me. "Your friend is in the ophan 'sylum," she yelled, and ran off.

I stood, numbed by her words, until one of the two moving men—those same men who carried out the belongings of evicted tenants and dumped them on the sidewalk—nudged me gently out of the way and clomped up the steps of The Flop Garden.

Libby's words still in my ears, I climbed partway up the adjoining building and sat, peering through the spiral-twisted bars of the banister.

An auto stopped in front of The Flop Garden. Mr. Fell got out and with a large metal key ring jangling in his hand, hastened up the steps. But he passed like a shadow against my thoughts of that darker than night, most terrible of all hells: the orphan asylum.

Had my father lied when he told me that Johnny and his brother had gone to a children's home? Was there no one I could believe? I tried to untwist the banister bars.

Someone stopped in front of the stoop and stared. I looked up only when I heard Carmella's, "Watchoo doing?"

"Nothing."

"How can you do nothing?"

"I'm doing it, that's all."

"You gotta be doing something."

"No I don't."

"You're talking to me, ain't you?"

I nodded.

"That's doing nothing?"

I wished she would go away.

"You want I should come sit down next to you so you can cry on my shoulder?" she asked. I wondered how she knew.

"No, I don't want to cry."

"You look like you're gonna flood the whole street. You listen to me, if you wanna cry, you better do it. If you don't you'll cry twice as much inside and then you'll drown from it."

So she, too, knew about inner eyes.

She sat down beside me. "Come on, tell Carmella what's hurting you so bad."

"Nothing, nothing's hurting me." I inched away.

"I'm giving you your last chance," she warned.

I began reluctantly, but after the first few sentences I described with relish the discrepancy between my father's and Libby's stories.

She listened attentively, even silently, until I had finished. "You know, I don't think I can be friends with you no more," she said with great seriousness.

"Why not?"

"Because birds of a feather stay together, and if I stayed with you I'm liable to become so stupid like you are."

"I am not stupid," I shouted indignantly.

"Oh no? Then how come you believe Libby, who's got a brain smaller'n a garbanzo, over your father, who's chief in a whole library and is one of the smartest people in the whole neighborhood? How come?"

I blushed.

"Besides," she went on, "you're stupid too because you don't know the difference between a children's home and an orphan asylum. 'Cause in a children's home they play games like Ring Aroun' a Rosie, and they sing "How Do You Do My Partner?" and eat lunch in the park like every day is Fourth of July except Sunday. *But* in an orphan asylum all the kids wear chains, and when they wanna eat they gotta stand around and hold up a little bowl and beg for it just like on the oatmeal box. Didja ever see the picture of the kid on the oatmeal box begging for a little bit of oatmeal?"

I said I hadn't.

"All right," she said decisively, "you stay here and I'll go get the oatmeal box that shows you how he looks." I promised to wait.

The moving men appeared carrying a small cabinet—one of its casters fell off as they came down the steps—a couple of chairs and a card table with the usual oilcloth cover.

They dropped things from their hands and backs like noncommittal shrugs.

A small, covered straw basket, the dead red color of an autumn leaf, rolled away. One of the men caught it and slammed it down on top of the cabinet.

The basket talked to me. It asked me to rescue it, to keep it from being sent to the orphan asylum for baskets. I promised it I would. Something had to be saved. Something!

I slipped down the steps, looked around carefully, not forgetting that there were eyes always watching; ran to the cabinet, jumped, grabbed the basket; then, hearing footsteps in the hallway, I hurried back to the stoop and sat with the basket behind me.

Mr. Fell came out of the building, sniffed the air and scurried away.

I turned my back to the rails and using my body as a shield, examined the oval beads sewed to its lid. One was a pale, summer-morning blue; another, like the clouded green of a playing marble; and a third, grape-purple. Attached to the center was a once-brass coin with a square-cut hole through which was drawn the glossy knot of a frizzled tassel. I knew at once what I would use it for: Johnny's bottle tops.

I heard the sound of a voice being cleared. Carmella! I slipped the basket behind me.

"Do you know what I am?" she asked, sounding as if she were mimicking my sister's actress-talk.

"A nice girl," I assured her.

"Don't give me any slop-silly, sugar-titty talk," she ordered. And asked again, "Do you know what I am?"

"No."

"I'm an Italian. Don't tell me you never heard people calling us Eyetalian?"

"I think so."

"You know so! And do you know why they call us Eyetalian? Because we got the best eyes of anyone in the whole world including everybody. And with my own eyes I saw a certain glom rat steal something from off these poor people's last things they have in the world. So stop acting like a saint before breakfast and hand it over."

Guiltily I sought an alibi that would rescue me. It came—not as a discovery, but as if it had been seeded in me all the time and had sprouted when the climate was right. "But I didn't take it to steal it, honest!"

"Oh no?"

"No."

"Then why? I double-dare you to tell me why."

"I took it, and when those men aren't looking I was going to bring it back to the poor family and put it in their house."

"You were?" She looked, sounded, dubious.

"Honest."

"How were you going to do it? Just show me. I'd like to see how."

The men flung down some rolled mattresses on the sidewalk and went back into the building.

"Come," I said to Carmella, "watch me."

Taking the basket, and with Carmella behind me, I followed them into the hall and hid in the area known as "under-the-steps" where baby carriages and bikes were usually left. We crouched and listened for their sounds, and when they became opaque, telling me that they were outdoors, we slipped out and ran up the steps to the second floor. An open door indicated the apartment.

I ran in, pushed the basket under a washtub in the kitchen, ran out.

Carmella started to go down but I caught her coat sleeve, motioned that I thought we should go up the steps, where we huddled on the halfway landing.

The men thumped up the steps. As soon as they were in the apartment, we descended carefully and ran out of the building.

"You know what?" Carmella said, her eyes victorious, "I got the biggest idea. It's so big it won't even fit in my whole head."

"What?" I asked, dimly fearful I knew what it was.

"Let's do it some more."

Before I could argue, she forced a nest of battered aluminum pans into my hands, took a large glassless frame containing the hand-colored photograph of an old woman with an idiotic left eye and a white scarf folded around her head.

We hurried to our hiding place under the steps. The men came down, we ran up.

In the middle of our third trip, while hiding on the halfway landing, we heard one of the movers say, "Hey, I thought I took this picture down once before."

"Maybe the old gal got cold outside and came back to warm up," the other mover jested.

The fourth trip. I dragged a pillowcase bulked with kitchen utensils. A hand chopper cut its way out of the slip, fell to the steps ringing, resounding. The noise was unexpected, frightening. We didn't take time to stash the things we carried but dropped them just inside the apartment door and fled up the steps.

The men returned. They whispered as they trudged down the steps, and we followed, hid. The men stomped up the steps. We ran out.

"No more," I told Carmella.

"Come on, don't be a yellow-belly. Don't you want to drive them crazy? Let's. Just one more time."

"No."

"Okay then, go ahead, be a wax nose. I'll do it myself."

She hoisted a sackful of clothing, the weight of which sent her reeling backward, and doubling to counter it, she stumbled forward. A long, rolled, pink object fell from the bundle. I picked it up, tried to push it back into the mouth of the sack.

"What the cripesake you doing?" Carmella asked.

"I'm trying to push it back. It fell out." As I went around to show her, I saw one of the men standing on the top of the stoop, watching.

"Run, Carmella," I shouted, and darted off.

"Hey you!" the man shouted.

Was he chasing me or Carmella? I turned in my flight. She had dropped the bundle, was halfway across the street. The long pink thing I still held fell open, and I tripped over the flapping ends of a large corset.

I felt myself being lifted. The corset dropped from my grasp.

"So you're the little devil!" he said.

From his face, his voice, I knew he wasn't really angry. From the way he held me, lightly shook me, I guessed it was only to frighten me. "What kind of a game d'you think you're playing?"

The word *sorry* had hardly left my throat when I heard a shriek. "Meh harget a Yiddish kind! Helf! Police!" a woman screamed from a window.

Another voice, shrill: "They're beating up a kid . . . a Jewish kid! Help! Help!"

Windows flew open. "Who's killing?" "What's happening?" "That murderer!" "What murderer?" "The one throwing out the furniture . . ."

And above it the first voice rode again, strident and terrible, "Meh harget a Yiddish kind! Helf!"

The man held me, turned a dumb look upward as more windows opened. Heads flashed out. Doors flew open. People ran. Someone yelled, "POLICE!"

As if in a kaleidoscope, I saw Mr. Fisher; Mr. Calabrese, a hair clipper held above his head; Mrs. Greneker, her face flashing fear; Mr. Goodman running, rolling a newspaper in his hands; faces; Mrs. Weissbaum, holding, pulling Marcia. Then, a snort of animal fury.

Carmella, her eyes a frenzy, threw herself at the man who held me, no longer at arm's length but pressed to his chest as if for protection, I heard the rip of his shirt as Carmella's fingernails raked down his back and she screamed, "*Let him go!*"

"Jes*us*!" he hissed, but didn't turn.

The other moving man was at his side, and with a shove of his forearm sent Carmella sprawling.

She rolled over like a cask, pushed herself up, all the time raving, "He tried to kill him. I saw. I was right here. He chased him. He grabbed him. He was going to choke him to death. I saw. I swear!"

"POLICE!" a woman's voice lacerated the air.

I was pulled from the man, tucked like a parcel under someone's arm.

"Take it easy. Nothing to go runnin' off at the mouth about," said Libby's father. It was he who held me. With his free arm, he elbowed the moving man. "What'cha try to do with this kid?"

The man began to explain. Carmella threw herself between them, hysterically. "Do something to 'im, Mr. Jackson, murder 'im, lynch 'im, skin 'im alive." Then, to the crowd, "What are you all standing around doing nothing for? Why?"

Mr. Jackson turned to push her away, and now I heard other voices, wondering, frightened women's voices:

"Who is it?" "It's the Hirshman's baby." "What happened?" "Who knows?" "Where's his mother?" "She's taking care of the one that's

253

dying." "Which one that's dying?" "In The Poorhouse. The top floor." "I didn't know there was someone dying there." "You shouldn't know from it. It's hopeless." "A Jewish woman?" "What else?" "Terrible."

I saw her running. Like fire before wind. Her face ran; her hair ran. She pushed people out of her way. Her eyes were overwhelmed.

She tore me from the arm that held me, clutched me, pressed, buried me to her. "Are you all right? Tell me. Are you all right? Did he hurt you? Tell me! Tell me!"

I heard her words. They were extinguished by the voices: "The one that's dying." "Which one that's dying?" "In The Poorhouse. The top floor." "A Jewish woman?" "Terrible."

"Bobby? Bobby? What's the matter? Are you hurt?"

"No." It was an answer to her, and to all questions. The sum of everything: No!

A woman: "Where's a cop?"

Another woman: "Go find! You could find a job quicker than a cop."

Carmella: "You're all a bunch of scared chicken-hearts. There ain't one man in the whole crowd with guts!"

Her father: "Every time you open da mouth, you open up my grave. Shud op!"

Mrs. Greneker: "How is he?"

My mother: "He seems to be in a kind of shock."

Mrs. Greneker: "Give him a little slap. It will help him come to."

I said, "No."

A woman: "That man's back is bleeding."

Another woman: "Let it. Better from him than from one of ours."

Mr. McClure: "All right, break it up."

A woman: "Finally, he's here. By popular demand."

Another woman: "I can smell the booze from here."

Carmella: "Mr. McClure! Mr. McClure! I saw it all happen. I was with him. The man tried to beat him up, even kill him."

Mr. McClure: "Take it easy, Carmella. Just take it easy."

254

Carmella: "Ask him yourself. I saved his life!"

Mr. McClure: "Hello, Mrs. Hirshman. How is he?"

My mother: "I don't know. He seems dazed."

Mr. McClure: "Hey, Bobby Shaftoe. Did the man hurt you?"

I said, "No."

Carmella: "It's a lie! I saw it with my own two eyes. I tell you if it wasn't for me, he'd be a dead bambino with a broken neck, maybe more."

Mr. McClure: "Rest your face, Carmella."

He walked to where the two men stood surrounded by the crowd, and Carmella, flinging words like grenades, followed. Mr. McClure spoke to the moving man who had caught me, but I couldn't hear. They were too far away, the noise of the crowd was too close, but nothing was louder than those words: "The one that's dying." "Terrible."

The man turned his back to Mr. McClure, and I saw the signs of Carmella's passion, bloody welts on his skin.

Carmella yelled, "You lie in your dirty black mouth. You were shaking his head off."

"Shud op!" her father warned.

She bared her teeth at him, went on to tell Mr. McClure her version of what had happened, referred to herself as Joan of Arc, Robin Hood, several saints.

Mr. McClure tried getting the moving men into the building where they had been working, but the crowd wouldn't let them pass. He ordered them to make way. The men, the sad men who had hung around day after day with their weary cigarettes, in their weary groups, moved forward, their faces like fists.

He shook his stick at them. Their faces became tighter. They settled their bodies into the ground like telephone poles. He shouted, asked them if they were all crazy. None replied, none moved.

Finally, Mr. McClure turned to the moving men and whispered, walked with them toward the corner. He looked back once. The men were set cement.

My mother quickly wheeled me away as if she didn't want me to see any more. Followed by Mrs. Greneker, she carried me into our building. In my room, she sat me on my bed, opened my coat, tugged it off, and searched my face. "Is anything wrong?" I shook my head. "Does anything hurt?" "No." "Shall I call Dr. Reuben?" *"No!"*

"Is that all you can say?" she asked. Worry, exasperation, dappled her face.

Martha, who had been craning and peering, trying to see around Mrs. Greneker, asked, "What happened?"

My mother looked up at her, "Where have you been?"

"Right here," Martha replied.

"Doing what?"

"Cleaning and cooking and things."

My mother looked at Mrs. Greneker. "She cooks healthy," Mrs. Greneker said.

"What does that mean?" Martha marshaled offenses.

"It means," said Mrs. Greneker, "that you know more about it than me."

"Oh, I don't know," said Martha sheepishly.

"Where's your father?" my mother asked.

"He said he had to go to the library for a few minutes and that he'd be back in time for dinner. I'm serving at two sharp."

"And Peter?"

Martha exclaimed, "How should I know?"

"All right," said Mrs. Greneker, nudging Martha from the room, "let's see how you're heating up dinner without losing a penny's worth of minerals."

"Tell me," my mother said when we were alone, "forgetting what just happened, have you been a good boy?"

"Sure."

"Just *sure*," she asked. "What became of the per cent system? You couldn't have been one hundred per cent good." I had forgotten that method of measuring my behavior.

"According to Carmella's radio station, that man tried to hurt you.

Is that true?"

The words were slow, as I told her what had happened.

"But," she said when I had finished, "he could have hurt you, couldn't he?"

I nodded. She looked at me as if trying to read behind my eyes, and sighed.

The women's voices whirled. A solid circle of sound, no beginning, no end. My mind slid back to the night I had heard her tell my father about Johnny's mother. All the way back to then. How could I ask her? She sat beside me, eagerly wanting something from me, anything. But how could I ask her if mothers ever died?

"A full heart has no voice, has it?" she asked. "I think this is the first time I have nothing to say to you but those same three words."

"What three words?"

"If you have to ask, it wouldn't help if I told you."

"Why?"

"Because they aren't words for the ear, they're for right here." She touched my chest.

I felt imprisoned. I had to free myself by saying something. Noticing that she was thinner than even before, I asked, "Do you eat a lot of deli over there?"

"Deli? Why deli?"

"Because you once told Martha that Jean Harlow keeps her figure and she only eats pastrami."

She half-smiled. "Did you really believe that?"

"I always believe you."

"Always?" she asked, her mouth crisping its corners.

I had been caught. Ashamed, I complicated my agony by wishing that she would go, but when she stood I began a frantic search for a way to detain her. I found none. She bent, kissed the top of my head and said, "It won't be long before I'll be home to stay. God willing, it won't be long."

She walked out and I heard her say: "Greneker, I'm going to sue you for alienation of affection. What have you done to him? I expected kisses, instead I got a shoulder as cold as a miser on Friday."

"That's the way it goes," said Mrs. Greneker, "you turn around for one minute and when you turn back, they're grown up."

"Grown up?" my mother remonstrated. "He's only five."

"The heart doesn't know from calendars," said Mrs. Greneker. "Did I ever tell you about my brother Chaim, he's dead now, he should rest in peace. It was in my town on the night of the first seder. We were all ready to sit down by the table, when all of a sudden my cousin runs in and tells us there is a pogrom going on right in the next town. I was only six years old, but I remember like it was yesterday. So my father put out all the lights in the house, and they locked the doors and pushed furniture against them. And the children they sent to hide in the cellar. So me and my sister and another brother hid ourselves under a big pile of straw in the corner. But Chaim—and he was only four years old, mind you—had to see what was happening. There was like a little window in the cellar, so that you should be able to look out on the street. And no matter how we begged him, Chaim wouldn't leave that window.

"We heard the screaming and the begging and the crying and the calling for help. We hung on to one another and shivered like leaves. It was so terrible that even if I should live to one hundred and twenty, I will not forget one second of it.

"When it was all over, my mother came down to us. She said that we couldn't have a seder because my father was out helping some neighbors, and she told us to take a little something to eat and go straight upstairs to bed with no lights because they might come back.

"I got up the next morning because my mother gave such a scream from downstairs, I thought someone was trying to kill her. I ran down in my nightgown with no shoes, nothing. And there was Chaim. His hair was white like a pigeon. And it happened overnight, just like that. And he didn't grow old only on the outside, it was on the inside, too. From that day he was an old man. He died from t.b. when he was sixteen. But he looked and acted like a man from seventy-five. So, you see, it has nothing to do with how old they are. Nothing, at all."

I stood on my bed to see my face in the mirror over the chest. My hair hadn't turned white, but it might overnight.

I heard my mother kiss Martha, thank her for helping; then something said to Mrs. Greneker; then her steps rapidly departing . . . departing. And the little hand inside me tightened, closed to keep her from going. The door opened; and the cry flew out of me, a wild bird escaping, "Mother, don't!"

I jumped from the bed, ran into the living room and into her body, waiting.

We wept.

Slowly, she walked me back to my room, sat, lifted me into her lap and gently rocking, she hummed my good-night song, but the voices, the women's voices, frayed the fabric of the music.

I awoke to familiar sounds, kitchen sounds, the radio lilting faintly. I didn't remember who had undressed me, had folded back the bed and had covered me, but I knew. "I'm up," I called.

" 'Oh, say can you see by the dawn's early light,' " Martha piped.

I padded through the living room into the kitchen.

The table sparkled with the old punchbowl as centerpiece, flanked by the brass candlesticks; the plates glistened; the cloth napkins were smooth as smiles; the silver plate shone.

"What's it for?" I asked.

"A meal should be inviting to the eye as well as the stomach," Martha recited.

"When are we going to invite it?"

Martha checked the clock. "In about twenty minutes. I'm serving two o'clock on the dot. And I'm not going to wait for anyone who's late, including Daddy."

Then, "Martha?"

"What?"

"Can I ask you a question?"

"Yes. But not a long one. I have to slice the radish to go with the calves' brains."

Quickly, timidly, I asked, "Do you think mothers can die?"

She looked vaguely around before saying, "Of course. Why should God play favorites?"

It wasn't the answer I hoped for or understood, but then it was only my sister. I told her I was going out.

"No you're not."

"You're not my boss."

"No, but I'm your sister. And it's my job to see that you don't get into any more trouble. Besides, Mother said you weren't to go out until Daddy came home."

"Why?"

"I'll die if you ask me another question."

"No you won't."

"Yes I will."

"Why?"

She shook her head briskly, chortled, and slumping over the drainboard, announced, "I'm dead."

"Good," I said, and left for my mother's room. I drew the chair up to the window and looked out.

The evicted family's possessions were no longer on the sidewalk, so I supposed they had already been removed. In their place, the men stood about in nervous huddles, examining cigarettes awkwardly, glancing up the street. Some sat or sprawled lazily on the steps of The Flop Garden, but like strangers, with furtive eyes.

Carmella busily marched from one cluster to the next, stopping to pound an angry fist into the cup of her hand, pointing an operatic finger first to one corner, then the other, throwing her arms wide and slapping them back across her bosom as if in this one motion she had captured all her enemies and had crushed them. The men ignored her.

Mrs. Weissbaum sauntered by casually, nodding to the men as she passed. When Marcia ran up to her, she gesticulated vociferously and slapping her behind, pushed her back toward their building.

Men drifted from one group to another.

Martha came into the room and peered out the window. "Anything happening?" she asked.

"What's supposed to happen?"

"Nothing, but in this crazy neighborhood, who can tell?" She left before I could ask another question.

I pushed up the window slightly to hear. The silence roared. Then all at once, heads cocked, shoulders drew back, faces hardened. The men drew together in the doorway of the building.

An official black car drew up in front of The Flop Garden. Its doors opened and four uniformed men got out. A police wagon followed cautiously behind.

The uniformed men brushed their clothes, reset their caps on their heads, looked at watches, pulled down their jackets, jerkily, nervously. When they seemed to have run out of gestures, they advanced, first slowly but after a few steps with greater resolution, on The Flop Garden stoop in front of which the men had become a boulder of faces and bodies.

One of the uniformed men, his hair gleaming white from under his cap, made a long, wide imperial gesture—the Lord parting the Red Sea—but the men moved closer together.

The officer turned to his colleagues, his shoulders slightly hunched, and then facing the stoop once more, raised a warning finger and like a diver, plunged into the body of men and tried to push himself through.

Hands shoved him back. His cap fell to the sidewalk.

Without warning, a squad of police erupted from the rear of the wagon. The four officers drew aside as if inviting their men to the attack.

A woman screamed.

From the stoop came a babel of thuds, slaps, cracks, yells, curses. The men fell back under the initial charge, but ferociously held onto their assaulters, hugging them as in an insane dance, to try to prevent them from swinging their clubs.

A man swerved, eluding the blow of a nightstick; crouching, he flung himself forward, rammed the cop's side and sent him crashing against a telephone pole. With his free hand he tore the club away; the cop sank and the man ran back to the melee.

Libby's father, his arms bearlike, waved a cop to come closer, feinted the swinging club and then fell unexpectedly to the ground, butted his opponent's stomach with his head, reared upward, pitched him backward, jumped on him, pinned his arms, twisted the stick out of his hand, cracked his head. And left the body lying.

I watched him, fascinated by his speed, his agility. One moment here, another there, jabbing a face with his fist, smashing ahead with the club, never hesitating. Then, turning from the free-for-all, he systematized his movements. He would come up from behind, crack the stick over a cop's heels, and when the off-balanced victim turned he'd swing it up under his chin. He decorated the sidewalk with crumpled heaps of blue.

Carmella was like a drunkard in a saloon. She would hurl herself into wherever the fighting was thickest, only to be heaved out a moment later. Once she emerged with a piece of cloth between her teeth, which she spat out, and ran back in. Another time she came out holding a hand over an eye and wearing an expression of abused innocence but a moment later dashed back, flinging her arms like mallets.

Mrs. Weissbaum appeared, with the American flag again pinned to the breast of her coat, and holding a carpet sweeper aloft. She sidled hesitantly to the edge of the fracas and seeing a police-capped head, brought the sweeper down with all her strength, then, looking amazed but pleased at what she had done, ran off dragging her weapon behind her.

Mr. McCarthy, who had been holding the top of the stoop as if playing King of the Mountain, was engaged in battle with a clubless policeman. Nobly and elegantly he searched for an opening while the cop bounced nervously, pawed the air with his left hand. Somebody hit the policeman over the head, but before he fell Mr. McCarthy's fist shot out, hit and flew back, all the while maintaining his form.

Once again Libby's father became the focus of my attention. I watched him being dragged away from the stoop by two policemen while a third ran behind and pummeled his head with a club. He writhed, strained like a chained Samson, refused to submit to the pounding. Mrs. Weissbaum came to aid him with her carpet sweeper, but one push from a policeman sent her scurrying off.

Carmella rushed in, fell to her knees, sank her teeth into a policeman's calf. He kicked her way, she bit his other leg. He mule-kicked her. She tumbled, got to her knees, held her stomach and with a look of embarrassed surprise, vomited.

A slim, tall man with a felt hat ran up behind the cop wielding the club over Libby's father, threw his arm around his neck, pulled him back and grabbing his stick, flicked the cap off and brought the stick down across the side of the policeman's head.

The others dropped Libby's father like a bloody pillow and turned to the newcomer.

One raised his club like the hooded lady on the Bon Ami label; the other held his in two hands like a baseball bat. Flinging his arm over his left shoulder, the man let the stick flash forward. It grazed the nose of the baseball player and crashed into the face of the Bon Ami lady; blood muddied his mouth.

But the man didn't stop. His stick boomeranged and collided with the side of the other policeman's head, which seemed to give that one pause; he dropped his club, went to the edge of the curb, sat and held his head.

The man pushed the hat back on his head. It was my father!

Amazement brought me to my feet on the chair. I called, waved.

Now he knelt in front of the half-conscious Mr. Jackson, tried to pull him away. The policeman with the bloody mouth had come up quickly from behind, when our window flew open and Martha—I didn't know she was there—screamed, "Daddy, look out!"

Whether or not he heard, he looked up, quickly rolled over on his back, pulled back his knees and shot them into the cop's stomach.

He could fight! My father could fight! I pounded the window.

He was now at Mr. Jackson's side, straining in an attempt to move him. Then, before I could tell it was going to happen, a policeman swatted the back of his neck. His hand flew to where he had been hit and he sank to both knees.

Martha and I were out of the house screaming, "Daddy! Daddy!"

We had fought our way through the crowd of frightened spectators when a hand and voice stopped me. "Stay here, Mr. Troublemaker," Mrs. Greneker commanded, and pulled me back.

Meanwhile Martha had reached my father, only to be told by my mother, who was rubbing his neck, to go back.

From seemingly nowhere, a tidal wave of boys appeared. They inundated the stoop, kicking, lashing, swinging bags filled with water. Peter climbed a policeman's back as if it were a wall, straddled it, stuck his fingers in the man's eyes, jumped off. Libby's brother lassoed a policeman's neck with his belt, pulled it tight and dragging him backward, jumped on his stomach.

Others bounded like flying squirrels, darted in and out of the fracas and then, following some mass instinct, withdrew to prepare for another onslaught.

But though they attacked again and again, and though it had seemed in all the battles I watched that the men were victorious, there were barely ten of the thirty left. And those the police had managed to back up the stoop and into the hallway.

When the last defender had been pushed inside, a voice roared, "THROW!" Pots, pans, dishes, pails, the back of a chair, a chamber pot, a hot-water bottle, light bulbs, the handlebars of a bicycle, the steering mechanism of a sled, and a shower of nails, screws, nuts, bolts and carpet tacks poured from The Flop Garden's windows.

The sudden storm forced the police down from the stoop, allowing the men to rush out of the hallway. But before long again they had to give ground.

Again the voice bellowed, "THROW!" and "LOOK OUT BELOW!" Everyone looked up. A steamer trunk teetered on the edge of the roof and as people screamed, came down in a flat dead fall. It hit the sidewalk in front of the stoop, stood like a man stunned and then burst apart.

The police, who had cringed against the doorway, looked at each other as if personally offended, as if the other side had resorted to unfair tactics. At a brisk sign from the white-haired officer, they collected their maimed and unconscious and hauled them back to the wagon. The officers got into their car and drove away, the wagon tailing closely behind.

Slowly the door of the Flop Garden opened. Mr. McCarthy put out his head, beckoned to the others inside and they came out. Seeing that car and wagon were gone, they walked jauntily down the steps and to the aid of their wounded.

I slipped out from under Mrs. Greneker's clutch and ran to my father. "I didn't know you could fight," I shouted as I came up to where he and my mother were sitting on the edge of the curb.

"Didn't you know his real name is 'Black' Jack Pershing?" my mother asked. He winked at me.

Martha, Mrs. Greneker, Peter came, all asking over and over if he was all right. If he was sure. If he wasn't just saying so.

From the colony that had formed around Mr. Jackson, there trumpeted a scream, "He's dead and I'm finished!" Libby's mother, with one hand on her head, the other pointing at the sky, while Libby held fearfully onto the hem of her coat, wandered as in sleepwalking and raved, "They have murdered him! They have taken the life of my husband! Women! it is over with him. And it is the end for me, and for my children. Where shall we go? What shall we do? I will go in the streets, in rags. I will beg food for my children. But for myself, there is nothing. Women! there is nothing! They have taken your husbands' jobs away. Now they have taken my joy away.

"Libby, go up and get the whitest sheet out of the closet, bring it down so we can cover your dead father so that no one will have to look at his poor, bleeding face. It is enough they will have to see my sorrow."

Libby clutched her mother's coat desperately. The men who were able flocked to Mr. Jackson's side, while the women tried to console his wife. I followed my father.

"Women, listen to me! Listen to a widow whose husband's body is still warm, his blood is still fresh on the stones." Mrs. Jackson brushed away my mother's hand. "Listen to what I have to tell you. Today it is my husband. Tomorrow it will be yours . . ."

A murmuring of, God forbid, filtered through the crowd.

"Today they tried to evict a family, so our husbands fought. But they will be back tomorrow and tomorrow and the day after until we are all in the streets. Women! the dream is over. America the beautiful is dead. If they don't murder you they'll starve you. Women, let the ground open up before us so that we can disappear into it. The suffering is too much."

I crouched next to my father, half watching Libby's mother and half looking on as my father felt Mr. Jackson's pulse.

His head moved. One eye opened. With a feeble motion he told my father to come closer. "Tell her she can stop already," he muttered. "She woke up the dead."

An ambulance arrived and the intern was led immediately to Mr. Jackson. As he knelt, dexterously adjusted his stethoscope, pushed it under the layers of Libby's father's clothes, peeled his eye back like the skin of a red onion, we heard the voice of Mr. McClure: "Stand back, folks. Let the man do his job." He elbowed a path for himself. People looked at him as if he were a bad debt.

Where has he been? The question whipped from mouth to mouth. Mr. McClure must have heard. He bent his head, muttered, "Excuse me," to the few still in his way and busied himself officially with taking down the intern's report.

Mrs. Jackson, oblivious to what was going on, continued her soliloquy. "God, be merciful, take me too. Don't leave me here to suffer to the end of my days. Answer my prayers. For once, give me my wish, I beg You. I am a good woman, a good wife, a good mother. You always take the good first, why not me? You didn't make this world for the good, only for the evil. Why leave me in it? Why? Why?"

The intern walked up to her. "Look, lady," he said tapping her arm, "there's no need to carry on like this. He's okay. Just a slight concussion. Nothing to worry about. Absolutely nothing."

Mrs. Jackson turned puzzled eyes to him. "Nothing?"

"He'll be fit as a fiddle in a day or two." The intern was all assurance, all authority.

"My husband, a fiddle?" she asked as if awakening. The intern left to attend to the others.

Mrs. Jackson turned to my mother, complained, "So if there was nothing wrong with him, why didn't he say so instead of letting me make such a damned fool of myself?" Taking Libby's hand and with lowered head, she hurried across the street and into the building.

The intern was examining my father. "They must've been told to take it easy," he said. "There isn't a serious case in the lot. You should see what's left over when they have a go at the commies. It's almost impossible to tell whose brains belong to who."

"No wonder I lasted as long as I did," my father observed.

Mrs. Mink was giving homemade shlivovitz to those able to swallow it, and offered some to my father. He thanked her, refused it.

She then went to the groaning Carmella, who begged for some. Mrs. Mink looked dubious, but then with a shrug indicating that perhaps it would be all right in view of the emergency, she poured a little into the thermos cup. Carmella gulped its contents, shot stricken eyes upward, clutched her throat and screamed. The intern went to her aid. My mother, who had been watching Carmella, nudged Mrs. Greneker and said, "I don't know why, but I can't help liking her." Mrs. Greneker responded with a terse, "I can."

We were on our way back to our building when everyone's attention turned to another black car, progressing slowly up the street. On its side was: "SOCIETY OF THE DAUGHTERS OF REBECCA." It stopped in front of The Poorhouse.

"Already?" Mrs. Greneker asked with more sadness than surprise.

"They said they'd send some of their members to stay with her," my mother answered.

"Now, they can't do enough."

"I'd better let them in. I have the key." My mother hurried up to the car and with a motion for them to follow, led the women who had emerged, up the steps.

Once upstairs, Martha took over nursing my father. She forgot about the minerals and vitamins and that the dinner had turned cold—although she did ask him to look at the table and to see how pretty it was. She chipped ice from the block in the box, rolled yards of bandage gauze into a pad, and despite his protests that he was fine sat my father on the couch and applied ice-packs to his head.

Peter arrived, aglow with triumph and swearing he was so hungry he could even eat her food. "Serve yourself," she said.

He turned the jets under all the pots and sat down at the table. "Did you see Daddy fight? He was great, wasn't he?"

I nodded.

"Did you see me?"

I nodded.

"How was I?"

"Stinky. You ran away before they could hit you."

"Well, you got one great, big hell of a nerve."

"I do?"

"You bet your sweet patootie you do. After all, it was all your cockeyed fault the whole thing started."

"It was not."

"It was so. You don't think they had a fight just to keep the cops from taking those few rotten pieces of junk from that apartment. The people don't even live there anymore. It was all because of you."

"No, it wasn't."

"It was all because you didn't have enough brains to get away from that dumb lummox in time. So it's your fault that Daddy's in there with a crack on his head, and Mr. Jackson's in the hospital. You and that nut factory, Carmella."

I left the kitchen and went to my room, sunk into further wretchedness over the thought that the fight had been not for me, but because of me; that I was alone on my side with no hurrays for me. I wandered back to that seemingly long ago when Johnny and I had first sat on the steps and he had told me about the jelly beans, and I wondered if he had felt even then as I felt now, and what his feelings were in the children's home—or was it really an orphan asylum, Carmella notwithstanding? I decided then I would not ask my father about it, but would test him and wait to see if he would take me there the next day as he had promised, without my having to remind him.

My mother arrived, asked Martha to go to the kitchen, she wanted to talk to my father. Martha left, saying, "Everything in this house is secrets." I crawled to the half-closed door.

"You won't have to borrow the money, after all," I heard her say.

"How come?" my father asked.

"I just found out from those women sent by the Daughters of Rebecca that they're more than just a home—they're mainly a society. I should have known, because when Jeanette told me that she wanted to be next to her mother, I asked her where it was. She told me to get in touch with the Daughters of Rebecca. Now I know why they were willing to take the children. You see, Jeanette's mother belonged to their society. She once bought a triple grave through them and the price of the grave includes the entire funeral except for . . ."

I clapped my hands over my ears.

chapter 13

After lunch on Sunday my mother said she had to go across the street "for a few minutes," Martha informed no one in particular that she and Henrietta were going to the movies, and Peter merely left.

I waited for my father to say something about visiting Johnny. He sat behind a wall of newspaper.

After forever, during which I coughed, cleared my throat, blew my nose, he lowered his paper and said, "How would you like to go for a walk?"

"Where?"

"St. Ursula's park."

He had forgotten. Or, even worse, he had never meant to take me to see Johnny. And I knew why—because it really was an orphan asylum.

"Why?"

"For one thing it's a beautiful day. It's Sunday. Besides, I have an experiment I'd like to try there."

"What's a speriment?"

"I want to test something."

"What?"

"Do you want to go or don't you?"

I considered it. Maybe the test had something to do with visiting Johnny. "All right." We put on hats, coats and left.

Girls were playing potsy, boys were playing stickball, women stood in little groups. The few men who were about looked satisfied. It was as if there had never been a yesterday.

We walked to the park in silence, the only exchange being when he took my hand crossing a street and I took it back on the other side. At the gate to the park, he asked if I wanted a bag of peanuts to feed the squirrels.

"No."

"Where's the 'thank you'?"

"No, thank you."

"You're welcome. I can use the nickel."

I reached into my pocket and felt the nickel in the envelope. I was certain I would never, never use it.

The park was alive with delights. Old men sat in the sun, children ran across the great cupped lawns, their mothers calling—always the mothers calling—lovers ambled, arms around each other.

The calliope wheezed, and the little band in the gray wood summer-house thumped and brayed. Footballs rocketed the sky, soccer balls rose like temporary moons, baseballs challenged birds. We walked the heaved and rutted lanes that wound meandering, making way for a jutting rock or the presence of a thick tree. A man passed and patted my head.

"Why did he do that?" I asked.

"He thinks you're a good boy," my father replied.

"He doesn't know me."

"You remind him of a boy he knows."

"Why doesn't he pat his head?"

"Because it's the boy he once was."

I didn't understand, didn't want to. "How far are we walking?"

"Until we come to a place that's right for my experiment."

"Where is it?"

"I'll know when we come to it."

A girl with silver-blonde hair in braids ran by, stopped, hopped on one leg, bellied her tongue at me and then ran off.

"Do I remind her of someone, too?" I asked.

"Of the man she wants to marry."

"With that face?"

"I thought she was very pretty."

"She looks like her mother hates her."

"Well, there's no accounting for taste."

We left the center of the park to where people were fewer, the grass mossier, brighter.

"Here's the place," my father announced.

I looked at the grassy semicircle framed by the path and on three sides by overgrown scarlet firethorn. "It is?"

"It's perfect. I couldn't have found a better place if I had made it myself."

"You couldn't?"

"Do you always do that?" he asked.

"What?"

"If somebody says, 'Here it is,' do you always ask, 'It is?' And then if they say, 'I couldn't have found a better place,' do you always ask, 'You couldn't?' "

"I don't know. Do I?"

"Never mind." He took a ball from his pocket.

"That's my ball."

"It's all right. I'm sure I paid for it."

"What are you doing with it?"

"I'm going to bounce it off your head if you don't stop asking questions."

"You will?"

"Stop that! Now, do you know how to play catch?"

I nodded, thought it a poor substitute for his broken promise.

"All right. You stand over there." He held the ball in the cup of his hand until I reached my position. With an underhand throw, he tossed it to me.

I held out my hand, but kept looking at him. The ball fell in front of me and rolled.

"I thought you said you knew how to play catch."

"I do."

"Don't you know you're supposed to keep your eye on the ball? All right, throw it back." He caught it. "Let's try again."

He threw it. I made an attempt to catch it, but it bounced off one of my knuckles.

"Throw it back," he ordered.

"I don't want to play catch," I called.

"Not with me, anyway," he added.

I knew the words were mine. I threw the ball, intentionally aimed it away from him, but he lunged, caught it. His ability defeated me.

"You want to try it again?" he asked.

I didn't answer. He tossed the ball, I made no move. Without a word, he walked to where the ball lay, pocketed it.

"Let's go." He held out his hand. I put mine in my pocket.

He began to walk, but not the way we had come. I followed until we reached the high black gates of a side exit.

"Aren't we going home?" I asked.

"Is that where you want to go?"

I wouldn't tell him. I had vowed it.

"Don't tell me," he said, after a moment, "that you really wanted me to take you to Johnny all the time?"

"You promised."

"I know, but you haven't mentioned it since."

"I thought you didn't want to take me."

"I thought you had changed your mind about going."

"I didn't."

"Let's go then."

I put my hand in his, hoping he wouldn't drop it.

We went through streets that were foreign to me, but he seemed to know them without hesitation. Smells were strange; sounds, musical. People were darkly beautiful with shining black hair; teeth, white and even. I wondered if this was where Carmella had lived before coming to our street.

I wanted to hurry, but he sauntered along. "Will we be late?" I asked.

He looked at his watch. "No. Visiting hours don't start until two. We've got a good half-hour."

So he must have been planning to take me all the time!

We were on a broad avenue with trolley tracks when a thought stopped me.

"What's wrong?" he asked.

"If I'm going to see Johnny, can I take him a present?"

He looked pleased. "Of course. What would you like?"

"I have to think hard."

"Think as hard as you like."

Candy came immediately, but it was too easy. So was a charlotte russe, cockamamies, whistles, marbles, checkers, tops, yo-yos, wind-up toys, push toys, balls, magnet and nails, pin the donkey's tail, snow-storm in the glass, jack-in-the-box, water pistol, popgun, slate and chalk, crayons, drawing books, storybooks, Cinderella. My mind hastened back to Johnny's brother, tearing my Cinderella book while we screamed with joy at the sight of our mothers getting out of that taxi. . . .

"Can I bring him a rose?"

"A rose?"

"Yes."

"What kind of a rose?"

"A very big one. A very red one."

"Are you sure that's what you want to take to him?"

I was certain.

We walked back about three-fourths of a block until we found a florist shop. The florist, it seemed, knew Mr. Goodman's game of picking jelly apples. He didn't pick the right rose until the third try. Then he drew it out slowly, laid it carefully on a table, rolled it together with a clutch of feathery ferns in soft green tissue and then in a cornucopia of brown paper, and pinned the ends. "Your mother will love this one," the florist said, handing me the package.

My mind hated him. I walked to the door, waited for my father to pay him.

Once outside, he said, "You didn't thank the man."

I muffled my anger in a snort.

"Why shouldn't he think you were buying it for your mother? Lots of children do."

"I wasn't."

"How did you expect him to know that? You don't think he can read your mind, do you?"

"No."

"So?"

"So that's why he should shut up."

"I get the hint." He said no more until we were up the steps. He purchased two tickets and we walked to the turnstile, beside which a man sat.

"How old's he?" he asked, examining me suspiciously.

"Five, and I have a full-fare ticket for him," my father replied.

Looking as if he had lost an argument, he took the tickets, dropped them into a glass-windowed box, turned the turnstile twice, and quickly grasping a wood-handled object projecting from the box, he chopped vigorously. The tickets fell from view. I imagined them in bits.

I asked why the man wanted to know my age and my father explained that under five would have been half-fare. I was glad I was five and full-fare.

From the station platform the city looked languorous in autumn sun, the buildings splendid in their mimicry of turning leaves. From one of three smokestacks rising in mid-distance a handful of blue smoke uncoiled dreamily. I asked it not to go away until the train came. . . . The incoming train slashed it from view. I had won.

We got in. I sat on my knees, looked out of double, dirty windows and watched fire escapes, curtains, faces, flowerpots, mops, then windows-windows flipping by like pages of a book quickly thumbed. After several stops the train went underground. Nothing to see. I turned around.

Opposite sat a woman in a dark brown coat, her hand clutching a purse as if it contained her world's possessions. She looked at me, and a silly little smile took shape in her eyes, on her lips. She nudged the man beside her, inviting him to look at me. He winked at me, then turned his eyes elsewhere. She continued to stare.

I wondered if she knew me; if I was supposed to make some sign of recognition; if she was somebody's mother; if she was going to the same place we were; if her husband was out of a job; if she was poor and, maybe, hungry; if she had just been evicted from her apartment and had no place to go; if she was crazy.

There was movement in the vicinity of her purse. My eyes went to it, and I watched a finger slowly release itself from the clutch and self-consciously wave at me.

She was playing itchy-coo with me. I itchy-coo'd back and she was sufficiently satisfied to stop staring.

Finally we got out. As we climbed toward light, my fear rose until at the last step I wanted to run back into darkness. I stopped.

"What's the matter?" he asked.

I knew only panic.

"Is there anything wrong?"

"I don't want to go," I blurted.

He didn't look surprised or annoyed. "All right," he said gently. "Do you want to go home?"

"Yes."

"Are you frightened?"

"No . . . yes . . . maybe . . . I don't know."

"Does the idea of seeing a children's home frighten you?"

"Is it an orphan asylum, too?"

"Is that what's frightening you?"

"Maybe."

"In that case, why don't we just look at it from the outside?"

I didn't want to see it at all, but I didn't want him to be disappointed again, like in the game of catch.

We turned a corner and came upon a playground loud and lively with children. Just like our playground. But there was a difference— their faces. Their faces were the same.

They shouted, ran, bickered just as we did. But their faces were the same. Also, they were dressed the same: blue knickers, blue shirts, blue jackets, blue caps with black visors, black stockings, black shoes.

I went up to the barred fence. My schoolyard had the same kind of fence. But their faces were the same.

"Is this it?" I asked my father.

He nodded. "Do you want to walk and see more?" I didn't, but said I would.

We passed the entrance. The usual many, many steps. The windows weren't barred as I had imagined. Some were even open. The walls were red brick, not gray granite, not rain-streaked. Some of the first-floor windows were decorated with paper half-moons, blue stars.

We walked until we came to another schoolyard. Girls skipping,

278

jumping rope, playing ball, jacks, dancing in circles; dressed alike in blue skirts, blue half-coats, blue berets, but they didn't look the same— not like the boys. I didn't understand.

"Shall we go home now?" my father asked.

The panic had dissolved to a tremble. "I want to see Johnny."

"Good boy," he said, and we started up the steps.

At the door he pointed to a sign and said, "If you could read you would see that it says, 'Society of the Daughters of Rebecca and Children's Home.' "

My father went to one of several windows in the entrance hall and spoke to someone behind it. We were directed to a line of people. We shuffled slowly forward, until it was our turn.

"Who would you like to visit?" a woman asked.

"John Schafer."

"Relative?"

"Friends."

"How many visitors?"

"Two, my son and I."

"How old is he?"

"Five."

"Isn't he too young?" she asked.

Tell her I paid full-fare, I silently urged my father.

"If I thought he was too young, I wouldn't have brought him," he said.

The woman said nothing to this, but pushed two cards out on the window ledge and gave him directions.

Down a long hallway, silent, clean, the mud-colored walls densely covered with pictures of old men in blacks hats with gray beards and predicting eyes, up steps to a double door leading to a waiting room. At a desk in the center a woman sat rigid. My father placed the passes on her desk and she motioned him to a seat.

A man appeared, called, "The party to visit Barry Grossman?"

A woman rose hastily, nodded to the woman next to whom she had been sitting as if apologizing for having been called first, and followed the man out.

In a similar manner we were called. My father took my hand, led me to a room containing long narrow trestle tables with benches attached, across which visitors talked to children in blue. Unlike the waiting room, this one had lightness, whiteness, and shone. Windows on three sides permitted the sun. The walls were naked except for a massive photograph of a man with a high forehead, round face, billowy chins and wealthy eyes. I asked my father if he was Rebecca. He gave me a *look!*

Johnny appeared. He had a haircut! A baldy haircut! I looked quickly at the other boys in blue, and they too had baldies. That— the absence of hair beneath their caps—was what made all the boys in the playground look alike.

His eyes searched the room with a restrained eagerness. I waved.

The man nudged him in our direction, and he came toward us with no sign of gladness or recognition.

"Hello, Johnny," my father said, and when there was no response, added, "Bobby wanted to visit you."

His look said, What for? Then, peering around vaguely, he motioned to the table. "You're supposed to sit down and then you can talk to me, if you want."

"That's a good idea," my father said. "Why don't the two of you sit here and have your talk. I'll be over there." He pointed to a window, and went to it.

We sat opposite each other, but he stared past me until I said, "I got a present for you," and put the paper cone on the table. "It's a big surprise," I said encouragingly, but he eyed it indifferently.

"What's in it?" he asked as he began to undo the paper.

"Wait till you see," I whispered, watching his face. He saw the rose. His eyes sang.

Letting the ferns fall, he picked it up and studied it as if the curl of every petal had to be memorized. He smelled it once and again; and then he asked, "My mother gave me it?"

It wasn't easy but I nodded.

"Did she give it to you to give to me?" the first small signs of excitement beginning to show.

"No," I replied cautiously, "she gave it to my mother and she—"

He interrupted with, "Isn't your mother in my house?"

"Yes, but sometimes she comes to my house and Mrs. Greneker goes to your house to make noodle soup like Columbus."

"Do you go to my house?" he asked quickly.

"No," I hastily replied.

"Why, isn't anybody in my house?"

"Sure, but you're here." The answer seemed to satisfy him and he went back to examining the rose in silence.

I stared at my father's back in the hope he'd sense I needed help finding something to talk about, but he didn't turn. Finally I blurted the story of the previous day's fight, carefully eliminating how it had all started; but even my offer to let him see where my father had been bruised brought forth no interest. We lapsed into silence again.

I asked him about his brother, but all he said was, "He likes it here."

I tried again with, "Do you go to school here?"

He nodded.

"Is it like ours?"

"Yes, but we have Hebrew school, too."

"You have two schools?" and when he nodded, "Do you know that Gerard Shuminsky is no more monitor? And that crazy Leatrice Aronowitz has radishes for brains is head monitor."

"We don't have monitors here," he said.

I sounded surprised, and he explained, "Because they say that monitors are for to make you afraid. And we're not supposed to be afraid of nothing. Everyone is so good and brave that we don't need monitors."

"But when the teacher leaves the room, doesn't she tell someone to watch?"

"No."

"Don't you fight or maybe even talk?"

"No, we sit and wait until he comes back."

"He? You have a man teacher?" I thought that having a man teacher was better than having Miss Diamond, and said so.

Once again silence, during which I went through a checklist of possible subjects. The one I finally found reached back to our first meeting.

"Do you still play giving jelly beans or gumdrops?" I asked.

He didn't answer.

"You don't have to anymore, because you know what happened to the bottle caps you gave me?"

He looked up.

"I put them in a red straw basket that I found and I took them to Miss Diamond and told her they were your collection," I lied. "You know what she did? She put them in the middle of the circle so we could see them. And she said that she thought they were better than Libby's stones and Gerard Shuminsky's bubble-gum wrappers and even better than my bottle caps. She clapped her hands a lot and everybody said, hurray for you. They said it very loud and over and over."

His disbelieving eyes forced me to continue. "And you know what's going to happen because you won the prize? Miss Diamond said she is going to paste all your bottle caps on a colored board and put it up all the way high over the blackboard. And when the mothers and maybe the fathers come to school on a special day they'll see them all the way on the top. And you'll have to stand in the middle of the room because you'll be the biggest winner."

"No they're not," he whispered fiercely. "They're not going to come. No one's going to come. And they're not going to see me because I'm going to be dead!"

282

I was stunned. He had made it sound true. But I had to say, "You can't be, because what'll your mother do if you are?"

He looked at me with amazement.

The man who had brought him returned and told us that time was up.

"Say good-bye to your friend," he told him.

"Good-bye," Johnny muttered.

My father joined us. Johnny repeated his farewell and walked away, his back straight, his hands stiffly at his sides.

I had nothing to say, but I wanted to call him. And as if he had heard my wish, he turned just before reaching the door and ran back. But he didn't even look at me—just caught up the rose, ferns and papers from the table and fled.

On the way to the subway, my father asked if we had had a nice talk. I said we had and he asked if I thought Johnny was happy. Because I knew of no way to tell him what I had heard, I said, "Yes."

We passed the playground. "They all sound happy, don't they?"

I nodded and said, "I think I know why they all have baldy haircuts."

"Why?"

"Because they don't have mothers to comb their hair for them."

chapter *14*

Next morning, I remembered the way my mother had come home the evening before dazed with exhaustion, saying she was too tired for anything. She had slipped to the floor in front of the couch on which I sat, rested the back of her head on one of the pillows and asked, "Was Johnny glad to see you?"

I was grateful my father was in his own room. "When can he come home again?" I asked.

"Did he say he wanted to come home?"

"He doesn't have to say because I know he hates it—they all have to have baldy haircuts and wear stinky blue, and they have to be so good and brave they can never have fun, and they never have so much fun that they don't even have to have a monitor, and I bet they have to beg for oatmeal—"

She caught one of my flying hands and kissed it. "He won't be there long," she promised. "It's only a matter of a few more days."

I awoke with the same question: *What* was only a matter of a few more days? Could it be that Johnny would be dead in that time? I knew he would die if his mother did . . . but mothers couldn't die. And now I had desperate need for greater proof than before. I had to know. I *had* to.

Libby and I left the apartment building on our way to school. I walked faster to build the distance between us and our mothers.

"Why are you walking so fast?" Libby asked.

"I have a secret question. I don't want them to hear," I confided. She became joyfully cooperative, skipped ahead. "What is it?"

"Do you think mothers can die?"

Without hesitation she replied, "No."

"How do you know?"

" 'Cause they always say, 'I'm gonna die,' and then they don't. Like my Aunt Bella. When my mother goes to see her, she always says, 'I'm so happy, I could die,' and then she don't. And sometimes when I kiss my mother good-bye in the morning and she has on her high blood pressure, she says, 'Libby, when you come home don't be surprised to find me dead.' "

"What do you say?"

"I say, I won't."

We had come to where the class line was forming when Libby stopped and said, "Ooh, what we forgot."

"What?" I asked. She pointed to the line. Most of the children were carrying empty cream-cheese boxes and paper bags. Gerard Shuminsky could hardly stand under the weight of a large potato sack and an enormous enamel bowl into which holes had been bored.

Libby then explained that this was the day we were to do indoor planting, that we were supposed to bring a planter and dirt with us, and that she couldn't imagine the kind of punishment we would get for having forgotten. All I could remember was Miss Diamond's shaking the packet of seeds at us, and nothing more. However, assuming that Gerard Shuminsky had more than enough dirt in his sack, I broke out of line and ran back to help him in the hope he would share some with me.

I took the bowl from him as he trailed behind, tugging at the sack and swearing eternal friendship between gasps.

The class was in the room when we arrived. Seeing us, Miss Diamond asked to know whose sack it was.

"It's mine," said Gerard Shuminsky proudly.

"What's in it?" she asked.

"Planting dirt," said Gerard Shuminsky, hurt that she did not recognize at once the greater effort he had made.

"It looks to me as if you're planning to bury somebody," Miss Diamond said, and throwing back her head, she cackled at the ceiling.

But instead of joining in as usual, the class became a hive. Every-one buzzed hatred for Miss Diamond into everyone else's ears. Gerard Shuminsky developed tears. Even the class knew he had tried so hard.

Miss Diamond's laughter snapped in mid-sound. She went to her desk, rapped with her ruler. "Quiet . . . quiet! What is the meaning of this whispering?"

The class gaped at her through sullen, pouting, even rebellious faces. We all knew to what lengths Gerard Shuminsky had gone to please her; that the only reason he wet his pants every day just before lunchtime was because he wouldn't raise his hand and interrupt her to ask to leave the room; that he thought she was the most wonderful person in the world; and that ever since she had been appointed first monitor, Leatrice Aronowitz had become as welcome as a pebble in a shoe.

I put the bowl down on the floor, went to my seat.

"I think we ought to bury her with it," Libby whispered as I sat.

Miss Diamond shushed her, warned her that she was supposed to be on her very best behavior or she would insist that her mother come to school.

Libby stood and said, "I 'pologize Miss Diamond for opening up my mouth." She curtsied, sat and quickly whispered, "That old shtinkfoose."

Miss Diamond, who had seemingly turned her attention to the rest of the class, barked, "What was that?"

Libby looked around and behind, her face as innocent as milk, her eyes assuring Miss Diamond that she must have heard someone else.

"Libby! Stand up!"

Libby obeyed.

"Now, what did you say?"

Twisting the ends of her neckerchief, Libby complained, "I don't know why you always pick on me like I did everything wrong in the whole class when I try to be as good as gold and maybe better. I didn't say nothing after I 'pologized so nice before. And now you say I said something and I'm always wrong and you're always right, even if someone else said it I have to be wrong. I wish the ground would open up before me so I could disappear into it. I suffer too much. I wish God doesn't leave me here to the end of my days. I am a good woman, a good mother, so if He takes the good first, why not me?"

"What are you talking about?" Miss Diamond looked lost. "What was that business about the ground opening up before you?"

"Oh, that was what my mother said before she found out my father wasn't dead."

"That, Libby Jackson," Miss Diamond spoke thunderbolts, "is all I am going to take from you now and forever." She strode across the room, grabbed Libby's arm; and as Libby tried to pull away, told Leatrice Aronowitz to keep the class in order and led a weeping, wrestling Libby from the room.

The door closed.

A blackboard eraser hit Leatrice Aronowitz. Leatrice Aronowitz demanded whoever threw it to stand up or else she would report the whole class. Another eraser sailed, missed Leatrice Aronowitz and hit Honora Wasserman. Honora Wasserman stood, looked around slowly, suspiciously, and having made up her mind who the culprit was, went to the blackboard, picked up the pointer and charging at Gerard

Shuminsky, hit him over the head. Gerard Shuminsky began to cry.

I ran over, pulled the pointer out of Honora Wasserman's fist and whipped it across her behind. Honora Wasserman, screamed virtuous rage. I lashed the pointer again for Johnny's sake—and again, for luck.

A girl, I suspected Felicia Bluestone but wasn't sure, dumped a bag of dirt on my head.

Solly Mink with a great battle-rousing "Yaaaaah!" ran into Leatrice Aronowitz, knocked her down and with the help of one or two other boys, dumped dirt into her bloomers.

Not that she felt sorry for Leatrice Aronowitz, but rather in the defense of all womanhood, Marcia Weissbaum slapped her hands and stamped her foot, ordered them to release Leatrice Aronowitz at once. For her efforts, Solly Mink stuffed a handful of dirt into her mouth. Marcia Weissbaum sputtered dirt and rage, flung whatever came to hand—and the full-scale war was on.

The boys were in one camp, the girls the other. The dirt flew in the first barrage. It was followed by bombardments of erasers, cheese boxes, tin cans, chalk, paper clips, paint boxes, raffia, rolls of colored paper, piano music sheets, storybooks, crayons, beanbags, the bird's nest, blocks, Libby's imitation-leather schoolbag and whatever else in the room proved throwable.

Just as the boys were beginning to show signs of conquering and as Herman Zuckerman and Generoso Puppi were stuffing Gazella Caccialanza into Gerard Shuminsky's sack, we heard Miss Diamond screech, "CHILDREN!" like a trolley making a sudden downhill stop.

We became stone.

When we had put our seats back in their places and stood penitent in front of them, Miss Diamond composed herself like a cat's fur. "You will all be punished very severely for this. And as for you, Leatrice Aronowitz—stop jigging when I'm talking to you—I cannot tell you how disappointed I am in you for not keeping this class in order. It seems to me that only Gerard knows how to keep such a bunch of ruffians in good behavior."

Gerard Shuminsky stiffened to attention. I was sorry. As long as it had lasted, I liked him better when he slumped.

"I want you all to sit on your hands," Miss Diamond continued. "And I want Gerard to stand up front right next to my desk. If anyone moves his hands from under him or says one word, I want Gerard to report him to me at once. And that person's mother will have to come to school tomorrow."

Gerard Shuminsky raised his hand to attract Miss Diamond's attention.

"What is it?" she asked.

"I can't be monitor now," he said sadly.

"Why not?"

"Because I got lots of dirt in my shoes and it hurts my feet when I stand."

"Then take your shoes off and empty them on the floor. I have to get the custodian up here anyway to clean up this horrid mess you children made."

"I can't take my shoes off," Gerard Shuminsky complained. He was very unhappy.

"Gerard," Miss Diamond asked loftily, "is this your idea of a joke?"

"No, Miss Diamond."

I thought he was going to cry.

"Then why can't you take your shoes off?"

"Because . . ." The words wouldn't come from between his lips. A tear swam up into each eye.

"Well, Gerard, speak up!"

"Because . . ." and then he quickly sputtered, "I can't tie my laces again."

"Neither can I," I volunteered.

"I can't neither," said Marcia Weissbaum.

At once, the entire class admitted and confessed that they didn't know how to tie their shoelaces.

Miss Diamond rapped the desk to bring us to attention. "In that case," she said, "after the custodian cleans up—and you are going to help him—we will spend the rest of the day, if necessary, learning how to tie our shoelaces."

We applauded, and Miss Diamond smiled and bowed, smiled and bowed like old Mother Niddity Nod.

All this time I imagined Libby standing, crying in the corner of Mr. Pierce's office. During lunch, I thought of her standing, crying, starving in Mr. Pierce's office. While we were having rest period, I could see her as a crumpled heap in the corner.

We were back to sitting with shoes in our laps, practicing tying, when there was a knock on the door. Miss Diamond crossed the room with the determination of a diver striding a springboard in preparation for a difficult jump, and opened it. "Yes?" With a gracious, flowing arm she waved in Libby and her mother.

That Mrs. Jackson should finally consent to appear raised Miss Diamond's stature a mile for me. Mrs. Jackson was, as she herself would have said, "dolled up," her lips were painted, her cheeks rouged. The tips of her ears shone with the frost of diamond earrings. And she wore high heels.

Miss Diamond led the way back to her desk, pulled a chair up on the platform for Mrs. Jackson, invited her to sit; and they bit and chewed words as if they had the opposite ends of a frankfurter in their mouths and were gobbling toward its middle. At times, Mrs. Jackson would glare at Libby, who stood in front of the desk as unconcerned as sunshine.

After the face-to-face conference was over, both women rose sighing with satisfaction. Mrs. Jackson stepped from the platform and loud enough for us all to hear, told Libby that she now had the "whole picktchoor."

Libby replied, "You do?"

"Yairse, I do," her mother countered. "And I orlso know how to straighten it owt!" She bowed once more to Miss Diamond and left tipper-tricking on her high heels.

School over, I found that Mrs. Jackson had waited and was taking me home with Libby.

I succeeded in my decision not to ask where my mother was.

The first thing that caught my eye on the way home was the jumble of furniture and bundles in front of The Flop Garden. I hurried across, examined them. They were the same that Carmella and I had tried to return; the little straw basket had lost its tassel.

I dashed across the street to find Carmella. She emerged from her father's store holding an Italian bread sandwich as if it were an enormous flute.

"Carmella?" I shouted.

"I can't talk with my mouth full. I'm liable to choke to death," she growled.

"Did you see across the street? They took all the things out again. Aren't we going to put them back?"

Swallowing, she said, "Naw, it ain't worth it. Besides, I don't want to fight again until maybe Wednesday. And then I'll only fight if they hit a little kid."

I didn't want to accept her decision. It would have meant that Peter was right and that the fight was not because they wanted to replace the possessions of the evicted family but because they thought the moving man had hurt me.

"But what about the fathers?" I asked. "Don't they want to put the things back?"

She shook her head. "You don't understand something. You can only win the same fight once. If you fight the same fight the second time you gotta lose. So, who wants to lose?"

Her meaning came to me only in terms of what had happened in school that day. We had rebelled against Miss Diamond and in a way, had won. But, in the end, Miss Diamond was still teacher and still in command of the class. And I knew we would never allow ourselves to have such a fight again.

I was about to leave and go home when the other question arose. It couldn't, however, be asked outright.

"I didn't know that you knew my father, Carmella . . ."

"Sure, I know him. Where do you think he gets his haircuts, in Hollywood?"

"He says you're smart." The lie, I thought, was necessary.

"And he sure knows what he's talking about. You can bet anything you want on that!"

"He says you read a lot of books."

"He's right, An' if I don't stop reading so many books, I'm going to have to wear dark glasses and have a cane and a cup. And anyone who doesn't put at least one nickel in that cup gets a WHAMO from my cane."

"Carmella, shud up da stupid mouth!" came her father's voice from inside the store.

Beckoning to me, she tiptoed away.

"Why does he always yell at you?" I asked.

"He has to. It's good for his digestion. If he doesn't yell, everything he eats stops right here"—she put her hand on the top of her chest—"and won't go down no further."

"Then why does he hit you so much?"

"He gotta do that, too."

"Why?"

"He's gonna hit me or my mother. And if he ever put one finger on my mother, you know what I'd do? I'd martyrize him right down to his last penny."

I didn't know what she meant, but I couldn't afford to lose the opening. "Carmella, do you know a lot about mothers, like you know about babies?"

She gulped a mouthful of sandwich. "A lot? I know everything from top to bottom about mothers. Why? Do you want to know something about your mother?"

"No," I assured her quickly. Then I wondered whether I should ask her at all.

"So, what do you wanna know? If it's about mothers, you came to the right office. What is it?"

Turning away, I asked, "Carmella, do you know if . . . if . . ."

"If what?"

"Can mothers die?"

Turning back slowly, I saw Carmella, her mouth full, shaking her head from side to side, "Uh-uhn, uh-uhn . . ." And when she finally swallowed, "Absolutely not! *Impossible!*"

A joyful "They can't?" popped out.

"Even if they wanted to, they couldn't. It's against the law. I don't mean police laws, I mean God's laws. You know what mothers have to do?"

"What?"

"They have to assumpt."

"What's that?"

Depositing the remains of her sandwich on the chair in front of her father's store, she crossed her arms, the tips of her fingers touching opposite shoulders, and rolling her eyes upward, she said, "They do like this, and then they go wheeeeee, straight up."

"In my religion, too?"

"It makes no difference what religion," she declared, "when it comes to mothers they all gotta assumpt."

"Thanks, Carmella. Thanks for telling me." I started to go.

"Okay," she said, returning to her sandwich, "if there's anything you want to get the real answer to, you know where to find me. My office is open twenty-four hours a day, except Sunday."

Carmella's opinion was satisfying, but despite her assurance I felt somehow it was restricted to her religion. Then, I remembered that Mrs. Greneker had gone to the rabbi to settle a problem. I was certain he would have the answer. But how to get to him? Only vaguely did I know the way to the synagogue.

The sounds of boys' voices playing stickball on Dawson Street promised a solution. I found Peter just as it was his turn at bat.

He picked up the stick, struck a wide stance, squinted.

I walked up to him, "Peter, will you take me—"

He dropped the stick, threw his head back in exasperation and yelled, "What in the hell's the matter with you, you loonybin? Don't you know I'm up. Scrammeroo!"

"I don't wanna scrammeroo. I want you to take me to see the rabbi."

"WHAT?" Peter gaped. "Hey Buddy," he called to Libby's brother, "get me a straightjacket. This kid's lost his marbles." Then to me, "Go 'way or I'll spit down your throat and charge you for a chocolate soda."

The boys began to snicker and crow. One of them shouted, "Gwan and say your prayers. You're holding up the game."

"I'll go myself," I said angrily, and stomped off in the supposed direction of the synagogue. I reached the corner, stopped a passing woman and asked her the way. "Ai tuck honly Chermann," she said, and departed. Another man pointed vaguely to the right and said, "It's somewheres up there, kid."

I walked until I came to a building that didn't look like an apartment house. A man stood near the door. "Is this where the rabbi is?" I asked.

"Dees is dee Amerigo Vespucci Soshull Culub," he replied. "You finda dee rabbi hoppa dee nexta block."

I thanked him and walked until I was certain I had reached the synagogue. Still, I sought confirmation from a man who stood near the curb, his hands held behind, swaying backwards and forwards.

"Can I find the rabbi here?" I asked.

"Yay-ess," he replied listlessly.

"Thank you." I turned and headed for the steps.

"Chusst ha second," he called to me, "vayer do you tink you har goink? YOU haf I suppose han happointmant."

"I just want to ask him a question."

I had started up the steps when he caught me by the arm. "Dunt you see da shul is clost?"

"But if I knock on the door maybe someone will answer," I argued.

"If you knock on deh door, I'm deh vun who vill henser."

"Are you the rabbi?"

"Hi am deh shamas. Go home, liddle boy, and *hurryup*." He shooed me like a flock of pigeons.

But instead of leaving, I rushed up the steps with the shamas close behind. I had time to pound on the door once before he caught me under my arms and carried me to the sidewalk.

Just then Peter, followed by Libby's brother, suddenly appeared. "Who do you think you're pushing around, you old geezer? Why don't you pick on someone nearer your size?"

The shamas, who had gone up several steps, shouted, "Go vay, you goy, you. You vant trouble, I'll gif it to you in your dirty fresh moud, you. You goy."

"If I'm a goy, so are you," Peter argued. "If you wanna know something, I was Bar Mitzvahed in that funeral home of yours. And if you wanna come off those steps, I'll show you something I never learned in Hebrew school."

While the shamas and Peter shouted at one another, Buddy flattened himself against the wall and slunk forward until he was directly behind the shamas. I knew what was going to happen and hoped it wouldn't.

Buddy knelt on the step, and Peter darted up, pushed the shamas, who fell back over Buddy, shouting, "Helf! Moider! Helf! Goyim! Poleece!"

Peter and Buddy zipped down the steps, flew past me, shouting, "Run, Bobby, run!" I was all ready to do so when I saw a man in a dark suit and black yamulka peer out from a small entrance next to the large double doors.

"Shmuel Yudel!" he called out in a sonorous, penetrating voice. The shamas stopped his bellowing at once.

"Are you the rabbi?" I called, and without waiting for his answer ran up the steps. "Are you?"

"Yes, my child, I am."

"Can I ask you a question?"

Before he could reply, the shamas came, hugging his body and huffing. "Dey tried to kill me, to moider me," he explained.

"Stop making a show of yourself," the rabbi ordered. "And close the front doors." The shamas looked as if he were going to weep.

Turning to me, the rabbi asked, "Would you like to come in, my son?"

I said yes, stepped across the threshold into a small waiting room, and immediately capped my head with my hands and closed my eyes.

"Why do you keep your hands on your head and your eyes closed?" the rabbi asked.

"Because I don't have a hat on my head and maybe something will happen to it."

He produced a yamulka. "Here, let me put this on for you," he said, fitting the cap to my head.

"It's true, you should have your head covered at all times, not only when you are in shul—but not because you expect God will punish you if you don't. Do you know why we always wear something on the head?"

"No."

"Not because we are afraid that God will strike us, but because we wish to protect our most precious possessions, our minds. Everything that is beautiful, everything that is good and wise, comes from right here." He lightly touched my forehead. "Tell me," he continued, "have you ever been inside?"

"Only when my brother was Bar Mitzvahed."

"Doesn't your father come here?"

"Not always," I lied, feeling that my father would understand I was trying to protect him.

"Tell him, the next time he comes, that he should bring you, too. Tell him the rabbi asked him to. You'll have a wonderful time. It's more fun than any games you play."

"It is?"

"Yes. Now what was the question you wanted to ask?"

The words clotted in my throat. Would his be the final answer?

Did I dare ask?

"Yes?" But not with impatience.

The words strained to escape.

"What's troubling you, my son?" In the softness of his eyes I saw understanding, and the words came loose.

"Rabbi, can mothers die?"

He knelt, took my chin in the cup of his hand. "So that is the question that is worrying your little head. I must say it's a very big question for such a little head. But here is my answer: Mothers are like time. Time passes, but it is always here. Times goes, but it always comes. So it is with mothers. Think about it. 'The Lord bless you, and keep you; the Lord make his face to shine upon you, and be gracious unto you; the Lord turn his face unto you, and give you peace.' "

He patted my head, stood and opened the door. I joined the sun. Peter and Buddy were waiting at the foot of the steps.

"What happened?" Peter demanded. "What did he do to you?"

"He talked to me."

"What did he say?"

"I won't tell you."

"Why not?"

"Because you didn't want to take me and you made fun of me."

"But I followed you. I broke up a good game just to make sure that you didn't get lost."

"I didn't want you to follow me, I wanted you to take me."

"Well, it's the same thing, isn't it? What did he say to you?"

"It's not the same thing. And I'm not going to tell you." I walked away.

"Where are you going?" Peter asked.

"Home."

"Home isn't that way. It's this way," he said, pointing in the opposite direction.

I didn't know whether to believe him, but there was one way of finding out. "Do you want to know what he told me?"

"Sure."

"I'll tell you when you take me home."

"Boy, you sure trust me, don't you," he growled, and threw his arm across my shoulder.

When we came to Herman's pickle store street, I said, "You know what the rabbi told me? He told me to tell Daddy that the next time he goes to shul he should take me and I would have more fun than any game I play."

"Oh sure," said Peter sarcastically, "some fun. It's the biggest chase game you ever saw. You come in and the first thing they take your hat away and instead you have to put on a yamulka and a tallis that's twice your size with long fringes so that you're sure to trip over it if you try to sneak out and they can catch you easier. Then there's a man standing up front and he's reading, 'Ebbele, bebbele, ebbele, bebbele'; but there's another man on one side who reads, 'Ebbele-bebbele-ebbele-bebbele,' faster; and then there's another man on the other side and he reads, 'Ebbelebebbeleebbele-bebbele,' even faster. So, you don't know where to begin reading. That goes on for a week and a half. Then somebody from the bleachers yells, 'Page two hundred and six,' so you turn quick to that page, and they start, 'Alla-balla-calla-dalla-falla . . . falla-dalla-calla-balla-alla,' and you have to follow on the opposite page in English. And they keep this alla-balla business up for a half an hour and you've read six or seven pages. Then everybody say, 'Amen.' And you look for an Amen, but there isn't any on your page, so you turn back one page and another, and another, and another, but still no Amen—until you're back on page two hundred and six, and there it is, only three lines after they first started. And that isn't all. You don't only have to chase them around for words, because first, everybody stands. Then you stand. Then some people sit and some keep standing. So you don't know if you should keep standing or sit. So you keep standing and everyone else sits. Then only some people stand. What should you do, so you sit. Suddenly someone behind you who you never saw in your life bops you on the head and tells you to stand or get out. So, you stand. Then some people put their shawls over their heads and rock back and forth, some don't put their shawls over their heads but they rock back and forth, and some don't do either. So you figure that maybe it's only the very holy ones who put the shawls over, so you copy them and just as soon as you do it, the guy behind you pulls it down and says, 'Gerrrrada, here, you trombone nick!' "

"What's a trombone nick?"

"I don't know, but you can bet it's not good. Anyway, all the time you've been chasing, you don't notice it but they draw out all the air and in its place some guy comes around with a spritzer and spritzes all this perfume over you; and then you're a dead-goner. All of a sudden everything becomes fuzzy and woozy and your head gets as heavy as a rock so that you can't keep it up and it falls once . . . it falls twice . . . and the third time you're out. But you're not really out, you're just like in a half-a-trance. Because after a few minutes while they're saying, 'Ebbele-bebbele-ebbele-bebbele,' you hear someone else saying something that in the beginning sounds like he's singing, 'Ebbele-bebbele,' but he's really singing, 'There - is - someone - in - the - tenth - row - on - the - right - side - who - is - making - like - this - is - a - hotel - where - he - should - go - to - sleep - and - if - that - someone - in - the - tenth - row - on - the - right - side - doesn't - quick - pick - up - the - book - will - the - kind - gentleman - in - the - back - from - him - give - him - a - knock - on - the - head - but - not - with - the - book - with - the - finger.'

"And you know it's you he's talking about, but you can't do anything about it, 'cause you're like paralyzed. And sure enough, you get a ping on the top of your head and you're back to chasing all over again. Some fun!

"Maybe," Peter said reflectively, "maybe if they just took the trouble to tell you what it's all about, maybe then it wouldn't be so bad."

We were in front of our apartment building.

I sat on the highest step. "Say," he said, flopping on the step below, "what did you want to go and see the rabbi for?"

The moment begged for the question. "Peter, can mothers die?"

"What kind of a question is that?"

"Just a question."

"You mean anybody's mother?"

"All mothers."

"You mean all the mothers in the whole world?"

"In the whole world."

"That's a lot of mothers."

"Can they die?"

"Well, that depends . . ."

"On what?"

"On what you mean by die?"

"I mean can they go away forever and never come back?"

"Oh, so that's the way you mean?"

"Yes."

"You're sure you don't mean like the sun goes away at night and comes back in the morning?"

"No, I mean never come back."

"I see." Peter leaned his elbows on his knees and tapped his temples with the tips of his fingers. "Do you know what a soul is?" he asked.

"No."

"I was afraid you wouldn't."

"What is it?"

"It's hard to explain. It's something inside you."

"Like a hand that opens very slow?"

"No, forget about it."

"Are you going to answer my question?"

"I'm trying to. Can't you see I'm trying?" He hummed and mumbled to himself.

"Don't you know the answer?"

"Of course I know it."

"So tell me it."

"All right! Now you really want to know the answer?"

"Yes."

"And remember, you asked me, I just didn't go telling you because I wanted to."

"All right, what's the answer?"

"The answer is . . . the answer is . . . the answer . . . is . . ."

"What?"

"I think so."

"That's no answer."

"Yes it is."

"No it isn't!"

"Hey, wait a second"—Peter looked up at me—"is that what you asked the rabbi?"

I nodded.

He turned his head away. "What did *he* say?"

"He said that mothers are like time, but I have to think about it."

"Why?"

"Because he said so and because I don't know how to tell time yet."

He took my hand and slapped it lightly in his palm. "You musta wanted to know the answer pretty bad to go all the way to the rabbi," he said, his face still averted.

"It's important. It's very important."

"Did you ask mother?"

"No."

"Well, don't."

"I won't—but why?"

"Oh, she'll give you an answer, all right. You know our mother, she has an answer for everything. But if she has to answer this one, it will hurt her a lot, and deep. I don't know if you get what I'm trying to say. But, you see, mothers are all tied up with things that get born and grow, things that live. They don't do so good with the things that die."

"Can I ask Daddy?"

"Sure, but why keep it up? I mean you can get a little dopey going around asking a question like that—it's a mile high. Besides, I don't think that that's the question you want answered."

"It isn't?"

"No." He let go of my hand. "You see, the question that I think is needling you is not so much about all mothers. You really want to know about Johnny's mother, don't you?"

I knew its truth as soon as I heard it.

"Well, if that's the question, then the answer is, I think so."

"That's the same answer as before," I objected.

"No, it's not. What I mean is that some sort of a miracle can happen, even at the last minute. But we'll find out pretty soon."

"How'll we find out?"

"The question box is closed for today."

"How'll we find out?" I insisted.

"I said the question box is closed for today. And that means"—he stood—"that if I answer one more question, my tongue will fall out of my mouth and my eyes will roll out of my head. So don't take any wooden nickels and twenty-three skiddoo to you." He ran off.

I turned to go upstairs as Libby came through the door.

"You're wrong," I said, "you Fifi la-la Libby, you're all wrong."

She looked at me strangely, and said, "I am not wrong 'cause my mother didn't do anything to me. She said that Miss Diamond has alley-toes and that she'd murder me alive if I told anyone, especially Miss Diamond."

I knew we weren't talking about the same thing but I had to ask, "What's alley-toes?"

"Her breath smells bad."

"And your mother didn't punish you, because of that?"

Libby nodded. "She says it gave her a headache that's so blind she can't see."

Before ringing the bell, I looked at the door. I knew that it no longer led to a land of nightingales and Nelly Belly Foos, where gingersnaps grew on blueberry bushes; that I would never pound on it, scratch it, kick it or make kissing noises into its crack again.

I rang; Martha opened the door. "Hurry up, change your clothes, wash your hands, and get ready for your dinner," she said, and walked toward my mother's room with a glass of water in her hand. "And," she added, "don't make any noise."

As soon as she opened the door I heard the sound of my mother weeping. It rose above Mrs. Greneker's shushing. Martha quickly shut the door.

She came out without the glass. I was about to ask her . . . but she said, "Please don't talk to me, I'm practicing self-control." A sob escaped. She hurried into the kitchen and turned on the water faucets.

I went up to the door of my mother's room. "Please, please Frances, don't carry on so," I heard Mrs. Greneker plead. Then my mother's tear-twisted voice, "I can't help it. I just can't help it . . . to be there, to hear her with her last breath calling for Johnny . . . Artie . . . Johnny . . ." Her words splintered into sobs.

No more. I didn't want to hear any more.

I went into my room, considered going under my bed, and then sat on it instead and thought . . . thought that I would never see the woman again with the bitter look that I had decided could only come from tasting laundry soap; that woman who long ago spoke to my mother while we stood on the registration line, who held her son's hand and would never hold it again; that woman who was the first mother in my world to die, to prove against all my proofs that I was wrong. But if I never would see her again, I would remember. I would remember the smell that riveted cleanliness into the nostrils; the yellow skin . . . the dusty voice . . . the scream that still lay curdled and soured behind my ears; and the rose.

Mrs. Greneker opened the door of my mother's room. "Frances, please pull yourself together. I just have to go up and turn the light down from under the holishkes. I'll be back in half a minute."

She was hardly out of the apartment when I heard my mother click for the telephone operator and ask the number of the Daughters of Rebecca. Was she going to take Johnny and Artie home? Bring them here? I silently begged that she would.

"Hello," she said, "I understand that. . . . Could you please tell me who is in charge of arranging for funerals? Thank you. . . . Hello, this is Mrs. Hirshman, I understand the Daughters of Rebecca are planning special funeral arrangements for the late Mrs. Schaefer. . . . Oh? Can you switch me over to his phone? Hello, Mr. Vogel?"

I imagined she was speaking to the man whose picture hung in the visiting room.

"This is Mrs. Hirshman. I understand that you are in personal charge of the funeral arrangements for Mrs. Schafer. I was the one who took care of her while she was ill, until your society sent a nurse and some members. What I wanted to find out was . . . well, I was there early this afternoon, just before she died, and one of the women from the Daughters of Rebecca told me that you were planning a special funeral—that instead of taking her to a funeral home, you were going to hold the service where she lived. . . .

"Mr. Vogel, I don't know if she should or shouldn't have told me. All I'm trying to find out is if it's true that you're going to have limousines, a rabbi, that you're going to speak, and . . . I'm not saying it isn't your business. But I've known her all my life. We went to school together. Of course she believed in God, but she wasn't orthodox. She wasn't even religious. Of course I agree she should be given a Jewish burial, but can't it be private? . . .

"No, I'm not a relative. She has no relatives. I don't know where her husband is. Your social service staff is supposed to be trying to locate him. But what's that got to do with your decision to make a three-ring circus out of her funeral? Whatever your reason for wanting to put on this spectacle, you mustn't forget the living. This neighborhood has many children. Do you know what mothers do when they find out there's going to be a funeral in the neighborhood? If it happens on a day when the schools are closed, they send them to the movies, or take them to visit relatives. Even if the funeral is small, they protect them from it. Isn't it bad enough that there have to be street funerals when families can't afford a funeral home? Do you have to make a block party out of it? Can you imagine when they find out it's a young mother? When they learn that her children are in an orphan asylum . . . ?

"All right, so you call it a home. I'm sure your place is a regular paradise, but children fear such places anyway. . . .

"I know that children aren't born being afraid of them, but whether it's the parent's fault or not, they're still afraid. I hope you're not planning to have *her* children there. . . .

"How could you? How could you be so cruel? They're only babies! Please! Please don't do it. How could it help? Who would benefit? Why must those children be punished so? Why?"

She fell to sobbing.

After a few moments, she said, "May God forgive you. I don't know a human being who ever could," and hung the phone.

Mrs. Greneker, who had returned while my mother was still talking, stood filling the door to her room. "So," she said, "you had to bang your head against the wall? Didn't I tell you that it would help like cups on a dead man?"

"I had to try. I just had to try. And you wouldn't believe what that man told me."

"These days, may they be forgotten as fast as they go, there is nothing I don't believe. Nothing."

"He said they were making it a big funeral because the home is in a bad financial condition. They haven't been able to raise money since the crash, and now they can't even afford to send out their appeals for donations. He said they need the publicity. Did you hear that? They need publicity, so they're going to parade a dead woman around like an advertisement."

"I can just see it, a funeral like an election with loudspeakers."

"Worst of all, they're bringing her children."

"This, the law shouldn't allow," Mrs. Greneker said angrily.

"He said he's doing it because it will make it easier to get them adopted. He called it 'building public sympathy for them.' "

"He's building more than that. He's building for them a picture they'll never forget as long as they live."

Martha called from the kitchen. "Bobby, come eat your dinner."

I heard a rustling in my mother's room and she rushed out into the living room. "Has he been here all this time?" Martha answered something from the kitchen. "Where is he?" my mother asked, anxious, fretful.

"Here," I said.

She was in the doorway of my room, looking as if I had been lost and she had just found me. "How long have you been here?" she asked, and came in.

"I don't know," I replied. And added without intent, "I can't tell time yet."

"You know you shouldn't wear your coat in the house," she said, unbuttoning. Mrs. Greneker left with a sigh.

My father came home, and my mother burst into tears. They went to their room.

Peter arrived; Martha served the dinner, he tasted it and pushed the plate away. "You put Vitamin R in it, I can tell."

"I did not," Martha argued. "I never heard of Vitamin R."

"How does it taste?" I asked.

"Rotten!" Peter announced, and left the apartment.

My father came into the kitchen, ate silently, sparingly. No one asked me why I didn't eat; Martha removed the plates.

The evening was sick. It lay shivering under many blankets of silence.

Martha rose suddenly, said, "I forgot something," took her coat and left.

My mother came out of her room, her face a colorless tangle. She walked through the living room, asked if I had my dinner but did not stop for an answer. Returning from the kitchen, she said, "Hardly anything's been eaten," took her coat, her hat, her black hat for places she respected. "I've got to go across the street, some of the neighbors will be there," she said. Then, to my father, "If I'm a little late, will you give him his bath?" The door closed.

As if it were a signal for which I had been waiting, I went to where my father sat and asked, "Can you teach me how to tell time?"

"Yes," he replied, "but it wouldn't be much good to know how without having your own watch."

"When is that?"

"A couple of years or so, but why are you in such a hurry to be able to tell time?"

"So I can know about mothers."

"Mothers?"

"Yes." I told him about the rabbi and asked if he would take me to the synagogue with him.

"Sure, whenever you want to go."

"When's the next time?"

"Saturday."

"Will you take me then?" He agreed to. "Do you know how to pray there, like ebbele-bebbele, ebbele-bebbele?"

"I don't know about the ebbele-bebbele, but I know how to pray."

"Will you teach me how on Saturday so I can pray to God for Johnny?"

"Why do you want to pray for Johnny?"

"Because."

"You don't think God will listen to prayers that are unnecessary, do you?"

I was perplexed.

"For instance, if you prayed to God to bring Johnny's mother back to him, He couldn't answer that prayer because it was He who took his mother away. Why should He bring her back?"

I didn't understand. I wanted to pray to keep Johnny from dying. "Did God take her away because Johnny did something bad?" I asked.

"No. He took her because He thought she should be free of pain and trouble forever."

This explained it then. Johnny would have to die to be free of pain and trouble too. The terrible inevitability of it made me feel grimly helpless, and I searched for some magic to prevent it from happening while my father went on with: "Johnny is unhappy now, that's true. But he has time on his side, time to remember only the good things and forget the bad. And maybe in that time he will be adopted."

"What's adopted?"

His explanation, which I couldn't fully comprehend, gave me hope that perhaps, by this strange method of becoming part of someone else's family, Johnny could remain alive. Now there was only the final, bitter question: "Why," I asked, "do mothers have to die?"

"Because they're like everyone else. Only God lives forever. And you wouldn't want your mother to be like God."

"I wouldn't?"

"Of course not. Would you like a mother you couldn't see—you couldn't talk to unless you prayed to her? Would you like a mother from whom you could only take? To whom you could give nothing because if she were God, she would have everything?"

The little hand opened inside.

"Would you like to have a bath?" he asked.

The difference was immediately apparent. Heretofore I had been told I was to be given a bath; now, it seemed, I had a choice in the matter. I was tempted to say no, to test his reaction, but another idea presented itself. I said, "Yes."

I went to my room and returned in my underwear. When he stood to follow me, I said, "I want to take my bath by myself."

"All right, I'll just sit and watch."

"And that's all?"

"That's all," he assured me.

"Then wait till I call you. All right?"

"Only if you call me before you get into the tub."

"I will." I turned on the taps to their fullest, and when the water was at the right height I called.

He came in, put down the lid of the toilet seat and sat on it. Putting his finger in to test the water, he asked, "Isn't this too hot for you?"

I put my finger in. It was, but I said, "No."

"If anyone else had turned on the water this hot, you'd be all for calling the fire department."

I put in one foot, stifled a yipe and waited for it to become used to the heat before daring the next step. When my back touched the water I almost jumped, but not wishing to concede that my father was right I sank as slowly as possible until I sat on the burning bottom.

I began to soap my arms. "Why don't you use the sponge?" my father asked. "Because it doesn't rub as hard as I can," I explained. "Do you want me to soap your back?" "No, I can reach it myself." "Suit yourself." I tried reaching my back, but couldn't. My father made no comment, but when I stood to wash my legs, he took my arm.

"Why are you holding me?" I asked, trying to pull my elbow away.

"Because you might slip and then whose fault would it be?"

"Mine."

"I'd have a hard time convincing your mother of that," he said, still holding my arm.

"But you said you would only sit and watch."

"What is all this don't-help-me, don't-touch-me business, anyway?"

Instead of answering, I asked how old he thought I would have to be before I could take a bath alone, without anyone even watching.

"Do you think you're old enough now?" he asked.

"Yes."

"Why didn't you say so in the first place?" he said, and left.

I was sorry, but didn't call him back until I had finished.

"What do you want?" he asked.

"Will you help me out?"

"If you're old enough to get in and take your bath, you're old enough to get out," he said.

He had seen through me. I was glad.

My mother returned while I was still drying myself and I boasted that I had taken my own bath.

"All by yourself, from beginning to end?" she asked.

"All by myself from beginning to end."

"But with the door open," she said, and slipped out of her coat.

I understood, at once, the meaning of doors.

I got into bed, waited for her to come, so I could ask the new question. Now, the most important one of all.

Time drawled. I was about to call when she came in, sat at the edge of the bed and said-sang, "How do you do, my partner, how do you today? Shall we dance in a circle? I will show you the way."

I didn't understand.

"It seems like it's been a long time since we've been partners," she said. "A long, long time since I was a nightingale and you were the prince who was good as gold; and I was the fake mother who found you in front of my door where your real mother left you by mistake; and remember when you gave me the hartichoke and then felt sorry, so you gave me your best cough medicine and a mustard plaster, and a hot-water bag under my feet and made me feel better?"

"And a half a aspirin, too," I reminded her.

"Oh, yes, I forgot. Without that half an aspirin I would have choked to . . . to smithereens."

I knew it wasn't the word she had meant to use.

"But now," she continued, "we can go back to being real partners all over again, can't we?"

"Yes," I replied. "But this time you're the real mother. And instead of buying me silver skates, maybe, if I'm old enough, you'll buy me a watch so I can tell time."

"Here I am, trying to turn time back a little and you want to push it ahead."

"Why do you want to turn it back?"

"Because it seems things were nicer then."

"Why can't you just think about them?"

"Think about them?"

"Yes, 'cause if you think about them, you can be there and here too."

"You mean, remember them?"

"Yes."

She clasped me to her, pressed my face against hers. "You're right, you're very right. We can always remember the nice things that once were and still enjoy the nice things that are now." Releasing me slowly, she added as if to herself, "Yes, we can't hold on. We can't even let go. Besides"—she shook back her hair—"there are lots of games you can play where you don't have to hold hands."

It seemed to me that she looked especially good and brave.

"What are you thinking?" she asked.

It had to be said like a sunshower, a sudden rain of words, all at once, and maybe the rainbow after:

"Why can't we adopt Johnny and maybe his brother? I wouldn't care if Artie slept in my bed, I promise. And I would give Johnny all my toys and my robe and slippers and even my whole kitchen chair. I could eat after he eats. And I don't need any baby books no more so it's all right if Artie tears them up. And you could give them the cookies you made extra for me after you baked the cake. I wouldn't care so long as you let them live here, please."

While smoothing back my hair, she carefully and gently explained that adopting Johnny and his brother would be a constant reminder for them and for us of their sorrow.

I could hardly wait for her to finish before I protested, "But if you don't, he'll die!"

Her face became immediately anxious. "Who told you that? Who?" she asked.

I was frightened. Perhaps I shouldn't have told her.

"Who?" she asked again, this time holding me away from her and examining my face. "Did Carmella?"

I shook my head. "He did," I admitted. "But I knew anyway—even before."

"But it's not so," she insisted. "Why should he?"

"Because he has no more mother and you don't want to let him live here. So, he has to."

"Would it happen to you if I died?" Her voice was a whisper.

The thought wounded, but I nodded.

"To every child whose mother dies?

Again I nodded.

"But it's wrong," she said. I looked up at her. My eyes must have shown doubt, for she shook her head and tightening her fingers on my arm with every word, she said, "Believe me, it is all wrong!"

I hoped she wasn't going to tell me some story to try and explain away what I felt to be the unalterable truth.

"Listen," she said. "Don't you know that Johnny's mother made him just as I made you and every mother makes her children? We make you to live . . . to live on after we go and have your own children and perhaps to give them our names so that we keep on living in them."

I stared at her.

"You see, every child is like a pearl that is added onto a long, long string of pearls. If children died when their mothers did, the string would stop growing. And it can't stop. It can't!"

I looked away.

Emphasizing each word as if she were trying to force them inside me, she asked, "If Johnny dies because his mother did, who would there be to remember her?" Before I could reply, she interrupted with, "Don't forget, Artie is still a little baby."

"You'd remember her," I said, "and I would, too."

She sighed, let go of my arms and slumped slightly.

Suddenly she shook her head and said, "You may not know it, but you have another friend . . . a little boy whose mother died. And he's still alive. He goes to school with you."

"Who?"

"Gerard Shuminsky," she replied. "His mother died a little less than a year ago."

Gerard Shuminsky! Everything I knew about him fell into place like nesting boxes: how he adored Miss Diamond, had to be her favorite, and especially monitor; how he had offered her his beads. It all made so much sense that I couldn't possibly accuse my mother of having made it up. Yet how could I have been so wrong about something I felt was so right?

"So, you see, little boys don't have to die because their mothers do. Do they?"

It was so difficult, almost impossible, but I nodded.

"Now," she said, her voice brightening, "you know what I hoped you would ask me?"

"No."

"I was hoping you'd ask me for your good-night song."

Although she smiled and her voice played, I sensed her sadness at having to ask me if I wanted her to sing me to sleep. "I thought that maybe because of Johnny's mother, you wouldn't want to sing," I said in excuse.

"But do you want me to sing it?" she asked. "I don't think it's going to sound the same as it used to. I've been out of practice."

I knew it wouldn't sound the same. "Please sing it," I asked.

She sang. Her voice, like a dusty-winged butterfly, swept the room. I closed my eyes, and even while listening wished she would never sing it to me again. It no longer belonged to me but to that little boy who once was a real prince and had a good mother, a fake mother and a dream that there was nothing in the world that the magic of his mind couldn't change to undiminishing joy.

She finished, kissed me, and thinking I was asleep, pulled the light cord and left, half-closing the door behind.

"I have a sneaking suspicion," I heard her say to my father, "that weather permitting, you will be playing 'catch' pretty soon."

"I tried once. It didn't work," he said.

"Next time, I'm afraid, it will."

chapter 15

I awoke to the sound of the door closing and with the fear that I was being shut out of something. Peter was already out of the room. I felt as if I had been alone for a long time and that something was about to happen, something very terrible.

The alarm rattled, louder than I had ever heard it, and I was about to burst from the room when my mother came in, quickly turned it off, pulled down the blanket and sheet, saying, "Early to bed, early to rise, makes a man healthy, wealthy and tired. Upsa!"

She tugged me up, began to unbutton my pajamas. Just seeing her calmed me; to assure myself that she was really there I had to oppose her in some way. I complained I could dress myself.

"I know, you're the smartest thing in shoes," she said, "but we haven't the time today."

"Why not?"

"Because we've got to be early for school."

"Why?"

"What would happen if one of these days you asked why and I didn't answer?"

"Nothing."

"Good. There's your answer."

I would have carried it further if it were not for the surprise of seeing Peter already dressed. "Is he going to school early, too?" I asked.

"You can see for yourself that he is," she replied, and slipped me into my underwear like sausage into its skin.

I was sent to wash. In the living room, Martha sat primly and cotton-faced on her made-up bed. "What are you doing?" I asked. "Nothing," she replied through minced teeth.

In the bathroom the sense of nothingness and detachment returned. I hurried through brushing my teeth, and was about to call my mother to comb my hair when I heard Peter whine, "Why do I have to go so early? The school isn't even open yet."

"So you'll be the first and get the door prize," my mother countered.

Just her voice and the happy sounds it made reassured me, and I could hardly wait for Peter to finish complaining, "But there won't be anybody there. What'll I do, haunt the place?" so that I could hear her reply, "You might take your life in your hands and go to the library."

"What'll I do there?"

"Let the books look at you. Maybe *they'll* learn something."

Peter gnawed his dissatisfaction with, "Aaaaaaaaw . . ."

These were the voices of my world. They were comforting and protective. But suddenly they were silenced by the sound of a horse neighing.

I ran out of the bathroom.

"What's that?" I asked.

Peter and Martha shot glances at my mother, at each other, and then lowered their lids.

Men's shouts could be heard from the street, the stomping of hooves.

Defeat darkened my mother's face. "They couldn't wait. They just couldn't wait, damn them!" she said fiercely and bitterly, and went into the kitchen.

Drawn by the excitement of strange noises, I ran with Peter and Martha to the front bedroom. Ignoring my father still in bed, we elbowed, nudged, wedged for viewing positions in the window.

"Ladies first," Martha announced.

"Come back when you get to be one," was Peter's retort.

Mounted police were supervising the placement of wooden trestles along the curbs, while those on foot were already herding people back from in front of The Poorhouse.

I only half-admitted to myself why this commotion was taking place. It was too loud and lively to have any connection with sorrow.

My mother came in.

"Have they started already?" my father asked.

"Funerals always start too soon and last too long," she said. And I forced myself to concentrate on the people hurrying along the street—noting that the men wore hats or caps and that most of the women were in black scarves or shawls.

My mother's "Bobby, come have breakfast," gave me a much-wanted reason to get away, but I pulled away reluctantly, not wanting to betray any signs of the terror crawling up inside. I fought against it by begging my brother and sister to be sure and let me know when something happened.

"You bet," said Peter, "just as soon as the main bout comes on."

"Shut up, you," Martha ordered, "this is serious."

I took the gloom of her last word with me. Breakfast was a blur of tastes and I rushed back to the window and fought my way into position. It was easier to watch than to wonder about it.

A truck had come during my absence and was now disgorging men and sound equipment. The crowd had grown to a solid mass that barely moved to allow the men pulling snakelike cables behind them to weave through.

Peter opened the window "to see better." My mother told us to get sweaters or to shut it. We flew from the window, scrambled back.

A ball of bright purple bobbed in the sea of black below. At one point it turned upward. It was Carmella. "Hey," she called up, "look at this." She flapped the purple scarf. "My mother got it for me. It's religious."

I nodded my approval if only because Carmella's was the only face in the crowd I could identify until now; recognizing her gave me a peculiar sense of confidence, which even Martha's remark, "Why don't they put her in a cage?" could not upset.

Noise was extinguished by the sounds of "One-two-three, testing. Testing, one-two-three." The weight of the crowd overturned a number of trestles. Horses reared, sashayed people back, threatened them with the nervous jigging of their hooves and their twitching rumps.

Mrs. Greneker arrived; all the windows in her apartment faced the rear. Peter and Martha were sent out on the fire escape to make room for her. Not to be excluded, I followed them and wedged myself between while Martha folded and refolded her skirt beneath her, complaining that anyone looking up from the street could see.

A long black sedan turned laboriously into the street. Police shouted and waved sticks to make passageway for it up to The Poorhouse. It stopped. A door opened, a tall thickset man emerged. The rear door was opened, a woman in black stepped out, leaned back into the car and I could watch no longer. Instead I looked up. Windows were crammed with more faces than they could hold. Fire escapes were perilously overloaded. Kids shimmied up poles, were ordered down by the police and shimmied up again. People peered from roofs.

While the police punctured the air with commands, the crowd murmured broodingly—like the slow scraping of feet on gravel. People waiting for grief.

It came.

In a freeze of silence, an ebony coach pulled into the street. The crowd drew back, cut a swathe of emptiness around it as it took its place behind the sedan.

"Aren't you going to school?"

Even Mrs. Greneker's head turned to look back into the apartment.

My father was dressed as if the day was every day—two books under his arm, his hat in his hand. My mother stood directly behind him. "I'm going to work," he said. "Come on, I'll help you through the crowds."

"Will you take me?" I couldn't contain the begging in my voice.

"Sure," Peter said as if glad of the chance.

Martha started to stand but changed her mind. "I think I better wait till the crowd's all gone," she said, and I caught her glancing first at Mrs. Greneker and then at my mother.

I followed Peter into our room and in a moment we were behind my father going down the steps. Just before opening the hall door, he took my hand and cautioned Peter to stay close behind.

The crowd was ponderously quiet. We twisted through it, my father repeating, "Excuse me, excuse me," continually.

I stared at legs as I passed; I imagined myself in a forest of legs. And then the realization came that with a few exceptions they were mostly women's; that there were no signs of children around. With the arrival of the coach they had fled around the corner as always.

A rich rolling voice came from the speakers: "Friends, we are gathered here today to honor the memory of a mother . . . a Jewish mother . . ."

The women wept. The women moaned.

We had just reached the edge of the crowd when the voice said, "A woman of such worth is not easily found."

My father stopped, looked at Peter, who immediately stashed his books between his legs, took his handkerchief out of his pocket, quickly made a knot at each end and put it on his head. I wondered if I was to do the same and was answered by feeling my father's hand resting lightly on my hair.

"For her price is far above that of rubies," the voice went on. "She stretches out her hand to the poor; she puts forth her hand to the needy. Strength and majesty are her clothing . . .

"Her children rise up and call her blessed . . ."

Lament.

I looked up and saw the dark jut of my father's jaw. Peter's head was turned up and away.

"O Lord, who are full of compassion . . ." but the weeping of the women engulfed his words.

The "Amen" was a kiss good-bye.

My father took his hand from my head. We turned and were about to start away when the sounds of deeper, more bitter grief broke from the crowd.

Once again my father stopped. He craned his neck and then looking at me, asked, "Do you want to see Johnny?" In the moment I wavered, he handed his books to Peter and lifted me onto his shoulder. I dared not look. Instead, I turned to our fire escape. Martha stood, holding her head high as if she were "practicing self-control." Mrs. Greneker was formless in her great black shawl. And just beyond her I could see the small rim of that black hat.

Then I looked over the heads of the crowd and I saw him. He held his brother's hand. The sun had caught the gleaming of their skull caps.

He walked stiffly to the top of the stoop. And just before descending he turned his face to me. It was as if there was no one else in the street or in the world. Just the two of us looking at each other, speaking with our eyes. It was agreed between us: that we would live . . . we would live even if out of Eden.

I shouted a silent, hurray for him. The little hand opened, stretched wide within me and finally let go of that fierce familiar dream. Then I felt it: the reverberations of, hurray for me, soared even as the cries of "the kinder . . . the children . . . oh, the children," floated upward like pigeons whose soft gray wings brushed past my face.